DEATH ANGEL

'*Suspense that'll keep you on the edge of your seat.*'

A striking beauty with a taste for diamonds and dangerous men, Drea Rousseau was once content to be arm candy for Rafael Salinas, a notorious crime lord. Then, when he loans her to a cold-blooded assassin as payment, Drea makes a fateful decision and a desperate move to escape, stealing a mountain of cash from the malicious killer. Though Drea runs, Salinas knows she can't hide – and despatches the assassin in hot pursuit. Left for dead, Drea miraculously returns a changed woman, but in order to stop looking over her shoulder, she needs to take down the man who marked her for death...

DEATH ANGEL

DEATH ANGEL

by

Linda Howard

Magna Large Print Books
Long Preston, North Yorkshire,
BD23 4ND, England.

MAGNA   13-10-09

British Library Cataloguing in Publication Data.
_____

Howard, Linda
    Death angel.

    A catalogue record of this book is
    available from the British Library

    ISBN   978-0-7505-3151-1

First published in Great Britain in 2008 by Piatkus Books

Copyright © 2008 by Linda Howington

Cover illustration © Douglas Black by arrangement with
Arcangel Images

The moral right of the author has been asserted

Published in Large Print 2009 by arrangement with
Piatkus Books Ltd.

Magna Large Print is an imprint of Library Magna Books Ltd.

Printed and bound in Great Britain by
T.J. (International) Ltd., Cornwall, PL28 8RW

To Logan Chance Wiemann, for all the smiles, and to Susan Bailey of the Exchange Bank, for answering all my questions about electronic transfers

1

'You did an excellent job,' Rafael Salinas purred to the assassin, who stood on the other side of the room, near the door. Either the man didn't like getting too close to other human beings, or he didn't trust Salinas and was giving himself an avenue of escape if the meeting turned sour – in which case he was smart. People who were wary of Salinas tended to live longer than those who trusted him. Drea Rousseau, curled close to Salinas's side, didn't care what the assassin's reasoning was, so long as it kept him at a distance.

He gave her the creeps, the way he never seemed to blink. She had seen him once before, and at that meeting he'd made it obvious he disliked her presence. He'd leveled his flat, un-blinking gaze on her for so long that she'd begun wondering if he made it a practice to eliminate people who could identify him – other than the people who paid him, of course, and maybe even them after the money was safely in his hand, or his account, or however assassins collected their fees. She had no idea what his name was, didn't want to know, because while truth was supposed to set you free, in this case she thought it might possibly be deadly. She thought of him as Rafael's assassin, but in fact he wasn't one of Rafael's

11

regular crew; he was a free agent, hired by whoever could afford him. At least twice now, that she knew of, Rafael had met the price.

To keep from looking at him and maybe finding that unnerving stare locked on her again, she unhappily examined the magenta polish on her toenails. She had put it on just that morning, thinking it would look interesting against the creamy white of the silk lounge outfit she was currently wearing, but the purple undertones were too garish. She should have gone with a shell pink, something delicate and almost transparent to compliment the outfit instead of contrasting with it. Well, live and learn.

When the assassin didn't reply, didn't rush to assure Rafael that he was honored to work for him the way others had, Rafael's fingers drummed impatiently on his thigh. It was a nervous habit he had when he wasn't comfortable, a telling little gesture, at least as far as Drea was concerned. She'd intensely studied his every mood, his every habit. He wasn't exactly *afraid*, but he, too, was being wary, which meant there were two smart men in the room.

'I'd like to offer you a bonus,' Rafael said. 'An extra hundred thousand. How does that sound?'

Drea didn't look up, though she quickly processed the offer and what it meant. She went to a lot of trouble to never show any interest in Rafael's business dealings, and when he'd occasionally asked her some very casual but leading questions she'd pretended she didn't understand what he was getting at. As a result, Rafael wasn't as careful around her as he might otherwise have been. As far as he was concerned, she had no interest in anything that didn't directly affect her, and in a way that was true, just not in the way Rafael thought. He assumed she didn't care who the assassin had killed for him, that she cared only about what she was wearing, how her hair looked, about making Rafael look good by being as sexy and glamorous as she could make herself.

She was definitely interested in that last part; making Rafael look good in the eyes of others always put him in an expansive mood, a generous mood. Drea studied the platinum and diamond anklet that circled her right ankle, enjoying the way the dangling diamond glittered in the sunlight, the way the platinum glowed against her tanned skin. The anklet had been one of Rafael's gifts when he'd been very happy about something. She hoped his pleasure with the assassin's success put him in an equally generous mood; she wouldn't mind a matching bracelet – not that she ever hinted. She was always very careful not to ask Rafael for anything, and to ooh and aah over everything he gave her even if it was butt-ugly, because even butt-ugly crap could be sold.

She had no illusions about the permanency of her position in Rafael's life. Right now she was at the top of her game, mature enough to be womanly, young enough that she didn't have to worry about gray hair or wrinkles. But in another year or two, who knew?

Eventually Rafael *would* tire of her, and when he did she wanted to have built up a nice little nest egg for herself, mostly in the form of jewelry. Drea Rousseau knew what it was to be poor, and she intended never to be poor again. She'd severed all ties with the girl she'd been growing up, white-trash Andie Butts, the target of malicious jokes because of her name as much as anything else, and made herself over into Andrea (pronounced *anDRAYuh,* which sounded French to her) Rousseau (to go with the fancier pronunciation).

'Her,' said the assassin. 'I want her.'

Her interest caught – who was *her?* – Drea looked up ... and the bottom dropped out of her stomach. The assassin was staring at her with the same cold, unblinking gaze she remembered. Shock slammed into her like a tidal wave; *she* was the *her* he was talking about. There were no other women in the room, no one else he could possibly mean. Icy fingers of sheer panic laced around her spine, but then common sense reasserted itself and she relaxed. Thank God Rafael was a posses-sive man; he would never–

'Ask for something else,' Rafael said lazily, looping his arm around her shoulders and snug-gling her close to his side. 'I couldn't give away my good-luck piece.' He pressed a kiss to her forehead and Drea beamed up at him, almost limp with relief, though she tried not to reveal that for a moment she'd been scared almost senseless.

'I don't want to keep her,' the assassin said dis-missively, without looking away from Drea's face. 'I just want to fuck her. One time.'

Reassured by Rafael's immediate rejection of the request, confident once more, Drea laughed. She had a sweet laugh, as harmonious as the chiming of bells. Rafael had once told her she reminded him of an angel, with her long, curly

14

blond hair, big blue eyes, and her bell-like laugh. She used the laugh as deliberately as if it were a weapon, reminding Rafael without words that she was indeed his angel, his good luck.

At the sound, the assassin's entire body seemed to tense, his attention so tightly focused on her she could almost feel the touch of it on her skin. Until then, if she'd thought about it much, Drea would have said he was already alert, but now he was somehow *more* so, as if all his senses were heightened, his focus so intensified she felt the burn of it on her skin and her laughter choked off as abruptly as if his hand had closed around her throat.

'I don't share,' Rafael said, an irritated note underlying the ease of his tone. The top man never shared his woman; if he did, then he lost an edge, an important one, in the authority he had over his men. Surely the assassin knew that. But they were alone in the penthouse apartment, with no witnesses to what Rafael did or didn't do, so maybe that was why he'd thought he could have what he wanted.

Again the assassin said nothing, merely watching, and though he didn't move there was abruptly something lethal stewing in the atmosphere between them. Curled against him as she was, Drea felt Rafael's almost imperceptible twitch, as if he, too, was aware of the change.

'Come now,' Rafael said, his tone cajoling, but Drea knew him well; she caught the uneasiness he was trying so hard to disguise, and because that wasn't something she was accustomed to seeing in him she almost darted an alarmed glance at

15

him, before catching herself and instead inspecting a fingernail as if she'd spotted a chip in the polish. 'That's a lot of money to throw away for something so brief. Sex is cheap; you can buy a lot of it with a hundred thousand dollars.'

Still the assassin waited, as silent as a tomb. He had made his request, and the only thing yet to be determined was if Rafael would grant it, or deny him. Without saying a word he made it plain that he wouldn't take the money that had been offered; instead he would walk away and at best Rafael would no longer be able to call on the assassin's services when needed. At worst – Drea didn't want to think about what the worst could be, would be. With a man like this, anything was possible.

Rafael suddenly looked at Drea, his dark gaze cool and assessing. She sucked in a breath, alarmed by that abrupt coolness, by the assessment. Was he actually considering the idea, weighing the cost if he continued to say no?

'On the other hand,' he mused, 'perhaps I have convinced myself. Sex *is* cheap, and I, too, can do a lot with a hundred thousand dollars.' He removed his arm from around Drea's shoulders and stood, straightening his pants with a practiced movement that made the hem break across his foot at precisely the right spot. 'One time, you said. I have business across town that will keep me tied up for five hours, which is more than sufficient.' He paused, then added lightly, 'Don't damage her.' Without even glancing at her again, he walked across the living room toward the door.

What? Drea bolted upright, unable to think straight. What was he saying? What was he doing?

16

This was a joke, right? *Right?*

Drea pinned her desperate, disbelieving gaze on Rafael's back as he walked to the door. He didn't mean it. He *couldn't* mean it. Any moment now he would turn around and laugh, enjoying his joke at the assassin's expense, never mind that he'd almost sent her into cardiac arrest. She didn't care that he'd scared her half to death, she wouldn't say a word to him about it, if he'd just stop, if he'd say, 'Did you really think I was serious?'

There was no way he'd give her to the assassin, no way–

Rafael reached the door, opened it ... and left.

Barely able to breathe, her lungs constricted by the tide of rising panic that threatened to strangle her, Drea stared blindly at that door. He'd open it now, and laugh. Any minute now, Rafael would come back in.

She didn't look at the assassin, didn't move, didn't blink, so thoroughly was she frozen. Her own pulse roared in her ears, her heartbeat like thunder. The hugeness of what Rafael had just done was so overwhelming she couldn't process it. Her body and most of her brain had gone numb, but a part of her mind still functioned, still grasped that Rafael had thrown her to the lion and then walked away without either a moment's hesitation or a single backward look.

The assassin moved into her line of vision, silently approaching the door and locking it – all the locks, the dead bolts, even sliding the safety chain into its slot. No one would be able to enter, even with a key, without alerting him.

Life flooded back into her body and she fled,

clattering in her four-inch heels across the marble tiles. Her body acted of its own volition, driven by desperation, without thought or plan. She dashed toward the hallway, then realization brought her to an abrupt halt as her brain caught up with her body. Down the hall were the bedrooms, and that was the last place she wanted to be.

Desperately she looked around. The kitchen ... there were knives, a meat mallet – maybe she could defend herself–

Against *him?* Any effort she made would be laughable to him – or, worse, make him angry, perhaps even angry enough to kill her. Within minutes her goal had changed from avoidance to simple survival. She didn't want to die. However brutally he treated her, no matter what he did, she didn't want to die.

There was no safe place, no haven where she could hide. Even knowing that, admitting it, she couldn't just stand there; with nowhere else to go, no way to stop him, she ran out onto the balcony, high over the city. She reached the wall and could go no farther, unless she tried to fly, and her sense of self-preservation was too strong to allow that. As long as she was alive, she would try to remain that way.

Blindly she reached out and gripped the iron rail set atop the wall, her fingers locking around the metal as she stared at nothing. Central Park spread out beneath her, a cool green oasis in the middle of the vast thicket of steel and concrete that was Manhattan. Birds soared below, and overhead fat white clouds drifted lazily across the pure blue of the sky. The hot sunlight touched her face, her bare arms and shoulders, while a breeze flirted with her curls. She felt disconnected from all of that, as if none of it was real, not even the heat of the sun on her cheeks.

She *felt* him approach, felt him halt when he was close behind her. She hadn't heard him, wasn't aware of a single sound other than the rustle of the breeze and the faint noise of the city far below; nevertheless she knew he was there. Every nerve in her skin was shrieking an alarm, telling her that Death was about to reach out and touch her.

His hand settled on the bare curve of her shoulder.

Panic exploded in her skull, mental fireworks that obliterated both thought and action. She didn't react; she couldn't. She stood there, violently trembling, because she was incapable of doing more, or even less.

Slowly, as if he savored the texture of her skin, he stroked down the length of her arm. His hand was hard and warm, his fingertips and palm rough with callus, but his touch was controlled, even ... gentle? She had expected brutality, been prepared for it, had so focused on simply surviving that she couldn't process the reality of the caress. Her senses reeled just as if he'd punched her.

His sliding hand reached her fingers, which were still tightly knotted around the railing, and lightly stroked over them before reversing direction and moving up her arm as slowly as it had descended. When he reached her shoulder he didn't stop, but continued onto her neck, where he moved the mass of her curls aside and slid his fingertips over her throat, the curve of her jaw, following the slender threads of muscle and tendon and sending chills chasing over her entire body. After a moment he moved his attention to the wide shoulder strap of her silk tank top, playing with it, sliding his fingers under it, tracing the line of fabric downward. If he hadn't realized before that she wasn't wearing a bra, he had to know it now.

'Breathe,' he said, the first word he'd ever spoken to her. His low, slightly rough voice made the word a command.

She did, gasping in air and only then realizing, by the acute relief in her lungs, that she'd been holding her breath for so long that she'd been in danger of passing out.

Slowly, still so slowly, he moved his hand down her side, the heat of his touch searing through the thin silk. He reached the bottom of the garment and his fingers dipped under it, exploring the elastic waistband of her flimsy, billowy pants, slipping beneath and around. Now he also knew that she wasn't wearing panties, either. Drea swallowed the lump in her throat and squeezed her eyes shut.

Closing her eyes was an instinctive move to shut him out, to distance herself from the here and now, but instead her action seemed to make all her other senses even more acute. Leisurely he moved his hand up her stomach and, with nothing else to distract her, her focus latched on to the touch with almost painful intensity. Her muscles contracted, her entire body tightening as he moved up, up, while she waited, once again holding her breath.

His hand closed fully over her left breast, and the air rushed from her lungs. He held her breast, stroked it, cupped it in his palm as if weighing it. He swept his thumb over her tender nipple, the rough pad rasping, until her nipple engorged and stood out firm and plump; then he moved on to her other breast and repeated the process.

Once again her senses reeled. The sheer pleasure of the caress scattered her thoughts, leaving her gasping and grasping for an anchor, something to hold her grounded. Whatever she had expected of him, it hadn't been ... this.

He bent his head and the heat of his mouth, the softness of his lips, closed over the sensitive cord in the side of her neck as he moved forward and pressed his body against her back, from shoulder to knee. Oh, God, he was so hot. She had felt cold, but his heat burned her. She had been braced for brutality, but he slid beneath her defenses with a touch that brought only pleasure.

'I won't hurt you,' he murmured, his lips moving over her skin as he slipped his other hand under her top. He played with her breasts, stroking them, plucking at her nipples, while his mouth on her neck made the bottom drop out of her stomach again as if she were on a roller coaster, rising and falling on a dizzying tide of sensation.

She had no idea how long they stood there, just that the disconcerting pleasure went on and on. She was lost, at sea without a compass. This was so far outside her experiences and expectations that she had no idea what to do. Pleasure? Her relationship with Rafael was all about pleasing him; *her* pleasure didn't factor into it at all. She had accepted that, concentrated on doing everything she could to make him happy. When had a man last even tried to please her physically? The memory was hazy, lost in the years, so long ago that she had ceased expecting any personal enjoyment. To feel it now, at the hands – literally – of a stone-cold killer, was staggering.

He pulled her nipples, gently pinching, and the sensation was just sharp enough to send a bolt of sheer sexual excitement straight to her groin. She felt herself reaching up and back, her body arching instinctively into his hands as her fingers slid around the back of his neck, feeling the hardness, the thickness of muscle. She clung, hearing the soft sounds of invitation she was making, feeling the hard ridge in his pants as she rolled her bottom across it. Her stomach muscles contracted again, this time in blind anticipation, and she tried to turn toward him.

He stayed her, holding her facing the rail, the city spread out before and around them. She felt him tugging on the elastic waistband of her pants, felt the sudden coolness of air on her bare ass as he dragged the silk downward, felt the tension of the elastic around her thighs.

Panic surged again, once more mixed with disbelief and horror. *Here?* On the balcony, in the open, where anyone might see them? The street was too far below for anyone down there to see, but what about people in the neighboring buildings? Telescopes abounded in this city, thousands upon thousands of people spying on their neighbors, on the buildings across the street, and surely the FBI or the DEA or *someone* was watching Rafael, which meant they were also watching her – and this man had her half-naked on the balcony.

He moved closer again, murmuring something low and soothing. He pressed against her nakedness, and his hand moved between them. She heard the muted rasp of a zipper, his knuckles briefly pushing between her buttocks, startling her into a stifled shriek, then she was aware of nothing except her own excruciating exposure and the heavy pressure of his bared penis at the opening of her body.

'Bend over a little.'

His hand on the back of her neck made sure she obeyed. His feet were between hers, pushing them as far apart as possible given the restriction of her pants around her thighs. He bent his knees, lowering himself for a better angle, and with his other hand he worked the thick head back and forth against her opening, moistening both her and himself. Then he pushed up and in, the intrusion slow and difficult.

Drea writhed, caught like a worm on a hook. Her thigh muscles tensed and relaxed, trembling. He caught her, pulled her back to him, held her braced as he slowly withdrew and thrust forward again. His right arm held her locked to him, while with his left hand he reached down and delved between her soft vaginal lips. He scissored his fingers around her clitoris, holding it captive as he moved inside her, back and forth, back and forth, the thick, hard length of his penis touching something inside her – her G spot, maybe – God, she didn't know, all she knew was that she was

23

rocketing toward climax so fast she couldn't think, then she was coming, hard, her inner muscles milking him, and raw animal sounds of completion were tearing from her throat.

She would have collapsed forward if not for his grip. He eased out of her and turned her around, holding her until she stopped gasping and shuddering, until she stopped crying. Why was she crying? She never cried, at least not for real. Yet now her cheeks were wet, her breathing hard and jerky. She fought for control and, when she could, she opened her eyes and looked up, met his gaze, and lost her breath all over again.

She'd thought his eyes were brown, but now she saw they were hazel, which was a completely inadequate word for the colors she saw there: not just brown and green and gold, but blue and gray and black added in, then shot with white striations. Up close the color reminded her of dark opals, full of surprising color. Nor was his gaze cold; she felt burned by the heat she saw there, the intensity of desire. He hadn't cooled down any, which ran contrary to any experience she'd ever had. Once a man came, he lost interest in continuing to play. But this man was still hard, still ready, and–

'You didn't come,' she blurted, struck by the abrupt realization.

He began walking her backward toward the open glass door, lifting her off her feet when her lowered pants threatened to trip her. 'Just one time, remember?' he said, his gaze glittering with both heat and fierce intent. 'Until I come, all of this counts as just once.'

24

2

In a building angled across from Rafael's apartment, a federal agent blinked at his monitor, then announced in a tone of astonishment: 'Hey, the girlfriend has a boyfriend.'

'What?' The senior agent walked over to the monitor and stared at it, at the couple on the balcony. He whistled. 'Talk about cutting it close; Salinas just left the building.' He frowned, studying the images. 'I don't remember seeing that guy before. Can we ID him?'

'I don't think so; not yet, anyway. He hasn't given us a good angle.' Despite that, the first agent, Xavier Jackson, danced his fingers across the keyboard, trying to clean up the resolution. Salinas had chosen his penthouse well; the angle, the height, the distance, all worked to make visual surveillance, at best, somewhat difficult – and as bad as visual was, what they had there was still a damn sight better than any audio they'd managed to get. Not only was the apartment soundproofed, but Salinas had also installed sophisticated equipment that thwarted all their attempts to eavesdrop. Nor had they been cleared to tap any of his lines, which to Jackson's way of thinking meant that some high-level judges were in Salinas's well-tailored pocket. That royally pissed Jackson off, because it ran contrary to his sense of justice, of right and wrong. Judges were human; they could

25

be stupid, biased, just plain bad, but, damn it, they weren't supposed to be dirty.

He froze a snapshot of the couple and sent it to the face recognition program, but he didn't have much hope.

The senior agent was Rick Cotton; he'd been with the Bureau almost twenty-eight years, had gone gray in its service. He was a quiet man, competent in his work, but neither talented enough at what he did nor politically savvy enough to rise any higher than his present position. He would retire in another year or so, collect his pension, and his absence wouldn't leave a gap, but at the same time the people who had worked with him would remember him as a solid agent.

In his own six years with the Bureau, Jackson had worked with some brilliant people who were also assholes, or, worse, slackers who were brilliant at ass-kissing, so he had no complaints about Cotton. There were a lot worse things in the world than working with a decent, competent man.

'This might be our break,' Cotton said as they waited to see if the computer program could put a name to the unknown man's face. Until now, they hadn't found a chink in Salinas's wall of security, but filming the girlfriend getting it on with some other dude was leverage they could use against her. Getting to someone on the inside would be an unbelievable break – not that it would shine up Cotton's reputation any, because some slick and savvy operator sitting in an office would find a way to take credit for it, and Cotton wouldn't protest, just plod on in his dependable way.

Jackson thought that he himself just might be

that slick and savvy operator, because damned if he'd let someone else take all the credit after the insufferably long, boring hours he and Cotton had put in on this assignment. He wouldn't leave Cotton behind, though; the man deserved better than that.

Jackson kept an eye on the split screen, looking for a better angle, but it was as if the bastard knew exactly where they were, because not once did he reveal more than a partial view of his face. His right ear, though – Jackson froze a very good image of the ear. Ears were good; they varied from person to person in shape, size, the way they were positioned on the head, and the interior whorls. People who disguised themselves often completely forgot about the ears.

The facial identification program surrendered, telling him there was no match, which he'd expected. 'Come on, look at the birdie,' he murmured to the man. 'Let me take your picture.'

He was focused so intently on his task that, until Cotton gave an uncomfortable cough, Jackson didn't realize what he was watching. 'Damn,' he muttered. 'He's doing her right there, out in the open.' Not that they could really see anything, but it was obvious from the couple's positions and movements what was happening on that balcony.

Then the unknown man swung them around, presenting his back to the camera, and half-walked, half-carried the girlfriend into the penthouse, pulling the sliding glass door shut behind him.

Not once had he provided them with a clear look at his face.

After the brightness and warmth of the sun-drenched balcony, the penthouse was blessedly cool and dim, and private. Drea clung to him for support; her legs were like cooked noodles and her brain felt like mush. He dipped his head to trail a line of slow kisses down her throat and across her collarbone. 'Is this place bugged?' he asked in that low, half-audible tone of his, his lips moving against her shoulder as he murmured the words on her skin. 'Cameras anywhere?'

'Not now,' Drea replied, then a sharp surge of combined lust and fear turned her insides to water. She worked hard to make people see her as ornamental, self-absorbed, and more than a little dumb: in short, nonthreatening. Having people underestimate her gave her an enormous advantage … but he didn't seem to under-estimate her at all, and that both pleased and frightened her. If he could see the brains beneath the act, then others might, too. At the same time, his easy assumption that she'd know the answer to a question so crucial fed a need that she hadn't realized was there, a hunger to be treated as an equal on some level.

At any rate, it was too late now to continue the dumb act. Recklessly she added, 'He used to, but he decided having a record of anything could be dangerous to him.'

At first, Rafael had had her followed everywhere she went, and hidden cameras had recorded her in her bedroom, as well as her bathroom. She'd had no privacy at all, and she had simply gone with the flow, keeping her activities completely

28

innocuous and boring. She had been with him for almost five months when she overheard him telling Orlando Dumas, his electronics whiz, to get rid of all the cameras and microphones, and to burn the tapes. Orlando hadn't bothered to tell him it was all digital, and there were no tapes, but Drea had had a private laugh at Rafael's expense.

If Rafael wanted to know how often she had her nails and hair done, fine, let him waste time having her followed. She shopped, she watched television, and she made a habit of going to the nearest library and checking out coffee table books of other countries. She would pore over the pictures, and in a deliberately careful manner read snippets about different customs and geographical features aloud to Rafael, until he impatiently told her he wasn't interested in ferrets and lemurs, nor did he care which waterfall was the highest in the world. Drea had managed to look faintly hurt, but thereafter kept the tidbits to herself. Shortly afterward, he'd stopped having her followed whenever she left the penthouse.

Most of the time, Drea didn't take chances, and behaved as she had when she'd been followed. She really did get her nails and/or hair done frequently, and she spent a lot of time shopping, both in person and on the Internet. She kept her bedroom television on a shopping channel, and a pad lying there with item numbers scribbled on it – numbers that she frequently scratched through, or changed, just in case Rafael had someone check. There were even real item numbers for clothing, should he check that far. She spent a lot of time doing exactly what Rafael expected her to be doing.

Occasionally, however, she did something entirely different. Rafael was ruthless and street smart, but he didn't think she was intelligent enough to slip anything by him, so she managed to slip quite a lot.

But this man, this killer holding her in his arms, saw beneath her carefully constructed façade, stripping away her defenses and exposing her as effortlessly as he'd stripped down her pants. She stared up into his narrowed gaze, wondering what else he saw. Was her secret safe with him, or did he see it as a card he could play whenever it was strategically useful? Maybe he'd want her to give him information about Rafael. Whatever he wanted her to do, she'd have to do it; she had no choice. That was actually an easy decision to make, because this man was one of the few people she'd bet on against Rafael.

Her thoughts had wrenched her from the control of her over-loaded senses, and as clarity returned she again felt the icy finger of panic. He wasn't finished with her. So far he hadn't hurt her – the opposite, in fact – but that didn't mean she was safe. Maybe he was just playing with her, getting her to lower her guard, relax. Maybe he got his jollies from sucker punches.

'You're thinking too much,' he murmured. 'You just tensed up again.'

Think! she commanded herself, willing the panic away. She had to think, get herself under control. God, how stupid could she be? Instead of acting like some twit who didn't know what her body was for, she should be using it, doing what

30

she did best, which was make a man feel special.

She stared at her own hands, her fingers digging into the hard muscle of his shoulders as she clung to him, and tried to force them into action. She should be stroking him, with both words and actions. She should go down on him, make him come, then – please, God – he would leave, and she could use the time to decide on her best course of action. She should be doing a lot of things, all of which right now seemed to be beyond her.

'Where's a bedroom?' he asked, lifting his head to survey their surroundings, his eyes alert. 'Not where you sleep with Salinas. Somewhere else.'

'We don't ... we don't sleep together,' she mumbled, once more jolted into telling the truth. His gaze returned to her and narrowed even more, and she shivered at the threat she felt lurking behind his every action. 'Sleep. We don't sleep. I have my own room.'

Her heartbeat thudded as he waited a beat before saying, 'You go to his room.'

It was a statement, not a question, as if he had also read Rafael with uncanny accuracy. Still, she nodded in confirmation. She *did* go to Rafael's room whenever he wanted sex. That was the way it was; people went to Rafael, he didn't go to them. Afterward she always returned to her own room, which she had deliberately made as feminine and frou-frou as possible, in keeping with the Barbie doll persona she'd cultivated.

'Your room,' he prompted.

Drea glanced to the right. 'Down this hall.'

He leaned down and stripped her pants to her

31

ankles. 'Step,' he said, and she did, lifting her feet out of the pools of filmy white fabric. She didn't have time to feel awkward for wearing a tank top and a pair of four-inch heels and nothing else, because he simply hoisted her up so she had to lock her legs around his hips to anchor herself, and he carried her down the hall.

His rock-hard erection rode her cleft, every step he took rocking him against her softly swollen flesh. Drea tightened the grip of her thighs and rubbed herself against the thick length, spreading her own dampness on it, trying to push him past the limits of his control. A hot pool of sensation gathered at the point of contact, then rapidly spread through her, taking her by surprise. She'd already climaxed, so she hadn't expected to get turned on again. Hell, she hadn't expected to get turned on at all. Nothing about this situation was what she'd expected, and though she kept struggling to gain control she kept getting her feet knocked out from under her and she'd go under yet again.

He reached her door and she managed to say 'Here' in a strangled tone, but she couldn't make herself release him so she could turn the doorknob. He did that himself, pulling her in more tightly to him with one arm under her bottom, while he opened the door with his other hand. The motion adjusted their positions just enough that abruptly his erection slipped into her; hot tingles shot along every nerve. The sensation was so electric that she moaned, every muscle in her body tightening. Helplessly she began rising and falling, trying to get as much of him as possible, her range

32

of motion limited by his grip on her. At this angle she could get only two or three inches of his penis inside her, and though the thick ridge of the head set off mini-explosions as she worked herself back and forth on it, that wasn't enough, she wanted more, she wanted all of it, deep and hard and fast.

The rhythm of his breathing hitched a little, the only sign he'd given, other than his erection, that he was the least bit excited. Abruptly Drea burned with humiliation at this evidence that, while he obviously wanted sex, he had no particular interest in *her;* she was here, she was available, and that was the extent of her use to him. She froze, and to her horror felt tears burn her eyes again. Doggedly she blinked them away.

What was happening? She wasn't the one who lost control; she used sex to control men, to get what she wanted from them. What was wrong with her, that she let this one man frighten her so much that all her usual defenses came tumbling down? Okay, so he was, like, king of the badasses, but she'd dealt with badasses all her life, and if there was one thing she'd learned, it was that when the little head lifted and took charge, the big head stopped thinking.

That didn't seem to have happened with him, but if she had a chance she could make him lose control; she knew she could. She wanted him to be as helpless as she felt, she wanted him fierce and hot and trembling, at her mercy instead of her being at his, but she wouldn't have any mercy for him at all, any more than he did for her.

He reached the side of the bed, lifted her off him, and tossed her onto the mattress. By the time she stopped bouncing, he had most of his clothes off and she held her breath as she watched him strip out of the rest. Naked, he was hard and muscled, almost lean. His chest was lightly haired, and at some time he'd been naked in the sun because he was tanned all over. For some reason, thinking of him naked and relaxed, drowsy in the sun, sent both her stomach and nerves trembling.

He bent over her and tugged her tank top up and off leaving her only in those lethal heels. His dark opal gaze fastened on her breasts, a look so loaded with male interest that her nipples puckered as if he'd licked them. She jerked, fighting an inexplicable urge to cross her arms over her breasts to shield them. Somehow she felt more exposed, more vulnerable, more *naked*, when he looked at her.

Reaching out, he lightly traced one fingertip around both nipples, then braced his hands on each side of her and leaned down to suck each breast in turn, his mouth so gentle on her that she felt the heat more than the pressure.

Her breath caught and her body arched upward, seeking more than he was giving her.

Desperately she groped for his erection, wanting, needing to seize some of the power, to balance the scales. Her fingers closed around the thick shaft, and a split second later his iron grip was on her wrist, firmly moving her hand away from him. 'No,' he said as calmly as if she'd offered him a slice of toast.

'Yes,' she insisted recklessly, reaching for him again. 'I want you in my mouth.' In her experience, no man could resist that offer.

But the hard line of his lips curved in faint amusement as he caught her hand and anchored it to the bed with an unbreakable grip. 'So you can make me come? You're in a hurry to get rid of me.'

Drea stared up at him, her emotions in such a toiling storm of lust and anger and ever-present fear that she trembled.

He secured her other hand, too, holding her firm as he moved over her and took what he wanted.

The hours that followed were a blur of lust and sex and fatigue, but a few moments were crystal clear. After her third climax she tried to squirm away from him, exhausted and over-stimulated and unable to bear any more. 'Leave me alone,' she said fretfully, slapping at his hands as he drew her back to him, and he laughed.

He actually laughed.

She stared up at the curve of his mouth, the flash of white teeth, by now expecting the way her stomach muscles clenched and the bottom fell away and she went rushing back down into the dark pit of longing that he'd uncovered. No other man had ever paid so much attention to her needs over his own, had lingered over her body, as he did, with slow touches and hot kisses. Orgasms, for her, had been what she faked with a man and provided herself when she was alone, and that had been partly her own choice because she couldn't concentrate on providing the maximum pleasure for the guy if she was distracted by her own reactions.

He had done to her what she usually did, taken

over her role, focused on her and provided so much pleasure she felt slightly drunk with satiation. He'd held back, stopping several times when he was on the verge of coming, and the strain was finally showing. His hair was damp with sweat, his face set in a hard, intensely focused expression; his eyes glittered with an intent so hot her skin should have scorched as he looked at her.

Until he laughed, and for a snapshot in time she saw him relaxed and momentarily – very momentarily – unguarded

He hadn't kissed her on the mouth. He'd kissed practically every other place on her body, but not her mouth, and suddenly she wanted that more than she wanted anything else he'd done to her. Impulsively she reached out and touched his face, her fingers lying lightly along the hard line of his jaw, feeling the faint roughness of whiskers and the heat of his skin. His dark brows lifted slightly in question, as if her touch puzzled him. Drea surrendered to the want, lifting herself and clinging her mouth to his.

For another of those frozen moments she felt him go as motionless as stone, as if he had to force himself not to pull away, and inside her chest something squeezed as she waited for him to reject her kiss.

But he didn't, and tentatively she tilted her head to deepen the contact. His lips were soft and warm; the heated scent of him filled her, called to her, jerked her from satiation to need. He hadn't opened his mouth for her and she craved that, but was almost afraid to ask for more. She dared the smallest touch of her tongue to those soft lips.

Abruptly he was kissing her in return, wresting control from her and pressing her back onto the mattress, his heavy body covering her. He kissed her as if some primal beast in him had slipped its leash and he wanted to devour her, his mouth hungry and hotly demanding, his tongue dancing with hers and forcing more response. She clung to him, arms and legs twined around him, and gave herself up to the storm she'd raised.

At another moment, lying exhausted and half-asleep, she realized she didn't know his name. That lack of knowledge hurt her, somewhere deep inside where she let no one touch. The way he'd kissed her emboldened her, let her reach out to rest her hand on his chest as he lay sprawled beside her. His heartbeat thudded fast and strong under her fingers and she flattened her hand over it as if she could link herself to that beat of life. 'What's your name?' she asked, her voice soft and drowsy.

After a moment of silence, as if he weighed her reasons for asking, he said calmly, dismissively, 'You don't need to know.'

In silence she removed her hand from his chest and curled on her side. She wanted to jump astride him and tease him, nag him, pry the information out of him, but one of the rules she'd developed over the years was not to nag, to always make herself agreeable, and the action, or lack of it, was so deeply ingrained she couldn't persist. Still, his lack of trust chilled her. She might feel as if some weird link had been forged between them, but he evidently didn't feel the same way. He was a killer, pure and simple, and he stayed at the top of his profession by trusting no one.

Some time later he lifted his head to look at the clock, and Drea did the same. Almost four hours had passed.

'Now,' he said, his tone going rough and deep as he moved over her, pushing her knees apart and settling on her, in her. His muscles tightened, and a stifled groan rumbled in his throat, his chest. He shuddered, as if being able to release his self-control was a pleasure so intense it bordered on pain.

She caught her breath at the power of his invasion. She was swollen and more than a little sore from everything he'd done to her, yet she didn't want this to end. 'We still have an hour left,' she heard herself say, and cringed inside at the small note of pleading in her voice.

A cynical expression hardened his gaze. 'Salinas won't honor the full five hours,' he replied as he began thrusting long and deep. It was as if a dam had been breached, and the power that had been restrained suddenly rushed forward. All she could do was cling to him and try to weather the storm, offer him the same generous use of her body that he had given her – and be surprised, yet again, by a response she hadn't thought herself capable of. He stiffened and began coming, groans tearing from his throat as he surged against her in powerful rhythm. She locked her legs around his and arched upward, her own raw sounds of pleasure piercing the air as her climax chased his.

When their bodies quieted, he extricated himself and immediately moved away. 'Is it all right if I use your shower?' he asked, walking toward the bathroom.

Drea searched for her voice and whispered, 'Sure,' a useless permission because he'd already closed the door behind him.

She lay amid the tangled sheets, knowing she needed to get up but unable to put thought into action. Her body was heavy and limp, her eyelids dragging downward with fatigue. Disjointed thoughts formed and disappeared. Everything had changed, and she wasn't yet sure exactly how. Certainly her time with Rafael was over, or almost over, and she needed to think about that, about what she should do. She knew what she wanted to do, and the idea was so new, so foreign to her, that she could scarcely take it in.

He came out of the bathroom within ten minutes, his hair wet, his skin smelling of her soap. Silently he began dressing, his expression calm and remote, as if he were lost in thought. She watched him, drinking in every inch of him, waiting for him to look at her. What they had shared for the past several hours had been so intense she almost couldn't remember what her life had been like before, a line of demarcation so plainly drawn it was as if everything before was in shades of gray and everything after was in Technicolor.

She waited, and still he was silent. She waited, certain that when he finished dressing he'd look at her and say ... what? She didn't know what she wanted him to say, only that pain was swelling in her chest again, a pain that threatened to suffocate her. She couldn't stay with Rafael any longer. She wanted more, she wanted to be more, she wanted... God, she wanted this man so intensely she couldn't let herself fully realize the breadth and depth of it.

He turned toward the door without saying anything and in panic she bolted upright, clutching the sheet to her breasts, he *couldn't* leave the same way Rafael had, as if she meant nothing, as if she *was* nothing.

'Take me with you,' she blurted, choking back the humiliating burn of tears.

He paused with his hand on the doorknob, finally looking at her, his brows drawing together in a faint frown. 'Why?' he asked in a sort of remote puzzlement, as if he couldn't understand why she'd said something so outlandish. 'Once was enough.' Then he walked out and Drea sat motionless on the bed. He moved so silently she didn't hear the penthouse door open or shut, but she felt his absence, knew the exact moment he left.

Silence closed around her, profound and tomb-like. There were things she needed to do, she realized, but actually doing them seemed beyond her. All she could do was sit there, barely breathing, considering the shambles her life had suddenly become. She had just been screwed, in more ways than one.

3

When the assassin left Salinas's penthouse, he didn't take the elevator. Instead he strode silently to one of the stairwells and went down four floors. Taking a key from his pocket, he unlocked the door to the luxury apartment he'd leased for a couple of months. He had to live somewhere, and though he moved frequently, he liked being comfortable. When he had to, he could – and did – endure long periods of wretched discomfort, but this wasn't one of the had-to times. Besides, it amused him to live right under Salinas's nose.

The silence wrapped around him like a welcome blanket. Only when he was alone did he relax – at least, as much as he ever relaxed. The rooms were spare, not because he couldn't afford to buy furniture, but because he liked the space, the emptiness. He had a place to sleep, and a place to sit. He had a television, and a computer. The kitchen was supplied with just enough for him to get by. He didn't need anything else.

When he moved from here, he would wipe everything down beforehand with a cleaning solvent to remove any fingerprints he'd left, then he would donate all the furnishings to a charity. Finally, he would have the apartment professionally cleaned, and it would be as if he'd never been here at all.

He would take some of his clothing with him,

but, like the furniture, he wore things only a few times before donating them. If a sharp forensics tech found a thread that had first escaped his own notice and then the attentions of the cleaning service, and if by some colossal stroke of good luck on an investigator's part led to him, nothing in his wardrobe would match that thread.

His computer was his Achilles' heel, but he couldn't do the necessary research prior to each job without it, so he did what he could to limit the risk, periodically wiping the hard drive, then removing it and installing a new one. As a final precaution, he would physically destroy the old hard drive. His safety routines were time-consuming, but they were simply part of his life. He didn't fret about them, he simply did them.

He traveled light, and he traveled fast. He had a sentimental attachment to nothing, so there was nothing from which he couldn't walk away. As for people ... they were much like his possessions: temporary. There were people of whom he was fond, in a distant way, but no one who elicited any strong emotions in him. He didn't even get angry, because he saw it as a waste of time. If the issue was minor, he walked away; if it was something he had to handle, he took care of the matter calmly and efficiently, and wasted no time worrying about things afterward.

Being a killer was neither something he worried about nor reveled in; it was simply what he was. The assassin was a man who knew himself and accepted that knowledge. He didn't feel what other people felt; emotions, to him, were mild and distant. Because of that, nothing ever overruled his brain. He was sharply intelligent, and physic-ally he was strong and fast, with the extraordinary hand/eye coordination that all truly superb marksmen possessed. Everything about him was perfectly suited to his chosen occupation.

While he might not have standards, as such – because standards seemed to imply some sort of moral guidance system – he did have rules. His number one rule was: never kill a cop. Never. Under any circumstances. Nothing would bring the full fury of law enforcement down on him faster than harming one of their own. Nor did he ever take a job involving romantic affairs, be-cause not only were they messy, they tended not to be lucrative. His prime targets were usually connected to the crime underworld, industrial espionage, or politics. The cops didn't really care about the former, the second category tended to be hushed up, and he never took a political job in this country. That kept his life as tidy and un-complicated as he could make it.

He went into his bedroom and removed his clothes, dropping them into a hamper in the closet, then went naked into the bathroom and carefully peeled the flesh-colored latex from his earlobes. He constantly changed his appearance in small ways, on the theory that he couldn't be too careful. Surveillance cameras were everywhere these days, thanks to the bastard terrorists. He always did his homework and located the most ob-vious places for surveillance to be set up, assumed he was being filmed, and worked the angles.

He could have showered here, instead of in Drea's bathroom, but she was far more astute than she wanted people to know. Short of an emergency, not many people would forgo washing off after four hours of sex – unless they knew they could shower very soon somewhere else, like maybe somewhere else in this very building. She might not have come to that conclusion, but he hadn't wanted to take the chance. Anyone sharp enough to pull the wool over Salinas's eyes wasn't a person he could take lightly.

The afternoon had been ... satisfying. Very satisfying. Not only had he learned a lot about Salinas, but he'd pushed the boundaries of his own self-control and had a great deal of pleasure from it. He'd wanted to know how much Salinas needed him, and the answer was obvious: very much – enough that Salinas had agreed to share his woman, which ran contrary to the basic foundation of his heritage, his position, and his ego. The only time someone in Salinas's position would give away his woman was when he was tired of her, and the assassin was damn certain that wasn't the case.

The identity of his latest target, a major drug trafficker in Mexico, had made the assassin curious. Salinas was a major distributor, but his operation was on the delivery end of the drug chain. Drug dealers were constantly knocking each other off, but for a distributor to have a supplier eliminated was ... odd. Something else was going on, something that could prove to be very lucrative to a man who was the best at what he did.

The assassin had carefully considered all the angles and possibilities, and devised a way to find out what he wanted to know. If the answer was 'yes,' then Salinas would soon desperately need

44

the assassin's services, which in turn meant the assassin could name his price for the job. If the answer was 'no,' no real harm was done, because while he'd have to stick by his implied threat to never work for Salinas again, there was never any shortage of jobs. There was, in fact, a surplus of people who wanted him to kill other people. Economically, there was no downside for him, and a 'yes' answer also gave him a nice physical bonus: Drea.

He was a solitary man by nature, but he wasn't a monk. He liked women and he liked sex, though he regarded both much as he regarded his own physical comfort: something he could do without if necessary. Normally he stayed far away from other men's women, because the situation could get sticky and he didn't want that much attention drawn to himself. But something about Drea had caught his interest the first time he'd seen her.

It wasn't her looks. He didn't have a particular type that he liked, but at the same time he'd never gone for the skinny, overly sexual, big-haired bimbos. Yet the attraction he'd felt for her had been instant and strong. He supposed skin chemistry outweighed all the negative factors, and led him to take a second look, which was when he'd realized that, regardless of how she looked and acted, she was far from dumb.

What had given her away wasn't anything she'd done, really. He had to admit, her act was flawless. Rather, it was his own heightened awareness of her. He'd always been, by nature and by practice, a skilled observer; the predator instinct

45

in him accurately read minute changes in expression, in body language. He couldn't pinpoint what had alerted him, only that he abruptly *knew* there was a sharp brain under all that hair, that she was playing Salinas like a violin.

Realizing that had only increased both his attraction and his admiration for her acting ability. She wasn't running a con, he had no doubt Salinas was getting good service for his money, but she was definitely running a risk. Salinas wouldn't blink at having her killed if the least thing made him suspicious of her.

The assassin respected survivors, and Drea was that. When he saw a way to have her, he didn't hesitate.

He'd been faintly surprised by her initial reaction. Women like her, who traded on their looks and bodies to get what they could from men like Salinas, usually saw sex as a commodity. At first he'd thought her reluctance was just an act, to pander to Salinas's ego, but when it became obvious she was truly terrified, he'd mentally shrugged and decided to drop the whole thing. He'd found out what he wanted to know, just by Salinas's reaction.

When she ran out on the balcony he'd started to leave, but an unusual impulse had sent him after her. She looked terrified enough to jump, and he didn't want that. Going out there had been risky – hell, the feds had to have Salinas under constant surveillance – but ultimately worth it. He'd touched her arm and felt the burn and sizzle of an almost electric connection, and within seconds she'd been responding – still frightened, but she'd felt that potent chemistry as strongly as he had.

He liked taking his time with sex, but today had been unusual. Once Drea had gotten over being so scared, she'd turned hot enough to scorch him. In the intensity of her response, he'd read how starved she was for attention, for being seen as she truly was, seen how much she needed to be stroked instead of being the one doing the stroking. Salinas had to be a lousy lover, selfish and lazy, to leave a woman that hungry.

As enjoyable as the afternoon had been, the assassin didn't plan a repeat. As he'd told her, once was enough. Now he would disappear until Salinas made contact again, and focus on turning this developing situation to his financial advantage.

Forty minutes later, an elderly gentleman with stooped shoulders and a slightly tottering gait left by the front entrance. He used a cane to steady himself as he made his way to the curb and waited for the doorman to hail a cab.

High above the street, Xavier Jackson and Rick Cotton noted the old man's exit, but they'd seen him coming and going several times before and a cursory investigation had revealed he was a tenant in the building, so their interest promptly moved on.

4

He was right, the bastard; Rafael would be early.

Drea forced herself out of bed; her legs were heavy and uncooperative, and her insides felt tender. She swayed, holding to the bed for support, her teeth chattering from a bone-deep cold. Ice had congealed in her veins, a coldness that permeated all the cells in her body and froze her from the inside out.

She had never before been so cold, but she couldn't allow herself the luxury of huddling under the covers. She had to do something to ward off disaster, and the only idea that came to mind was a long shot. Laboriously she smoothed the sheets and pillows, then hobbled to the kitchen and grabbed a can of Febreze. Returning to her bedroom, she sprayed the bed linens before tucking everything in tight and drawing the silk duvet in place. She stacked her decorative pillows on the bed in their usual order, then sprayed the air deodorizer around the bedroom and in the bathroom. Maybe she was just imagining it, but she would have sworn she could *smell* him.

Why was she so cold? The air felt freezing, but she couldn't take the time to stop and adjust the thermostat. After replacing the Febreze in the kitchen, she gathered her scattered clothing and took the garments into the bathroom with her, where she carelessly dropped them on the floor the way she normally did. Then she turned on the water in the shower, made it as hot as she could stand it, got in and swiftly soaped herself, cleaning away the stink and stickiness. At least the water lent her some of its warmth.

Think! She had to think.

She couldn't. Rage bubbled in her like a thick tar, coating her brain in icy blackness. How could she have been so damned stupid? Stupid, stupid, *stupid!* She was disgusted with herself. She *knew* better than to believe in that happily-ever-after fairy-tale bullshit, but let her spend a few hours with some guy who knew how to use his dick and she was all but begging him to take her with him. No, not just 'some guy,' but a man who killed as easily as most people brushed their teeth.

Self-ridicule clogged her chest until she felt as if she were suffocating. What had she thought? That because he'd been slow and easy and made sure she came he'd fallen in love with her? Yeah, right. His technique was different, that was all. Like every other man she'd been with, once he got his rocks off, he lost interest.

Humiliation gnawed at her like a hungry animal. Why couldn't she just have enjoyed the sex stuff and not let her emotions get involved? Instead she'd acted like the naive, idiotic girl she'd been at fifteen, thinking a man would make everything in her world right, instead of screwing things up even more.

At least she'd been young, the first time she'd made a fool of herself for a man and ended up alone and pregnant – and then just alone – so that was some excuse for being stupid. Not now.

Not this time.

She rinsed off and got out of the shower, and despite an almost nauseating distaste made herself use the towel the assassin had used. Rafael noticed details, and too many towels would be a dead giveaway.

The blast of air-conditioning was frigid on her damp skin and she began shivering again as she blotted her wet hair with the same towel, which was now too wet to do much good. Tossing the towel aside, she grabbed the thick terry robe hanging on a hook and pulled it around her, then went to the marble vanity to get her comb and drag it through her hair.

As she stared into the mirror, she realized her face was wet, and with distant surprise she realized she was crying. Again. Twice in one day had to be a record for her.

She would *not* cry over this. Crying didn't help a damn thing. She all but slapped the tears off her cheeks.

They came back. She stood there, watching the woman in the mirror and the slow trickle of tears down her face, and had the disorienting feeling she was watching someone else, someone who had disappeared a long time ago. Her face was white, the expression in her eyes stark. Without her makeup, and with her long hair slicked back from her face, she was the girl whose baby had died and taken all her dreams with it.

Drea fled the bathroom, choking on bitterness. She should dry her hair and put on makeup, make herself look as pretty and sexy as possible, but she couldn't do it. Staring at herself in the mirror long enough to do that – *no*.

Her momentum carried her into the living room, where she faltered to a stop, her head down, like a wind-up toy with a broken spring. What now? What should she do? What *could* she do?

She was so cold. The death chill seemed to swirl through her and around her, turning her shivering into teeth-rattling shudders. Even though the floor was carpeted her bare feet were icy and bloodless, the magenta polish garish against her colorless skin. She hated the color of that polish, hated the way it had looked as he lifted her feet over his shoulders–

A raw, guttural sound burst from her chest as she shoved the memory away and lurched toward the sliding doors and out onto the balcony, into the warmth it offered.

She barely registered the soothing heat from the stone tiles under her feet. Besides warmth, the balcony also offered memories she didn't want, couldn't bear. She avoided looking at the railing where she'd stood earlier, and instead sank down on the tiled floor and leaned her back against the wall. The bright sun had warmed the brick, too, and welcome heat began to leach through to her skin. Whimpering with relief, she drew her legs up to her chest and pulled the robe around her so she was completely covered, and curled forward to rest her forehead on her knees.

Choked sobs tore free, born from a despair so deep she couldn't understand it, or her own reaction. What was wrong with her? She never just gave up like this; she was always maneuvering, managing, looking for an advantage. She needed to pull herself together, make an effort to seduce Rafael–

No! The word erupted from her subconscious, reverberating through her entire body. The savagery of the instinctive reaction shook her; she never allowed herself to feel that deeply about anything. Then something inside her settled and she felt the utter rightness of it. She and Rafael were over, finished. He'd given her away as if she were nothing to him – as if she were nothing, period.

She hated him, hated him even more than she hated herself. She'd completely subjugated herself to him, bitten her tongue and smiled and gone along with him no matter what he wanted, and for what? For him to treat her as if she were a common whore? She trembled with a primitive need to hurt him, to see his blood, to physically beat him and bite him and tear at him with her nails.

She couldn't; she knew that. His goons would either shoot her on the spot or drag her off to be disposed of at their leisure. Admitting her own helplessness against him was even more galling.

The ruthlessly logical part of her brain ordered her to pull herself together and just deal with this, but she couldn't seem to shove all these turbulent emotions away. They were like giant waves that kept crashing over her protective walls, and she was going under for the third time.

Rafael had to pay. She didn't know how, but she had to make him pay. She couldn't live if she let him get away with grinding her into the dirt the way he had. No matter how low life had pushed her, she'd always managed to reassure herself that at least she hadn't been reduced to prostitution. She'd seen herself as Rafael's mistress, not his whore, which maybe was splitting hairs but to her way of thinking it was a damned important hair.

She no longer had the comfort of that illusion. To him, she was nothing more than goods to be traded for a service, and the mirror she held up to herself reflected back only what he saw. Her entire body shuddered from the force of her sobs, her throat under such strain that she began gagging, but her stomach was empty and the spasm produced only dry heaves.

Finally she heard him enter, closing the door more loudly than he usually did, as if to emphasize his lack of remorse. He'd wanted to retain the assassin's services more than he'd wanted to keep her, and–

The bitter thought stuttered to a halt, and for a moment she felt her brain almost freeze in a sudden burst of comprehension. *He'd wanted to retain the assassin's services...* There was someone else he wanted dead, wanted it desperately enough that he'd swallowed his pride and given – loaned – his mistress to another man. Maybe that meant he valued her more than his actions said; maybe this gave her an advantage.

Her brain felt as if it were gummed with molasses; before she had time to work through her thoughts, Rafael stepped through the open sliding doors onto the balcony, halting when he saw her. 'Why are you out here?'

His tone was so casual that the thick, sulfurous rage surged again inside her, and she had to clench her fists on the folds of her robe to keep from launching herself at him and tearing at his eyes with her nails. She gulped in huge breaths of air, fighting for control, fighting to *think*. She had to do something, say something.

She lifted her head and he flinched, his eyes widening with shock. Drea was acutely aware of how she looked, with her swollen eyes and ravaged face. She'd never before let Rafael see her looking anything less than perfect, but this time she didn't care how she looked.

In another sudden burst of clarity, this one even more stunning than the first, she suddenly knew exactly what she was going to do, what she had to say. The enormity of the plan was so stunning that if she let herself hesitate she might chicken out. Rafael had to pay, and she knew exactly how she would make him do it.

She sucked in a deep, shuddering breath, bracing herself. 'I'm sorry,' she choked out, tears streaming down her face again from the effort it took to apologize to the bastard. 'I didn't know... I didn't know you were t-tired of me–' Her voice broke and she covered her face with her hands, her shoulders heaving from the force of her sobs.

She heard the scrape of his shoes on the tiles as he moved closer. Then there was a hesitation, as if he either didn't know what to do, or knew but didn't want to do it. Finally his hand settled on her shoulder. 'Drea...' he began.

Drea jerked away from him, unable to stand even a casual touch from him. 'No, don't,' she said raggedly. She wiped her face with the sleeve of her robe. 'I don't want your pity.' More tears slid down to take the place of the ones she'd removed. 'I knew you didn't love me,' she whispered, 'but I-I thought I had a chance, I thought one day you might. I guess now I know better, huh?' Her lips and chin quivered as she stared out into the distance, though most of the view was blocked by the wall. She didn't dare look directly at him, afraid he would see in her eyes the utter loathing she felt for him. Thank God for these damn stupid tears that wouldn't stop, even if she had to make Rafael believe she was crying because of him, instead of–

No. She was *not* crying because of that damned killer. She didn't know why she was crying, but it definitely wasn't because of him. Maybe she'd gone crazy, or something. But crazy or not, she'd play it for all she was worth. She was banking on Rafael's ego, banking that he'd be so flattered that she'd actually fallen in love with him that he'd be willing to buy the line of bullshit she was handing him.

He crouched beside her, his dark eyes searching her face. Drea kept staring straight ahead and once more wiped her face. Maybe she couldn't handle anything else that had happened today, but she would damn sure handle Rafael Salinas, or die trying.

'Did he hurt you?' Rafael finally asked, his voice quiet, the tone deadly and underlaid with something unlike anything she'd ever heard from him before.

She didn't take the time to analyze it, just went with her instincts. 'He didn't touch me. I was upset and he got– He said I wasn't worth the trouble, and left.' She gave a short, bitter laugh. 'I guess

55

you still owe him the hundred thou. Sorry 'bout that.' Rafael was Latino; knowing the assassin had had sex with her would lessen her value in his eyes, maybe even so much he wouldn't try to keep her. She wasn't ready to go, not yet, so she had to make him think nothing had happened.

'He didn't touch you?' Rafael's tone now held pure shock.

'That makes the two of you, huh? He didn't want me, either.' She hadn't meant to say that, the bitterness was too sharp and violent, but the words burst out of her. She regretted giving him even that much of a window onto her true feelings, though the emotion was genuine and that would carry some weight.

Once was enough.

Well, damn him to hell and back, once was more than enough for her. She knew now what he'd been doing: playing some kind of game with Rafael, one so subtle Rafael didn't have a fucking clue he was even supposed to have been on the field. It was a game of sexual one-upmanship, and the assassin had won, giving her such an overdose of pleasure that she'd lost her mind and actually begged him to take her with him. She'd been fucked straight into stupidity, and she still didn't have her brains back or she'd be able to stop this stupid crying.

Anguish washed over her again, still fresh and powerful, and she buried her face against her drawn-up knees as she wept.

Rafael hovered beside her, as if he couldn't decide what to do. Nothing in their relationship had prepared him for this; Drea had always been accommodating, smiling, shallow and ornamental. He'd never seen her upset, or even annoyed. She would be willing to take bets that he thought she was interested in nothing except shopping and getting her hair and nails done, but then, she'd gone to extraordinary lengths to make him think that.

Finally he said, 'I'll get you some water,' and disappeared inside.

Water! As if a drink of water was going to comfort her. She was upset, not thirsty. Still, the gesture said something, because Rafael didn't fetch anything for anyone; it was always the other way around, with others catering to him.

He was gone far longer than simply getting a glass of water would take, and she knew he was looking through the penthouse, searching for signs that she'd lied to him. Mentally she ran through everything she'd done, wondering if she'd overlooked anything.

He stepped back out onto the balcony and crouched beside her once more. 'Here,' he said. 'Drink some water.'

The tears had subsided enough that she thought she could talk, so Drea lifted her head and wiped her face before reaching for the glass and taking an obligatory sip. 'I was going to pack,' she said wretchedly, her throat so clogged she was barely intelligible. 'But I don't have a-anywhere to go. I'll start looking for a place, if you'll let me s-stay here for a couple of days.'

'You don't have to go,' he said, putting his hand on her shoulder again. 'I don't want you to go.'

'You don't want me,' she said, shaking her head

and finally daring to look at him, or at least look in his direction; her vision was so blurred with tears he was just an undefined shape. Her voice wobbled, but she swallowed hard and managed to keep going. 'You *g-gave me* to him. You could have just told me to go, you didn't have to do that. Maybe I should have seen you were getting tired of me but I guess I hoped so much you might love me that I–' She interrupted herself, shaking her head. 'Never mind.'

'I *don't* want you to go,' Rafael insisted. 'I would never have– Look, he had me over a barrel and he knew it.' He looked around, as if assessing their vulnerability to electronic eavesdropping, and said impatiently, 'Let's go inside, we can't talk out here.'

Drea let him pull her to her feet and usher her inside, his hand resting possessively on her waist. Triumph roared through her, pushing the tears away, at least for now *Yes!* She'd bought herself the time she needed to put her plan into action. She just had to hide her true feelings from him a little while longer, but she had so much practice at that it wouldn't be a strain.

Rafael would pay, and pay big.

'What do you make of that?' Xavier Jackson asked in astonishment, blinking at what the parabolic microphone had just picked up. The sound quality wasn't great, because of the wind, the distance, and other factors, but the computer program could filter out a lot of the interference.

'I think we need to find out who the mystery man is,' replied Cotton, 'if he's important enough to make Salinas share his girlfriend. He hasn't left the building yet?'

'If he has, we missed him. But then, we haven't seen him entering the building, either. Ever.'

'Then he either has a tunnel, or he's in disguise.'

'I don't rule out the tunnel,' Jackson said wryly. There were all sorts of abandoned tunnels under the city. None of their city blueprints showed a tunnel there, but that didn't mean there wasn't one. It was something to check out, even though he'd go with the assumption the man had disguised himself somehow. He'd go back over all the surveillance video and compare every person who'd left with the video he had of the man on the balcony. 'I wonder why the girlfriend's trying to convince Salinas nothing happened between her and the guy, when Salinas evidently gave her to him?'

'Who knows?' Cotton sighed, rubbing his hand over his head in frustration. 'That shot the hell out of using this to get to her, though, because even if Salinas found out they did do the nasty, he issued the invitation. Damn it all to hell.'

They both stared at the computer screen in frustration, even though right now it was showing them exactly what they had: nothing.

5

Rafael Salinas quietly opened Drea's bedroom door and walked to her bedside. He had seldom been in this room, though he'd had his men regularly search it to make certain she wasn't up to anything. Her chosen decor was so fussy and frilly it was cloying, and normally he didn't like being reminded that his mistress had such bad taste. Tonight, for some reason, the excess not only didn't bother him, but in a strange way was almost touching. Her room was like the room of a young girl whose doting mother had let her decorate however she wanted, almost innocent in its exuberance.

She was asleep, lying on her side facing away from the door, curled in a tight knot on the very edge of the bed. She looked smaller than usual, as if she'd been diminished. The light from the hallway spilled across the slightly exotic cast of her cheekbones, tangled in the heavy mass of her curly hair. She had cried until she was exhausted, and even in the dimness he could tell how swollen her eyes were.

He wasn't a man who suffered from self-doubt; that was for fools and pussies who either didn't know what they were doing or didn't have the guts to do what they wanted. Still, for the first time in years – decades – he felt crippled by un-certainty.

60

Equal amounts of panic, anger, and confusion churned in his gut. How had this happened? Why was he feeling this way about *Drea*, of all people?

He sat down in the bedside chair, moodily watching her. She'd been with him for two years, longer than any other woman, but only because she was placid and undemanding. He didn't have either the time or patience to deal with whines, pouts, and demands. Being with Drea, however, was easy; she was even-tempered, slightly dumb, and interested in nothing except shopping and looking pretty. There was never any drama from her, no tantrums, no demands for expensive gifts or, worse, his time. He never gave her much thought; she was just *there*, smiling and complacent, whenever he wanted sex.

If he'd had to think about it, though, he would have said sex was the only reason he kept her. He hadn't wanted to let that bastard have her, sure, because no man worth his *cojones* shared his woman, but his options had been limited, and all of them bad. If he'd said 'no,' which his pride and ego wanted to do, he'd have lost the killer's very valuable services – services he would very much need when the time was right. There was also the real possibility that the killer would take his refusal personally, and while Rafael wasn't afraid of anyone, he was smart enough to know there were some people you just didn't fuck with – and the assassin was one of those people.

So he'd swallowed his pride, his temper, and said 'yes,' and he hadn't liked it one fucking bit. He'd stewed about it all afternoon, imagining *his* woman naked with another man, and he'd even caught himself, damn it, wondering if the bastard's dick was bigger than his. He didn't have to worry about shit like that, so he was pissed that the little niggle of doubt had intruded. He had the money and the power, and that was what mattered to women like Drea.

But even though he'd seen the shock in her eyes when he agreed to let the assassin have her, he hadn't expected her to really care very much. After all, sex was how she paid her way. No big deal, right?

Part of him really thought he'd find her filing her nails, or watching that damn shopping network she loved so much, as placid as always. Instead he'd found her huddled on the balcony, crying her heart out, and he felt as if he'd been punched in the stomach. Her appearance had shocked him: her hair wet and slicked back, no makeup, eyes swollen from crying. Her face had been pinched and white, as if she was in shock, and the expression in her eyes–

Broken. That was the only word he could think of to describe her. She'd looked broken.

At first he'd thought she'd been hurt physically, that the bastard was the kind who got his rocks off by hurting women, and once again Rafael had been knocked off balance by an unexpected reaction, this time his own: he'd been swamped by pure rage that anyone would dare harm what was his, that simple, harmless Drea had been hurt. No matter what it cost him, now and in the future, he'd have the assassin hunted down and killed.

But that wasn't what had happened. Instead, she was devastated by this proof that he, Rafael, didn't love her, and she had given up hope that he ever would. He mentally fumbled all the pieces together, setting himself up for another punch to the gut.

The last blow was the one that leveled him, put him down for the count. *Drea loved him.*

Rafael still couldn't get his head around the idea. Love wasn't part of their deal. But here she was, making plans to leave him because now she knew he didn't love her and she didn't have any hope he ever would. The assassin hadn't even touched her. As unbelievable as that seemed, she had no reason to lie about it, because he'd arranged it, expected it. There was nothing to hide from him, nothing that needed to be hidden. Suspicion was second nature to him, so he'd checked the penthouse. No bed in the place showed signs of having been used. Drea was fresh from the shower, the bathroom still humid, the clothes she'd been wearing dropped on the floor as always, one towel used and carelessly discarded. He had to figure she was telling the truth.

He felt betrayed, because she wasn't what he'd expected, what he'd become accustomed to having. She wasn't there because of convenience and money and protection, or any of the other reasons a woman like her usually hooked up with a man. She was there because she loved him. He was confused, and furious, and – *fuck!* – flattered. He didn't want to be flattered, he wanted everything to be exactly the way it was before. He didn't want it to matter to him that she loved him, but it did.

It shouldn't matter to him if she moved out; he

could replace her without effort. Women always came to him, he never had to go out looking for one. He knew that – he *knew* it, and yet the thought of losing her made him sick with panic. He, Rafael Salinas, was worried about a woman. It was enough to make him laugh. And yet, there it was: he didn't want to lose her. He didn't want another woman. He wanted Drea. He wanted to keep her in clothes and shoes and give her money to buy all the silly pampering she wanted, and most of all, he wanted her to love him. That was the most ridiculous part of all this, that he should care at all if she loved him, if anyone loved him.

Slowly, sitting there in the half-dark, he began to think that maybe he had fallen in love with her. It couldn't be, but how else could he explain this sense of panic, this confusion, this *pain?* He hadn't loved anyone or anything since he'd been a kid, growing up in the toughest barrios of Los Angeles, when he'd learned that valuing someone merely gave your enemies a weapon to use against you. He had to stop this line of thought, shut it down now.

But it was heady, this feeling that made his heart race, and his stomach jump, and for the first time in his life he understood why people did such stupid things when they were in love. This weird mixture of euphoria and dread felt as if he'd mainlined a mysterious drug, so instantly addictive that already he wanted more.

Drea stirred, drawing his attention to the bed. A tender ache settled in his chest as he watched her roll over and once more draw her legs up into a tight curl, as if even in her sleep she tried to protect herself, to make herself small and insignificant. She needed him, he thought, needed him to stand between her and the world, so she could feel safe. Someone like her, dumb and sweet and gullible, would be a sitting duck if she was on her own.

Either she hadn't been sleeping soundly or the intensity of his gaze awakened her. She opened her eyes, and for a moment she didn't appear to notice him, sitting there in the shadows. Then she registered the open door, and she blinked a few times, then rubbed her eyes. When she saw him she said 'oh' in a small voice that still sounded exhausted and raw from crying.

Rafael wanted to do something he'd never done before, for anyone: he wanted to comfort her. He wanted to take off his clothes and slide under the covers with her, hold her close and whisper reassurances to her – anything to take that empty broken expression from her eyes. The only thing that stopped him was an uncertainty that she would welcome him, something that would never have occurred to him before. His pride and ego had taken a battering already that day, and he didn't want to risk being rejected. Tomorrow would be time enough to push his luck a little.

'I was just checking on you,' he said, keeping his voice low and trying to sound matter-of-fact, as if he did that sort of thing all the time.

'I'm okay.'

She didn't sound okay. She sounded as if there was no spirit left in her, as if she'd never smile again.

There was a squeezing sensation in his chest

that made talking difficult. He licked his lips, then swallowed nervously. He'd done this to her, hurt her so deeply that he'd destroyed the almost childlike joy she'd taken in life. He'd make it up to her, he thought fiercely. Somehow, he'd talk her into staying. He could always make it impossible for her to find another place to stay, thereby forcing her to stay here. He didn't care what means he used, so long as they worked.

Just that morning, less than twelve hours ago, she would have been asking if there was anything he wanted, catering to him, fussing around him to make certain everything was just the way he liked it. Now she simply lay there, making no effort at all to even have a conversation, and the chasm that separated them felt as if it were a thousand miles wide. If only she got mad the way other women did, he thought in frustration, then he could get mad in return, and he wouldn't be feeling this helpless. But Drea never lost her temper; he didn't even know if she *had* a temper.

He'd joked with someone once that she had all the depth of a petri dish, and now he wished that were true.

He'd made fun of her, dissed her to others, and he hadn't realized or appreciated that all this time she'd been, very simply, devoted to him. If loving someone else was a bitch, *being* loved was insidiously worse, imposing a subtle burden of care on him. Twelve hours ago he'd been free. Now he'd been ambushed by emotion, and chained as effectively as if feelings were made of steel.

'Do you need anything?' he asked as he made himself get to his feet. He couldn't just sit by her

66

bedside like some idiot.

She hesitated a few seconds before answering, seconds in which his heart leaped in hope, but then she said, 'Just some sleep,' and he realized that her pause had been caused by exhaustion rather than indecision.

'I'll see you in the morning, then.' He leaned over the bed and kissed her cheek. Once, twelve hours ago, she would have turned her head to meet his mouth with hers, but now she simply lay there. Her eyes were already closing before he turned away.

Rafael had barely shut the door behind him when Drea's eyes popped open, and she shuddered. She was a good actress, but she knew she wasn't good enough to hide what she felt if he tried to have sex with her. She couldn't do that again, not with *him;* she had to escape before he really pushed the issue, because she didn't trust herself to maintain control if he did.

At least tomorrow Rafael would be surrounded by his usual retinue, whom he had sent away this morning so he could deal with the assassin without any of them knowing what he was up to. Usually having his inner circle of muscle constantly around got on her nerves, but now she was grateful for their anticipated company. Rafael would take care to treat her normally, so none of them could guess what had happened today; his ego wouldn't stand letting that become public knowledge. He would have to go about his scheduled business, whatever that was. It would be nice if he had to fly across country, but she'd have known if he had a trip scheduled.

He was acting ... weird. She had expected him to be flattered that she was in love with him, but she hadn't expected him to completely derail. Bringing her water, checking on her ... sitting in her bedroom in the dark, for God's sake! He was acting as if he'd had a character transplant, and it was creeping her out. She would think he'd fallen in love with *her* if the idea wasn't so ridiculous. Rafael didn't love anyone. She doubted he'd loved his own mother.

But if he thought he was in love with her, at least for now, that gave her some leverage. That leverage, of course, came with strings, because he might want to stick close to her, and that was the last thing she wanted. She needed a little alone time, so she could get her plans organized and launched.

From the beginning of her relationship with Rafael, she'd taken steps to secure her future. He'd given her numerous gifts of jewelry, but at no time had she ever assumed he'd let her take the jewelry with her when he dumped her. To circumvent him there, she'd taken photographs of each piece and had them all duplicated in paste – very good fakes that had cost her hundreds of dollars to have made, but the cost was well worth it. Each time she'd worn a piece of the real jewelry; when she gave it back to Rafael for him to lock in the safe, she'd swapped the costume piece for the real thing. Rafael guarded the fakes, and when she could, she slipped away to the bank where she had a safe-deposit box he didn't know anything about.

She could live for a while, and live well, on the money she could get from selling the jewelry, but that wasn't enough. Taking the jewelry would make him angry, but it wouldn't be a slap at him, an insult that would cut him to the quick. Besides, he'd *given* the jewelry to her, so it was hers anyway. She wanted to do something that would make him a laughingstock, that would eat away at him.

Yeah, it was dangerous. She knew that. But she'd thought things out, and once she was out of the city she had an advantage; Rafael was purely Big City. He'd lived his entire life in either Los Angeles or New York. Rural America was as foreign to him as Timbuktu, but she'd grown up in a small town in the middle of the country, and she knew how to make herself inconspicuous, how to blend in. There were a lot of places where she could reinvent herself. He wouldn't be expecting that, because he thought she was too dumb to pull it off. On the other hand, he also thought she was too dumb to steal him blind, and pretty soon he'd know better.

She'd have to move fast and keep on moving, and have an alternate plan she could go to each step of the way, in case something went wrong. She should *expect* things to go wrong, then she wouldn't panic when they did.

She would have, at most, a few hours' head start. If she wasn't out of New York City by then, she was as good as dead.

6

Drea overslept, and finally dragged herself out of bed feeling as if she'd been battered, in both body and mind. Four hours of sex, even really good sex, might sound good in theory, but it wasn't something she wanted to do again, even without all the emotional upheaval that had accompanied it. She couldn't deny the physical pleasure, but she liked to be the one in control. She'd rather have a clear head during the act, and take care of her own needs later, when she was alone. Look how stupid a few orgasms had made her, even if the dumbing effect was only temporary. She'd never make that mistake again; if anyone was made stupid, it would be the guy, not her.

This morning she didn't let herself wimp out in front of the mirror; she squared up to it and focused on what she saw now, not the reflection that had been there years ago. She wasn't that stupid, vulnerable girl any longer, so thinking about her was a waste of time.

The present was bad enough, she thought critically, turning her head from side to side as she examined herself. Her face was colorless, unless she counted the bruised-looking shadows under her swollen eyes, and her hair was so snarled it looked as if a nest of rats had been wrestling in it. Maybe it was just ego, but she didn't want to look *pitiful*. She couldn't wipe away every trace of yesterday, but she could certainly look better than this.

For the first time ever, she locked the bathroom door before undressing. She didn't care what Rafael thought, didn't care if he didn't like it.

She picked up a comb and fiercely attacked the knots and snarls in her hair, then got in the shower and scrubbed with her favorite perfumed shower gel. Yesterday afternoon she hadn't had time to put conditioner on her hair, which was why it was such a mess this morning. She took the time now, and felt the thick strands turn silky under her fingers.

The first thing she'd do, she thought grimly, was cut most of this mess *off*. Not only was her hair too identifiable, but she didn't like her hair this long, or this curly. She had some natural wave in her hair but these corkscrew curls resulted from stinking chemicals and hours of maintenance. She'd deliberately chosen the look, knowing it made her look more frivolous and less capable, but, *damn,* she was tired of it. She was tired of pretending she didn't have a brain, tired of putting someone else's needs and wants ahead of her own.

She pulled on her robe and tightly belted it, then swiftly began putting on her makeup, feeling as if time were slipping away and she had only a few hours in which to escape. She shouldn't have slept so long, she should have set her alarm, but she hadn't, and now she had to move fast. With Rafael weirding out on her the way he had, as if he'd suddenly discovered this deep love for her – yeah, right – she couldn't predict what he'd do next, and the uncertainty scared her. He was a dangerous man, and a smart one. All it would take to tip him off was for her to make one slip of the tongue, or forget to guard her expression. She hadn't made that mistake in the two years they'd been together, but she'd never before been so on edge, either. She didn't trust him, and she no longer trusted herself to hold things together.

An idea struck, something that might give her a small advantage if it worked. If not, then at least her situation wouldn't be any worse. She forced herself to cough. The sound was mild, at first, but as she did it again and again the cough became deeper, rougher. She stopped after a minute and said 'Damn it' out loud, to test her voice. Already she sounded hoarse, but not hoarse enough. She coughed some more, pulling the effort from deep in her chest, and felt her throat burn. If she were sick, she'd have a ready-made excuse for keeping Rafael at a distance if he tried to have sex with her – and she'd also have an excuse for looking so pale, which was nothing but her ego talking, but after yesterday she needed every bit of ego she could rustle up. Between the two of them, Rafael and the assassin had pretty much ground her into dust.

She heard a faint sound in her bedroom, and a chill ran down her spine. Rafael! She whirled and unlocked the door, pulling it open in the same motion and stepping out without looking, as if she hadn't heard anything and didn't know he was there. She all but bumped into him, and jumped with a fake yip of surprise. 'I didn't know you were in here,' she said, pleased with how hoarse her voice sounded.

72

He put his hands on her waist and frowned down at her. 'Are you sick? You sound terrible.'

'I might be catching something,' she mumbled, looking down. 'I woke up with a cough.'

He tilted her face up, his dark eyes sharply examining her pallor, the shadows under her eyes. Drea could barely force herself to stand there and let him touch her. He was a handsome man, with thick black hair and chiseled features, but she had never loved him and at the best of times had found only mild pleasure in being with him. There was no pleasure left now, only hate burning so strong and hot she could barely contain it.

Still, she managed to put suffering in her expression as she looked back up at him, then she closed her eyes and swallowed. Straightening, she gently removed herself from his grasp and went to her closet. Opening the door, she turned on the light and stared into the small room, at the shoes scattered across the floor and the laden hangers jammed together without any sort of system. 'I need to find a job,' she said in a wobbly voice, the tone a little lost and bewildered. 'But I don't know what to wear.'

The truth was, there was nothing in her closet appropriate for job-hunting, and nothing she would mind leaving behind. Every garment had been chosen with the purpose of showcasing her assets, and was either too flamboyant or too revealing. There was nothing tailored, not a single skirt long enough to reach her knee – or, if it did, there was also a side slit to add oomph.

Rafael came up behind her and this time he slid his arm around her, pulling her close against his side. He bent his head, pressed his warm mouth to her temple. 'I think you have a fever,' he murmured. 'You should stay home today, and when you're feeling better you can worry about what to wear.' He gave a small, indulgent smile, as if he were talking to a child.

'But I have to—' She knew damn well she didn't have a fever, because she wasn't sick, but that was exactly what she'd wanted him to say.

'No,' he interrupted. 'You don't have to leave, and you sure as hell don't have to hunt for a job. You don't have to do anything, except rest.'

She pulled back from him and searched his face with a desolate gaze. She let her lips tremble a little 'But ... yesterday...'

'Yesterday, I was an idiot,' he said forcefully. 'Listen to me, babe: I don't know how many times you want me to say it, but I'm not tired of you, I swear I don't want you to leave. I want you to stay here and let me take care of you the way I always have. You can't make it on your own. You're not qualified for any job except looking pretty; but you're damn good at that.'

Drea let a weary sigh leak out of her, and she leaned her head into his shoulder, let him support her weight. 'I don't know what to do.' The vulnerability of her posture disarmed him, and also gave her the chance to make certain she could control her expression. She was incredulous that he'd actually admitted he'd been in the wrong about anything – a first – and enraged that he so completely dismissed her capabilities. Logically that last shouldn't matter, because she'd worked damn hard to make him think exactly what he'd said, but to hell with logic. She was in an emotional free fall, and the only handholds she could grab were those of hate and rage. She clung to them, because without them she'd never stop falling.

His hand slid up and down her back, gently rubbing. 'That's what I'm telling you: you don't have to do anything. We'll go on the way we did before. Nothing has to change.'

He had no idea how much things had already changed. She didn't say anything, pretending to think things over, then she threw in a bout of coughing just to be on the safe side. The last thing she wanted was for her voice to begin recovering and sounding normal.

He hugged her close, squeezed her. 'You should take it easy today, see if you feel better tomorrow. How about if I bring you a present tonight? What would you like?'

'I don't know,' she said, and sighed again. 'I think I will just stay in today. I don't feel like shopping. What are you doing today? Are you staying here?' She injected a faintly hopeful note into her raspy voice as if she actually wanted him to stay around, though she felt relatively safe in assuming he wouldn't; Rafael rarely spent the day at the penthouse. He liked to see and be seen, and unless there was some party to attend he never took her with him.

'No, I have business I have to attend to. I'll leave a couple of the guys here, okay? Anything you want, anywhere you want to go, just tell them.' He never left the penthouse empty; someone was always there, making it difficult for the FBI or anyone else to slip in and plant surveillance devices. At first she'd always had two babysitters watching out for her; one would stay behind while the other kept watch on her if she went anywhere. Later, after Rafael decided he could trust her, just one man stayed behind to watch the penthouse and if she went out she went alone. It had been awhile since she'd had one assigned specifically to her; Rafael probably thought he was giving her a perk, when instead he was making her plan that much tougher to play out.

'Who?' Not Orlando, please, she prayed. Orlando Dumas was the sharpest arrow in Rafael's quiver, especially with computers. The last thing she needed was someone computer-savvy looking over her shoulder. When she'd first moved in with Rafael, Orlando had been her most frequent babysitter, because Rafael knew Orlando was the most likely to spot anything suspicious.

'Who do you want?'

'I don't care,' she said listlessly. If she expressed a preference at all, Rafael would wonder why; even asking whom she *didn't* want would trigger his suspicions, so it was safer to let him choose the person he wanted. She'd deal with it regardless. 'I guess I'll look at some things online this morning, and if I feel better later on I'll go to the library.'

'You do that.' He kissed her again, this time on the forehead. 'I don't know what time I'll be back, so eat without me, okay?'

'Okay.' *Perfect.* Eating without him wasn't unusual. They usually shared breakfast, which she wouldn't have to do today because she'd overslept and was late, but most of the time she ate her other meals alone. She'd never been a big part of his life, she realized; how could she have deluded herself that she was anything more to him than convenient sex? She was easily replaced, easily forgotten – and easily bartered.

That was about to change. By the time she was finished, Rafael would *never* forget her.

Satisfied that he'd weathered the threatened upheaval to his domestic arrangement, Rafael gave her another hug and kiss and strolled out. Drea blew out a huge breath, her legs going weak with relief. Maintaining her act, schooling her every expression and word, had never been a problem, but now it took real effort and she felt the strain. In her head she could hear a clock ticking, warning her that she couldn't keep this up for much longer.

Still, she played it safe, because he might look in on her again before he left the penthouse. She turned on her television, put it on a shopping channel with the sound turned very low, and curled up in a chair with a cashmere throw pulled over her legs. Then she waited, closing her eyes and straining her ears for the sound of the door closing. She'd have muted the television if she'd been certain Rafael wouldn't reenter her room, but until he actually left she had to assume he would. How much of her life had she wasted doing this, setting the stage and making certain every detail was perfect, on the off chance he might notice?

This time it paid off. He opened the door without knocking. Drea opened her eyes as he crossed the room, and to her astonishment saw he had a cup of coffee in his hand. 'I brought your coffee,' he said. 'It'll help your throat.'

Impatience roiled inside her, made her want to clench her teeth, but she stopped herself just in time. He'd notice the motion of her jaw muscles, and he'd know she was putting on an act. God in Heaven, would he just *leave?* He must have some worm in his brain, to be acting like this.

'That's so sweet,' she said, and coughed some more as she took the cup from him. 'Thank you.'

'Cream and three sugars, right?'

'Right.' No, it was two sugars and skim milk, which told her how much attention he'd paid. Now she'd have to skip her morning toast to make up for these extra calories. She sipped the too-sweet, too-rich brew, and smiled at him. 'Perfect.'

A faint blush tinged his high cheekbones, and it was all she could do not to gape at him. Rafael Salinas, *blushing?* The world as she knew it must have ended, and she'd been too damn busy being traded around like a whore to have noticed.

She let her head rest against the back of the chair, and sighed as if she felt really miserable. Maybe the bastard would take the hint and leave her alone. She had to be careful not to overdo it, though, or he'd be strong-arming some doctor to check her over. She also didn't want him checking on her all day long. He never had before, but today was a day for firsts.

'Call me if you need me,' he said.

'I will.'

He was clearly torn, wanting to go about his business but at the same time not wanting to leave her. For once, she was out of ideas. She just wanted him to go, and couldn't think of any maneuver that would steer him out the door, so she curled deeper into the chair and closed her eyes; that way, at least, she wouldn't have to look at him.

But, wonder of wonders, either that worked or he couldn't think of any more reasons to delay. She heard him leave her bedroom, then the rumble of masculine voices, and finally the blessed sound she'd been waiting for: the closing of the main door. She could still hear the television in the parlor, and an occasional comment as the two men he'd left behind settled down to watch some sports on the tube.

She resisted the urge to peek and see who Rafael had chosen to babysit her. She was supposed to be sick, and lying down; she didn't want to make anyone suspicious by bouncing out of the bedroom as soon as the door had closed behind Rafael. Her timing didn't have to be down to the minute, but she wanted to leave Rafael as little time to react as possible.

There were plenty of things she could do to get ready, though. She tiptoed over to the door and turned the lock in the doorknob. Locks like that were flimsy and wouldn't slow down any of Rafael's men for more than a few seconds, but she felt safer having that little bit of warning.

Going to the closet, she pulled out a large leather tote. First into it went one of her few pairs of flat-heeled shoes. Once she managed to slip away from her babysitter, she'd have to do some fast walking, and the four- and five-inch heels she preferred might be glamorous but they were hell to walk in.

One thing that worried her was that she didn't know how much influence Rafael had in specific areas. Cameras were everywhere in this city, recording people in stores, walking down the sidewalk, getting on a subway. Everything that went on in a bank was definitely recorded, but she felt safer about that because Rafael didn't know about her safe-deposit box, or which bank she had used. But if he had any pull with the city, the traffic engineers, or the cops, he might be able to get access to recordings and be able to track her movements. That was a chance she'd have to take, because if dematerializing was a learnable skill, she hadn't yet found the class that taught it.

Almost everything here would have to stay. She selected some basic cosmetics, enough to get her by but not enough that Rafael would ever notice part of her stuff was missing. The rest she left scattered across her vanity, as if she were expecting to return. She rolled up a pair of black cropped pants, and a skimpy black shirt, and added them to the bag. Black was the least noticeable color in New York, because so many people wore it, even during the summer. Another bag, smaller and plainer, also went into the tote.

That was it. She'd buy everything else she needed as she needed it. She was satisfied that no one, looking at this room, would think anything other than that she'd gone shopping and would soon be back. Rafael, knowing how she loved clothes and makeup, would never believe she'd willingly left all this behind, and that would buy her precious time – she hoped. She'd have to make a clean escape; if the babysitter saw her, tried to catch her, then she'd have no grace period at all.

She paced. She watched the clock. After a while, hunger pains drove her from her room to the kitchen. Rafael didn't have a cook because he didn't trust people outside of his network, and generally thugs didn't develop their culinary skills, but he did have food delivered so there was always something available.

She made herself walk slowly, as if she didn't have a lot of energy. The two men sitting in the living room looked around. To her relief, neither of them was Orlando Dumas. Their names were Amado and Hector, and if she'd ever heard their last names she'd promptly forgotten them. They were okay, sort of middle of the pack: not the smartest, not the dumbest. Cool. She could handle that.

'You feelin' better?' Hector asked.

'Some.' She'd forgotten to keep coughing, but her voice was still a little raspy. 'I'm going to heat some soup for lunch. Do you want any?' She doubted it, because she could see plates and glasses on the coffee table, indicating they'd already eaten, plus Amado had his hand in a huge bag of Doritos.

'Nah, we've already had lunch. Thanks, though.' Hector had fairly good manners, for a thug.

Drea went into the kitchen and nuked a bowl of soup, ate it standing up at the counter. Her heart was kicking into high gear; she could feel the rhythm of the beats picking up in speed, feel the

81

excitement beginning to race through her veins. She looked at the clock again: two p.m.

Showtime.

7

After locking her bedroom door, Drea got her laptop and logged on. She had carefully researched this, not because she'd been planning all along to wipe out Rafael's bank account and go into hiding, but sort of as a 'just in case' type of thing.

If Rafael had played straight with her, she'd have been content to rock along at the status quo for as long as he wanted her, then she'd take her jewelry and leave. That was what she'd expected to happen, and she'd played her part to convince him that she was completely harmless, so he wouldn't worry about something she might have seen or overheard.

Besides all that, what if Rafael had been killed? Things like that happened to people like him. She hadn't seen any point in letting all that money sit in the bank, his accounts frozen, until the feds stepped in and took it all.

So she'd planned for the future – her future.

So she truly had no idea where or how Rafael kept his other set of books, for the big money that hadn't been laundered. She hadn't tried to find out, judging that effort way out of her league in terms of the risks she was willing to take. But the bank account that Rafael used for his personal needs, and the one from which he made transfers to the account he'd set up for her, well, that was different.

The penthouse had a hard-wired router for their computer use; Orlando had told Rafael to go that route instead of wireless, as a wireless router made it easier for someone else to capture his information. Drea's laptop's IP number was different from that of Rafael's laptop, but from the router outward only one IP number showed up at the other end, meaning that, if she accessed Rafael's bank account, as far as the bank was concerned, the access came from the correct IP number.

Getting Rafael's password had taken months of watching, catching glimpses whenever she could, watching his hands and working out what keystrokes he was using. If he'd changed his password regularly she'd never have been able to figure it out, but like most people he didn't bother. Nor was his password particularly imaginative: he used his cell phone number. He had two cells, an encrypted one Orlando had gotten for him, and another one that he used for ordinary stuff. Drea didn't know the number for the encrypted phone, but she'd often called his regular cell. After she'd figured out three of his keystrokes, she'd known what the password was.

She went to the bank's website, then logged on as Rafael, holding her breath until the account information actually flashed onto the screen. First she went into his account preferences and changed the e-mail address so that any notifications would be sent to her e-mail address instead of his. From the research she'd done, she knew that a bank would send an e-mail when any unusually large transfers were made, and she didn't want Rafael getting that e-mail today.

How long it would be before he – or rather, Orlando – thought to check her e-mail account was anyone's guess. At first, when Rafael realized she had disappeared, he'd check her room. He'd never expect her to leave all her clothes behind, so he'd be concerned something had happened to her, and he'd have his men searching for her. Unfortunately, that meant she also had to leave the laptop behind, because he'd notice immediately if it were gone. She didn't care; there were no files she needed to keep, no photos saved on it.

Besides, she *wanted* Rafael to know what she'd done – after she'd had plenty of time to get away, of course. She wanted him to know that she'd made him pay. He might not find out about his empty bank account until he bounced a check, which could be days. That was the best-case scenario, but sometimes the ball bounced her way. She wasn't counting on it, though; she intended to run far and run fast. She'd have to change her name, spend some money to get a new ID that would hold up under at least a first round of scrutiny, but she knew all about reinventing herself and the prospect didn't bother her.

The e-mail problem taken care of, she went back to Rafael's account information and took her first look at the bottom line. A savage glee filled her. Two million, one hundred eighty-eight thousand, four hundred thirty-three dollars and two cents. She'd leave him the two cents, she thought, because she was transferring only round numbers.

Maybe she'd be smart to take only the two

million, and leave the hundred and eighty-eight thousand. That way he wouldn't immediately bounce any checks, which might stack the deck in her favor. On the other hand, as he'd said, a hundred thousand was a hundred thousand. That was the Judas price he'd put on her, so evidently she was worth a hundred grand. Why shouldn't she take it?

Two million, one hundred thousand dollars. It had a nice sound to it. She typed in her account information, jumped through all the electronic hoops, and with a keystroke was an instant millionaire. She waited a minute, then logged into her own account and stared in satisfaction at the nice big numbers. In case Rafael somehow discovered what she'd done, to keep him from simply transferring the money back into his account, she changed the password. He couldn't get to the money now, because as far as the bank was concerned, he'd given it to her and it was hers to do with as she pleased.

The next step: move all that nice money to a different bank. Not right now, though; it was too soon. A routine e-mail alerting him to the transfer was one thing, but the last thing she wanted to do was trigger a personal telephone call. She'd wait an hour, maybe less, before the bank's closing time to move the money to two separate accounts: part of it to a bank in Elizabeth, New Jersey, but the bulk of it she'd put in the little independently owned bank in Grissom, Kansas, where she still maintained the very first bank account she'd ever opened. The bank here wouldn't, by law, be able to provide Rafael with any information about what she'd done with the money after it landed in her account.

She couldn't help smiling. Rafael had insisted she open the account at his bank to make it easier for him to transfer money to her as she needed it. He had intended his name to be on the account, too, but he hadn't been with her and somehow she'd 'forgotten' that part of his instructions, though she'd dutifully had the statements sent to him so he could keep track of her spending. He'd been annoyed, but not enough to do anything about it, because he had assumed that, because he controlled how much and when any funds were deposited in her account, he also controlled her. He'd been wrong then, and he was wrong now.

Pacing, she reviewed the steps she'd taken so far, trying to think of any additional details. She added a thin black hoodie to her tote bag, so she'd have something to cover her hair with until she could get it cut. She could take a pair of scissors with her and hack it off herself, but she didn't want anyone finding long hanks of hair in a trash can and putting two and two together. She'd get her hair cut tomorrow, in a hair salon, where people got their hair cut all the time and no one would pay any attention to her.

She checked the charge on her BlackBerry, tossed it in the tote, then added one final item: an empty wallet. That was all, she decided. What she was taking was minimal, just what she needed now. She was ready.

Crap, no, she wasn't. Mentally smacking herself on the forehead, she hurried to her closet and retrieved the key to her safe-deposit box from where she had taped it to the inside top of her satin house slippers. Without the key, she wouldn't be able to retrieve the jewelry she'd stashed there, or the bank routing numbers and her account numbers that were also in the box. She couldn't believe she'd been about to walk out without the key. She'd have been helpless, unable to do anything, and she would have to either walk away without anything, or risk coming back here for the key, which would have meant Rafael possibly could discover what she'd done while she was still within his grasp. The thought made her shudder. Even if he didn't, he would want to make love to her tonight, and she knew she couldn't bear it. She couldn't pretend yet again, couldn't hide what she was thinking and feeling.

Going to the door, she coughed several times to cover any sound as she unlocked the door, then pulled it open. She went to the living room and paused at the entrance. Both Amado and Hector looked around at her. 'I'm feeling a little better,' she said hoarsely. 'Is it okay if I go to the library?'

She knew their orders, but she phrased it as a question anyway. She'd never given Rafael's men any lip or attitude, acting as meek and mild as possible, and she didn't change her act now.

'I'll get the car,' Amado said, looking resigned as he got to his feet. He and Hector must have discussed the possibility beforehand, and Amado had drawn the short straw. Hector got to stay at the penthouse and watch sports, while poor Amado had to find a nearby parking space, then sit in the car and wait for her call.

'I'll change clothes and be right out,' Drea promised. She knew they didn't believe her, because she usually took forever getting ready, but today she moved with a speed and purpose she normally kept hidden. She pulled on a cream-colored pair of silk pants and matching tank, then slipped on a cropped silk jacket in hot pink. She was now so noticeable, and so easy to spot, that Amado wouldn't recognize her after she changed clothes, even if she walked right past him. He'd be looking for the pink jacket and her mass of curly hair.

Slipping the straps of the tote bag on her shoulder, she looked around the room for one last time, saying good-bye to Drea Rousseau. The act has served her purpose, but good riddance.

'Bye, Hector,' she said as she left the bedroom and went to the door. 'See you later.'

He waved a hand in reply, not looking away from the television. Drea let herself out, and stepped into the elevator. She was alone. As she pushed the Down button and the car began to move, a sense of lightness and relief began to seep through her, as if chains were falling away. *Soon,* her subconscious whispered. Soon – just minutes now – she would be free. She would be herself again. A few more minutes of pretense with Amado, and she'd be able to close the door on this part of her life.

Exiting into the lobby, she gave the doorman her usual friendly, empty-headed smile. Amado pulled to the curb as she stepped onto the sidewalk. He looked faintly surprised to see her so promptly, but hopped out and opened the rear door of the black Lincoln Town Car for her.

There were thousands of cars just like it in New York; all the car services used them. Rafael used them as his personal cars because they blended with all the others, making it easier for him to shake anyone following him.

As Drea stepped into the car she thought she saw the assassin and panic froze her heart, her blood. She stumbled, almost falling, as her feet suddenly refused to work. Amado grabbed her arm. 'You okay?'

Her gaze darted around, looking for whatever had alarmed her, made her think of him. He wasn't there. She hadn't seen him. Armies of people marched up and down the sidewalks, but he wasn't one of them. She didn't see anyone with that lithe way of moving, or that particular way he held his head. She closed her eyes, sucking in deep breaths as she tried to calm her skittering pulse.

She let herself lean on Amado for just a moment. 'I turned my ankle a little,' she said, managing a faintly helpless tone. 'Sorry.'

'Did you sprain it?'

'I don't think so. Not much, anyway.' She gingerly rotated her right ankle. 'I'm okay.' As she got into the car she took another quick look around. Nothing. There were a lot of dark-haired men, but no one like him. A brief glimpse of something, someone, had reminded her of him, but that was all. He wasn't here. She would know if he were here.

Drea wrenched her thoughts away from the killer. She couldn't let herself get distracted, or she'd make mistakes, any one of which could be fatal. She had to concentrate, and she had to move fast.

By the time Amado pulled to the curb in front of the library, she had herself focused again. 'I'll be about an hour, I guess,' she said vaguely as he helped her out.

'Take your time. Call me when you're ready to leave.'

She could tell from the resignation in his tone that he expected her to be much longer than an hour. The Drea he knew, who they all knew, didn't have much concept of time and was habitually late. If she thought something would take 'just a few minutes' it would invariably take at least an hour, whatever 'it' was.

'What's your number?' she asked. 'I think I have a pen...' She let her voice trail off as she began rummaging in the tote.

'Let me have your phone,' he said as a couple of irate drivers blew their horns at him.

She pulled the BlackBerry out of its little pocket and gave it to him. He was very patient; he didn't sigh or anything as he quickly pro- grammed his number into the device. 'You know how to use your contact list, right?' he asked, just to make certain.

'Rafael showed me,' she said, nodding her head and mentally rolling her eyes.

The cacophony of horns was growing more insistent. 'Take your time,' Amado said as he got back into the driver's seat. Despite the increas- ingly impatient drivers, he still watched as she crossed to the steps and began climbing them. She put on a small limp, just enough that he would notice. Details added up. Not only would he be looking for her bright pink jacket, but also that telltale little limp.

Once inside, she went straight to the ladies' room. Locked in a stall, she swiftly changed clothes and shoes, packing her things in the tote to be disposed of later. She switched wallets, removing her driver's license and all her cash from the Gucci wallet Rafael had given her, and stowing them in the generic one she'd picked up at Macys. She left the credit cards in the designer one. Not only would using the cards be suicidal, but if someone less than honest found the wallet and used the cards, it would muddy her trail that much more.

She couldn't leave it lying out in the open, though; that would be too easy, too obvious. Tucking the wallet back in the tote, she flushed the toilet as if she'd used it, and left the stall.

Two other women were at the row of sinks. Drea dawdled, washing her hands, fiddling with her lipstick and generally primping, until they left. Quickly she wet her hands and began dampening her hair, the water both darkening the color and straightening the curl. When her hair was wet enough, she combed it straight back, flattening it to her head, and twisted it into a tight knot that she haphazardly secured by sticking a pen through it. The knot didn't have to hold for long, just long enough.

Just one more thing. Dampening a paper towel, she washed off as much of her makeup as she could. Then she exited the bathroom with her normal stride, just another busy, hurried, focused New Yorker. No one looked twice at her.

She strode out the exit. Removing the designer wallet from the tote, she held it down by her side, and paused by a trash can. As unobtrusively as possible she let the wallet drop, and used her toe to nudge it behind the can where it was mostly out of sight. Someone would find it, and soon. An honest person would turn it in to the library personnel; a dishonest one would take the credit cards and go on a spending binge. Either scenario worked for her, though the second one would be most troublesome to Rafael.

Quickly walking a couple of blocks away, she hailed a cab and gave the driver a destination. A direct route would have been faster but would also make her easier to track. When she exited that taxi, she walked another couple of blocks and took another one. She changed cabs a third time before reaching her final destination in Elizabeth, New Jersey.

Time was getting short, the afternoon sun sinking lower. Drea went into the bank and requested access to her safe-deposit box. She signed in, retrieved her key from her bag, and a slim, young Asian-American woman ushered her into the small room lined floor to ceiling with boxes.

Drea's was a small box, located near the floor. She had to squat to insert the key. The young teller inserted the bank's key, turned both of them, and unlocked the door. Drea murmured her thanks and the young woman smiled as she left, leaving Drea alone.

Getting out what she needed took just a minute. She removed her clothing from the tote, then from the safe-deposit box she took the velvet bag containing her jewelry, and dropped it in the tote. The only other item in the box was the manila envelope containing the paperwork on her accounts. That, too, went into the bag. Then she stuffed her discarded clothing in the safe-deposit box, relocked it, and dropped the key in her bag.

She left the bank without looking left or right, intent on getting out of sight. Once out on the sidewalk, she hailed yet another cab and asked the driver to take her to a respectable motel. He grunted in reply. While he drove, Drea got out her BlackBerry and her account information, and set to work.

Five minutes later, it was done. Two million dollars had been wired to her account in Grissom, Kansas, and a hundred thousand dollars to her small account at the bank she'd just left. It was too late for her account to be credited with it today, but it would be there first thing in the morning. She'd wait until after she'd used the BlackBerry to confirm that the transactions had been posted before she disposed of the PDA. She sighed; she would miss the little gizmo.

She turned off the BlackBerry, and sighed again as she leaned back in the seat. It was done. She had moved fast, and she was as exhausted as if she'd run a marathon. With luck, Amado was just now beginning to be worried and impatient. He hadn't called her, so he definitely hadn't yet gone looking for her. Soon, though. When she didn't answer the phone, he'd go looking for her, figuring maybe something in the library blocked cell calls, the way casinos did.

When he didn't find her in the library, he'd get

worried. Because he thought she'd been sick, he'd get the library personnel to check all the bathrooms. After that failed, he'd call Rafael.

Given Rafael's suspicious nature, he'd first have Hector check her bedroom, to see if she'd taken her things. Only when Hector reported that her makeup was still in the bathroom, her laptop was still there, her television was still on, and that she hadn't taken any luggage with her would Rafael begin to think that something might have happened to her and he'd have his men start searching for her. They would concentrate on the area around the library. If some honest soul had found her discarded wallet and turned it in to the library personnel, then he might even call the cops.

Now there was an entertaining scenario: Rafael Salinas, going to the police for help. She'd almost pay money to see that.

He'd check with the hotels in the area, to see if she'd registered. Given how much he thought of her brainpower, he'd expect her to do something obvious, which was a big point in her favor.

She wasn't that far away in terms of actual distance, but she was in a different state, and Rafael would never in a million years think she'd go to Elizabeth, New Jersey. He wouldn't even expect her to leave Manhattan.

Later, when he discovered that she'd robbed him blind, he would focus on her hometown. She knew he'd had her investigated, that he knew her real name and all that, but that didn't matter because she wasn't going back to her hometown. She had no intentions of ever going back to that place. She thought some cousins still lived there, but she hadn't contacted them since she'd left and had no reason to ever get in touch with them.

Jimbo, her older brother, had left before she had, and she'd never heard from him again. Good riddance, anyway. He was nothing but a loser. Her parents were divorced and had both sort of drifted away, too, focusing on their own lives and not much caring about their two offspring. Drea had deliberately cut ties with them, too. She had only herself, which was the way she liked it.

The taxi deposited her at a motel that at least looked clean, which was the best she could say for it. For just one night, she figured she could stand a lot worse than this.

She registered with a fake name, and paid cash. The bored clerk rattled off a list of rules and instructions, and slid a key to her. She was on the second floor, which was fine with her as she didn't have any luggage to haul up and down.

The carpet in the room was stained and worn, the furniture was rickety, but at least the room didn't stink. Drea ignored her surroundings and looked for a phone book. When she finally found it – secured on a chain – she flipped to the yellow pages and looked for a hair salon that was close to the bank, then she began calling. She called four before she found one that could give her an appointment at ten in the morning.

That was that. When the bank opened in the morning, she would withdraw her hundred thousand dollars, then go straight to the hair salon to have her hair cut and colored, and she'd be good to go. She'd buy some secondhand car, pay cash, and head west.

She was free.

8

Raphael tried to let only anger show; he didn't want any of his men to think Drea was actually *important* to him. Anger, though, was the smallest part of what he was feeling. Uppermost was fear, a gut-wrenching fear that he couldn't shake. Until Amado showed him Drea's wallet, which some kid had found behind a trash can outside the library and turned in – honest little fucker – Rafael had thought Drea was maybe trying to teach him a lesson, except that was foreign to everything he knew about her. But now he couldn't console himself with that theory, what with the evidence of her wallet, which was empty of cash and ID, but all her credit cards were still there.

A stupid thief would take the cash and the credit cards and go on a spending spree that would lead the cops right to him. A smart thief would take the cash and leave the cards. Her driver's license was gone, too. Identity theft was a big business, and a valid driver's license was a valuable thing to have. When he added Drea's disappearance to the fact that the credit cards were right there, not a single one missing, the most probable scenario wasn't a good one. He couldn't even hope the feds had picked her up – though fat lot of good Drea would have done them, unless they wanted to find out all she knew about shopping – because they wouldn't have

98

stolen her cash and tossed the wallet.

He had enemies, a lot of them. If one of them had grabbed Drea, then she was as good as dead. She might be kept alive for a while to be used as leverage against him, but he'd never see her again except in bits and pieces. In his world, violence was commonplace; the only things of value were money and survival. It was a world he thrived in, a business model he excelled at, but now it made him sick to his stomach to think of sweet, dumb Drea being raped and tortured.

He had all of his men gathered in the penthouse, the one place he was certain his conversations couldn't be monitored. Orlando knew what he was doing, so Rafael had sprung for all the fancy safeguards that kept the feds from listening in on everything he said. 'Somebody had to have seen something. There are cameras on all the entrances and exits, right?' He directed the last question to Orlando.

'Should be, but who knows what kinda security they got? Who breaks into libraries? I'll see what I can find out.'

Obtaining a search warrant was out of the question – no one even suggested it. Call the cops? What a laugh. The cops would piss around with all their legal shit – and that's assuming they'd do anything at all. Rafael wasn't wasting time with that; he'd do things his way. He'd find out who had snatched Drea, and then he'd hit the fucker with everything he had.

'Maybe, when she found out she'd lost her wallet, she went looking for it,' Hector offered.

'Dumb ass,' Amado replied in a sour growl.

'Why doesn't she answer her cell phone?'

'So maybe somebody grabbed her purse, and she chased after him and got lost.' Hector was grabbing at straws, and the sadness in his dark eyes said he knew it, but he still felt compelled to offer every possible alternative to what they knew had probably happened.

'She wouldn'ta done that,' Amado said. 'She turned her ankle getting into the car, and she was limping. She couldn'ta chased nobody down. Besides, if somebody grabbed her purse, she'd of screeched to high heaven, and everybody in the library would've known about it.'

'Whoever grabbed her was slick,' Orlando said. 'When she comes out, put an arm around her like you're friends, only your other hand is holding a gun shoved in her side. She'd have gone with him without making a sound.'

If the snatch had happened outside, the library cameras might not have caught anything, Rafael thought, then he realized it didn't matter. Whoever had grabbed Drea would want him to know, because they'd grabbed her for a reason. Just to take her and kill her didn't make any sense; probably whoever had done it would be contacting him soon, asking for money, or maybe something else. He thought furiously, wondering if whoever it was knew what he'd hired the assassin for and had figured out who was behind it. He was pretty sure there was no way. And even if someone had, if killing Drea was vengeance for what he'd done, whoever had done it would want him to know, otherwise there was no point.

'We don't have to check the library's security,' he

100

said heavily. 'Whoever took her will call.' One way or another, whether Drea was dead or alive, they would call. Until then, all he could do was wait.

Unable to stand there in front of his men any longer, Rafael abruptly turned and left the room, going down the hall to her bedroom. Pushing the door open, he stepped just inside, then halted as if he'd hit an invisible wall. Her presence was so strong he could almost touch it. The scent of her perfume hung in the air. The television was on, as usual, the voices of the shopping channel hosts so cheerful they reminded him of chirping birds. Her laptop was open, because she never closed it, and though the screen was dark the power light told him it was in sleep mode and would come to life at the touch of a key. The closet door was standing ajar, the light on inside so the jumble of her clothing was clearly visible. Costume jewelry was scattered across the top of the dresser.

Drea was like a magpie, going for the shiny and colorful. She was messy, careless, and childlike in her enthusiasms. She deserved better than to die a brutal death at the hands of men to whom she meant nothing.

His vision clouded, and to his dismay he realized he was getting teary-eyed. He couldn't let anyone see him like this, so he forced himself to walk farther into the room, to look into her bathroom where the vanity was littered with cosmetics and the air was even thicker with her scent, a feminine mixture of perfumed bath gel, scented candles, lotions, and sprays. Drea loved – had loved – all the frills of being a woman.

There was a huge weight on his chest, and an

emptiness inside. He could barely breathe under the pressure, and even his heartbeat seemed labored, heavy and slow, from his misery. He'd never before felt such pain, as if he would never be free of this ache. She was gone. It wasn't fair; he had realized he loved her only to lose her the very next day. He resented her for being upset with him yesterday, for forcing him to really *see* her, resented her for the weakness she'd caused in him, resented her for being gone. Damn her – and damn himself, for being such a fool.

Drea woke in the middle of the night, gasping for air, fighting the sheet as if it were a rope twisting around her. She bolted upright, looking wildly around the room. Enough streetlight seeped in around the edges of the curtains that the room wasn't truly dark; if it had been, she might have had heart failure, but as it was she could plainly see that no one was there. She was blessedly alone.

She'd dreamed of the assassin, dreamed he somehow found her here in this motel and got inside the room, and that this time, after he had sex with her, he really was going to kill her. She couldn't see him, but she'd sensed him there in the shadows, watching her. In the weird way of dreams, she knew that as long as she stayed awake he wouldn't be able to do anything, but in spite of her best efforts to keep her eyes open she got sleepier and sleepier until finally she couldn't resist and fell asleep – now, there was something she'd never done before, dreaming about trying to stay awake and falling asleep instead – only to

102

wake with him on top of her, inside her, and with his hands wrapped around her throat.

That was when she woke up for real, struggling against a phantom, freezing cold from the panic that held her in its icy grip.

Even dreaming, even knowing he was going to kill her, the feel of his penetration had been so real that she'd been close to climax. Fully awake now, angry and humiliated even though no one knew what a fool she was, Drea got out of bed and went to the sink to get a drink of water.

She flipped on the light and stared at herself in the harsh fluorescent glare. She was naked, because she had no clothes other than the ones she'd had on. She had washed her underwear out by hand, and draped it over a clothes hanger to dry.

Normally she wore pajamas; was the abnormality of sleeping nude what had triggered the nightmare? Because that's what it had been, a nightmare. Even knowing she was alone, she looked behind herself in the mirror, as if expecting him to appear there.

The layout of the room was typical of motels, with the sink and vanity area in an open alcove at the rear of the room, and the toilet and tub/shower in a tiny room by themselves. There was no rear exit, she realized; if she was caught in here, she had no way out. Knowing that made her want to immediately bolt, but common sense kicked in. She was relatively safe here; even if Rafael had found out about his bank account so soon, which would be unbelievably bad luck, and somehow got the security video from the library so he had a current description of her, she had changed cabs

103

often enough, and done enough zigzagging across the city on foot, that it would take time for him to put all of it together and follow her trail.

She could afford to wait until she had her money, until she got her hair cut and colored, until she had a chance to buy more clothes and a secondhand car. She shouldn't let herself panic. The dream had her spooked, that was all.

Still, though she turned out the light, she couldn't go back to sleep. She didn't want to dream about him again, didn't want him close, even in her subconscious. Lying awake in the dark, she endured the slow tick of minutes slipping away, bringing dawn and her new life closer and closer. Thinking about the past was useless; she focused instead on what was ahead of her. She was a millionaire now; maybe she'd buy a house, her very own house. She'd never owned a home before. Come to think of it, there hadn't been anywhere she thought of as home, not for a very long time anyway.

Morning came, and Drea ventured out to get something to eat. She was starving, having made do the night before with crackers and chips from the vending machine next to the stairwell. She found a small diner that was so crowded she had to stand and wait for a stool at the counter, rather than having a booth to herself. Finally she was sitting, crammed between two burly guys who looked like construction workers, or truck drivers maybe. She didn't make eye contact, and they didn't speak, just devoted themselves to emptying their plates.

She ordered sausage and eggs and toast, a meal

she would never have eaten if she'd still been with Rafael, out of fear she might gain a few ounces. Once the first bite hit her mouth, Drea forgot about watching the clock and lost herself in what was maybe the first complete meal she'd had in ... she didn't remember how long. Since way before she'd met Rafael, so ... years. She hadn't eaten a complete meal in years.

Screw men. She didn't need a man now. She was rich, and she'd eat whatever the hell she felt like eating.

Finally, filled with a sense of well-being that went beyond food, she walked back to the motel. It was almost time for the bank to open. Sitting in her shabby little room, she waited until nine-fifteen, then turned on her BlackBerry, which immediately buzzed an alert that she had messages, which she ignored, and accessed her account. Nothing. The transfer hadn't been posted yet. Tranfers should have been handled first thing. There was no point in even checking the Kansas account, because Kansas was on Central time and it would be another hour before she could realistically expect anything there.

Had something gone wrong? A chill ran down her spine. Legally there was no way Rafael could have stopped the transfer, but illegally ... yeah, hold a gun to the bank manager's head and maybe he could have done it, if Rafael had somehow found out almost immediately.

He didn't, as a rule, write a check for anything he wanted to buy; he used plastic. For that matter, Rafael didn't normally write a check at all, even to pay bills. Orlando had told him not to get a debit card, that someone could get the number and wipe him out, so Rafael still paid bills the old-fashioned way but he didn't actually do it himself. His accountant, the legal one, did that for him.

No, she was almost certain Rafael couldn't have found out anything.

Ten minutes later, she tried again. This time, her account showed the hundred-thousand-dollar deposit.

Limp with relief, Drea fell back across the bed, clutching the BlackBerry to her chest. She looked at the amount again, and began laughing. It was there, and it was all hers, every last penny of it.

And she was going to be late for her appointment at the salon if she didn't hurry. She bounced off the bed, called a taxi, and left the room key and a couple of dollars on the bedside table before going out to wait for her ride.

Things went downhill when she got to the bank and began closing out her account. After providing her identification, and information for the paperwork, she asked for the hundred thousand in cash. The account manager, a middle-aged woman with wine-red hair, stopped what she was doing and stared over the desk at Drea. She looked perturbed. 'I don't know if we can do that, at least not for the full amount,' she said apologetically. 'Usually we give customers a cashier's check when they close out accounts. Obviously we don't keep a huge cash reserve here. If you'd given us some warning we could have had additional funds on hand, but ... let me talk to the bank manager. I'll see what we can do.'

Drea bit back the stinging remark she'd been about to make. A bank didn't keep a lot of cash on hand? What the hell kind of bank didn't have cash? Antagonizing the woman wouldn't help, though, would probably even prevent her from walking out with any cash at all, so instead she said, 'I'm sorry. Everything happened so fast... I wasn't thinking.'

She didn't specify *what* had happened so fast, but her apology seemed to work because the woman said, 'Maybe we can work something out. I'll be right back.'

As the woman disappeared into another office, Drea thought furiously. What good would a cashier's check for a hundred thousand do her? All she could do with it was open another account. She needed cash, untraceable cash.

Glancing at her watch, she saw that time was getting short if she intended to make her salon appointment. She could skip the appointment, get her hair cut farther on down the road, but she'd like to change her appearance before she bought a car. Maybe if she gave the bank some time, and came back after her salon appointment, she could get more cash, but that would mean the account manager would know how she'd changed her hair, which would make it easier for Rafael to trace her.

This wasn't working. She'd have to adjust her plan. Okay, so she'd give the bank more time to get the cash together, maybe even another day – God, what kind of risk would she be running by staying in Elizabeth another day?

An unacceptable risk, she decided. She needed

to leave today.

She didn't have a lot of cash left, though, so she'd have to get some money right now. She didn't have to have the entire hundred thousand in cash; twenty thousand would do, and the rest in a cashier's check. Ten thousand would buy a car reliable enough to get her to Kansas, the remaining ten would be plenty to pay for motel rooms and food. How long would it take her to get to Kansas, anyway? Two days? Three? She'd have plenty of cash to spare.

The account manager came out of the office, her brow furrowed in a way that told Drea there was no way she could get the entire hundred thou in cash. 'I'm sorry,' she began, but Drea shook her head.

'It's all right. How about twenty thousand in cash, or even fifteen, and the remainder in a cashier's check. That would be plenty. I don't know what I was thinking; I sure don't want to be traveling with that much cash.'

The woman's expression cleared. 'I know we can do fifteen in cash, but let me see about twenty–'

Time was getting too short. 'I've taken up too much of your time,' Drea said. 'Fifteen would be great.'

'Are you sure? It won't take a minute to check–'

'Thank you, but don't go to the trouble.'

Finally she had her fifteen thousand in cash, one hundred and fifty hundred-dollar bills, and a cashier's check for the remainder. The cash was surprisingly bulky, which made her glad she hadn't been able to get the entire amount in cash. She'd have had to buy a small suitcase just to hold the money, which would be a tad conspicuous. At least the fifteen thousand would fit in her bag.

She had to sign a couple of forms, then at last the transaction was finished. 'Thank you so much,' she said, then looked at her watch and hurried from the bank.

She was almost twenty minutes late getting to the salon, and the stylist was in a pissy mood because of it, but he cheered up when she indicated her mass of long corkscrew curls and said, 'Cut it off and I want to go smoother and darker.' Like most stylists, he loved cutting long hair and going for a drastic change.

An hour and a half later, she walked out of the salon a brunette, her hair in a shaggy cut that was a little spiky on top. It looked sharp as hell, and she loved it. Her entire face looked different, stronger, the bone structure more evident. She wasn't Drea Rousseau now, she was someone else, a woman who didn't take any crap from anyone.

She'd have to think of a new name, a name that would fit her new self. Somewhere along the line she'd have to get a new driver's license, but she'd worry about that later. Right now, she needed wheels.

A little over five hours later, she crossed into Pennsylvania, heading west. Her car was a maroon Camry, a little the worse for wear with some rust eating at the metal and a collection of dents and dings on the fenders, but the tires were good and the engine ran okay.

Soon, she thought, she'd be driving a Cadillac. Or maybe a Mercedes. In a couple of days she'd be in Kansas, and from there, who knew? She could pick anywhere she wanted, and Rafael Salinas could kiss her ass.

9

Raphael almost didn't take the call when he saw it was from his bank. He'd been awake all night, fueled by coffee and anxiety, but hour after hour had passed with no word from whoever had taken Drea and he'd lost whatever faint hope he'd had, which had never been much, that she might somehow he ransomed or exchanged.

'Salinas,' he said curtly. 'What is it?'

'Mr. Salinas, this is Manuel Flores, with–'

'Yeah, I know who you're with, I saw the Caller ID.' He just wanted the guy to get to the point and get off the phone. He didn't have the patience today to deal with penny-ante shit, not when he knew Drea was probably dead somewhere and he couldn't even grieve without looking like a pussy in front of his men.

'Ah … yes, well. The bank did send an e-mail yesterday alerting you to the transfer that was made, but I wanted to follow up and–'

'Transfer?' Rafael was exhausted, but not so exhausted his attention wasn't caught. He sat up straight and snapped his fingers at Orlando, pointing to the phone and then his bedroom. 'What transfer?'

Orlando strode into the bedroom and a second later there was a click as he picked up on the call.

'Ah … the transfer of funds from your account into Ms. Butts's account. The, ah, account that was listed as Drea Rousseau.'

'Yeah, yeah.' Like he didn't know Drea's real name? He didn't have a problem with her using Rousseau as her last name instead of Butts. Hell, who would? He sure as hell hadn't wanted to introduce her as Drea Butts. 'I didn't make any transfer yesterday.'

A distinctly worried note entered Flores's voice. 'A sizable transfer was made yesterday afternoon, and even though the transfer was verified as coming from your ID address, with your password, the amount was unusual so as a matter of policy an e-mail notification was generated alerting you to this transaction. Then, this morning, when I became aware that all of the funds were transferred from Ms. Butts's account late yesterday afternoon, I thought a personal phone call was in order–'

'I didn't transfer anything into her account yesterday!' Rafael bellowed, getting up and walking into his bedroom where Orlando was already sitting in front of Rafael's laptop, checking his e-mail account. With everything going on yesterday, Rafael hadn't bothered with crap like that.

Orlando scrolled quickly through the messages, then looked up at Rafael and shook his head. 'There's no message from the bank here,' he said.

'I didn't get any e-mail,' Rafael snapped. 'If I had, I'd have called, because I didn't transfer any money yesterday. How much we talking about?'

'Ah ... two million, one hundred thousand dollars.'

Rafael felt as if his head was going to explode. 'What?' What the hell was going on? Had whoever snatched Drea forced her to give them the money in her account? But who in hell had transferred it from his account into hers in the first place? Drea didn't have his password, and it wasn't like he had it written down anywhere for her to get, not that she'd have recognized it as anything other than his cell phone number anyway.

'Ah–'

'If you say "ah" one more time I'm going to reach through this phone and rip your fucking throat out,' Rafael said harshly 'I didn't transfer anything yesterday, I sure as hell didn't transfer any two million bucks, and I didn't get a fucking e-mail. So put the money back in my account!'

'I–I can't,' Flores stammered. Rafael could almost hear the 'ah' he'd barely stifled. 'The transfer was made from your ID address using your password, and in any case, as I told you, the entire amount was transferred out late yesterday afternoon. Our bank no longer has control of these funds.'

'Somebody ripped me off and I don't give a fuck what the bank controls and what it doesn't. You people let somebody get my money, so you can damn well get it back.'

'We can't do that, Mr. Salinas. Legally, the bank's hands are tied–'

'There's no way in hell the transfer was made from my computer, because I didn't do it, so don't tell me about legal!'

Orlando got a very peculiar look on his face. Abruptly he got up and left the bedroom, leaving Rafael shouting into the phone. He was back in less than a minute, carrying Drea's laptop. He placed it beside Rafael's laptop on the desk, disconnected Rafael's machine, and connected Drea's. Then he opened her e-mail program and began scrolling. She had about twenty messages, most of them junk from various stores where she'd done some online shopping, so going through them didn't take long. Orlando stopped scrolling and pointed at the screen.

'Hold on,' Rafael said into the phone, bending down to look at where Orlando was pointing. Orlando opened the message and there it was, the e-mail the bank had sent. What was his e-mail doing on Drea's computer?

'We found your e-mail,' he snarled. 'It didn't come to me, it went to my girlfriend. You couldn't even get that right, so–'

'I assure you, Mr Salinas, the e-mail went to the address that's specified in your account information.'

'I set it up myself and I sure as hell didn't use my girlfriend's e-mail address, I used my own.'

'Nevertheless, that's the address that's on our records now, and any change came from you using your password, so we have to assume you knew what you wanted to do.'

'I'm telling you, I didn't–' Rafael stopped, breathing hard, as an awful possibility began dawning on him. Despite the sudden feeling in his gut, his brain automatically rejected the idea. It wasn't possible. Drea was computer literate enough to order stuff off the Internet, but that was about it – and even then, Orlando had had to walk her through the process several times before she grasped that all she had to do was follow whatever instructions were on the screen. She'd had it in her head that whatever she'd done on one website was what she had to do on every site.

Rafael remembered how she'd kept saying helplessly, 'But it doesn't make sense!' Was he supposed to think this same woman somehow got around his password protection and into his bank account, transferred out almost all of his cash into her account, then promptly moved it yet again to God knows where? The Drea he knew not only wouldn't have been able to do it, she wouldn't even have thought of it.

Her attitude toward money had been almost like a child's. She'd never asked him for a penny. The way she looked at it, if she had plastic, or a checkbook, then she had money. If he hadn't kept track of her account himself, she'd have had overdrafts all over the place, because she never paid any attention to her balance.

To accept that she could possibly have done this was to accept that she'd duped him, duped everyone, for two years. His ego violently rejected that, because he wasn't a dupe, he was Rafael Salinas, and anyone who had ever tried to dupe him had died regretting it. He trusted no one. He'd had Drea investigated, he'd had her followed, and he'd kept a check on her. Not once had she said or done anything that would make him think she was anything other than exactly what she appeared, which was sweet and dumb.

'I'll get back to you,' he said abruptly to Flores, and ended the call. He stared hard at Orlando, who was staring back at him. 'Tell me how this could have happened. Tell me how someone got into my bank account and ripped me off for the tune of two fucking million dollars.'

'It had to be done from here,' Orlando said. He clicked on the computer's history, and there it was, plainly showing that someone, using Drea's computer, had accessed the bank's website. 'On the receiving end, both your laptop and hers would show the same IP address, because they go through the same router. If she got your password, as far as the bank's concerned, you're the one who made the transfer.'

'I didn't give her the password,' Rafael snapped. 'I never wrote it down, either.' Not even Orlando knew what his password was.

'She got it somehow,' Orlando kept his expression blank as he pointed out the obvious. 'If you ever accessed the account while she was in the room, she might have paid enough attention to figure out the keystrokes.'

'This is *Drea* we're talking about. She could barely figure out how to turn on the shower.' Okay, so that was an exaggeration; they still weren't talking about a mental giant here.

'That much money's a powerful motivation, and the proof is right here.' Orlando tapped the computer screen. 'I don't think anybody grabbed her, I think she took the money and ran.'

Rafael stood there, rage and humiliation burning through him. He'd let himself care about her, and the slut had played him for a fool. He never should have let his guard down, never for a minute let himself believe that she cared at all about him. She had to be the best actress in the world, to keep up that act for two years without a single slip, to produce all those tears the day

116

before yesterday. And he'd fallen for it; that was what ate at him like acid. He'd bought the whole enchilada, fooled himself into thinking she really loved him, hell, even that *he* was in love with her.

She'd pay for this. No matter what it cost him, she'd pay.

'She can't run far enough,' he said flatly. He'd like to take her apart with his bare hands, but he'd learned to put some distance between himself and the actual act, so even if he ordered it, he had some deniability. He could do without killing her himself, so long as he knew she was dead. He might regret not having the satisfaction of personally meting out justice, but vengeance would do almost as well, and he knew exactly how he was going to get it.

The assassin waited three days after receiving Salinas's latest summons before he got in touch. He wasn't doing anything else, but he was in the mood for some downtime and he was an independent contractor, not one of the bastard's employees. Whatever Salinas wanted could wait.

He didn't trust the summons; it came too soon after his afternoon with Drea. Maybe Salinas had changed his mind about the offer and was, in retrospect, feeling as if his machismo had taken a hit. It had taken a lot more than a hit, but the assassin didn't think Salinas had figured that out yet. Drea was too good at what she did; she'd keep quiet about how much pleasure she'd gotten out of the deal.

So he waited, and he watched. He was as curious as ever about Salinas's future plans, but while he didn't have many virtues, patience was one he possessed in abundance. Something was going on; he could tell by the expressions on the faces of Salinas's goons, on Salinas himself. The assassin had observed the man coming and going several times, and it was obvious he was in a bitch of a bad mood.

When he judged Salinas had waited long enough, he first indulged himself with a leisurely tour of the Metropolitan Museum, which was one of his favorite places in New York. He didn't mind the tourists, or the gaggles of children; the exhibits were their own reward. When he was finished he stood on the broad steps and made the call.

'Come to the penthouse,' Salinas ordered. 'When can you be here?'

'I'm nearby,' the assassin said calmly, 'but it's a nice day. Bethesda Terrace, in half an hour.' He disconnected, then turned off his phone and slipped it into his pocket. Not only would Salinas have trouble setting up an ambush in such a short time, but the Terrace was a public place, full of both tourists and city residents. It was also wide open, so his avenue of approach wouldn't be limited. From there he could disappear into the depths of Central Park, should Salinas be of a mind to have him followed.

He had no idea exactly where Salinas was, so half an hour might be an impossible deadline for him to meet. For himself, though, Bethesda Terrace was a pleasant walk. If Salinas was up in the penthouse, he'd have plenty of time to get there. If he was across town ... tough. For something important, he'd make contact again.

The assassin enjoyed making things difficult for the bastard, even in such a small way. Pleasure came where he found it, though, so he followed both his instinct to play it safe, and his inclination to jerk Salinas's chain.

He walked into the park, pausing to get an ice-cream cone. Though he knew the park fairly well, he nevertheless bought a map, and spent a few minutes studying it because he liked to know exactly what his options were if he happened to need one. He kept the map in his hand, knowing Salinas would spot it, and draw the conclusion that the assassin didn't live locally and therefore wasn't familiar with the layout of the park. The conclusion would be half right, because he didn't really *live* in any one place; he stayed in various places for various lengths of time, and right now that place happened to be a few floors below Salinas.

He found a vantage point and watched. If he saw anything that looked suspicious, he'd call off the meet. He knew Salinas wouldn't meet him alone; a man like that couldn't afford to go anywhere without his muscle in attendance. The assassin didn't worry about the thugs he could see, though; it was the ones who weren't out in the open that he looked for.

Finally he saw Salinas, only a couple of minutes late, and with three men behind him. The assassin studied the surroundings, but didn't see anything suspicious: he knew many of Salinas's men on sight, so he didn't have to rely only on behavior in judging whether or not it was safe to approach. No one appeared to be lurking without reason, no one seemed to be trying to stay out of sight. Finally he left his own concealment and strolled forward, still eating his ice cream.

Salinas was irritably checking his watch when he looked up and saw the assassin. 'You're late,' he snarled as he gestured his men back.

'Long line at the ice-cream stand,' the assassin said lazily. 'What's up?'

Salinas looked around, then took an old-fashioned transistor radio from his pocket and turned it on. The volume was loud, so loud that if Salinas hadn't taken a step closer, the assassin couldn't have heard him.

'Drea stole two million bucks from me, four days ago, and took a powder. I want you to find her and take care of the matter. Permanently.'

A rivulet of melted ice cream trickled down the cone. The assassin caught it with his tongue, hiding his surprise. 'You sure? She didn't seem bright enough – though I guess that would be the proof, right?'

'I'm sure.' Salinas gave a grim smile. 'And, yeah, on the list of stupid things to do, ripping me off is right at the top.'

10

Never piss off a smart woman.

Given the timing, he didn't have to be a genius to understand what had happened. Drea had been more than upset by Salinas giving her away; she'd been furious. This wasn't just an 'I'm leaving you' message, but an 'I'm leaving you and take *that* you bastard!' gesture. As gestures went, it was an attention-getter.

Amused, he took another lick of ice cream. He was more inclined to applaud her than go hunting for her. Still, a job was a job. 'Make your best offer,' he drawled. 'What's it worth to you?' He couldn't decide if he'd take the job until he knew how much was on the table.

Salinas looked around and thumbed the volume on the radio even higher. The people passing by gave him annoyed looks, not that he gave a shit. 'The same amount she stole.'

Two million, huh? That definitely put a different light on the situation. He'd have to think about it, but in the meantime he didn't want Salinas looking for anyone else to take care of the situation. If he didn't take the job, his delay would at least give Drea a better chance of getting away clean and the thought gave him a certain satisfaction. He didn't have to like his clients, but he had nothing but contempt for Salinas.

'Half up front,' the assassin said. 'I'll let you

know where to wire it.' Then he tossed the rest of the ice-cream cone in a nearby trash can and strolled away, his manner relaxed, though his eyes never stopped searching his surroundings. He spotted someone who was almost certainly a fed, too suit-and-tie for his surroundings, stooping to tie his shoe while keeping his head slightly turned in Salinas's direction. That would be Salinas's tail, hurrying to catch up.

The assassin wasn't particularly concerned. His meeting with Salinas had taken less than a minute, not enough time for a tail to get in place and snap some photos. By the time the tail had arrived, the meeting was over and he was already walking away. He went across the Bow Bridge then into the heavily wooded Ramble, where there was plenty of cover. Though the day was hot and humid, the temperature hovering close to ninety, there under the thick shade the air was cooler, and he could feel a slight but pleasant breeze against his skin.

He deliberately didn't think about the offer; time enough for that later, when he was certain he wasn't being followed. As a matter of habit he focused intensely on the right now, aware of everyone around him, whether or not anyone was approaching him from behind, what his ever-changing avenues of escape were. Paying attention to details had kept him alive this long, so he saw no reason to change his habits. That was why he spotted the second tail almost right away; this guy wore jeans and running shoes, so he wasn't the fed who'd been following Salinas.

The assassin calmly analyzed the situation. Just

because this new tail wore casual clothes, didn't mean he wasn't a fed. It just meant he was better prepared. The FBI wouldn't have any reason for having him followed other than his meeting with Salinas; it was possible they were exploring any and all contacts. Or the tail could be one of Salinas's goons, following him for God knows why. Maybe Salinas was pissed because he'd had to walk to the park, and he thought an attitude adjustment in the form of a beating was needed – though, in that case, he'd better send more than one man. Maybe he wanted to know where the assassin lived, no more than that, on the theory that there was no such thing as too much information.

He kept a steady pace. Up ahead the path took a sharp turn, and the tail's view would be blocked by trees and shrubbery for ... he considered how far behind him the tail was ... about seven seconds, which was plenty long enough. The tail must have noticed the same blind spot, because he picked up the pace. The assassin didn't respond by speeding up, which would have telegraphed his awareness he was being followed. He was close enough that it didn't matter, though his time was down to about five seconds.

He made the turn, whirled, stripped his white shirt off over his head and crumpled it in his hand as if it were a towel, then burst into the steady loping pace of a runner as he rounded the turn going back in the direction from which he'd come.

The tail didn't even glance at him as he loped by; instead, the guy was hurrying to get around the turn and get him back in vision.

Good luck with that he thought as he cut off the path and disappeared into the thick growth. He was just another shirtless runner, among hundreds, maybe thousands, who were sweating through their routines in the park that day. His dark gray pants, at first glance, would resemble sweatpants enough that no one would think twice about him. Only his shoes would be a giveaway, because who went jogging in Gucci loafers? Evidently he did, but it wasn't something he recommended.

When he was a hundred yards away, he paused to pull on his shirt. The humid heat had caused sweat to sheen his skin, and the fabric stuck to him as he tugged it into place, but he wasn't breathing any faster than normal. Keeping a leisurely pace, he made his way out of the park.

'Did you get a shot of the meet?' Rick Cotton asked, his expression calm as he listened to the answer.

Xavier Jackson marveled at Cotton's forbearance. He hadn't said, 'Did you at least get a shot of the meet?' and there was nothing in his tone that implied any hint of impatience. Most SACs would have been biting heads off left and right, but not Cotton. He was always fair, even when the results weren't what he'd hoped for.

They hadn't been prepared for Salinas to *walk* anywhere, much less into Central Park. By the time the agent on the street had realized Salinas wasn't being picked up by a car, he and his entourage had already been halfway down the block. Then, though he'd been hurrying as un-

124

obtrusively as possible to catch up, a traffic signal had caught him and forced him to wait before he could cross the street. As a result, the meet had already happened before the agent could catch up, and all he could give them was a partial description of the man Salinas had gone to meet, for all the good it did them. *About six-one, two hundred pounds, short dark hair* described at least a hundred thousand men in the area, if not more.

'I think it was the same man on the balcony with the girlfriend,' Cotton said when he hung up.

Jackson thought so, too. The big question was, where was the girlfriend? She'd left four days ago, and hadn't been seen since. They had stopped following her months ago, because their budget and manpower was limited and using it to follow Salinas himself had been deemed more productive. Besides, she'd never done anything interesting, at least not until that scene on the balcony.

Maybe her absence was due to nothing more dramatic than a break-up with Salinas, but something was going on. Salinas and his men were stomping around as if they were spoiling for a fight with someone, anyone. If it were just a breakup, Salinas might – *might* – be upset, but his men wouldn't be.

And now Salinas had met with probably the same man who'd been on the balcony making love to Salinas's girlfriend. Something was going on, but it was more than likely personal crap, and they weren't interested in that. Unless they could use it against him somehow, Salinas's love life was his problem, not theirs.

There were over twenty-three hundred known street surveillance cameras in New York City, and God only knew how many hidden ones. If anyone was on the street in the city odds were he, or she, would be caught on camera, which was why he was always so careful to change his appearance on a regular basis. Even if he happened to be tracked on camera, his trail would be lost when he entered a building as one person and left as someone else. Only extensive analysis would, with a lot of luck, pick him up again, and he went to great pains, in this country, to ensure he wasn't worth taking that much trouble.

Drea was smart enough to change her appearance, too; he took that for granted. What he didn't know was where she'd changed, or how she'd looked afterward. He could've asked Salinas what was known about Drea's movements on the day she disappeared, but where was the fun in that? Finding her without Salinas's help would keep him sharp, sort of like doing math in his head instead of using a calculator.

He had considerable computer skills, but in this case the cons associated with doing his own hacking outweighed the pros. There was no point in taking the chance of setting off an alarm when he could find out what he wanted to know by another avenue. A lot of things truly did revolve around the old truism that it wasn't what you knew, it was who you knew – and it so happened he knew someone who worked for the city of New York, someone who owed him a debt so huge it could never be repaid, and who could access that network of security cameras.

He'd caught a break in that nothing important had happened in the city over the last four days – just the usual number of muggings and murders. There hadn't been any terrorist attacks, no bicycle riders hurling bombs, no sensational happenings of any kind. Because things had been quiet, no one would be paying any attention to a back access to the video records from several days ago.

On the other hand, did he want to go to that much trouble before he even decided to take the job?

Hell, yes. For his own amusement, he wanted to know how she'd done it. He was even a little proud of her; she hadn't let any grass grow under her feet. Salinas had seriously insulted her, and the very next day she'd taken action. He knew the banking hoops she would have had to jump through, knew the timing issues, because he'd played that game himself.

He was seldom amused, and never proud, so the fact that he actually felt both of those emotions was a little puzzling.

Or not. Another thing he didn't do was play games with himself. The way he felt was directly tied to the admitted chemistry he'd had with her – not that chemistry would save her life if he decided to take the job. Attraction was one thing, but two million was two million.

Using his disposable cell phone, he placed the call. When the Brooklyn-accented voice answered with a terse *yeah*, he said, 'I need a favor.'

He didn't identify himself; he didn't need to. There was a long pause, then the voice said, 'Simon.'

'Yes,' he said.

Another pause, then: 'What do you need?'

There was no attempt to blow him off, or stall him. He hadn't expected there to be. 'I need access to the street cameras.'

'Live feed?'

'No, from four days ago. I know the starting point. After that–' An invisible shrug was evident in his tone. After that, his search could go in any direction, though after he did some background work on Drea he'd have a better idea of what she was likely to do.

'When do you need it?'

'Tonight.'

'You'll have to come to my house.'

'What time's best?' He could be considerate. In fact, he made an effort to be considerate; it didn't cost him anything, and a little goodwill could one day make the difference between living or dying, escaping or getting captured.

'Around nine. The kids will be in bed by then.'

'I'll be there.' He hung up, turned to his computer, and went to work.

Finding out Drea's real name was Andrea Butts took no time at all. He wasn't surprised that her name wasn't Rousseau, though the 'Butts' was a bit unexpected. He'd have been surprised if her name really had been Rousseau. Once he had her real name, he went into the DMV records and got her driver's license information. Her Social Security number was a bit tougher, but he had it within an hour; after that her life was an open book.

She was thirty years old, born in Nebraska,

never been married, no children. Her father had died a couple of years ago, and her mother ... her mother was back in Drea's hometown, so that was somewhere to check, even though he thought Drea was probably too smart to go back there. But, she would be comfortable in the area, and she might contact her mother. There was one brother, Jimmy Ray Butts, in Texas, currently serving the third year of a five-year sentence for burglary, so she wouldn't be going to him for anything.

That was it for immediate family; if he dug deeper he was likely to find aunts and uncles, cousins, maybe some high school friends. But Drea struck him as a loner, trusting no one except herself, depending on no one except herself.

He understood that philosophy. As far as philosophies went, it was the least likely to result in disappointment.

At exactly nine p.m. he leaned on the buzzer, and in a few seconds the Brooklyn-accented voice said 'Yeah' in the same way he answered the phone.

The assassin said, 'Simon,' and the door was buzzed open. The apartment was on the sixth floor, and he took the stairs instead of the elevator.

The apartment door opened as he approached, and a whippet-thin mixed-race man of about his own age gestured him inside. 'Coffee?' he said, by way of both greeting and invitation. Scottie Jansen's real first name was Shamar, but he'd been called Scottie most of his life, because kids in school had started calling him 'Shamu' and thereafter he'd refused to answer to Shamar.

129

'No, I'm good. Thanks.'

'This way.'

As Scottie led the way into a cramped bedroom, his wife appeared in the kitchen door and said, 'Don't start something that's gonna take you four hours to finish, because I'm going to bed at eleven.'

Simon turned and winked at her, and said, 'I don't mind,' and her tired face broke into a grin.

'Don't even try sweet-talking me. I'm immune to it. Just ask Scottie.'

'Maybe you're only immune to *his* sweet-talking.'

She snorted and returned to the kitchen. 'Close the door if you need privacy,' Scottie said, swiveling a battered office chair, the seat patched with duct tape, and plopping his skinny ass in it.

'No state secrets involved,' said Simon, and the unspoken words *this time* echoed in the room.

Scottie flexed his long fingers like a concert pianist about to tackle a difficult score. He began typing commands, his keystrokes so fast they were a blur. Screens zipped past. Occasionally he stopped to stare at one, muttering under his breath the way all geeks seemed to do, then he'd continue. After a few minutes he said, 'Okay, we're in. What's the starting point?'

Simon gave him the apartment building address, and the date, and parked his own ass on the foot of the bed, leaning forward so he could see. The room was small enough that they were almost shoulder to shoulder.

Unless you were watching either sex or assorted violence, there was nothing more boring than a surveillance tape. He told Scottie he was looking for a woman with long, blond, curly hair, and that helped, because he could speed through all the comings and goings of people who didn't have long blond curls. Finally Simon spotted her and said, 'There,' and Scottie immediately paused, then backtracked.

He watched Drea leave the building, carrying a large, bulging tote bag – he'd bet his life she had a change of clothes in there – and stumble as she got into a black Town Car. Scottie finessed the commands, skipping from camera to camera, following the car until it double-parked in front of the library. Drea got out, limping a little, and went in, and the car left.

Simon leaned closer to the screen, intently watching the exit. This would be where she changed. There were a number of things she could do with that mane of hair, but she would also need to ditch that light-colored jacket. What could she do to blend in with most New Yorkers? Wear black, that was what. And she'd pull her hair back, maybe stuff it under the back of her shirt, or wear something with a hood. A hood might be a tad unusual, given the heat, but people did weird shit all the time.

He looked for the shape of her body, the tote bag, anyone wearing black – which was almost everyone – any woman with her hair covered or slicked back.

He was gratified by the speed with which he spotted her. 'There she is,' he said.

Scottie stopped the tape. 'You sure?'

'I'm sure.' He knew every line of that body;

he'd spent four hours kissing and stroking every square inch of it. It was her, beyond a doubt. She hadn't wasted any time; she was out within ten minutes, maybe even before her driver found a parking space nearby. Her hair was darker, maybe she'd wet it, and it was slicked back, she was wearing head to toe black, and she walked without a trace of a limp, striding along without a hint of sway or jiggle.

Good girl, he thought with approval. Bold, decisive, paying attention to detail – way to go, Drea.

She didn't make it easy for Scottie. She walked a few blocks, got a taxi, and after she got out of the taxi she walked a few more blocks before snagging another ride. She zigzagged her way across the city, but finally she entered the Holland Tunnel and the network of cameras lost her. Still, the fact that she'd used the Holland instead of the Lincoln Tunnel told him a lot.

He was on the hunt. Drea might be good ... but he was better.

11

It really pissed Drea off that getting her own money from a bank had been so much trouble.

She'd taken her time on the drive to Kansas, because she didn't want to get tired and make stupid mistakes, or maybe even have a car wreck. She had to fly under the radar, which meant paying cash for everything and otherwise not getting herself noticed. Once she had the two million she'd have more options, but until then she was limited.

Taking her time meant the drive had taken her three days instead of just two, but that was okay, because she'd enjoyed herself. She was alone, blessedly alone answering to no one but herself. She didn't have to act like a brainless twit, didn't have to constantly smile and hide any hint of temper or impatience, or even a too-sharp sense of amusement.

How pitiful was it that for two years she hadn't been able to laugh spontaneously at a joke? If she'd laughed at all, she'd had to ask questions first, as if she didn't get the punch line. Rafael and his goons had spent a lot of time laughing at her in addition to the joke. Bastards.

She'd never have to make herself look stupid again, because she'd never again depend on a man for what she wanted. On the trip she ate whenever the mood took her, stopped to see anything that looked interesting, bought clothes based on what she wanted rather than some image she had to project. Instead of trying to look sexy, she went for the comfort of cotton pants, T-shirts, and sandals. After all, she was spending hours every day in the car, in the middle of summer.

Remembering the lessons learned from the bank in New Jersey, she knew she wouldn't be able to waltz in and get the two million. All she'd get was another few thousand in cash, and the rest in a cashier's check. She was already holding a cashier's check for eighty-five thousand, for all the good it did her. Unless she was buying a big ticket item, she couldn't spend it. Yeah, like she could drop a couple of hundred bucks and ask for eighty-four thousand eight hundred dollars in change.

There was also the difficulty in carting that much money around with her. She couldn't do it. She'd had to convince herself of the impossibility, so, with time on her hands, the first night on the road, she'd actually measured her remaining hundred-dollar bills. The way she calculated it, a thousand dollars, banded, was one tenth of an inch thick, so a ten-thousand-dollar stack would be an inch thick. That meant, roughly, ten inches for every hundred thousand, in which case a million would be a hundred inches, and two million would be two hundred inches, or a stack over sixteen feet high – kind of tough to carry around, and even tougher to stash out of sight. She'd be practically advertising for someone to knock her in the head and take her dough.

So, the money had to be kept in a bank, but

she'd like to break the paper trail of cashier's checks, even though by law the banks weren't allowed to give out any information to Rafael. That didn't mean he couldn't get it, just that he'd have to go to a good deal of trouble, and how much trouble he went to depended on how angry he was. Two million dollars worth of angry, plus the insult to his machismo, meant he'd be willing to spend twice that much money to find her. That kind of revenge might not be cost-effective, but it would definitely be satisfying.

In order to break the paper trail, at some point she'd have to get the two million converted into cash, even if for just long enough to drive to another state and stash it in another bank. The problem was, banks didn't like to hand out two million in cash, even to the person it belonged to.

Remembering that the bank in Elizabeth needed time to get in a large amount of cash, on the second day Drea stopped in Illinois, bought a cheap prepaid cell phone, and activated it, then she went out to the car to call the bank in Grissom, Kansas. With the doors safely locked and the air-conditioning running, she placed the call and said she wanted to speak to someone about closing out her account.

'Just a moment, I'll switch you to Mrs. Pearson.'

After several moments, there was a click and a pleasant voice said, 'This is Janet Pearson. How may I help you?'

'My name is Andrea Butts,' Drea said, wincing as she used the hated name. One way or another, she was ditching that name, forever. 'I have an account with you, and I'd like to close it out.'

'I'm sorry to hear that, Ms. Butts. Is there a problem, or–'

'No, nothing like that, but I'm moving out of the area.'

'I see. We hate to lose you as a customer, but life happens, doesn't it? If you'll come in, in person, I'll take care of the paperwork for you.'

'I'll be there sometime tomorrow afternoon,' Drea said, estimating her travel time and hoping she was at least in the ballpark. 'The thing is, it's a large amount, and I want the bulk of it in cash.'

There was a small silence, then Mrs. Pearson said, 'Do you have your account number?'

Drea recited it, and she could hear computer keys clicking as Mrs. Pearson pulled up her account information. After another, longer pause, Mrs. Pearson said, 'Ms. Butts, for your own safety I really, really don't recommend taking this amount in cash.'

'I understand the difficulty,' Drea said. 'That doesn't change the fact that I need this in cash, and I'm calling ahead of time so you can have that much available.'

Mrs. Pearson sighed. 'I'm very sorry but we can't even order this much cash until we've verified your identity.'

Drea struggled for patience, but she'd been on the receiving end of rudeness too many times for her to start snapping at someone who was just doing her job and had to follow bank policy. She couldn't, however, hold back her own sigh. 'I understand. As I said, I'll be there tomorrow afternoon. That's too late to get the money, isn't it?'

'Actually, it's too early. We're a small bank, and we order our cash supply from the Federal Reserve just once a week. The head cashier places the order on Wednesday, so our order just went in yesterday. She won't order again until next Wednesday.'

Drea wanted to beat her head against the steering wheel. 'She can't make a special order, as this is such a large sum?'

'She'd have to have special authorization, I'm sure.'

Rapidly she assessed the situation. 'How long after she places the order does it take for you to receive the cash? The next day?'

Mrs. Pearson hesitated again. 'I'd be glad to discuss this with you in person, but I really don't like to give out that information over the phone.'

Again, she couldn't fault the woman, who didn't know her from Adam's house cat; for all she knew, Drea was planning to rob the place and was trying to find out when they'd have the most cash available.

Things were not working out the way she'd planned. Instead of getting the cash and disappearing, it looked as if she'd have to hang around Grissom for at least a week. Grissom was a small town, and from what she remembered had only one tiny motel, which would make finding her incredibly easy.

She could limit her vulnerability though, by staying, say, within a hundred miles but moving around and never staying more than one night in each place. This was turning out to be a pain in the ass, but if she wanted to break the paper trail she had to do it somewhere, and she'd prefer sooner rather than later.

'I understand,' she said. 'I know this is a problem. I'll be there sometime tomorrow afternoon.'

'I hope we can work something out,' said Mrs. Pearson, which Drea thought was probably bank-talk for I hope you come to your senses.

She made it to the bank the next day about twenty minutes before closing; she had miscalculated how long the drive would take her so she'd had to get up at four that morning and drive hard all day long. She was tired, a little punch-drunk from three days of driving, and definitely frazzled. Her hair was a curly mess because she hadn't had time that morning to use the blow-dryer to straighten out the permed-in curls, but at least with curls she more resembled the photo on her driver's license. She couldn't imagine what a mess it would be if the bank didn't believe she was who she said she was. How could she prove her identity? Get a letter or something from Rafael? Yeah, right.

As it happened, her bedraggled appearance worked in her favor. Mrs. Pearson turned out to look like a fugitive from the old *Dynasty* television show, but her eyes were kind and her big-shouldered power suit was buttoned over a motherly heart. By that time Drea had worked up a sob story to use, involving an abusive ex-husband, who had been stalking her, but the story was useless. The bank manager's mother had died overnight; he had left for Oregon and wouldn't be back until after the funeral. No one wanted to bother him, and likewise no one at the bank would take responsibility for placing such a huge order for cash outside their normal routine.

God in heaven, Drea thought despairingly, why couldn't she have gotten an account at a large national bank that probably got cash every day or several times a day, rather than this podunk bank in a podunk town of not-quite three thousand residents?

She could drive to a larger town, maybe Kansas City, set up another account, and wire the money there, but larger cities meant more drug money came into play, and that gave Rafael more influence. She would be able to get her money faster, but she'd be in more danger while she did it.

As this was now late on Friday afternoon, the earliest she could set up an account would be the following Monday. Even if she then transferred the funds immediately, they wouldn't be posted, probably, until late that day. So it would be Tuesday before she could request cash, and the bank might or might not be able to get in that much the same day. On the safe side, she had to figure the following Wednesday would be the earliest she could get the money from another bank, whereas it would take her two days longer, the next Friday, to get the money here.

Two days longer, weighed against the greater danger. Neither choice looked great, but they were the only two choices she had. The only better possibility was if the bank manager's mother was buried this weekend and he came back to work on Monday which she doubted would happen.

'I suppose I'll be staying for a few days,' she said with a thin, exhausted smile. 'Can you recommend the motel, or should I go to the next town?'

She would need three things, Simon thought: cash, a car, and a cell phone. As smart as she was, she probably had a secret bank account somewhere nearby, so he'd assume she had the cash. A car, though; where would she get a car? Not in New York; she had last been seen in a taxi entering the Holland Tunnel, crossing into New Jersey. A different state made more sense, so he'd look in New Jersey. And somewhere nearby; she wouldn't waste money taking a taxi any great distance.

Not a new-car dealership, either; she'd try to fly under the radar, which meant a used car, fairly good condition but nothing spectacular.

He hacked into the DMV to get a copy of her New York driver's license. A native of the city might not have a license, might not even know how to drive considering how available public transportation was, but in his experience people who moved to the city tended to keep their licenses up-to-date. Once he had the photo, he played with the image, using his computer to cut her hair and darken it. Then he printed out the result, because now was the time for some legwork, and he had to have a picture to show.

He hit pay dirt on Monday and a hundred bucks later had the make and model of the car, plus the tag number. New Jersey issued two tags, one for the front bumper and one for the back, and some unscrupulous individuals made money by stealing just the front tag and selling them to people who wanted a tag on the rear, just to avoid being pulled over for having no tag at all, and who weren't

140

intending to stay in New Jersey. It was amazing how many people passed through New Jersey and how many needed just one tag. Once out of state, a smart person could play license plate roulette and keep ahead of the computer system.

A cell phone, though, was more problematic. She could buy a prepaid cell phone and keep her name out of the system. Damn it, that was probably a dead end.

That left the IRS.

He was like everyone else; he didn't like to fuck with the IRS, but the taxman was the only way he could find where Drea had sent the money. Any currency transaction involving ten thousand dollars or more triggered a report to the IRS, which was why he moved his own money in increments, and all of it to an offshore destination. Handling money was a hell of a lot of work.

The IRS, however, had a really pissy computer system, which was good luck for him and really bad news for Drea.

On Tuesday he learned that she had transferred her two million dollars to a bank in Grissom, Kansas.

12

If boredom was lethal, Drea thought, then she wouldn't live long enough to get her money. She'd left her hometown and eventually worked her way to New York City precisely because she didn't want to live in a town like Grissom, Kansas. She'd grown up in a small town; the life wasn't for her.

It wasn't the people. The people were generally nice, if not nosy. And even though her life in New York hadn't been all glamour and excitement and an endless round of parties– Rafael wasn't one of the Beautiful People, unless there was a subgenre of Beautiful Thugs – and she'd spent a lot of time in her room, at least it had been an extremely comfortable room. She hadn't gone to the theater or movies, but there was always pay-per-view on the television. She didn't have even that in the tiny, dingy room she got that Friday night at the tiny, dingy Grissom Motel, which lived down to its unimaginative name. And she couldn't go to a movie, because Grissom didn't have a movie theater – or much of anything else.

There was a small café, and one fast-food restaurant staffed by bored teenagers. For shopping, there was the hardware store, the feed store, the farm-supply store, and a dollar store. For a wider selection, the citizens drove to a neighboring town thirty miles away, which had a Wal-Mart. Big whoop.

She could remember when going to WalMart had been a big deal to her, because that was where she'd bought most of her clothes. If she'd managed to scrape together enough money to buy something at Sears, she was as proud of it as if she'd gotten it at Saks Fifth Avenue.

And here she was again, wearing Wal-Mart clothes. The difference was that she had two million bucks in the bank, and she knew that soon she could wear anything she wanted. In the meantime, living in the boondocks again was driving her nuts. Maybe she hadn't done much when she'd been in New York, but at least she *could* have.

Nerves ate at her; she felt as if the waiting was scraping her skin raw. After one night in Grissom she checked out of the motel and drove thirty miles to the town that boasted a strip mall, but on second thought kept going, to the next town down the road. The extra distance from Grissom would make it just that much more difficult for anyone to find her.

The next day, she checked out of that motel, and drove some more.

She did that for the next three nights. Living out of a cheap suitcase, not bothering to unpack because she was spending just one night in each place, bothered her on some bone-deep level. Every decision she'd made since the day she'd left home, such as it was, had been made with her eye on one goal, which was to have money, security and a home. She had money now, even if she couldn't get it yet. A home? She was afraid to stay in one place long enough to unpack her suitcase. She'd had somewhere to stay, but it

143

wasn't *hers,* a place where she belonged and could let her guard down. Maybe 'home' and 'security' actually meant the same thing – in any case, she knew she hadn't found it yet.

She was holding her breath, waiting to start living.

On Wednesday she found herself driving in a wide, meandering circle around Grissom, as if she were circling a drain. There was nothing to see except miles and miles of flat land, green with the summer crops, and the wide blue bowl of sky overhead. Traffic was sparse, because I-70 was a long way to the north, and down here in farm country the only people driving around were the people who lived here – and not many did.

Maybe it was the long days of solitude, or the mostly empty road that meant she likely wasn't in grave danger if she let her mind wander, but with nothing to occupy her time except her thoughts she began to feel ... uneasy. That was the only way to explain it. She'd made a mistake some- where, somehow.

All the steps she'd taken ran through her head, and she examined each one. She tried to think what she could have done differently, and other than transferring all the money to the Elizabeth bank and taking her chances with an extended stay in the area, she came up blank. On the other hand, was she taking a bigger chance by hanging around Grissom for so long?

Was she relying too much on the assumption that Rafael wouldn't go to the police? She didn't think so. Rafael would want to take care of her his way, the permanent way, which precluded any cops. Her other assumption was that Rafael, who had lived his entire life first in Los Angeles and then New York, would have no idea how to track her through middle America. This was her territory, not his. But what if she was wrong?

What if he hired out the job?

A chill shot through her. That was what she'd overlooked. Rafael wouldn't try to hunt her down himself, he wouldn't send his men out to beat the concrete bushes of New York. She'd stolen two million dollars from him, smashed his ego, and thrown his newfound 'love' back in his face. To him, the last two reasons would be even more powerful than the first. For an offense that serious, he'd hire the best.

And the best was ... *him*.

Her heart began hammering and her breath came too fast. Jerkily she pulled to the side of the road and gripped the steering wheel as she fought off the panic attack. She couldn't panic; she couldn't afford the wasted time. She had to *think*.

Okay. The bank wouldn't give out information about her account to anyone without a search warrant, which obviously Rafael wouldn't be able to get. But ... what about a hacker? The assassin made his living tracking down people, and he was damn good at what he did, or he wouldn't be able to charge the huge amounts he did. He earned the money by producing results. It followed, then, that he'd either be really good himself at getting into supposedly secure computer sites, or he knew someone who was.

Drea took a deep breath and held it for a few seconds, did that several times to slow her heartbeat. *Think it through, think it through.*

To hack into a bank's computer system, he'd first have to know which bank, but, damn it, he'd have the starting point because he'd know which bank Rafael used. Or he could get into the IRS system, knowing that every transaction over ten thousand dollars triggered a report to the tax agency, and from what she'd read the IRS didn't have the best computer system around. By the same token, Rafael's bank was one of the huge national banks with billions and billions in assets, so it followed that the bank would have a kick-ass security system on its computer network.

While she'd been wasting time driving aimlessly around looking at fields and sky and not much else, he could have tracked the bank transfers, and be waiting for her in Grissom.

The best thing she could do was walk away from the two million, at least for now, and stay safe. She still had the cashier's check for eighty-five thousand from the bank in Elizabeth, so it wasn't as if she was broke.

As soon as she deposited it somewhere, though, so far as she knew that would trigger another of those damn currency transaction reports, which would lead him straight to the bank where she'd put it.

There had to be a lag time, though, even a short one, between the bank and the IRS. She had an advantage with the cashier's check, because that should mean it would be immediately honored. She needed to go to a large city, use the cashier's check to open an account at a large national bank, let them know ahead of time she was wiring in two million dollars, and make arrangements to get at least a chunk of it in cash.

Suddenly, she knew how she'd work it. With the cash, she'd open up several different bank accounts, in different but neighboring towns, always less than ten thousand dollars so the bank wouldn't have to file those damn reports. Then, in a flurry of activity, she could wire smaller sums out of the Grissom bank to all those other banks, and one by one she could go to those other banks, close out the accounts and get the money in cash. She would fly under the radar. Getting the entire two million would take longer – a lot longer – but unless he could hack into the bank's computer system she should be home free.

Well, almost home free. At the least she would buy enough time to get a new identity and start over. With a new name, a new Social Security number, she could disappear.

Pulling out her cell phone, she checked the level of service. One bar. Not good enough. She'd have to get closer to a town. That was another thing about the wide-open spaces; they were *too* wide open, too many long miles of no people, no traffic, no houses, just fields as far as the eye could see. An ear of corn had no need for a cell phone, whereas her ear definitely did.

She drove for almost an hour, keeping an eye on the service indicator on her phone. When the number of bars abruptly jumped to three, she decided to give it a try, and pulled over.

Her first try, she got Mrs. Pearson's voice mail. 'Mrs. Pearson this is Andrea Butts. Something has come up and I *don't* want the two million in cash. I hope your head cashier hasn't put in the order yet. I really need to talk to you, but I'm afraid to come to the bank. Please call me back at–' She stopped, completely blanking on the number for her new cell phone. 'I'll call you back,' she said hurriedly and ended the call.

Damn it, what *was* that number? She turned off the phone, then turned it back on, and watched the screen as it flashed the info. Grabbing a pen from her bag, she scribbled down the number and called Mrs. Pearson again.

To her surprise, Mrs. Pearson herself answered. 'Hello, Ms. Butts, I just got your message. I was seeing some clients off and missed your call by seconds. I'm giving a note to Judy right now, about the cash order. I have to say, I'm relieved you've changed your mind, but ... is something wrong?' She lowered her voice. 'You're afraid to come to the bank?'

'It's my ex-husband,' Drea said, glad that her hard-luck spiel was making itself useful after all. 'I don't know how, but he's followed me this far, and knows I have an account with you. I'm afraid he's watching the bank, and if I show up there, he'll follow me.'

'Have you called the police?' Mrs. Pearson asked, a gratifying amount of alarm in her tone.

'So many times I've almost worn the numbers off the phone buttons,' Drea said wearily. 'It's always the same answer: until he actually *does* something, they have no grounds to pick him up. He's a salesman for a large agricultural firm, so he has a good reason for being in just about any area, and I don't have a right to keep him from doing his job, blah blah blah. I guess this is what I get for covering for him all those times he hit me, saying I fell down the steps, or closed the car door on my hand when he's the one who broke my finger.'

'Oh, you poor thing,' Mrs. Pearson murmured. 'No, you certainly shouldn't come here if you think he's watching. But ... what are you going to do?'

'I don't know.' She did know, she just hadn't worked out the particulars yet. 'He thinks he's entitled to the money because we were still married when my parents died and I inherited my share of their estate.'

'Ah ... an inheritance is the personal property of the heir, I think.'

'So the law says, but he thinks he earned it by putting up with me.' Drea put bitterness in her tone. 'I just need to break the paper trail, so he can't keep following me.

'Your account information is confidential. How does he–'

'He has a friend who works for the IRS.'

'I see.'

The fact that nothing more needed to be said told Drea that her reasoning about the IRS was more on target than she wanted it to be.

'I'll have to work something out, but I don't know what.'

'I'm afraid that any transaction you do will have to be reported to the IRS,' Mrs. Pearson said regretfully. 'Banks are required to make currency transaction reports on any movement of funds involving ten thousand dollars or more, so your two million will certainly leave a paper trail.'

'I don't want to cause any trouble with the IRS, and I'm certainly not trying to avoid any taxes. I just need to get my money and move it to another location before he can find me.'

'Your best bet of getting a lot of cash on short notice is to be in a city that has a Federal Reserve Bank. We're in the Kansas City district, but there's a branch in Denver, which is a bit closer to us here. The only thing is, when you get to where you're going and deposit the money, that bank will have to make a CTR, too.'

Not if the bank wasn't in this country, Drea thought grimly. If she could ever get her hands on this money, she was taking it offshore as fast as she could, to get out from under the ever-prying eyes of the government. When she got her new ID, she was getting a passport – a legitimate one – and then at least she could go on vacation to the Cayman Islands and take her money with her. She was tired of this crap.

'The safest way to move this money is to do it online,' Mrs. Pearson continued.

'I don't have a computer,' Drea said. 'Can I use a computer in an Internet café, or a library?'

'Umm, it would be better if you kept the same IP number. Can you do it from your cell phone?'

'This is a cheapie. It doesn't have Internet capability.'

'Get one that does. Then you can manage your account wherever you are. Or get a laptop, which I really recommend.'

'Then what do I do?'

'Go to our website, and follow the instructions.'

150

'Don't I have to sign something?'

'Yes, there's an agreement you have to sign. I can mail it to you–'

'I don't have a mailing address,' Drea confessed, feeling as if she was once again beating her head against the wall.

After a moment Mrs. Pearson said, 'I wouldn't normally do this, but if you'll get a laptop and Internet service, then call me, I'll print out the agreement and meet you somewhere. Where there's a will there's a way, Ms. Butts! We can get this done.'

Getting Internet service would also require putting her name in the system, Drea thought, but what the hell, she wasn't getting anywhere by any other means, and she sure as hell wasn't showing up at that bank in person.

'I'll do that,' she said wearily. 'Thank you. I'll call back when I get things organized.' She disconnected the call and let her head drop back against the headrest. Who knew stealing two million dollars would be so damn much trouble?

13

Was she crazy? Drea wondered as she plowed through her to-do list with ruthless determination, but no matter how determined she was, the damn thing kept getting longer.

Every step she took seemed to spawn two more steps, without which the first step wouldn't work. Because she didn't have a credit card, she had to pay cash for the cheapest laptop she could find at Wal-Mart, and she was beginning to run low on cash. Unless she wanted to risk going to the Grissom bank in person, she had to use the cashier's check for eighty-five thousand to open an account at a bank in the same town as the Wal-Mart, which would cause another currency transaction report to be issued.

Still, what choice did she have? She had to have Internet service in order to electronically move the two million bucks. But before she signed up for Internet service, she needed a laptop. And to get a laptop, she needed cash.

Everything seemed to loop back on itself. When she went to the cell phone store to get a wireless card for her brand-new laptop and sign up for the company's wireless service, she either had to have an address to which the bill could be sent, or she had to arrange for the bill to be automatically deducted from her bank account every month.

'Sure, why not?' she murmured to the slim

152

Hispanic kid who was helping her. All of her bank account info was right there in her purse, of course, considering she'd opened the account just two hours before.

And still, she was going purely on supposition. While she was certain Rafael was looking for her, she had no proof he'd hired anyone to track her. Maybe he just had Orlando on the job. That was her best-case scenario: while Orlando was good with computers, she knew he didn't have the expertise to hack into the IRS system.

Not only that, Rafael wouldn't let him. The very last thing Rafael wanted was to bring the IRS down on him, poking into his finances. It was the IRS, after all, that had brought down Al Capone. This past week had taught her how difficult it was to clandestinely move money around. No wonder money-laundering was such a big-time business; how else were all the drug dealers supposed to move their massive amounts of cash into the mainstream so they could openly spend it?

Even if Rafael had hired someone to track her, he might not have wanted to go to the expense of hiring him. The assassin was expensive – very expensive. Rafael had to be aware he wasn't going to get his two million back; he'd know the difficulties she faced, and he'd know that, once the money was credited to her account, he couldn't get to it. Would he be willing to add the cost of the assassin to the two million he'd already lost?

Yes. She was almost positive the answer was yes. Rafael would be in a rage and capable of anything. And considering his profession, the assassin would be well aware of the ins and outs of moving money around and converting it to cash.

That was the one thing she hadn't researched properly, the one weakness in her plan. She had acted hastily, pushed by emotion, and now she was paying the price. Was she never going to learn? she wondered bitterly. All emotion did was cloud the issue and make things more difficult. She should have shrugged off what Rafael had done, steeled herself to endure, and planned better. She could have waited until she had something set up off-shore, away from the prying of the IRS, *then* made her move.

She still had the bag of jewelry that she could liquidate, but probably her best bet would be selling it on eBay or something, and that would take time. Yet now that she had the laptop, she could get started on that. She wasn't broke and helpless, not like the first time. She had options.

What she didn't have was time. Days had passed since she'd left New York, plenty of time for him to track her. Unless she was willing to walk away from the two million, at least for a while. And how long would it be before she felt safe to access it? A year? Two years? Five? She had to move fast.

She didn't even have the eighty-five thousand now, at least not in her hand. Accessing it came with the same risks as accessing the two million. She had some more cash, and she had the jewelry, but while she could probably live off that she wouldn't be able to get that new ID so she could disappear There wouldn't be a house, a home just for her. She'd have to work at a job that paid her under the table, probably waitressing in some dump. She'd lived that life before, and she didn't intend to do it again.

The way she saw it, risky or not, she had to act.

Finally, with everything in place, she called Mrs. Pearson. 'I'm set,' she said. 'I have a laptop, and I have wireless service.'

'Good! I have the application ready. I get off work at five o'clock; I can meet you at ... where's a good place?'

'I don't know. Let me think.' In a town the size of Grissom, there was no good place. The café wouldn't work; Drea didn't want to be caught in a small place, on foot, with the only exit through the kitchen. She'd been in the café, and plates were handed out of a large pass-through to the waitress. There was a door at the back of the café that led to the restrooms and maybe to the kitchen, but she hadn't checked it out when she was there so she didn't know for certain. Unless she wanted to clamber through the pass-through, which she didn't because the grill might be right there under it, the café was a trap.

This was another example of not being thorough in her planning. She should have checked out everything, because her life might depend on it. From now on, she'd assume he was just one step behind her, and act accordingly. She wasn't safe until she'd broken the paper trail, and that would take time.

'How about the parking lot of the dollar store,' she finally suggested. There was more than one entrance; even better, it was on a corner, so she had more than one street to choose. No one who knew anything about her would ever look for her at a dollar store.

This was like a chess game, Simon thought with relish. He enjoyed matching wits with someone like Drea. Most of the time, his prey was clueless, even people who should know better. Most of his targets took security measures but then they felt very secure and relaxed their guards. Big mistake. *Fatal* mistake. The way to stay alive was to never relax, never assume you were safe.

He'd taken a flight out the previous afternoon, rented a pickup truck so he'd blend in with the population in the rural area, and driven the rest of the way. He was dressed in jeans, black work boots, and a short-sleeve, dark blue work shirt like mechanics wore. His shirt even had a name, *Jack*, embroidered above the left pocket. Everyone knew a Jack. Jacks were everywhere, and it was such a common name no one paid any attention to it. A stained ball cap, sunglasses, and beard stubble completed his disguise.

He was somewhat limited in his disguise choices, because he couldn't pull off the wheelchair routine in a town this small. People would be stopping to help him, they'd ask where he lived, wonder why they hadn't met before. Still, he was satisfied with his appearance; he blended in, which was exactly what he wanted.

If Drea hadn't realized before how difficult it was to get a large amount of cash, by now she did. She might be like the majority of his targets and assume she was safe here in this backwater because she hadn't used a credit card anywhere, and she'd driven instead of flying, but he

156

expected she would be sharper than that.

She had so far played it smart, but by now she'd have figured out the weakness in her plan, and realized how she could be traced. Would she expect him to be the one on her trail? It was possible. She knew Rafael well enough to play him, which meant she was damn accurate in predicting what he'd do.

She'd have to have Internet service to move the money electronically, and she'd have to fill out paperwork to set up the process. That meant the Internet service would have to come first. Last night he'd surfed through the systems of the companies serving this area, and she wasn't listed. Until she was able to get a new ID she'd have to use her real name, and all new paperwork cost more cash than he figured she had. Until she could change identities, she wouldn't be able to shake him.

Sitting in the pickup truck, he used his laptop to tiptoe through the wireless records again, starting with the largest company – and there she was. In the efficient way of cell phone service providers, she'd immediately been entered into the system.

Now she had to deal with the bank's paperwork, which meant she either had to come to the bank in person, or she'd already established a relationship with someone at the bank who would be willing to bring the paperwork to her. Because this was Drea, he was betting on the latter.

A bank employee wouldn't leave the bank by the front door; they all exited through the employee entrance at the side. He parked where he could keep an eye on that entrance; anyone who left, at any time other than closing, would be his number one prospect.

He watched patiently. At four-thirty, the front doors were locked. Okay, this wasn't going to be easy, but he'd have been disappointed if it was. He'd have to visually sort through the bank employees as they left, and follow the most likely.

Not a man, he decided immediately. Drea didn't trust men, with good reason. She was contemptuous of the ones she could play, and distrustful of the ones she couldn't. Eliminating men from his list wasn't much help, because most bank employees were women.

His most likely suspect would be a middle-aged woman, he thought; someone with experience, someone who would be in a position with some authority. An older woman would be more likely to feel protective of someone Drea's age. She would also be carrying papers, either in her hand or in a briefcase or large tote bag. With his parameters in place, he waited, and he watched.

He spotted her immediately. For one thing, she left promptly at five, which suggested she had a purpose. That purpose might be nothing more than cooking supper, but she carried a file folder in her hand. Bless her heart, he thought with mild amusement. She was willing to help, but she was completely out of her element. How much more obvious could she be?

She got into a beige Chrysler. He hated beige cars; they didn't stand out. At least the traffic here was light.

The big question was, where was she going?

Grissom was limited in its public choices. Maybe she'd arranged to meet Drea at her own home, which could make things dicey as far as following her went.

He didn't immediately pull into the street, but instead let another bank employee get between him and the Chrysler. He hung back, not wanting to spook her, though he thought there was little chance of that.

She drove two blocks, and at the second corner turned right, into the parking lot of a dollar store. Simon didn't touch his brakes, didn't look directly at the Chrysler as he cruised by, but with his peripheral vision he studied the parking lot looking for cars with someone sitting in them. Would Drea get in the Chrysler, or would the bank lady go to her? He bet on the bank lady being the one to leave the cover of her car; Drea was too smart to parade around in public when she suspected someone was looking for her.

In his rearview mirror, he saw the bank lady get out of her car, pause, then begin walking purposefully across the parking lot.

'Bingo,' he said softly. 'Your ass is mine, sweetheart.'

14

A chill ran down Drea's spine and she whipped her head around, looking in all directions. A sense of imminent danger seized her, making her want to put the car in gear and floorboard the accelerator. She couldn't see anything out of the ordinary, but her lizard brain was screaming Run! and she actually trembled from the effort it took to remain where she was. He wasn't here. She knew he wasn't, just five more minutes and everything would be set. She could leave. She could go to Denver and soon have her two million in cash, and then she could disappear so thoroughly even he would never be able to find her.

She had checked out the parking lot when she arrived fifteen minutes ago, even though there was no way he or anyone could have known where she was meeting Mrs. Pearson. The only vehicle with anyone sitting in it was a battered, four-door Chevy. The motor was running, to keep the air-conditioning going in the ninety-degree heat. Sitting in the front passenger seat was an older woman, her face lined with years and fatigue; a whining toddler was imprisoned in a car seat in the back. No threat there, unless the kid escaped.

She recognized Mrs. Pearson as the older woman pulled into the parking lot, then she immediately switched her attention to the passing traffic. Right behind Mrs. Pearson was a red sedan, driven by a woman, then a guy in a pickup truck. Drea stared at the guy, but she couldn't get a good look at him because of the sun's reflection on the window. She could tell he was wearing a ball cap, though, and he was focused on his driving because he didn't turn his head to look in Mrs. Pearson's direction.

Both the red sedan and the pickup disappeared down the street. As Mrs. Pearson, file folder in hand, hurried across the parking lot toward her, Drea anxiously watched the street behind her, wondering what had given her the willies. Another car, this one also driven by a woman, went by just as Mrs. Pearson reached for the door handle.

Drea quickly hit the unlock button, and Mrs. Pearson got in. As soon as she slammed the door, Drea locked the doors again. Every car had a blind spot, and she didn't want anyone slipping up behind her, then getting into the back seat and putting a gun to her head.

'Have you seen him?' Mrs. Pearson asked, her head swiveling as she looked all around them.

'No, not yet.' But he was around. She knew he was. The tingle in her spine, the lizard sense of danger, warned her he was near.

She was more vulnerable now than she'd been yesterday, or even this morning, and she knew it. By getting Internet service she'd put her name in the system, verified her presence in the vicinity. She'd been caught on the security cameras at the cell phone store, so she had to assume her changed appearance was no longer a secret.

Maybe she was assigning way too much power

161

and skill to him, but she didn't think so. If she had any skill at all it was in reading men, and her gut said he was capable of finding her. It also said he was the most dangerous man she'd ever met, and while she'd met some stone-cold killers who could curdle your blood, he was head and shoulders above them, which was why he scared the shit out of her.

Mrs. Pearson opened the file folder and removed several sheets of paper. 'Fill these out, sign them, and everything's set.'

Drea took the papers, giving one more long look around. 'Keep an eye out while I'm reading. He's tall, about six-one, good-looking and in very good shape. Short dark hair.' The thumbnail description seemed very inadequate for a man whose very presence seemed to suck all the air out of a room, as if he not only commanded his space but everyone else's, too. But how could she describe the way he moved, the grace and speed, and at the same time get across how very *still* he was? Saying his eyes were like dark opals was useless, because you couldn't see all those colors unless you were very close, and then it was too late.

Mrs. Pearson took her job as lookout seriously; she didn't say anything while Drea turned her attention to the papers, but Drea was aware of the almost constant movement of the older woman's head. People came and went in the parking lot, but they were mostly harried mothers, wilting in the heat, usually with a kid or two dragging behind to the accompaniment of flip-flops slapping on the pavement.

The paperwork took only a few minutes. Drea

scribbled her signature, then replaced the sheets in the folder. 'I can't tell you how much I appreciate the trouble you've gone to,' she told Mrs. Pearson, returning the folder to her and taking a long look around as she did so. There was still nothing out of the ordinary, and she still had that worrisome tingle running up and down her spine.

'You shouldn't have to live your life in fear,' Mrs. Pearson said, her kind gaze a little sad as she looked at Drea. 'I hope you can finally get free.'

'I hope so, too,' said Drea.

After Mrs. Pearson left, Drea sat and watched the traffic for a few more minutes. She hadn't parked at the curb but rather in an open-ended slot, so she wouldn't have to waste time backing up if she had to leave in a hurry. From where she sat in the parking lot she could see behind the store, see the vacant lot, overgrown with weeds, that separated the store from some residences. Was that a dead-end street, or could she use it to come back onto the main drag at a different point?

Once again, she hadn't done her homework, and fury at herself shot through her. How could she expect to get out of this alive if she didn't start paying more attention to detail? She should have bought a map of the town as soon as she got here, studied it, acquainted herself with every street and road. *He* probably knew exactly where that street went.

She looked at the vacant lot, wondered briefly how much broken glass was hidden by the weeds, then gave a mental shrug and put the car in gear. Steering it around the back corner of the store, she

163

threaded between two parked cars that probably belonged to store employees, jolted over one of those movable concrete forms that had once blocked the end of the parking slot but had now been pushed half out of the way, and plowed across the lot. The ground was uneven, bouncing her around, and the tall weeds whipped against the side of the car. Then there were two hard jolts as she shot over the curb and into the street, the back wheels fish-tailing a little as they tried to grab traction. Then the rubber grabbed the pavement and the car gathered speed, hurtling toward the end of the street two blocks away where, hallelujah, she could see a stop sign and another street.

From where he was parked down the block, facing the store, Simon watched her circle to the back of the building, then cut across the vacant lot in the rear before heading north on the short side street. The truck was in gear, so he briefly checked for oncoming traffic – none – then let off on the brake and pulled away from the curb, executing a U-turn in the street and heading west.

The side street ended after a couple of blocks; she could go either east or west. He bet on west. The closest Federal Reserve bank was in Denver, and she'd be in a hurry to get that two million converted to cash. Not only that, the farther west she went, the emptier the country was, at least until she hit the West Coast. People could and did disappear all the time in the vast emptiness of the region, but they were people who lived outside the system without bank accounts or cell phones, or even electrical service unless they happened to rig up a generator. He couldn't see Drea living that lifestyle. If possible, she'd go for comfort.

If he miscalculated and she headed east, locating her again might take him a couple of days, but there weren't that many secondary roads out here that she could use. Not that they didn't exist, but they tended to wind around for miles and then just stop, and you had to either backtrack or cut across country, in which case you better know where in hell you were going and have a four-wheel-drive vehicle with heavy-duty suspension. Her middle-aged car wasn't capable of going cross-country, and Drea was too smart to try.

She might deem it worthwhile to ditch the car and get something more durable, though, if she had squeezed out enough cash to give her some reserves. In fact, he'd bet on that. As soon as she got to Denver, where she'd feel safer because she could blend in with the much greater population, she'd change cars.

He had a full tank of gas; he was ready to go in any direction she chose. But how much gas did she have? If she had to fill up, she'd likely stop at the Exxon station on the western edge of town. It wasn't a huge station, but it was at an intersection and had four pumps on each side of the station, so she wouldn't feel hemmed in.

He still didn't know what he was going to do. Indecision wasn't one of his traits, but this wasn't one of his usual jobs. Maybe it was because he was aroused by her sheer guts in ripping off Salinas the way she had done, or maybe it was

165

because of that afternoon of hot sex they'd shared, but at this point he was tracking her because, until he decided on his course of action, he didn't want to lose her. Maybe he was simply enjoying the chase, wondering what wrinkles she would throw at him.

On the other hand, two million was two million. And, unlike Drea, he already had an offshore account – several of them – so he wouldn't have the difficulties she'd been facing.

At some point, though, he'd have to make a firm decision, and that point was fast approaching. Let her go or collect the two million? Let her go or take the risk of making a hit here in the States? Killings could and did go unsolved all the time, but he never lost sight of the fact that things were different here than they were in an underdeveloped country.

He glanced at his navigation system. The road she was on had a stop sign at every intersection – that would slow her down. He was on the main drag, which had two traffic lights back in the business district, such as it was, but the rest of the way the stop signs were all on the intersecting streets. He'd be at the gas station a couple of minutes before she reached it.

When he got there, he pulled in front of the air hose station and got out, so no matter which side of the gas pumps she chose, he could move around and keep the truck between them. She might have a full tank and not need to stop, which was okay; she wouldn't be able to get so far ahead of him that he'd lose her, not in the couple of seconds it would take him to get back in the truck.

He spotted her, coming toward him at a measured speed, not so fast she'd get pulled over but not poking along, either. He moved as she came closer, keeping the truck cab so it always partially blocked her view of him, in case she happened to glance his way.

She didn't pull in. She stopped at the intersection, looked both ways, and went straight across, heading west toward Colorado.

Good girl, he thought approvingly. She'd already filled the tank, instead of leaving something that important for the last minute. He went around the truck and climbed into the cab, and pulled back onto the highway just a hundred yards behind her.

15

Drea looked in her rearview mirror to make certain no one was coming up behind her, and saw the man getting into the pickup truck. Her heart gave a huge lurch, then skipped several beats. The road swam before her eyes as blood drained from her head. He was too far away for her to see his face, but she'd seen the way he moved, all grace and lethal power. She'd seen the way he held his head, the set of his shoulders, and she *knew*, knew in a way she couldn't explain but that went all the way to the bone.

That pickup. She'd seen that pickup before, or one very similar, and she couldn't stretch coincidence that far. It was the same color and make as the truck that had gone by just after Mrs. Pearson had pulled into the dollar store parking lot. It was him, and he'd been watching her even then. Somehow he'd figured out what she was doing and who to follow, and knowing that terrified her. He was too good at what he did; how could she possibly get away from him?

She had just enough control that she didn't jam the gas pedal all the way to the floorboard, but she steadily increased the power until the speedometer needle edged toward ninety and the front end began shimmying, then she eased off just a little. Her only hope was to get far enough ahead of him that she could take a side road or hide behind some structure, but she wouldn't be able to do that if the car fell apart.

The geography of Kansas didn't help. The land wasn't completely flat, but as good as. There was no way–

She was breathing too fast again, her heart pounding so hard and so rapidly she could barely think. She couldn't let him get to her like this; she had to be on her toes, she had to think, and she couldn't let herself panic.

She fought her nerves, fought her instinctive reaction, and forced herself to ease up on the gas pedal until the car had slowed to a far more reasonable speed. She couldn't outrun him; she'd be stupid to even try. The pickup was a full-size truck, with a more powerful engine than the six-cylinder she was driving. He was sitting higher, too, so he'd be able to see her for quite a distance, and she couldn't pull far enough ahead of him that she was out of sight for even a few seconds.

The question was, would he try to catch her now, when the countryside was so wide open that any other vehicle at a distance might be able to see him, or they might pass a farmer in his fields at any time? Or would he be content to shadow her and wait until nightfall provided him with cover?

He'd have to pull even with her to have a decent shot. He could force her off the road, but, contrary to the movies, cars didn't usually explode and burn when they crashed, and the combination of seat belts and air bags meant the people inside often survived. Of course, if he forced her off the road and her car was so damaged it was

169

undrivable, then he could take his shot at his own leisure, but unless she hit a power pole or something, being run off the road wasn't going to accomplish much; she'd tear up a field of wheat, but that would be about the extent of the damage.

In her favor was the fact that he didn't know if she was armed. She wasn't, damn it, because guns hadn't been part of her arsenal. Sex and guile were her weapons, along with makeup and perfume, but he didn't – couldn't – know if she'd acquired a gun in the past eight days and he'd have to use caution.

She glanced at her fuel gauge, and wondered what his gas mileage was. Her six-cylinder got pretty good mileage, certainly better than his big engine would get. Maybe she could go farther than he could on a tank of gas. If he ran out of gas – no, fat chance he'd let that happen. But if he had to stop for gas, she'd have a chance to get away, to turn off the road and hide, take some other route to Denver.

He'd know that, though. If he began getting low on gas, he'd be forced to make a move. Maybe *she* could stop at a gas station, run inside, and ask for help. Hell, she had a cell phone; she could call 911 and say she was being followed by a strange man.

Except ... except she didn't want to draw a cop's attention, and a cop would pull *both* of them over. The license plates on this car weren't kosher. She'd stolen two million dollars, and even though the cash wasn't in her possession, she sure as hell didn't want her name on the cop computer network. Not only that, he was behind her; he could simply say he had no idea who she was; all he was doing was driving down the highway. She didn't even know his name, so she couldn't claim he was an ex-boyfriend or whatever.

She checked the rearview again. He was still there, closer than he had been before. He wasn't gaining fast, but he was gaining.

Had he realized yet that she'd made him? She hadn't taken any evasive actions, but unless she pulled over, ran into the wheat, and crawled on all fours for the next fifty miles, her options in evasion were limited.

Still, she wasn't going to give up. She was in a moving vehicle and so was he, so the odds of him getting off an accurate shot were very low. She knew from listening to Rafael and his men talk when they were watching some action movie on television how improbable things like that were. Just to see if they'd known what they were talking about, she'd done some research on it and found that, in this instance, they were right. Even the best snipers in the world had to shoot from a fixed position, or luck mattered more than skill.

Unless he tried to run her off the road, she was safe enough for the moment. If he started closing on her fast, then she'd know he had decided to make his move. She couldn't let herself panic, because if she did then it was all over. So long as she kept her head, she had a chance.

She'd made him. He knew it as soon as he saw the car gaining speed like a rabbit running from a hound. He also knew the exact moment she reined in her galloping panic and began thinking again, because she let off on the gas and slowed

171

to around sixty.

He was content to lie back and keep her in sight. The miles spun by beneath their tires, and after about an hour they crossed the state line into Colorado, but this part of the state was damn near as flat as Kansas and she didn't have any opportunity to shake him. He watched the clock, and he watched his fuel gauge. The truck had a bigger gas tank than her car, but it also guzzled gas at a faster clip, so it was a toss-up which of them would need gas first.

He'd have to time his move; as they got farther west the country would get rougher, and nightfall became more imminent. He couldn't let her get so far ahead that she could cut her headlights and turn off the road – a risky move, but he had no doubt she'd try it. He'd have to tuck in close behind her when it began getting dark, and if she hadn't been forced to stop for gas by the time his gauge read lower than a quarter of a tank, that was when he'd make his move.

What he did depended on what she did. She could be armed. If she pulled a weapon on him, then he'd have no choice in the matter and he'd take her out. His own weapon, a Glock 17, lay on the seat beside his right thigh. He didn't worry about being caught with a weapon; he had a federal license that would pass inspection by any cop, state or local. The license was fake, but discovering that would take digging through several layers of camouflage. The weapon had no serial number on it, couldn't be traced to him, and if he needed to he'd ditch it without a second thought.

The time was fast approaching when he'd have

to make up his mind. Take her out, or peel off and go back to New York? Why go to this much trouble unless he intended to do the job? Amusement and entertainment weren't good reasons for being here. He was spending too much time and money following her unless he collected his fee at the end of the ride.

None of his previous targets had meant anything to him, pro or con. Human life, as a theory, was no more valuable to him than, say, the life of a housefly. His hits weren't motivated by notions of right and wrong, politics, religion, love, hate, or anything else other than the fee he earned. Drea, though, was different. He knew her, and not just physically, though their skin chemistry was stronger than anything he'd ever experienced before.

He knew her intelligence, knew her guts and her determination. She was a fighter, a survivor. He hadn't seen her relaxed, completely herself, but then he suspected she hadn't let down her guard in years. She had decided on her course of action, then never looked back.

He might disagree with the wisdom of hooking up with someone like Rafael Salinas, but he didn't know what Drea's circumstances had been before. Maybe Salinas was a huge step up, though that was difficult to fathom. Salinas was a thug; smarter than most, but still a thug. For Drea to keep up her act, without a single false note, for as long as she had indicated a level of self-discipline he hadn't seen before – except in himself.

Was that why he'd hesitated for so long? Because he saw something in her that reminded him of himself? Not his lack of emotion, because Drea had enough emotion for the both of them, but the things she'd hidden from Salinas were what he saw and enjoyed. Maybe that was why he hadn't yet taken action. On the other hand, he hadn't yet told Salinas where to wire his down payment, either, and he didn't do a job until he verified the specified amount was in his account.

Everything kept circling back to the same thing: yes, or no? Do the job, or drive away? Let her go, or take the two million?

If he didn't take the job, Salinas would send someone else after her. But she had a big head start, and once she had her stolen millions in cash her options were pretty much unlimited. If she got caught, it would be through pure bad luck. The only way she'd be truly safe, was if Salinas thought she was dead.

He could do that, take the money and tell Salinas the job was done, but he'd never faked a job before. His value lay in his reliability, and his accuracy.

On the other hand, if he was ever going to screw a client, it would be Salinas. He had nothing but contempt for the son of a bitch.

He glanced at the sky. There was probably another hour, hour and a half of daylight, and the terrain was getting noticeably rougher as the earth began wrinkling as the land rose toward the Rockies. The actual mountains were still a good distance away, but they didn't rise from a flat nothing; it was a gradual lift, an increase in the folds of the earth's crust, and then the big eruption. The longer he waited, the rougher the land,

and the more opportunity she'd have to give him the slip.

He pressed his boot on the accelerator, and the truck began eating up the distance between him and Drea.

16

The truck was gaining on her. Drea hadn't looked in the mirror for several minutes as she paid attention to the road, which was developing some twists and turns at the same time the elevation was rising and falling. Right now they were climbing a low ridge, with the land falling away to the right; not an extremely steep drop nor a long one, but throw in the occasional sharp curve and her driving skills were being tested. She was out of practice, despite the past week, and most of her driving had been done on flat land anyway.

It had been a while since she'd seen a road sign that gave her the highway number, and she began to worry that she might have missed a crucial turn, because they hadn't met another car for at least five minutes and the road was noticeably narrower. Was she still on her chosen route to Denver? She couldn't exactly pull over and look at her map; there was no shoulder to the road, not to mention there was a killer on her ass.

Then she dared a glance in the mirror and saw the truck was no more than fifty yards behind her, and closing the remaining gap at a frightening pace.

Her heart leaped into her throat, and her hands tightened on the steering wheel until her knuckles turned white. He'd evidently decided now was the time, that the road was deserted enough and he didn't have to wait any longer. She'd hoped for night to catch them, hoped...

She didn't know what she'd hoped. That he'd wait until she had the best chance of giving him the slip? Yeah, like that was going to happen. She should have expected this.

He'd tightened the gap by another twenty yards and was close enough now that she could make him out in the truck cab, see the dark sunglasses he was wearing.

How much was Rafael paying him? Maybe she could pay him more. Maybe – Why was she letting herself get distracted with this crap, as if she'd be able to negotiate with him? He wouldn't mess around and talk about the situation, he'd kill her and leave – thirty seconds, tops.

Damn it! Drea was suddenly furious with herself, with him, with Rafael, with every damn thing. It couldn't end like this, she refused to let it end like this. Rafael was *not* going to be the death of her, not when the bastard *owed* her for two years of putting up with his bullshit, for smiling when she wanted to slap him, for giving him blow jobs and acting as if it made her happy. What kind of stupid-ass fool thought *giving* a blow job was satisfying? He owed her for giving her to another man, for treating her like a whore and making her feel like a whore.

And damn that other man for being *him,* for not treating her like a whore, for being gentle and giving her such incredible pleasure before walking out without a single backward look, throwing at her the careless words, 'Once was enough.' Was he her punishment for all the men she'd played, all the men she'd used? How damn ironic was it that the one time she thought– Never mind what she'd thought, forget that she'd begged him to take her with him, because regardless of what she'd thought, their minds certainly hadn't been running in the same direction.

She went around a curve too fast and the back end of the car slid a little; the landscape, so clear in the hot, mellow light of the setting sun, was suddenly blurry. Her eyes stung with tears that she refused to let fall. She had cried enough over him already. She had learned never to look back, never to give fate a second chance to kick her in the teeth.

'Screw you,' she said to the reflection in the rearview mirror, to the expressionless man behind the dark sunglasses.

The road corkscrewed on her, an S curve so sharp she was in it before she realized how extreme the angle was. She hit the brakes as she felt the back tires skidding once more, pulling her to the right, toward where the pavement fell away to nothing.

'Slow down,' he said sharply, knowing she couldn't hear him, as he watched the rear end of the car skid around. He took his foot off the gas, letting the truck slow itself as he entered the series of curves behind her. Maybe if he backed off a little she wouldn't push the curves so hard; the truck didn't corner as well as a car did, anyway.

Her back tires slid off the pavement, throwing up a spray of gravel. He watched in futile anger, knowing there wasn't a damn thing he could do.

Drea's heartbeat stuttered wildly as the car slid toward the edge, a debilitating sense of helplessness filling her because the laws of physics had her in their grip and there was nothing she could do to get loose.

She was in the most acute part of the curve, with empty air in front of her and to the right. Time froze for an instant, then clicked forward to the next frame, then the next, like watching a slide show with someone else controlling the clicker. In each frame she knew exactly what was happening, her thoughts flying much faster than the frames were advancing.

First frame: in that instant she knew that if she steered into the skid, she would drive straight off the road, down into the tree-studded bowl contained between the two halves of the S-curve. Even if she survived, any wreck at all would be the death of her, because he was right behind her and he'd be able to take his shot anytime he wanted.

Second frame: in the split second that the back tires skidded over closer to the edge, the car began tilting backward and the bottom dropped out of her stomach, as if she were on a roller-coaster ride. Through the rearview mirror she caught a glimpse of the big pickup truck behind her and the man inside, and a surge of pain hit her so hard that her skittering heartbeat faltered under the impact. *He hadn't wanted her.* If only he had. If only he'd held out his hand to her when she begged 'Take me with you.' But he hadn't, and he never would.

Third frame: the back tires suddenly found traction, digging into the crumbling edge and sending great fans of dirt and gravel arcing outward. The steering wheel wrenched to the side, turning with a life of its own and tearing out of her white-knuckled grip. The car shot forward, and took her over the edge. Maybe she screamed; she might have screamed the whole time, but she was aware only of an all-encompassing silence.

Fourth frame: the car seemed to hang in midair for long, agonizing seconds. She looked across the gap to where the road curved in the second half of the S, thinking inanely that if this were a movie the car would make that jump and land on the pavement on the other side, jouncing wildly and maybe losing a bumper but otherwise miraculously unscathed. But this wasn't a movie and the moment ended. The weight of the engine pulled the front end down, and she saw the trees below rushing up at her like spears from a missile launcher.

Just split seconds, slices of time, yet her vision was crystal clear, her thoughts ordered and full. This was the end, then. She had thought about death; unlike most young people, she had met death when her placenta separated during her twenty-second week of pregnancy. She had almost died; her baby *had* died, died while still inside her body, then cut from her body still warm and motionless, taking all of her dreams and agonizingly intense love with him. He'd been so tiny, so frail and limp and turning blue even as she sobbed and begged God or whoever to let him live, to take her instead because he was innocent and she wasn't, because he had all the possibilities of the world lying before him while she was worthless, but that must not have seemed like a good trade because her baby hadn't lived.

She had, in a way. She'd gone through the motions. She'd survived, because at the core of things she was a survivor even though there would never be another baby for her. And she had never loved again, never felt anything for anyone until a little over a week ago, when he, the nameless he, had broken through her shell and touched her.

And now he'd killed her.

The first impact popped the windshield out like a false fingernail. If the car had had an air bag when it was new, it no longer did, because no big white pillow blew up to smack her in the face even though the force of impact was like a huge body blow that shutdown all her senses except for a very small sense of awareness that lingered and held on because holding on was such a part of her.

Not having an air bag didn't matter, though, because it wasn't the first impact that killed her. It was the second.

'Shit!' Simon said violently as he slammed on the brakes and fought the truck to a tire-smoking halt, shoving the gearshift into the park position and leaping out while the truck was still rocking. *'Fuck!'*

He paused briefly on the crumbling road edge, judging the best path to take, then went sideways down the sharp slope at a breakneck pace, half kneeling here, grabbing a bush there, digging his heels in when he could. 'Drea,' he yelled, though he didn't expect an answer. He paused briefly to listen, and heard nothing other than what was almost a vibration in the air, a sensation rather than a noise, as if the violence of the impact still reverberated.

The drop was too long, and there were too many trees. When a car took on a tree, the tree usually won. Still, maybe she wasn't dead; maybe she was unconscious. People survived car wrecks every day, even those that looked unsurvivable, while one that seemed not much worse than a fender bender would pop someone's spine and that was that. It was position, it was timing; hell, it was luck.

He couldn't explain why his heart was pounding and his stomach felt as if it were filled with ice. He'd seen death many times, up close and personal. And most of the time he was the cause. The transition was fast, the blink of an eye, the flight of a bullet, and that was it: lights out. No big deal.

But this didn't feel like no big deal. This felt like– God, he didn't know what this felt like. Panic, maybe. Or pain, though why he'd feel either of those was beyond him.

He pushed through scrub brush, lost his footing, and slid the last twenty feet on his ass. The car was to his right, half-hidden in broken tree limbs and bushes, a heap of tangled metal from which dust still floated. Broken glass from the headlights and taillights was everywhere, shards in red and white and amber, glittering in the sun. One wheel had come completely off, the tire exploded by the force of the impact. Other pieces of twisted, sheared metal lay here and there.

He reached the rear end of the car first. He could see the top of her head, just above the headrest; she was still in the seat. The driver's door was completely gone, and he could see her left arm dangling limply, blood slowly dripping from her fingertips.

'Drea,' he said, more softly.

No response. He shoved through the brush and wreckage until he reached her side, then momentarily froze.

God. A pine sapling had come through the windshield – or rather, where the windshield used to be – and impaled her chest. She was sitting upright only because she was pinned to the seat, which was already soaked black with her blood. He reached out his hand, then let it fall. There was nothing he could do.

A breeze fluttered the trees around them, and a few birds sang their evening songs. The heat of the setting sun burned his back and shoulders, and bathed everything in a clear golden light. Details were crystal clear, but oddly detached. Time was moving on around them, but he felt as if they were enclosed in a bubble where everything stood still. He had to make certain, for himself. He leaned half into the car reaching out to feel for the pulse in her neck.

In the strange way things happen, her pretty face had only a few small cuts. Her pure blue eyes were open, her head turned toward him as if she was looking at him.

Her chest rose in a slow, shallow breath, and with a jolt that ran all the way to his feet he realized that she *was* looking at him. She was going, and going fast, but for this moment she saw him, she recognized him.

'God, sweetheart,' he whispered, abruptly remembering exactly how she tasted, how soft and silky her breasts were, the sweet scent of a woman underlying the expensive perfume she wore. He remembered how she'd felt in his arms, how hungry for affection she'd been, the tight slick heat of her body as he slid into her, and the lost look in those blue eyes when he left her. He remembered how her laugh sounded as musical as bells, and the realization that he'd never hear it again was a punch in the chest that left him winded.

He didn't think she heard him. Her expression was as calm and serene as if she'd already gone, her face porcelain white. Yet her gaze remained locked on his face and slowly her expression changed as it softened and filled with wonder. Her lips moved, shaped a single word ... and then she was gone. The blue eyes set, began to dull. Automatically her body took one more breath, still fighting for a life that was already gone, then it, too, stopped.

The breeze flirted with a tendril of her hair, blowing it against her pale cheek. Gently, Simon reached out one finger and touched the tendril, dark and straight now, but still as silky as it had been when it was blond and curly. He smoothed it back, tucking it behind her ear then he stroked her cheek. There were things he needed to do, but for the moment he could do nothing except stay exactly where he was, looking at her and touching her, feeling as if the ground had dropped from beneath him. He watched her, waiting, hoping for another breath, but she was gone and he knew it. There was nothing.

He drew several deep, ragged breaths, then forced himself to straighten from the car. Sentiment had no place in his life; he couldn't allow anyone or anything to matter, to get inside his emotional and mental shields.

Moving briskly, he did what had to be done. He looked around until he found her purse, lying several yards away. Swiftly he removed her cell phone and the driver's license from her wallet, slipping both into his pocket. She didn't have any credit cards, no other identification, so he returned the wallet to her purse and tossed it onto the front floorboard. Her laptop was easier to find, because it was in the backseat, though getting to it was far more difficult. Finally he reached it and dragged it out.

One thing more: the bill of sale for the car. He worked his way around to the other side of the car and used his pocketknife to pry open the crushed glove box. Removing the bill of sale, he paused a moment to think if there was anything else that could give away her identity. No, he had it all.

The last thing he did was use his cell phone to take a picture of her. It was ghoulish, but necessary.

Carrying the laptop, he climbed back up to the road. No more than five minutes had passed since the accident, if that long. No other vehicles had come by, but then this wasn't exactly an interstate highway. Opening the door of the still-running truck, he put the laptop on the passenger seat, then took Drea's cell phone out of his pocket and checked to see if there was any cell service out here. There was, but not much; maybe he could make himself understood. He punched in 911, and when the operator answered he said, 'I want to report a car accident, with a fatality, on highway...'

He gave the pertinent information, then, when the operator began asking questions, he flipped the phone closed and ended the call.

He'd wait until he heard the sirens. He'd stand watch over her body, guarding her and keeping her company, until he knew someone was coming to take care of her.

Standing with one boot on the running board and one arm resting on top of the truck, he watched the sun set behind the far mountains, watching the purple twilight begin its rapid progression. Finally a faint wail reached him, carried by the clear dry air, and several miles away he could see the flash of red lights.

He got in the truck and sat for a moment, his arms crossed on top of the steering wheel, remembering the way she had looked at him and the way her expression had softened, then she had said one word: 'Angel–'

And died.

He cursed, and banged his fist once on the steering wheel. Then he put the truck in gear and drove away.

17

She didn't hurt. Drea thought she probably should be hurting, but she didn't. That was okay; because she wasn't a fan of hurting.

Everything seemed distant and unreal. She knew she should be trying to get up, that there was an urgent reason why she should run, yet she had no desire to move. Moving didn't seem to be an option, anyway. Maybe after a while she'd get up.

No, no, she couldn't lie to herself, even now. Especially now. She was dying. She knew it, and it was okay. If she'd had a choice, yeah, she'd keep trying, but choice had been taken away and letting go was almost a relief. She could feel herself dying, feel each breath coming slower and slower. Her heartbeat – was her heart even beating? She couldn't feel it at all. Maybe it had stopped. That was okay, too, because it had just been going through the motions since her baby died and it was tired of the act.

Her baby... She hadn't named him. She'd been in shock from blood loss, close to dying herself because the doctor hadn't been able to stop the bleeding, and they had taken the tiny body away. No one had ever brought any birth certificate forms for her to fill out, because he'd never taken a single breath. Stillborn. That was the term for it. He'd been so still when he was born, even though, up until an hour before, he'd been entertaining himself by turning flips and trying to kick her ribs out. Then there had been the sudden, severe pain, and the bleeding that soaked her clothes. She didn't have a car, she didn't even have a license, because she wouldn't turn sixteen for another month and she was at home by herself. By the time she got to the hospital, it was already too late. Her baby never had a name.

The memories floated in and out of her head, as vivid as if she were living through the experience all over again, except this time when she saw his little body she knew that soon she'd be joining him in the nothingness of death. *Soon, sweetheart,* she promised him.

Her vision was weird, all foggy and dark, but abruptly there was a face in front of her, a face she knew. She saw those dark opal eyes that had been both dream-come-true and nightmare to her, the strong bone structure, the lips that she knew were soft and gentle. She had been terrified of him, yet now she wasn't. Now she wanted to reach out and lay her hand along his jaw, feel the scrape of his beard stubble, the coolness of his skin overlying the heat of muscle, but her arms wouldn't work. Nothing worked.

Was he really there, or was she seeing him the same way she'd seen her baby? She heard a whisper of sound, an odd echo of the promise she had made just a moment ago. Watching him, she also felt the echo of an emotion she'd thought she would never feel again, and she wanted to tell him, she tried to tell him, but her vision was going even darker and she couldn't really see him any longer.

Then the light came, a bright pure light behind him that seemed to grow and grow until he was nothing but a silhouette against it. She saw something, something at once beautiful and terrible, and she knew it had come for her.

'*Angel,*' she whispered, and died.

Death wasn't supposed to be like this. It was supposed to be *nothing.* She seemed to be hovering, looking down, watching him get something out of her purse, take her laptop, but none of that meant anything. Then a strong compulsion began pulling her away from the scene, taking her somewhere else, but she had no sense of distance or speed or even really *moving.* It was more like a transition, as if one instant she was one thing and the next instant she was something else.

Drea kept waiting for the lights to go out, for her sense of consciousness to shut down. She kept waiting for the nothing, though she wondered how she'd know, since only consciousness could comprehend the lack of consciousness and self. But her thoughts remained, her sense of self remained, and it was all very confusing.

So maybe there was no nothing, maybe there was something. Maybe death really was more of a passing than an end. Well, if that were true, wouldn't she be someone else now? Or would she always be herself, just somewhere and someone else.

In that case, wasn't there supposed to be some sort of tunnel, with a bright light at the end of it, and people who had loved her and were already dead should be waiting to greet her, right? She'd seen a bright light, and she'd seen something that she thought was an angel, but she'd never seen an angel before so how would she know if that was one? But there was no tunnel, no line of people waiting to greet her, and she began to get agitated.

'Where is everyone?' she asked irritably, the sound curiously flat, as if she hadn't really spoken and hadn't really heard anything. This didn't make sense. If she existed, then she had to exist somewhere, and she didn't seem to be anywhere. There was nothing around her, nothing and no one.

If death turned out to be a lack of being rather than a lack of consciousness, well, then, that sucked.

'Where *am* I?' she snapped, unable to control her annoyance. She'd gone years without showing any temper at all, but here she was dead for just a few minutes and already she was losing control.

'You're here,' a woman's voice said, and abruptly Drea *was* there, in an actual place, though she had no idea where that place was. She stood on a rolling green lawn, with fragrant grass soft beneath her feet. The air was rich with the scents of spring, and at such a perfect temperature that it was neither warm nor chilly, but was almost indecipherable. She could hear the drone of bees, and see a bright kaleidoscope of flowers, huge beds of flowers, dotting the landscape. There were trees, and a blue sky dotted with white clouds, and a sun. There were buildings gleaming whitely in an indefinable distance. She saw all of that, and the absolute harmony of it was so beautiful it

190

almost hurt to look around her. What she didn't see, despite the voice she'd heard, were other people.

'I can't see you,' she said.

'Ah, give it a moment. You came very fast. Give time a second to catch up.' With that, a woman came into view. She was about Drea's age, slim and glowing with health, her dark hair pinned up in a haphazard way that looked completely charming. What was disconcerting was the way she came into view; because while she didn't just appear out of nothing that was almost what happened. It was as if she had lifted aside a curtain and stepped onto a stage with Drea, parts of her becoming visible before the rest of her did.

Other people began appearing, also stepping onto the stage, and with every second that passed Drea saw more and more people, some of them there with her, others walking around and going about their own business. Nine more people joined her and the woman, standing in a loose circle around her. Were they real, or was her dying brain hallucinating? She didn't know if she herself was real anymore. She touched herself, to see if she still had any substance or if all she had left was a sort of cellular memory of what she had been. To her surprise, though her sense of touch felt oddly off, she seemed to retain a physical body.

Another strange thing was the almost physical sense of ... of peace; that was the only word that came to mind. Peace. She began to feel soothed and comforted, and *safe*.

Gradually she noticed something about the

small group of people surrounding her. They all seemed to be her age, roughly thirty, all fit and healthy, all of them attractive even though she could see at least half of them had features that, before she died, she would have said weren't attractive at all. Now they were. It was that simple. Her eye could make the distinction between attractive and unattractive, but her mind couldn't. But her eyes didn't operate independently of her brain, did they? Her brain, then, still had the ability to understand the difference between beauty and ugliness. Was her mind, then, somehow a thing separate from her brain? She had always thought mind and brain were the same thing, but ... they weren't.

Another thing. When she looked at these people, she could sense what they had been before, and that was confusing as all hell because some of them hadn't been the same sex they were now. The woman who had spoken first was the least confusing, because her image was somehow more solid, less blurred by the overlay of a recent carnation, as if it had been a very long time since she had been anything other than exactly what she was now. Drea concentrated on her, because that gave her mind and eyes a rest. She was tired, and dealing with conflicting layers was more than she could handle right now.

'You see them,' the woman said, faint surprise in her tone, and by 'them' she didn't mean just the other people, but all their other layers of existence.

'Yeah,' said Drea. There was a wealth of communication going on here, things understood beyond what was actually said.

192

'So soon. You're very observant.'

She'd had to be, to survive. All of her life she'd watched and studied, judging the best approach to take to get, first, what she needed to live – food. Later, when she was older, she'd studied people more deliberately, to decide how she might manipulate them to get what she wanted.

'Why is she here?' a man asked, not in a nasty tone but in true puzzlement. 'She shouldn't be here. Look at her.'

Drea looked down at herself, though she couldn't honestly tell what she was wearing. Clothes, yes, but the details were so vague she knew only that they were there. Or, was he seeing the stains of her life layered over her the same way she saw their lives? The details of her life reeled through her mind and she saw them as a film of dirt overlying everything she was and did. Anger flared; she'd done the best she could to survive, and if he didn't like it–

Just as abruptly as it had flared, her anger died and was replaced by a wash of shame. She'd never done the *best* she could do. She'd been very skilled at manipulating men to get what she wanted, she'd been a damn good lay, she'd used sex as a weapon, she'd lied, she'd stolen, and though she'd been very good at all of those things, none of her decisions had been based on the *best* of anything, except maybe the best of two bad choices. She had certainly never looked for a *good* choice.

She looked squarely at the man, reading him. He'd been an undertaker, she saw; he'd made a living from death, helping families through the

193

grieving process by walking them through the traditional steps. He'd seen everything; he'd prepared bodies ranging in age from babies to the very old. He'd taken care of people whom hundreds had loved and mourned, and those no one had mourned. Death held no surprises for him, and no fear. Death was part of the natural order of things.

Because he'd seen so much, he'd long ago lost any blinders he might have had. He saw people as they were, not as they wished they had been.

He saw what she was, and he knew she was worthless. *Worthless.* Without worth. She had no excuses, no defense. She bowed her head, accepting that she shouldn't be in this place of peace. She didn't deserve it. Everything she'd ever done, everything she'd touched, was poisoned by her lack of regard for anyone except herself.

'She's here for a reason,' said the woman, though she looked just as puzzled as the man. 'Who brought her here?'

They all looked at one another, searching for answers, but there didn't seem to be any. This was a ... a tribunal of sorts, Drea thought, though not a formal one. Perhaps a better description was 'gatekeeper.' Today was their turn at the gates, to guide people to their correct places.

Except this wasn't her correct place, she thought miserably. She'd never done anything to earn this place. The ignominy of being unwelcome made her ache with embarrassment. This was the good place, and she didn't belong here because she wasn't good. Yet, she hadn't come here on purpose. Maybe it was stupid of her, but

194

she didn't know how she'd gotten here, and she didn't know how to leave.

It stood to reason that, if this was the good place and she didn't belong here, then she belonged at the bad place. Perhaps the great nothing she'd expected was the bad place, the true end with no form of continuing life, but perhaps that was wishful thinking and there was a really bad place, the way the fire and brimstone preachers always said there was. She wasn't religious, never had been. Even as a child she'd thought, *Yeah, right,* because her own life was proof that no compassionate spirit was holding her safe.

And maybe this wasn't heaven the way it was traditionally imagined, maybe the setup wasn't the same, but there was definitely goodness, and peace, so maybe this really was heaven. Or maybe this was the next life, and only those who had proven themselves worthy got to go on. For the others, like her, there was no going on, no continuity of her spirit or soul or mind.

She looked at her life again, weighed it, and found herself wanting.

'If you'll show me how to leave,' she whispered wretchedly, 'I will.'

'I would,' said the woman with some sympathy, 'but someone evidently brought you here and we need to find out–'

'I did,' said a man, striding up to the group and joining the loose circle, with Drea standing in the middle. 'Sorry to be late. Things happened very fast.'

The others turned to look at him. 'Alban,' said the woman. 'Yes, they did.' Drea wondered if

195

Alban was his name, or a greeting. 'There are extenuating circumstances?'

'There are,' he said gravely, but he smiled at Drea with piercing sweetness, and his serious dark eyes searched every detail of her face as if committing it to memory, or reaffirming some old memories.

She stared at him, knowing she'd never seen him before, but there was something so achingly familiar about him that she felt she *should* know him. Like everyone else there, he seemed to be about thirty, as if prime adulthood was the oldest anyone ever got. She looked for those layers that would tell her about him, but like the woman, he was mostly free of the blurring overlay of past lives. He drew her, somehow. She wanted to be close to him, wanted to touch him, yet there was nothing carnal about her longing. Pure love welled in her, poignant in its simplicity, and unconsciously she held out her hand to him.

He smiled and took her hand, and it was then that she knew. Beyond all doubt, beyond reason, she simply *knew*.

Tears welled in her eyes and rolled down her cheeks, but she smiled through them as she clung to her son's hand, lifted it to her lips, brushed a gentle kiss across his knuckles. This was her son, and his name was Alban.

'Ah,' the woman said softly. 'I see.'

Drea didn't know what the woman saw, and in that moment didn't care. After all these years of empty pain, she was holding her son's hand and looking into his eyes and seeing the spirit that had once resided, however briefly, in her baby's tiny form. This form wasn't the one her baby would have had, these features weren't what he would have grown into, but the essential part of the person ... yes, this was her child, who had lived after all, just in another existence.

'She loved me,' Alban said, still smiling that perfect, radiant smile. 'I could feel it, and you see how pure it was. When I was leaving her and coming back home, she tried to save me by offering her life in exchange.'

'That shit never works,' said the undertaker, in the weary, slightly cynical, but sympathetic tone of someone who had seen the same heartbreaking scene played out many times, always with the same result.

'Gregory!' said the woman in a tone that was both amused and an admonishment. To Drea she explained, 'He hasn't been here all that long, this time, so he–'

'Still remembers a lot,' Drea finished for her. She couldn't help smiling, because Alban was smiling and holding her hand, and no matter what happened now everything was okay.

'She meant it,' said Alban, and he duplicated her action of a moment before, taking her hand to his lips and lightly kissing her fingers. 'She was a child herself, just fifteen, but she loved me enough to sacrifice herself to save me. *That* is why I brought her here, because though there has been a lot of darkness in her life, there has also been love of the purest kind, and that deserves a second chance. I stand as witness.'

'I say yea,' said a blond woman, tall and willowy. 'There was love, she wears it still. I stand as witness.'

'And I,' said a man. His layers said that he'd endured a lot, that his previous body had been bent with a painful deformity that had confined him to a wheelchair for most of his life, but here he was tall and strong and straight. 'I stand as witness.'

Of the eleven people surrounding her, three thought there was no point in giving her a second chance, but even those three were free of any sense of malice. They simply thought she didn't belong there. She didn't resent them, because there was no room for resentment here even though there was evidently room for disagreement.

The woman stood there for a moment, her face lifted slightly to the sky, her eyes half closed as if she were listening to some song only she could hear. Then she smiled and turned to Drea. 'Your mother-love, the purest form of love, has saved you,' she said. She touched Drea's hand, the hand that still clung to Alban's hand. 'You've earned a second chance,' she said. 'Now return, and don't waste it.'

The medic was packing up his bag because there was nothing he could do, nothing that could have been done even if he'd been there when the accident happened. Blue and red and yellow lights strobed the highway above, while blindingly bright emergency lights had been rigged to shine down on the car. People were talking, radios were crackling, and the rumble of the wrecker's engine gave a bass underlay to all the other sounds. Still, he heard something strange, something that made him stop and cock his head, listening.

'What?' asked his partner, pausing too, and looking around.

'I thought I heard something.'

'Like what?'

'I don't know. Like ... sort of like this.' He demonstrated, taking a quick, shallow breath of air through his mouth.

'With all this noise, you heard something like that?'

Yeah. Wait, there it was again. Didn't you hear it?'

'Nope, not a thing.'

Frustrated, the medic looked around. He *knew* he'd heard something, twice, but what. It was coming from his left, from the direction of the wrecked car. Maybe a branch had finally snapped under the strain, or something.

They had covered the woman's body with a blanket, draping it over her as best they could, given the fact that she was pinned to the seat with a damn tree through her chest. God, this one was bad. He tried not to let it get to him, but he knew this was one he wouldn't forget. He didn't want to look at the pitiful sight again, but, damn it, there was that sound for a third time and it was coming from that direction, for sure.

He stood, leaning closer to the wreckage, straining to hear. Yes, there it was. He heard it – and he saw the blanket move, as if the fabric was being sucked in a little, then blown out.

He froze, so astonished he literally couldn't move for two long, very long seconds. 'Shit!' he said explosively, when he could move again, when he could speak, and he whipped the blanket back from her face.

'What?' asked his partner again, leaping to his feet in alarm.

It was impossible. It was fucking impossible. Still, he pressed his fingers to the side of her neck, feeling for a pulse. And it was there, though he'd have sworn on his life that there hadn't been one just minutes ago, but now he could feel the beat of life under his fingers, faint and rapid, but there.

'She's alive!' he yelled. 'God! Get a chopper in here! We got a live one!'

18

She swam in and out of consciousness. She preferred 'out,' because then she wasn't aware of the pain. The pain was a bitch. It was the biggest bitch she'd ever tackled, and most of the time it kicked her ass. There were times, when the drugs were either wearing off enough to let her think but still keep the pain somewhat at bay, or when the drugs were taking hold with exactly the same result, when she knew that this was the price she had to pay for that second chance. There was no magic healing, no easy trip back to the land of the living. She had to grin and bear it, though there was no grinning and an awful lot of bearing.

Every decision she'd made in her life, every step she'd taken, had led her straight to that deserted road and the accident. That was the point at which she'd exited, and the point at which she'd been tossed back. No detours allowed, no shortcuts from dead to perfectly healed.

She remembered, with a clarity even the drugs couldn't affect, every moment of what had happened after she died. Real time, though, was more hazy. Sometimes she would hear the nurses talking when they were in her ICU cubicle, the words drifting in and out of her brain and sometimes making sense, but just as often not. When she did understand the words, she felt a detached wonder: a tree stuck in her chest? That was ridiculous. But hadn't she looked down and seen something like that? Her memory of that time before, or between, was fuzzy. Though if she'd had a tree stuck through her, it would certainly explain how she felt physically, and why the agony in her chest seemed to expand to every cell of her body. She had no sense of time, of what day it was, or anything beyond the bed she was on and the unceasing battle she fought with the Great Bitch of Pain.

The nurses talked to her, too, explaining over and over what had happened to her, what they were doing, why they were doing it. She didn't care, so long as they delivered the drugs that kept the Great Bitch at bay. Of course, there came a time – way too soon, by her way of thinking – when her surgeon ordered a decrease in the drugs. He wasn't the one in agony, with his sternum cut in two, so what did he care? He was the one wielding the saw and scalpel, not the one on the receiving end. She had only a vague idea which of her visitors was the surgeon, but as her mind began clearing she memorized some particularly salty things she wanted to say to him. Okay, so he'd had to cut her sternum in half, but cutting her *drugs* in half? Bastard.

If everything she'd seen and experienced was supposed to make her sweet and forbearing now that she had a second chance, she'd already failed that test. She didn't feel at all sweet or forbearing. She felt like someone who'd had her sternum sawed in two and her heart hauled out and used as a soccer ball.

As she gradually left the drug-induced fog, for

202

a while she couldn't think of anything except the Great Bitch and how she could get through the next hour, because without the full power of drugs she and the Bitch were constant companions. By then the nurses were getting her out of bed a couple of times a day, moving her to a chair so she could sit up – yeah, as if the hospital bed wouldn't crank to a sitting position and she wouldn't have to choke back the screams of agony every move brought. All they had to do was press a button and the head of the bed would rise and, hello, she could just lie there and ride it like a wave.

But no, she had to get up. She had to walk, if what she did could be called walking. She called it the hunched-over-in-agony shuffle, accomplished by sliding her feet instead of actually lifting them, and dealing with all the tubes and lines and needles and drains in her body, and trying to keep her ass covered at the same time because all she could wear – sort of wear – was one of those miserable cotton hospital gowns and it wasn't even tied, just kind of draped over her with just one of her arms actually through a sleeve. What modesty she'd had was quickly abused; a hospital wasn't the place for privacy, of any kind.

The nurses talked to her all the time, encouraging her each and every step, whether it was actually making it the two steps to the chair they made her sit in, or managing to take a sip of water by herself, or even the spoonful of applesauce she took on her own when they started letting her have some actual food. They constantly asked questions, trying to get her to talk, trying to get information out of her, but something more had happened to her than a miraculous second chance: she had stopped talking.

When she was conscious, her brain never stopped working – slowly, perhaps, but it still worked. After the surgeon began weaning her off the drugs, she felt as if her head was teeming with thoughts, more thoughts than her skull could hold. At first the lack of connection between her brain and her tongue bothered her, but as her thoughts gradually cleared she realized that the cause of her silence wasn't brain damage, it was a sort of information overload. Until she had things sorted out for herself, this verbal short-circuit was her mind's way of protecting her.

There was so much she needed to think about. They didn't seem to know who she was, because on each shift, a nurse would ask her name. But why wouldn't they know? Where was her purse? Her driver's license was in her wallet. Had her purse been stolen? She didn't think so. She had a memory, she thought it was a memory, of him – the man, the killer – getting her purse, then tossing it into the car. Would he have gotten her driver's license? Why on earth would he want it? But even though she couldn't think of a reason for him to take her license, that had to be why no one knew who she was. Had he inadvertently done her a favor?

She wasn't certain who she was, not any longer. Drea, the creature she'd invented, was dead. She had *been* Drea, but now she wasn't. She wasn't certain who she was now. Names … what did a name mean? To Drea it had meant a lot; the plain

Andie had been left in the dirt, and the fancy Drea had taken her place.

There was nothing wrong with fancy, but there had been a lot wrong with Drea. Lying in the windowless cubicle, unable to tell if it was day or night, time marked only by the shift change of the nurses who took care of her, she looked at herself, her old self, in the harsh light of a new reality.

She had been incredibly stupid. Instead of using men like Rafael, and taking pride in it, they had been using her. They had wanted only her body, and that was what she'd given them, so exactly how had she been using them? They'd been willing to pay her and she'd been willing to be paid, so that had made her exactly what she'd always sworn she wasn't: a whore. Not one of them, and especially not Rafael, had cared one whit if she had a thought in her head or any emotions or interests, likes or dislikes. Not one of them had seen her as a person, because none of them had cared, one way or another. She'd been completely disposable to them; the only value she'd had was a sexual one.

But they had held her cheaply because she'd held herself cheaply. She couldn't remember a time in her life when she'd ever valued herself, when she had ever held herself to a higher standard. Not once as an adult had she ever made a decision based on what was right, what she *should* do; instead, she had gone for whatever paid her the most, benefited her the most. That had been her only criterion. Maybe most people also used that as the basis of their decisions most of the time, but they also went out of their way to help friends, they sacrificed their own material needs to provide for their children, or their aged parents, or they gave to charity or *something*. She'd done none of that. She had looked out for Drea – first, last, and always.

Now the harsh eye she turned on herself was merciless. She saw all of her faults, the basic dishonesty with which she'd lived her life. The only time – the *only* time – she hadn't played a role was when she'd been with *him,* but she'd been too frightened then to hold the act together, and in any case, he'd already seen through her. He was the only man who ever had. Was that why she had such an over-the-top response to him, both emotionally and physically? She couldn't say he'd broken her heart, because obviously she didn't, hadn't, *couldn't* love him – hell, she didn't even know his name! – but at the same time his rejection had hurt her more than anything except losing her baby, so obviously something had been there. But she didn't know what – just something.

Alban. Dorky name; she'd never have named him Alban. But for there, that place, the name fit perfectly. She knew, without knowing how, that it was an old name, dating back centuries. And the woman ... she hadn't introduced herself, but her name was ... Gloria. One by one, mentally reviewing the eleven people who had looked at her and decided whether or not she deserved a second chance, she knew their names as well as if they'd worn signs. Gregory, the undertaker. Gloria had used his name, so that one was obvious. But what about Thaddeus? And Leila?

And all the others whose names sounded so gently in her head when she saw their faces?

In her mind she drifted between that world and this one. She didn't want to leave that world, and she sure didn't want to be in this one, with her constant companion, the Great Bitch. Her second chance wasn't really at this life, it was a second chance to earn *that* life. If she wanted that, then she had to do *this*.

It came down to good decisions and bad decisions, she thought as she drifted. Bad decisions were everywhere. Making one was easy, like picking fruit off the ground. The good decisions were mostly the ones that were difficult, like climbing a tree to get to the fruit at the very top. Yet sometimes the good decision was right there, lying on the ground in front of her, and all she'd have had to do was bend over and pick it up. But instead, she'd looked around and picked a bad decision – sometimes even going out of her way to get it. That was how wrong-headed she'd been.

Making good decisions didn't mean being a saint. That was lucky, because even with her new knowledge she didn't think she could ever reach *that* level. In fact, she was beginning to feel cranky about this whole business. Okay, she'd try. She'd try like hell, which maybe was a bad analogy, but she wanted to go back to that place, she wanted to see Alban again. She wasn't his mother there, she understood that, but for too short a while they had shared the closest of connections, her body giving him life, and she wanted to feel the echo of that love again.

Her thoughts were interrupted time and again

by the hospital staff, who were growing more and more perturbed by her lack of speech. The nurses constantly asked her questions, talked to her, even gave her a notebook and pen to see if she could write. She could, but she didn't. She had no desire to write anything, just as she had no desire to speak. She simply stared at the pen in her hand until they gave up and took it away.

The surgeon, against whom she still held a big grudge, shone a bright light in her eyes and asked questions, none of which she answered. She didn't even punch him while he was that close, though she thought about it.

The surgeon called in a neurologist. They did an EEG on her and discovered her synapses, or whatever, were firing wildly. They did a brain scan, looking for damage that would explain her loss of speech. They discussed her, standing right outside her cubicle, as if the sliding glass door wasn't open and she couldn't hear every word.

'The medics made a mistake,' the neurologist said flatly. 'She couldn't have been dead. If she'd been without oxygen that long, she would, at the least, have significant brain damage. Even allowing for the most extreme variables, and we've both seen cases like that, if she had no heartbeat and no oxygen for an estimated *hour*, for God's sake, there's no way she could come through without any brain damage at all. I don't see anything that would explain her lack of speech. Maybe she couldn't speak before; maybe she's deaf? Have you tried ASL?'

'If she were deaf, she'd be using sign language herself, trying to communicate,' the surgeon said

208

drily. 'She doesn't. She doesn't use another language, she doesn't try to write or draw pictures or even indicate she hears us. If I had to compare it to something, I'd say this complete lack of communication is symptomatic of autism, which I don't think she has because she makes almost constant eye contact, and she does everything the nurses want her to do. She understands what we say. She cooperates. She just doesn't *communicate*. There has to be a reason.'

'Not that I can see.' She heard the neurologist heave a sigh. 'The way she looks at people ... it's almost as if we're another life form and she's studying us. We don't try to communicate with bacteria. It's like that.'

'Right. She thinks we're bacteria.'

'She wouldn't be the first patient to feel that way. Look, my recommendation is you call in a psychologist. What happened to her was traumatic, even by our standards. She may need help getting over it.'

Traumatic? Had it been? What had come before had been traumatic as hell, but her actual death ... no. She couldn't remember being impaled. She knew it had happened, had that hazy memory of seeing herself but all in all she was glad she'd died, because otherwise she wouldn't have seen Alban, she wouldn't have known that wonderful place existed, that there was something else waiting out there. This life wasn't all there was; there was more, much more, and when people spoke of death as 'passing' they were exactly right, because the spirit passed on to that other level of existence. Knowing that was the most comforting thing she could imagine.

So a psychologist, Dr Beth Rhodes, came several times to talk to her. She said to call her Beth. She was a pretty woman, but there was trouble in her marriage and she was truly more concerned with that than she was about any of her patients. Drea/Andie – or was it Andie/Drea? Which one was first, now? – thought Dr. Beth should take some time off and concentrate on what was important, because she loved her husband and he loved her, and they had two kids to consider, so they should really get their shit together and work things out, and then Dr. Beth would be able to give her full attention to her patients.

If she'd been talking, that's what she would have said. But she felt no compulsion to answer Dr Beth's questions, at least not now. She still had some thinking to do.

For instance: no one knew who she was. As far as the world was concerned, Drea Rousseau/Andie Butts was dead. She was safe from Rafael, safe from the assassin. She truly could start anew, as the person she chose to be. That could be a problem, because one of the people who came regularly to her cubicle was a cop, a detective, who wasn't investigating her for any crime or anything except driving a car with a tag that didn't belong to that car, and not having a license, nothing of a hugely felonious nature, but still things that had to be resolved. She was also officially a Jane Doe, and he was as interested as the hospital staff in finding out who she was.

The day came when she was transferred from

ICU to a regular hospital room. As her nurses got her ready for transport, removing tubes, chattering to her, telling her how great she was doing and that they'd miss her, suddenly she focused on one nurse in particular. Her name was Dina, and she was the quietest of the nursing squad, but she was invariably gentle and unhurried, and her concern was evident in her touch.

Dina was going to fall. Andie/Drea saw it happen. Not clearly, the surroundings were fuzzy, but she saw it. Dina was going to fall down some stairs ... drab, concrete stairs, like the stairs in a hotel or in a ... hospital. Yes. Dina was going to fall down the stairs here in the hospital. She would break her ankle, and that would be a bitch because she had a ten-month-old baby who could crawl at the speed of light.

She reached out and caught Dina's hand, the first time she had initiated any interaction with them at all. The nurses looked at her in surprise.

She wet her lips, because after all this time she had almost forgotten how to form the words, the connection tenuous between her mind and her mouth. But she had to warn Dina, so she pushed harder and finally the words actually happened.

'*Don't ... take ... the ... stairs,*' said Andie.

19

'I hear you've been talking.'

The charge came from the foot of the bed. Andie opened her eyes, and hovered for a moment between asleep and awake, reality and ... other reality. Her perception of time, space, and what was real had been radically altered, the defining lines gone. Maybe with time, and once she no longer needed any painkillers at all, she would regain the sharpness of *now*, though she didn't want to lose her sense of connection to the other place.

In the *now* she had to deal with the surgeon, Dr. Meecham, who was sprawling in a chair a couple of feet from the foot of her bed. His arms, big and muscular and hairy, were revealed by the short sleeves of his scrubs – and they were crossed over his chest, telling her he was feeling stubborn and in the mood for answers.

She ignored him for the moment, her gaze drifting to the windows. Sunlight poured through the glazed reflective glass, which made the sky look as though a thunderstorm were forming but gave her both sunlight and privacy. It was nice to have an actual room, to see the progression of sunlight to darkness, nice to have a little more privacy even though the nurses had the extremely annoying habit of leaving the door open. Someday soon she'd tell them to close it.

But not now. Not today. Telling them would require talking, and she couldn't bring the words up. Speaking to Dina had been driven by need, and the effort had exhausted her. Answering the surgeon's questions didn't meet that level of need.

Besides, he'd cut down on her drugs while she still needed help battling the Great Bitch. Let him stew.

'You might be interested in what happened to Dina,' he said.

Was she? She thought for a moment and decided that, yes, she was. She'd cared enough to speak, cared enough to make the words travel from her brain to her mouth, across an empty no-man's-land. Slowly she brought her gaze back to him.

Despite his callousness with the drugs, she liked him. He had a calling, and he was ruthless about answering that call. He went into battle every day, plunging his hands into bloody body cavities and working to help people live, then doing what he had to do to get them back on their feet. So she would have liked a couple of more days of help in fighting the pain; weighed in the balance, she would rather have pain than develop a drug dependency. Maybe she'd forgive him.

On the other hand, he really needed to stop screwing around on his wife.

'Dina took the stairs anyway,' he said, his sharp gaze watching her closely. 'But she said she felt uneasy about what you said, so she was extra careful. She kept an eye out for anyone who might be hiding in the stairwell, and she held on

213

to the stair railing. She usually runs down the stairs, but this time she held on to the railing. She was on the third flight when she slipped. If you hadn't warned her, if she hadn't been holding on, she'd have gone to the bottom of the flight and could have been really hurt. As it is, all she has is a mild ankle sprain.'

That had worked out, then. Good.

He was silent a minute, she guessed to give her a chance to talk if she were so inclined. She wasn't.

Giving up on that tactic, he uncrossed his arms and leaned forward, watching her intently. He opened his mouth to speak, closed it again, and rubbed his hand over his jaw. Andie watched him with faint puzzlement. He acted as if he was perturbed by something; surely he wasn't that upset because she hadn't made this huge breakthrough in speech.

'What was it like?' he finally asked, his tone suddenly hushed, a little unsure.

Her own mouth almost fell open. She blinked at him in astonishment and a tide of red washed into his face. 'Never mind,' he muttered, getting to his feet.

Was he asking about the other place? Surely he wasn't crass enough to ask what it was like to have a tree puncture her heart. Besides, he was a surgeon; traumatic injuries would be nothing new to him.

He *knew* she'd been dead, that the medics hadn't made a mistake. Yet here she was, a living, breathing, walking – well, sometimes, when they made her – miracle, and what she'd said to Dina had somehow tipped him off that she'd been to

214

that other place. Maybe he'd seen it before. Maybe another patient had told him about it, and he was curious. Maybe he wanted her to say that she didn't remember anything, so he could put his trust completely in science, where he felt most comfortable.

She lifted her hand to keep him from walking out the door, and a beatific smile lit her face. 'Beautiful,' she managed to say, the single word taking so much effort that she felt winded.

He stopped in his tracks. Swallowing, he came to stand beside her bed.

'What do you remember? Can you tell me?'

He looked torn, as if he wanted to hear something that would allow him to disregard what she said as an oxygen-deprived brain producing hallucinations, but at the same time he wanted to believe in something more.

She needed to talk. She needed to get through this barrier, once more make the connection between the world inside her head and the world on the outside. The breach had been helpful, giving her the time she needed to adjust, but now it was time for her to fully rejoin this world, because it was the only world she had.

With that thought, her surroundings suddenly popped into sharper focus, as if everything had been blurred while she lingered between both places. She had made the final decision to stay, she realized. Until now, she had been in a limbo of sorts, lingering there while she thought things over, but now she had decided: she would stay here, and try to earn herself a place in that other world.

Talking suddenly became easier, a Mission Possible, even though it was still an effort.

'I remember everything.'

Relief washed over his face. 'Was there a tunnel? With light at the end of it?'

Describing the other place wasn't going to be easy, because words literally couldn't impart the utter tranquillity and joy, the quiet beauty. But right now he wasn't asking where she'd gone, just the process of getting there.

'Light. No tunnel.' Had she missed out on something, or had she gone too fast?

'Just light? Hmm.'

There it was, the doubt, the instinctive fallback on the science he knew. Bright light could be explained by a misfiring, dying brain. She wondered how he could square that with her lack of brain damage. Because she didn't want to steer him wrong, and because she held a grudge against him, she voiced the random thought that had earlier popped into her head. 'Stop screwing around on your wife.'

He paled, then turned red again. 'What?'

'She's going to find out, if you don't stop.' Suddenly irritated, she pulled the sheet higher, as if she wanted to shut him out. 'If you don't love her, then get a divorce, but keep your pants zipped until then. Act like a grown-up.'

'Wha–? What?' He said the same word for the third time, his mouth opening and closing like a guppy's.

'Believe me now?' She scowled at him. She would have flounced on her side and turned her back on him, but flouncing was out of the

216

question. Instead she just narrowed her eyes at him and silently dared him to deny her accusation, though he was more likely to tell her to mind her own business.

She could see him struggling not to do exactly that. He was in his early fifties, a man who had spent his entire adult life perfecting the science and the skill with which he saved lives. Like most surgeons, he had a healthy ego, which was a polite way of saying it was monstrously huge. Doing what he did required a huge helping of self-confidence, and he was accustomed to being the boss. Finding himself abruptly called on the carpet by a woman whose life he had saved, and who undoubtedly owed him a large amount of money for his services, wouldn't go down easy.

He started to snap back at her. She saw it, and scowled harder at him. 'Don't start doubting just because I didn't see a tunnel. I guess some people do. I didn't. I had a tree stuck through me – a small one, but still a tree – and I went fast. So sue me.'

He crossed his arms again and rocked back on his heels, a man who wasn't inclined to surrender without a fight. 'If you had a real near-death experience, you're supposed to be mellow and happy.'

'I didn't have a "near death" experience, I had a *death* experience. I died,' she said flatly. 'I was given a second chance. So far as I know, having that second chance doesn't mean I have to fake being in a good mood. If you want to know what I remember, how about this: I remember looking down and seeing a guy go through my purse, then steal my laptop. Did he get all my money?'

He was so easy to read, even now, when he was trying to school his expression. His shock was evident, at least to her.

'No, I believe there was a considerable amount of cash still in your purse, but no ID, and no credit cards.'

She hadn't had any credit cards, but she didn't tell him that. So only her ID was missing? Strange. Why take her driver's license and not her cash?

'You didn't have any vehicle registration in your car either. I believe Detective Arrons wants to discuss that with you.'

She imagined he did, plus the bogus license plate. She'd worry about that later. For now, she waved it away. 'If the money was still there, it can go to my hospital bill. I'm not a charity case.'

'I'm not worried about–'

'Maybe you aren't, but the hospital is.'

'While you're in such a chatty mood, what's your name?'

'Andie,' she said promptly. 'What's yours?'

'Travis. Last name?'

She had always thought fast on her feet, but all of a sudden she was drawing a blank. Nothing, absolutely nothing, came to mind. She simply couldn't come up with a fake last name. She stared at him, frowning. 'I'm thinking,' she finally said.

His brows knit a little. 'You don't remember?'

'Of course I remember. It's there. Give me a minute.' If Rafael thought she was dead, there was no reason for him ever to check to see if anyone with her name popped up anywhere. To be on the safe side, though, she should use a different name. Would that be completely screwing up her second chance, lying to protect herself? Maybe lying was bad when it hurt someone else, but not so bad otherwise.

She should have asked for training, or at least a set of guidelines.

'Andie,' she said again, hoping for inspiration.

'You've already said that. Is it short for Andrea?'

'Yes.' What else could she say? She couldn't think of any other female name that started with A-n-d. She wasn't about to tell him her last name was Butts, no matter what. Finally she gave up, shrugging. 'Maybe tomorrow.'

He had his pen out, making a note on her medical records.

Immediately her attention zoomed in another direction. 'I'm not brain-damaged,' she charged irritably. 'It's all your fault. I'm just drugged enough that I can't think, but not drugged enough that it stops me from hurting. Have you ever stopped to think how it feels, having your chest sawed open and pulled apart and your heart manhandled? Huh? I have *staples* in me. I feel like a legal file or something, I have so many staples in me. You could build a house with my staples. And what do you do? You *cut down on my painkillers*. You should be ashamed of yourself.'

She stopped, confused by her own lack of control. She never went off on anyone like that. She smiled, and acted sweet. Why was she turning into a bitch? But she also stopped because he was laughing. *Laughing.*

She could be friends with this man. 'Sit down,'

she invited, 'and I'll tell you about the other place.'

Simon had made a lifelong habit of resisting temptation, but this one wore him down. The idea was always there, nagging at him, and he couldn't let it go.

He couldn't forget Drea's death. He couldn't forget her face, or the way her expression had suddenly lit with joy just as she died. He couldn't forget *her*. Her death had left an ache in him that he couldn't explain, or get rid of.

He'd shown Salinas the picture he'd taken with his cell phone, showed him Drea's driver's license. Salinas had blanched when he saw the picture, then sat silently for a moment. Finally he said, 'Tell me where to wire your fee.'

'Forget about it,' Simon had said. 'I didn't do the job; she had a wreck.' He'd tracked her, though, and driving too fast trying to escape him was why she'd had the wreck. Had it been anyone else, he'd have taken his fee without hesitation. While he hadn't killed her, he had definitely caused her death; still, for the first time he couldn't take a fee for someone's death.

This was different.

He didn't want it to be different. He didn't want to feel as though a huge hollow had opened up in his life, as though he'd lost something so important he couldn't even begin to imagine the depth of that loss. He wanted to forget the utter bliss with which she'd met her death.

But he couldn't, and in the weeks since, he'd been driven by a gnawing compulsion to find her grave. There had been more than enough cash in

220

her purse to pay for a decent burial. Would the state try to identify her first, keep her in a morgue while a slow-motion search for family was made? Or would she be photographed, DNA samples taken, then promptly buried?

If it was the first, maybe he could claim her body. He'd buy the most beautiful, serene cemetery plot he could find, and put her there. A granite headstone would mark the beginning and end of her life. He could put flowers there, and visit her occasionally.

And if she'd already been buried, he could make certain a stone was put there, and he could still take flowers to her. He just needed to know where she was.

Finding her should be easy, he thought. He knew where the accident had happened, so all he had to do was check the newspapers for the area. A traffic fatality, an unidentified woman – five minutes, tops, and he'd know.

He gave in to temptation, and sat down at his computer. Finding her didn't take five minutes. It took two minutes and seven seconds.

He read everything twice, shaking his head in disbelief. It wasn't possible. The newspaper had got it wrong; happened all the time. He checked the next day's edition for an update, a correction. Instead, it said the same thing. Her name wasn't known, she was a Jane Doe, but–

God. He felt as if he'd grabbed a live wire and had the hell knocked out of him. The shock was so great that he realized, with an odd kind of remoteness, that he was breathing hard and fast, and his vision had narrowed until he saw nothing but the lit computer screen. It wasn't possible. He'd watched her die, watched her eyes dull and her pupils fix. He'd felt for the pulse in her neck, and there hadn't been one.

But something had happened. Somehow the medics must have revived her, kept her going long enough to get her to a hospital. He didn't know how, it had to be a fucking miracle, but right now the *how* didn't matter.

Drea was *alive*.

20

Simon flew into Denver that night. He carried only one small bag, so he could leave directly from the arrival gate instead of dealing with the hassle of luggage claim. He had no weapons on him, and no need to procure any. He just wanted to see Drea for himself, to make sure it was really her, and to find out what had happened.

There must be some mistake. The woman in the hospital probably wasn't Drea. It would be a hell of a coincidence if there were two Jane Does, one alive and one dead, and the live one would be more newsworthy than the dead one. Drea's accident had happened a good distance away, in a far less populated area; the report of an un-identified accident victim might not have made it into any newspaper at all.

Or, worst case, the medics had somehow revived Drea, but she was either brain dead or had very limited function, maybe just enough activity in her brain stem to keep her lungs working and her heart beating, though how her heart could beat after what had happened, he didn't know. He couldn't imagine any surgeon doing the kind of extensive repair job that would be needed, if one were even possible, on someone who was either brain dead or in a severe vegetative state.

That was why he thought the woman couldn't be Drea. He didn't want it to be Drea, not with the brain damage she would have suffered.

But if it was, if the woman really was Drea and some damn fool had kept her body alive even though her brain was gone, he'd take care of her. He'd find the best place in the country for her, someplace where her body would be tenderly cared for. He might visit her occasionally, though seeing her like that would be even tougher than watching her die. He had no legal right to make any decisions concerning her care, but fuck that. He had the money to make it happen, and if anyone stood in his way he'd simply take her. He made a living being where he wasn't supposed to be, and doing things he wasn't supposed to do.

He checked into a hotel for the night. There would be more people coming and going at the hospital during the day, making it easier for him to blend in. Days were busy, with outpatient tests, visitors in and out all day, flowers and newspapers being delivered, food and medical supplies coming in; he would be one more face in the crowd. In his experience, people working the night shift lived in a smaller world and tended to notice strangers more.

First, he'd have to find out if the Jane Doe was still in the hospital. Over two weeks had passed; if the woman in question wasn't Drea, she might already have been released – or she might have simply walked out because people without ID usually had something to hide. If she was no longer there, then obviously she wasn't Drea, and he could go home. If her injuries had been severe and she was still there, then he'd have to see her to make certain she was or was not Drea. Back before hospitals got so pissy about privacy he could have placed a call and learned all he needed to know, but now information was given out only to immediate family. Still, that didn't mean he couldn't find out things, just that it would be a little harder.

He was at the hospital before six o'clock the next morning, waiting for the shift to change. Could be some of the hospital staff worked twelve-hour shifts, which might be from six to six, or seven to seven, and he didn't know who his target would be. He'd have to work fast; he might have hours, depending on how alert the target was – though, coming off a long night shift, probably not all that alert – or he might have no more than thirty minutes. But shift change was the time to move in, when distraction was high.

He went in through the emergency room entrance, which was always busy, then located the elevators and the directory. ICU was on the seventh floor. A harried-looking woman, her face lined with exhaustion and worry, hurried in just as the elevator doors were closing. She had probably been to the cafeteria, because she carried a large cup of coffee. She punched the button for the fourth floor. After she exited, he rode the rest of the way alone.

The glassed-in ICU waiting room was full of bleary-eyed people camped out in the cramped room, some almost literally, bringing sleeping bags, snacks, books, and anything else to make the long dreary hours more comfortable. A coffeemaker was set up on a table, making popping noises as it spewed out a fresh brew. Several tall stacks of polystyrene cups stood sentinel next to the pot.

The heavy doors to the ICU, operated by a pressure plate, the wall, were directly across from the waiting room. The glass walls allowed him to watch the doors from inside the waiting room, and while he waited for a shift change he might be able to glean some information from the relatives who had stood watch through the night, desperately hoping their loved ones would live or stoically waiting for the end. Sharing an ICU waiting room was almost like sharing a foxhole; everyone was in a crisis situation and information flowed like water.

He found an empty chair where he could watch the ICU, then leaned forward and propped his elbows on his knees, his head hanging down. His body language suggested despair, an emotion with which everyone in that room was on intimate terms. He kept his head just high enough that he could still see the ICU doors.

He didn't make eye contact, didn't look around; he just sat there, the very picture of misery. Within a minute, the gray-haired woman on his left asked in a sympathetic tone, 'Do you have a family member here?'

She meant in the unit, of course. 'My mother,' he said in a strained voice. An ICU always had plenty of elderly people in it, so that was a safe choice, plus appearing as a devoted son always put people at ease. 'Stroke.' He swallowed hard. 'A severe one. They think ... they think she might be brain dead.'

'Oh, that's tough. I'm so sorry,' she said. 'But don't give up hope yet. My husband works construction. A month ago he fell from four stories up, broke almost every bone in his body. I thought I'd lost him.' Her voice trembled with remembered despair. 'I'd been trying to talk him into retirement and he'd finally promised me next year, then this happened and I just knew he'd never get to enjoy all the hunting and fishing trips he'd planned with our son. No one thought he'd make it, but he's still holding on, and now they think that maybe next week he can be moved into a regular room.'

'That's good,' he murmured, looking down at his hands. 'I'm glad. But my mother–' He broke off, shaking his head. 'I found her too late.' He threw in a bit of guilt, to make the pot bubble. 'They're running tests now, but if she's brain dead...'

'Even the best doctor doesn't know everything there is to know about the human body,' broke in a burly, red-faced guy seated on the other side of the gray-haired woman. 'A couple of weeks ago they brought in a woman who'd been in a car wreck, ran off the road and hit a tree. Tree branch went right through her chest.'

There it was, exactly what he needed to know, and he didn't even have to get into the ICU itself. Simon controlled his expression as his attention was caught with a painful jerk. That was Drea. Beyond a doubt, that was her. The relief came as a roller-coaster ride in his stomach, but then abruptly it knotted with dread. She might have survived the wreck, but in what kind of shape? Would she ever be able to function? Walk, talk, recognize anyone? He tried to speak and couldn't, his throat so tight he could barely breathe.

The gray-haired woman patted his arm in sympathy, evidently thinking he was on the verge of tears. The simple, compassionate gesture start-led him. People didn't touch him so casually, so easily. There had always been something about him that made people keep their distance, something cold and lethal to which this woman was evidently impervious. Drea had touched him, though; she'd put her hand on his chest, she had clung to him and kissed him, her mouth as tender and hungry as if she couldn't resist the urge. The memory made him swallow convul-sively, and that loosened his throat enough that he managed to talk. 'I think I read something about that,' he lied, choking the words out.

'The medics said she was dead at the scene. They were packing everything up when one of them heard her gasping. They swore she hadn't had a pulse, but all of a sudden she did. They had to cut the branch off so they could bring her in, because they figured if they pulled it out they'd do even more damage, plus the branch must somehow have been pressing against her aorta, kept her from bleeding to death.' The burly guy crossed his arms over his massive chest. 'They thought for sure she'd be brain dead, but she wasn't. Took over eighteen hours of surgery to patch her up, then ... was it three days ago when they moved her?'

'Two. Day before yesterday,' said the gray-haired woman, picking up the story.

'They moved her into a regular room. I heard

she's doing fine, but I also heard she can't talk, so maybe there was some brain damage.'

'She's started talking,' someone else said. 'She said something to one of the nurses. They were all talking about it.'

'That's amazing,' Simon said, his stomach doing the loop-the-loop again, this time joined by his heart. With distant amazement, he realized he might pass out – or vomit. Or both. She was *doing fine*. She was *talking*.

'It's a miracle, for sure,' said the burly guy. 'She was a Jane Doe. She didn't have any kind of ID, and nobody seemed to be looking for her. They couldn't get her to write her name or anything. Now that she's talking, though, I guess they know her real name.'

No, they wouldn't, Simon realized. Drea was too sharp for that. She'd give them a fake name, which presented him with a problem: how was he to find her? Even if he gained access to a computer, which he had no doubt he could manage, he had no idea what name she'd told them. Swiftly he abandoned that idea; he'd have to tackle this from a different direction.

'Who was her doctor?' He had no reason to ask a question like that, but people talked about any number of subjects in a hospital waiting room. They talked to pass the time, they talked to distract themselves, they formed relationships that might not last beyond their loved one's stay in the ICU, but while they were enclosed in this glass cell they laughed and cried together, comforted one another, passed along family recipes and birthdays – anything to get by.

'Meecham,' was the prompt answer. 'Heart surgeon.'

The surgeon would make his rounds every day, visit all his patients. When someone had a traumatic injury like Drea had suffered, the surgeon's ego got all tied up in how well that patient was doing, especially when the patient had defied all odds and survived. Finding Dr. Meecham wouldn't be difficult; following him around wouldn't be, either.

He thought about hospitals, about how they were organized. Patients weren't assigned willy-nilly to an empty bed; different floors were for different situations, which streamlined different types of care by concentrating it. There was the maternity floor, the orthopedic floor – and the post-op surgical floor, which was where Drea would most likely be.

Doors to the patients' rooms were left open a lot, whether it was from carelessness, haste, or for the nurses' convenience. The odds were at least fifty-fifty he could walk down the hall on the surgical floor, glance in all the rooms that had open doors, and find her. If not, then he'd trail Dr. Meecham. One way or another, though, he *would* find her. There had never been anything more important to him than that.

He had never cared about anything before, much less so intensely that he couldn't let it go and walk away. He didn't like it, but he still couldn't let it go. Drea represented a weakness that could be used against him, by Salinas or anyone else who figured out that he had this one chink in his armor.

230

Across the hall, the double doors to the ICU swung open and a small knot of nurses, both male and female, came out of the unit. He didn't need access to the unit now, so he didn't follow them. If it turned out he needed to lift an ID tag so he could go into controlled areas, he'd get one, but first he'd see if he could locate Drea the easy way.

She was here, she was alive, and she was talking.

Abruptly he couldn't sit there another minute, another second, couldn't hold his act together and pretend he was concerned about his nonexistent mother when all he wanted to do was get somewhere he could be alone until he had himself back under control.

'I'm sorry,' he said, breaking into the conversation that had been flowing around and over him, then getting up and striding out of the waiting room. He looked around, spotted a restroom, and all but bolted for it. It was, thank God, a one-seater; he locked the door, then stood trembling in the middle of the tiny room.

What in hell was going on? He'd spent his entire adult life, and some years before that, perfecting his control. He tested himself, learned his own limits, and then pushed those limits. He didn't fall apart, had never fallen apart. Everything he did and everything he said was deliberate, chosen to produce the response or result he wanted.

He could handle this. Finding out she was alive and at least functional was good news – still a shock, but nothing to send him over the edge. If he could find a way to talk to her without scaring

231

her to death, he'd tell her she had nothing to fear from him, that as far as Salinas was concerned she was dead and to go on with her life. Not now, though; physically she would still be too weak, and he didn't want to do anything to put a strain on her heart. God only knew what kind of damage she'd sustained.

Besides, there was always the possibility that she truly didn't remember who she was, in which case she wouldn't remember him, either. Just because she was talking didn't mean she was mentally unscathed. He had to get a grip, and find out exactly how she was instead of letting his imagination run away with him.

Shit. *Imagination.* When the fuck had he started having an imagination? He dealt in facts, in hard reality, in what *was.* Reality was solid. He could depend on reality, depend on it being a cold, hard bitch. That was okay with him, because he was a cold, hard bastard. They were a good pair.

He took several deep breaths and shook off whatever the hell it was that had him so on edge. All he had to do was find Drea, and discover for himself exactly what her condition was; then he could get back to New York. There were things he needed to do, he'd been in the same location long enough, and it was time he moved on. He'd check on Drea, and if she was all right he'd walk away for good.

21

Surgical post-op was one floor down, so Simon took the stairs instead of dealing with the elevator. He preferred the stairs anyway; they gave him two directions of escape, while an elevator not only trapped him in a small box, it followed its electronic commands in the order in which it received them. If it was going 'down' and had already received a call from a lower floor, he couldn't punch the button for a higher floor and make the elevator go 'up' instead.

The hospital's general shape was a giant T, but it was lying down instead of standing up. He came out at the end of the long hallway and systematically walked the floor. Each room had a small plaque outside the door with the patient's last name as well as the doctor's name, which was damn convenient for his purposes.

The nurses' station was situated at the intersection of the T, but the nurses couldn't see down the hallways unless they stepped out from behind the divider. At the moment, with the shift change just ending and the morning meals being delivered, the hallways were a beehive of activity and he blended into the general hub-bub. He kept an easy pace, looking into all the rooms with open doors but taking care to move only his eyes and keep his head steady, so to the casual observer he wouldn't be paying any attention to the patients.

At least half the doors were closed, but with one reconnaissance he was able to eliminate all of those patients whose doors were open, because none of them were Drea. As he walked he noted the rooms that had Dr. Meecham listed as the doctor, marking their location in the three-dimensional map of his surroundings that he carried at all times in his head.

Then he saw the name 'Doe,' and he almost stumbled.

Room 614. Meecham was the doctor listed.

The door was closed, but he knew he'd found her. She was there, just on the other side of that door. He knew it was Drea. There were people with the actual last name of 'Doe,' but what were the odds one of them would be on this floor, at this time, with Meecham as the doctor?

His hand closed around the door handle almost before he realized he was reaching for it.

Slowly, carefully, he forced himself to release the handle. If he walked in there she'd scream the place down – assuming she recognized him. He still didn't know her mental state.

The name 'Doe' didn't tell him anything. If she'd come through without brain damage, she would take full advantage of the circumstances and not tell them her real name. If she did have brain damage, which was likely, then she might not know her name.

Belatedly he noticed the sign on the door: *No Visitors*.

There were two layers of meaning to the sign. The first was obvious: no visitors. The second was 'why not?' Who had put it there? The hospi-

234

tal, because curiosity-seekers and/or the press had been annoying/agitating/gawking at the patient, or had the patient herself requested the sign be posted? Drea certainly wouldn't want any press, and she would want to keep any cops at bay, too, until she had cooked up a suitable story and felt able to handle them.

But he now had the name she was registered under, and he knew her room number. He'd be able to find out everything he wanted to know. He didn't have to actually see her, didn't have to talk to her; he could safely ignore the weird compulsion he felt to do exactly that.

Looking down the hall, he saw that the big cart laden with food trays was just three rooms down. The door to the room next to Drea's was closed, too, so he moved farther down and leaned against the wall right outside the door, as if a nurse or tech had gone into the room to perform some duty and asked him to wait outside. He kept his gaze on the floor.

The cafeteria lady worked quickly, delivering the food trays to the proper rooms. She pushed the cart toward him, stopping it just past the door to Drea's room. He glanced up, ready to give a quick, polite smile if she looked at him, but she ignored him as if he were so much furniture. People who worked in hospitals saw a lot of people leaning against walls.

She pulled out a tray, which looked as if it held only orange gelatin, fruit juice, coffee, and milk, but any food at all meant Drea was capable of feeding herself; rather than being fed by a tube. The cafeteria worker knocked quickly on the door, then opened it without waiting for an answer.

'Is that real food?' he heard Drea ask, her tone grumpy.

The cafeteria lady laughed. 'You've graduated to Jell-O. If your stomach handles that without any upset, maybe tomorrow you can have mashed potatoes. We just bring what your doctor says you can have.'

After a brief silence, Drea said, 'Orange! I like orange Jell-O.'

'Would you like to have two?'

'Can you do that?'

'Sure. Any time you want more, just let us know.'

'In that case, yes, I definitely want another Jell-O. I'm starving.'

While Drea was talking to the cafeteria lady and concentrating on her food, Simon straightened away from the wall and walked quickly past her door, not turning his head to look at her.

For a moment he was walking blindly, and did not see the young woman who stepped out of a room until he bumped into her. 'Sorry' he said automatically, without looking at her, and plowed ahead.

The next thing he knew, he was crushed into the back corner of a crowded elevator and had no memory of getting on it. He, who always knew not only exactly what he was doing but what everyone around him was doing, who even studied a public restroom from a strategic standpoint before entering it, had let himself get so wrapped up in his thoughts he hadn't paid any attention to what he was doing or where he was going.

He exited on the ground floor, but the elevator

he'd taken wasn't in the same bank as the one he'd used going up. Instead of coming out close to the emergency room entrance, he was in the main lobby, which boasted a soaring, two-story atrium in which live ficus trees grew.

Numb, his brain sluggish, he walked to the exit until he remembered his rental car was in the parking lot outside the emergency room. He stopped, looked around, but didn't see any signs pointing the way to the ER.

His usually infallible sense of direction told him to take the left corridor, so he did. He wanted to laugh, and he never laughed. Relief fizzled in his blood like champagne, making him giddy. His heart pounded in his chest, the cage of his ribs feeling too tight, as if it were closing in around his heart and lungs, restricting them.

A discreet sign caught his eye and he paused. On an unexplainable impulse he opened the door and stepped in.

As soon as he closed the door behind him he felt the silence, as if the room was soundproof. The unceasing noise and motion of a hospital halted at that doorway, as if he had entered another realm. He stood there a moment, wanting to go but feeling compelled to stay. He wasn't a coward. No matter how ugly reality was, and it was often a real bastard, he'd always dealt with it and in it. Mercy wasn't one of his qualities, with himself or with others. Some people misled themselves about their true nature, but Simon never had. He was what he was because no life, his own or anyone else's, had ever meant anything special to him.

Until now

Until Drea.

The room was dim, there were sconces on the side walls, and on the front wall a panel of stained glass was backlit, bathing the small room in colour. The air was cool and fragrant, the scent coming from a bouquet of fresh flowers sitting on a table in front of the small altar. There were three padded pews, each large enough to hold maybe four people, but he was the only person in there.

He sat down in the middle pew and closed his eyes, letting the silence wash over him and calm him. There was no music. If hymnal music had been piped in, he probably would have left, but there was only the peace and the silence.

Drea was alive. He couldn't yet take in what that meant, hadn't yet been able to accept that the ground beneath his feet had caved in and he was clawing at air. Just for a moment he let himself relax, the softly glowing light of the stained glass painting colors on the inside of his eyelids. The scent of the flowers enticed him to take deeper breaths, drawing the cool air deep into his lungs, easing the constriction in his chest.

Ruthlessness was as much a part of him as his skin. His own character made it impossible for him to shrug off what he'd seen, what he knew. Drea had died. He'd heard her last breath, seen the light leave her eyes. He had felt the difference in her flesh when he touched her, because dead bodies immediately begin cooling. Her soft skin had lost its heat, its vibrancy. On an even deeper level he'd felt her absence, the absence of the person, the spirit, the soul, whatever you wanted to call it. Without that animating spark, the body is different, and no longer that person.

He'd stayed there with her too long to think he'd somehow been mistaken about her death. She hadn't had a pulse, and she hadn't been breathing. By the time the emergency vehicles got there, at least half an hour, maybe longer, had passed. She should have been long past resuscitation; the brain began dying after just four minutes. She would have been completely brain dead, beyond even the most heroic efforts to revive her. The guy in the waiting room had said the medics had been packing up their stuff when she began gasping on her own. Had they even tried to revive her? Add that to the length of time she'd been dead.

Yet she was sitting in a hospital bed, obviously alive, talking normally, rejoicing in the fact that she'd been given orange Jell-O to eat.

That she was alive at all, in any condition, was a miracle. That she had come through the ordeal with no apparent brain damage was a second, even larger, miracle. He didn't believe in miracles. If he'd had any philosophy in life it ran along the lines of the classic 'shit happens.' Usually it was bad shit, sometimes it was good shit, but it was always random shit. You lived your life, and when the run was ended, that was it. Nothing.

But this ... this was something he couldn't explain. This had him by the throat and balls and wouldn't let go, and he had to face it.

Something had brought her back to life.

He opened his eyes and stared at the stained glass, looking but not seeing.

Could there be something between birth and death, something more than an organism reaching the end of its viability? Could there be something with enough power to give life back to a cooling body? If so, that meant ... that meant there was something after death, that death here wasn't the end.

If there was life after death, then there had to be another place, another when and where. If death truly was passing onto that other place, then it followed that how lives were lived really did matter.

Good, bad – the concepts had never meant much to him. He was who he was, and he did what he did. The average person on the street was perfectly safe from him. He meant them no harm, felt no contempt for them; he might even have sometimes felt distantly fond of citizenry in general, because they carried on with their lives no matter what. They worked, they went home, they ate dinner and watched some television, went to sleep, got up and went to work again. Armies of them went through that routine, and the routine was what made the world work.

Those who preyed on these ordinary people were the ones he held in contempt. They thought it was okay to take what these people had worked for, that only fools and idiots worked for a living. For his part, he thought it was okay to kill the scum.

And yet, if he looked at it logically, his life was much worse than theirs – not in a material way, but in the wasteland that was his soul.

The black chasm beneath his dangling feet was what awaited him, what he'd earned, and yet he

240

had this chance to change the course of his life here. Because of Drea, he saw things he'd never seen before, accepted that there was more. Was there truly a God? Was that what this was?

Because of Drea, he saw that Death walked with its arm around him. If he went on as he was, he knew what would be waiting for him. But if he could judge himself, walk away from that life, would the outcome change?

It sounded simple enough, but the concept was a complete sea change.

A huge, choking pain filled him, and his throat closed on a sound like that of a wounded animal, helpless and suffering.

A door off to the side of the small room opened. Simon hadn't realized it was there, a lapse on his part that was unbelievable, and unforgivable, because such a lack of awareness could be deadly.

'I don't want to intrude,' a man's quiet voice said, 'but I heard—'

He'd heard the muted howl of agony. Simon still didn't turn.

'If you'd like to talk...' the man began again, when Simon didn't respond.

Slowly Simon stood, feeling as weary as if he'd been awake for days on end, as battered as if he'd fallen off a cliff. He turned and looked at the small, middle-aged man who wore a regular suit, no vestments or white collar at his throat. Physically the man was unprepossessing, slight and balding, but there was an energy to him that kept him from being insignificant.

'I'm giving thanks for a miracle,' he said simply, and wiped the tears from his face.

22

Seven months later

'Andie, order up!'

Andrea Pearson gave a quick glance over her shoulder at the pass-through to the kitchen, where Glenn was loading the shoulder-high bar with plates piled high with hamburgers and steaming hot french fries, then resumed unloading heavy plates off the tray she carried. Glenn, owner and cook at Glenn's Truck Stop, was shoveling food onto plates as fast as he could. It was Friday night, truckers were headed home, and the place was packed. The work was grueling, but the tips were great and Glenn paid her under the table, which was even better.

'I'll be right back with refills,' she said to the three truckers in the booth, then hurried over to get the newly plated orders while the food was still hot. After dispensing them to the proper table, she loaded her tray with the coffeepot and tea pitcher and made the rounds, refilling cups and glasses. All the other waitresses were hustling as fast as she was, swivel-hipping their loaded trays through the tangle of chairs and tables.

'Hey, Andie,' a female driver said as she passed by, 'tell my fortune for me.'

Her name was Cassie, her hair was blond with dark roots, and she wore a lot of makeup, along

242

with tight jeans and high heels. She was very popular with a certain segment of the male drivers; the more settled ones left her alone. Tonight, though, she was with some other female drivers, and they were ignoring the guys for some girl time.

'You don't have one,' said Andie, not even slowing down.

The next time she went by, Cassie signaled for her check. The group was laughing and joking, trading stories about their men or their kids or their pets, though Andie was hard put to tell which story was about which group. When she took the check over, Cassie said, 'Whaddaya mean, I don't have a fortune? You mean I'm not going to marry some good-looking rich guy and have a life of leisure?'

The other women hooted, because in their world things like that just didn't happen.

'Nope,' said Andie in a matter-of-fact tone. 'You won't ever be rich. But if you don't start making better decisions, you're going to end up broke and eating cat food to make ends meet.'

Silence fell on the little group, because Andie's tone wasn't joking.

'Better decisions?' Cassie asked after a slight hesitation. 'Like what?'

'Andie! Order up!'

'Gotta go,' she said, hurrying to the bar. Her left arm was aching from toting the heavy trays for the past five hours, and she had three more hours to go. She hadn't had time to grab anything to eat, either, so she wasn't inclined to waste any of her precious minutes trying to give Cassie life lessons.

Hell, how much brains did it take not to screw every guy who came down the highway – in Cassie's case, almost literally? Besides, it irritated her that Cassie had asked her to 'tell her fortune.'

Andie didn't tell fortunes. She didn't have a crystal ball, she couldn't tell where crazy Uncle Harry had buried his coin collection or which horse was going to win at what track. If she could, she'd be playing the ponies herself. Sometimes she got impressions about people, that was all. She might warn somebody to slow down on his run, or tell him to have his cholesterol checked, stuff like that. Working as a waitress meant she saw people doing stupid things that were bound to get them into trouble, and if she warned them and they didn't listen, why was it so surprising to them when, lo and behold, they got into trouble? Cause and effect: do something stupid, and bad things will happen. Big duh.

But in the few months she'd been working at Glenn's, she'd gotten sort of a reputation as a psychic, and nothing she said could dissuade anyone from that idea. The only way she could disprove it, she supposed, was to not tell anyone whatever it was she thought they should know, but she couldn't in good conscience let a driver sit there wolfing down fried food when she was fairly certain he was going to have a heart attack in a couple of weeks.

She'd done some research on the afterlife and near-death experiences, and several times she had come across references that a person who had died and been revived sometimes came back with the gifts of prophecy and vision. The only thing close to a vision that she'd had was when she saw that nurse, Dina, falling on the stairs – and she'd been on painkillers at the time, so that could have had something to do with seeing things. As for prophecy ... wasn't that about big things, such as the end of time, or 9/11, or a president getting shot? She hadn't experienced anything like that.

But she had definitely come back with a knack for some small stuff – for everyone except herself. When it came to herself, she didn't have even the smallest inkling of a premonition. She had to flounder along, and it seemed to her that most of the time her choices were all bad, and she had to take the least worst of the lot. She wasn't racking up many points that way.

Like the two million bucks. For the life of her, she couldn't decide what to do with it. Sending it back to Rafael was out of the question. Yes, she'd stolen it from him, but he'd gotten it by running drugs and then laundering it through all of his penny-ante businesses. Giving it back to him would just make him that much stronger in the drug world.

On the other hand, she couldn't just keep it. It wasn't hers. She'd had to use part of it to live on after she was released from the hospital, because though she'd had a couple of weeks of physical rehab before Dr. Meecham would release her, she hadn't been in any shape to get a job and work. She'd been able to bathe and dress herself, and take short walks, but that was about it. Getting strong enough to actually get a job had taken weeks more of physically pushing herself;

ignoring the protests of her chest muscles, which hadn't wanted to do *anything.*

She'd been driven by the need to escape, and not because of any legal issue. Her ability to lie had come through in a pinch, and she'd sailed through her interview with Detective Arrons. Once she settled on a name – Pearson, in honor of the kind-eyed Mrs. Pearson at the bank in Grissom – the rest of it was easy. For the most part, she told the truth. She bought the car in New Jersey and hadn't bothered to register it there because she'd been leaving that day, moving out here, and figured she'd wait until she got settled and knew what her address would be before applying for a Colorado tag.

Okay, so that wasn't exactly the truth. He could have pressed the issue, because she didn't have a driver's license either; there were a number of factors figuring into his decision to let it drop. First and foremost, the car hadn't been reported stolen anywhere. Two, while still drugged up she'd asked about her laptop, but no laptop had ever been found, which opened up the possibility that her belongings had been pilfered. A man had made the 911 call, but no one had been there when the emergency crews arrived, so the unknown man could easily have taken her things. She had also been in a horrific car accident and her survival was nothing short of a miracle, so the detective wasn't inclined to hassle her. Once she came up with a name for him, and a cursory check didn't turn up any warrants, he considered everything square.

No, what really spooked her was that someone

246

had paid her hospital bill – and Dr. Meecham's bill. And the anesthesiologist's, the radiologist's, and every other ologist involved in her care. When she peppered Dr Meecham with questions, he'd shrugged. 'The payment came in the form of a cashier's check. I don't know who sent it. The envelope was tossed in the trash, so I can't even tell you where it was mailed from.'

Andie supposed someone, out of sheer charity, could have been moved by the brief mention of her accident in the newspaper, but the story had never been given the big human-interest treatment, evidently because she'd lived and wasn't an amnesiac. There hadn't been any public fund-raisers, and if anyone had bothered to ask she'd have told them she could pay the bills – using Rafael's money, of course, but that didn't bother her at all. It alarmed her that someone had, out of the blue, anonymously shelled out some big bucks.

She had no idea who that someone could be, but she was afraid he, or she, somehow knew who she really was. Her instinct told her to leave Denver as fast as possible, so that's what she'd done.

She'd bought another secondhand car, headed northeast on the interstate, toward Nebraska, and traded that car in for another as soon as she crossed the state line. Driving long distances had been a challenge, because she tired so easily, but she kept moving steadily eastward until she got to Kansas City. Three interstates came together in the K.C. area, giving her a lot of options if she had to move on. She kind of liked that idea, and somehow she'd ended up getting a job at Glenn's.

She also shelled out the cash needed for a new ID, for Andrea Pearson, so she now had a valid driver's license in that name – well, as valid as a license could be if the name on it was fake. Her red 2003 Ford Explorer was duly registered to her, and she had insurance on it and everything.

She rented half of a duplex in a rundown neighborhood and actually lived on what she made at Glenn's. After spending most of her life trying to score all the luxuries she could, she was oddly content with her life, with three smallish rooms in a house with a sagging roof. At least the tenants in the other half of the house weren't on drugs. Just thinking of her time with Rafael made her feel dirty.

But she still had the two million, or most of it, sitting in the bank. She thought about writing one big check to a charity or something just to get rid of it, but she couldn't seem to just *do* it. What if that was the wrong thing? She wasn't sure how donating to a charity could be wrong, but what if that wasn't what she was meant to do with the money? What if there was some other cause she was supposed to give it to, if she could figure out what that cause was? The American Cancer Society, maybe. Or St. Jude's Hospital. There were a lot of great organizations that could use the money, but she couldn't work her way past this weird paralysis in decision-making.

She didn't know what was wrong with her unless it was a reaction to the trauma. Dr. Meecham had given her some literature on it, and evidently people who had heart surgery often went through some emotional upheaval afterward. Because her case was so extreme, she should probably expect some difficulties in dealing with stuff. She could get through the day, she could handle the physical demands of her job, she could buy groceries and pay her bills, but other than that she wanted to spend her time curled up on her secondhand couch, wrapped in a blanket to keep her warm during the grueling midwestern winter, reading a book from the library. Deciding which books to check out was the toughest decision she could handle.

When her shift at Glenn's was over and she trudged out into the snow, she wished she could make the decision to move farther south, but hell, winter would be over soon.

Spring might be close, but snow was still falling. The night sky was a thick, dark gray that said more snow was coming. She pulled her thick wool scarf up to cover her head and wrapped the ends around her neck to keep out the icy wind. Lowering her head into the wind, she trudged through the snow toward her red Explorer.

'Hey, Andie.'

Turning her head, she recognized Cassie as the woman climbed out of the cab of her Peterbilt. The big diesel engine was running, because a diesel was a bitch to start in cold weather. No matter how much fuel cost, having to pay for a jump-start and then factoring in the time lost meant that the rigs were never cut off during a run.

Inwardly Andie groaned. She didn't want to get into a discussion about Cassie's fortune, or lack of it, but other than walking off it didn't look as if she had any other choice. She actually kind of liked Cassie, so she stopped and waited for her.

Cassie slipped a little bit on the ice, then reached Andie's side, 'Come on, I'll walk you to your car,' she said. 'Where is it?'

'Over there,' said Andie, indicating the gravel lot off to the side, where the employees' vehicles wouldn't get in the way of the big rigs coming in or going out of the truck stop.

'I saw some guy watching you through the windows,' Cassie said, pitching her voice low so only Andie could hear her.

Andie skidded to a stop as her heartbeat kicked into a gallop. 'A guy? What guy?'

'Just keep walking,' said Cassie calmly. 'I don't see him now, but I thought I'd make sure you got to your car okay.'

Words failed her, that someone she barely knew would go out of her way to make sure Andie was safe. 'I'll drive you back to your truck,' she managed to say. 'That way you won't be in any danger either.'

Cassie smiled down at her. She was a tall woman, lean and rangy, and even though she'd exchanged her high heels for boots she was still a good five or six inches taller than Andie. 'We women have to watch each other's asses, toots, and I don't mean that like I'm hitting on you either.'

Andie snorted. She had watched Cassie in action often enough to know that the trucker didn't swing that way. Immediately her attention switched back to the man Cassie had said was watching her. 'What did he look like – that guy?

Are you sure he was watching me?'

'Absolutely, positively. He watched you for a good five minutes, going back and forth. As for how he looked, hmm.' Cassie thought about it. 'Tall and in good shape, but he was wearing a thick coat with the hood up, so that's about all I can tell you. Even with the coat, though, you could tell he wasn't a porker or anything.'

Most truckers weren't what you'd call 'in good shape,' but enough of them came through the truck stop that a guy who took care of himself wasn't all that unusual. In the four months she'd worked there, Andie had probably seen a couple of hundred who matched that vague description. But none of them would have stood out in the snow watching her; each and every one of them would have come inside, ordered a cup of coffee, tried to talk to her there if he was interested.

A chill that had nothing to do with the weather ran down her back. The uneasy feeling that had chased her from Denver told her someone was on her trail. But who, and why? She had died. Short of actually staying dead and being buried, wasn't that enough to shake *him* off her tail?

What if it wasn't him, though? Who else could it be?

Someone knew who she was and where she was.

23

'You're running from someone, aren't you?' Cassie asked as they reached the Explorer. 'You know who this guy is?'

'God, I hope not,' Andie muttered, unlocking and opening the door. The interior light came on and they both checked the backseat as well as the luggage compartment in back. Both were empty. 'I thought I'd lost him.'

'In this day and age, honey, it's tough to shake someone who's hell-bent on finding you. If he's got your Social Security number, he can find you anywhere.'

'He doesn't,' Andie said, certain of that. He might have her old Social Security number, but there was no way he could have the new one. Besides, Glenn didn't report her earnings to the IRS, so even if she had been using the old number nothing would be reported on it. She began walking around the Explorer, looking for footprints in the snow that would tell her if anyone had been around or under her vehicle.

'Don't forget about phone records,' Cassie continued. 'When you call home, he can access your folks' phone records and track you that way.'

'I don't have any family. I haven't called any old friends.' Not that she had any, unless she reached way back to middle school. Once she'd lost the baby she'd turned her back on every emotional connection she'd ever had, not wanting to feel anything ever again. All she'd wanted to do was forget, to walk away and never look back, because to look back was to remember the crippling pain. She couldn't go through that again, not ever.

She finished her circuit of the Ford – the snow was undisturbed. As she got behind the steering wheel, Cassie tromped around to climb into the passenger seat. 'So maybe you have an admirer,' she said to Andie. 'Has anyone been flirting with you?'

'Who has time to notice? We're run off our feet in there. Unless someone pinches me, or pats my ass, I don't even look at their faces.'

'Yeah, I've seen you look at their faces a time or two. I thought one asshole was going to faint. What did you say to him?'

She knew exactly the incident Cassie was referring to, because her eyes and voice must have telegraphed her absolute sincerity to the driver, and he'd turned dead white. 'I told him if he touched me again I'd stick a fork through his nuts.'

The old Andie – Drea – Andrea ... hell, she didn't know who she was anymore ... would have pretended not to notice the pinch or the pat. She'd have been sweet and slightly vacant, not causing any problems but inside she'd have been sick with anger and contemptuous that no one realized she was faking everything. Being dead had changed her in more ways than one, because she couldn't act sweet and vacant now. She had buried her temper years ago, but in the past few months it had clawed its way to the surface and seemed determined to stay there.

Cassie threw back her head and laughed in appreciation. 'I'm surprised he didn't tell Glenn.'

'He did. Glenn told him to keep his fucking hands off the waitresses if he didn't want his balls ventilated.' Andie smiled in memory. That was what she liked best about Glenn. Some guys would have been jerks and told the waitresses to put up with it, that he didn't want to lose any customers but not Glenn. One of his daughters had helped pay her way through college by working in a restaurant, so he had a different view of what waitresses sometimes endured.

As Andie carefully steered the Ford through the long lines of rumbling trucks toward Cassie's rig, Cassie cleared her throat, then said hesitantly, 'That thing you said about better decisions, what did you mean?'

'Little things. Like, maybe, instead of buying a flashy bracelet you like, you put that money in an interest-beating savings account or a CD.' Cassie liked jewelry. None of it was expensive – probably the most she'd paid for anything was a couple of hundred dollars – but she liked a *lot* of jewelry.

'I don't spend that much...' Cassie began.

Andie reached the rig and put the car in park. 'It adds up.' She ran an expert eye over what jewelry she could see: earrings, several cocktail rings, four or five bracelets. 'What you have on cost you roughly three thousand dollars, total. That's three thousand dollars that could be in a bank. What you should be doing is saving up enough to invest in a good mutual fund.'

Cassie wrinkled her nose. 'God, that sounds so *boring.*'

'Yeah, it does,' Andie agreed. 'Boring and hard are usually good signs that's what you should be doing.'

'I'll be okay. I make good money.'

Cassie was shrugging off what Andie had told her. Normally Andie would have done her own shrugging and let it be, but Cassie had gone out of her way tonight to help her so that favor got turned around.

'One wreck will wipe you out,' she said, her voice going kind of distant the way it sometimes did. 'You'll be hurt, out of commission for about six months. You have insurance on your rig, but you won't be able to work and you'll lose your house. It's all downhill after that. I wasn't kidding about the cat food.'

Cassie froze with her hand on the door handle. In the glow of the dash lights, her face suddenly showed her age, and more; it showed fear. 'You see something. You really do see something, don't you?'

Andie wasn't about to get into whether or not she 'saw' things, so she waved the question away. What she'd just said was common sense. 'Another thing: you should start respecting yourself more and stop hooking up with losers. One of them's going to give you an STD.' She turned to face the woman. 'You're smart, you're successful. You should act like it, because doing stupid things will stop you from being more successful. Trust me, I'm an expert on doing stupid things.'

'One of them being this guy you're running from?'

'He's at the top of the list.' Proof of her stupidity, Andie thought, was that even though he was a hired killer and no doubt would have shot her if she hadn't saved him the trouble by having a wreck, in unguarded moments she'd have flash-backs to that afternoon with him and the pain would almost bring her to her knees. She was stupid enough that she really *would* have gone anywhere with him, if he'd only said the word. She was stupid enough that, even now, her terror of him was mixed with a longing that cut at her heart.

What she wasn't stupid enough for was to believe that, if he'd found her, she'd still be alive right now. She laughed in relief at the realization. 'It wasn't him,' she said. 'Watching me, I mean.'

Cassie raised her eyebrows. 'Yeah? How do you know?'

'I'm still alive.' She smiled wryly at her own fear. If he had found her, she wouldn't have survived the walk across the parking lot, whether Cassie was with her or not.

'Holy shit! You mean he's trying to *kill* you?' Cassie's eyes went round, and her voice rose.

'That's what he does, and he's very good at it. I pissed off some bad guys,' she said by way of explanation.

'Holy shit!' Cassie said again. 'I guess so, if they're trying to kill you! And you think *I* make stupid decisions?'

'I told you I'm an expert at it.' She drummed her fingers on the steering wheel, feeling a sudden urge to confide in Cassie, in someone. She'd been alone since she was fifteen, not physically alone but mentally and emotionally isolated, and other than Dr. Meecham no one knew about her death experience. On the other hand, she couldn't talk openly about it; that would be like stripping naked in public, and she didn't want what had happened to her to become common knowledge. She settled for something short of full disclosure.

'I had a near-death experience a while back,' she said. 'Let's just say I saw the light, in more ways than one.'

'Near-death? You mean that business with the tunnel, and your dead friends and family greeting you, that kind of near-death?' Cassie's tone was eager, curious, the way she turned to Andie somehow full of hope.

Most people hungered for that, she realized, the knowledge or proof that they didn't end with death, that they somehow carried on. They wanted to believe their loved ones were still alive, somewhere, healthy and happy. They might *not* believe, they might reject anything they couldn't hear and touch and see, but they would be very happy to be proved wrong. She couldn't prove anything; she could tell what she'd experienced, what she'd seen, but *prove* it? Impossible.

'I didn't see a tunnel.' Cassie's face fell, and Andie had to smile. 'But there was light, the most beautiful light you can imagine. I can't describe it. And there was an angel. I think it was an angel. Then I was in the most beautiful place I've ever seen. The light was clear and soft and sort of glowed, and the colors were so deep and rich they made you want to just lie down in the grass and soak everything in.' Her dreamy voice trailed off as for a moment she drifted, remembering; then she

257

shook herself, both mentally and physically.

'I want to go back there,' she said firmly, 'and I realized I had to change if I was going to have a shot at it.'

'But you were already there,' Cassie pointed out, bewildered. 'Why would you have to change?'

'Because I wasn't supposed to be there. It was temporary, so I could have a sort of ... review, I guess. Then they voted to let me have another chance, but if I screw this one up, that's it, no more chances.'

'Wow. *Wow*. That's deep shit.' Cassie thought it over for a moment, maybe even thinking about her own life and some changes she could make. She put her hand on the door handle. 'I guess that *would* make you rethink some things, wouldn't it?' She hesitated another moment, then shook her head and shoved the door open. 'I could talk your head off, asking questions, but I need to get home. You be careful. Whether or not this guy I saw's the one after you, you should still be careful, because he *was* watching you. I know that for a fact, it was kind of creepy.'

'I'll be extra careful,' Andie promised, and she would. Getting killed, again, wasn't the only bad thing that could happen to her. She might even have a little bit of a death wish now, if she could be certain she'd changed enough or earned enough points, or whatever. But she didn't want to get raped, she didn't want to get mugged, or a whole bunch of other stuff, so she would definitely be careful.

After Cassie got out, Andie waited until she saw her new maybe-friend climb safely into her rig, then she drove home. Hyper-alert, she watched for any car that seemed to be following her, but traffic was light this late on a snowy Friday night and for the most part there was no one behind her.

By the time she got home, the adrenaline rush of fear had faded and she was yawning with exhaustion. The porch light was on, just the way she'd left it, a welcoming pool of yellow light in the icy darkness. There was a streetlight at the corner but the trees blocked most of the light from her house and she hated coming home in the dark. She always left a small lamp on, too, to make it look as if someone was there.

The duplex didn't have a garage, or even a carport, so she parked by the porch and pulled her coat and scarf more snugly into place before getting out of the Ford. Snow immediately slipped down inside her shoes; it was deeper here than it had been out by the interstate, undisturbed by hundreds of trucks roaring in and out. Sighing as the icy wetness hit her already cold feet, she unlocked her door and slipped inside the warmth of her shabby sanctuary.

She was safely home. From his parking spot down the street, Simon watched her go inside. He'd been waiting here since that trucker had spotted him watching her. The trucker couldn't have gotten a good look at him, not with the hood of his heavy shearling coat pulled up, but he'd moved on anyway.

He'd kept an eye on Drea – she went by Andie now – since she'd left the hospital. He'd done what he could, paying all of her medical bills, and for a while he'd stayed close by in case she needed help with anything, but only dire circumstances would have forced him to step in. She was too scared of him; he couldn't predict what she'd do if she saw him.

When she left Denver, he'd trailed her. When she made contact with someone to get a new ID, he'd smoothed the way for her – first, because that way he had inside information on her new name and Social Security number, and, second, because he didn't like the looks of the bastard she'd contacted. He made sure she wasn't ripped off and that the guy knew she wasn't without protection.

She had gotten a new cell phone, too, and the one real chance he'd taken, as soon as she was settled, was to break into her duplex apartment and install a UPS locator in the phone. He also had one on the Explorer, but she would probably hang on to the phone even if she traded in the Explorer.

After that, he pretty much left her alone. He checked on her about once a month, just to make sure she was okay, and he kept his ear to the ground to make sure Salinas hadn't somehow gotten word she was still alive, but that was it.

He started the car and pulled away from the curb, not hurrying. If she heard the engine start, enough time had passed that she wouldn't think anyone had been sitting in a car at the curb when she pulled into her driveway.

She looked good, he reflected, much better than she had even a couple of months ago. When she'd first been released from the hospital she'd been so frail he had been tempted to snatch her off the street, just to keep her from driving. She'd been cadaverously thin and ghostly pale. At first she'd been able to drive maybe half an hour before tiring out and being forced to stop at the nearest motel. Sometimes more than a day passed before she ventured out again, which made him afraid she was doing without food all that time.

Several times he'd considered having a pizza delivered to her room, but that would seriously spook her. He'd hung back and watched, hoping she got to where she was going and got settled before her strength gave out completely.

She'd made it to Kansas City; he didn't know if that was her intended destination all along, or if she got that far and decided to rest for a while, then made the decision to stay. When she rented that ratty little duplex, he'd heaved an inner sigh of relief.

The weight she'd put on looked good; she was heavier now than she had been even in New York, but she'd been too thin anyway and all the weight she'd lost after the accident had been a loss she couldn't afford. He'd watched her work, knew the pace was nonstop, but she was getting enough to eat and her arms showed the muscle she'd gained from lifting heavy trays all day long.

She had two million bucks sitting in the bank in Grissom and she lived in a neighborhood that was just an inch from qualifying as a slum, while she worked as a waitress in a truck stop. The irony was, he didn't wonder why; he knew why she wasn't using the money.

Salinas had contacted him again, so he figured

it was time for the next hit in whatever scheme Salinas had going. He hadn't answered the summons. He hadn't taken a job in the past seven months, though sometimes he wondered idly if there wasn't one more hit on the books for him, because it pissed him off that Salinas was still breathing.

He'd have to think about that. In the meantime, everything was okay in Kansas City.

24

'Is dog food bad for kids?'

Andie stopped in her tracks and stared at the two women in the booth. They were both youngish women, clad in jeans and sweaters, hair pulled back in ponytails, and with almost identical harried expressions. They looked nothing alike, but they were the same in their situations: young mothers, multiple children, impossible schedules. That they were here in Glenn's at three p.m. on a Tuesday afternoon suggested they were grabbing some time for themselves while the kids were either at day care or grandma's.

'Don't mind me,' she said, shamelessly eaves-dropping. Waitresses overheard a lot of interesting conversational tidbits but this one made her want to laugh.

The woman picked up a fry and swabbed it in ketchup before heaving a sigh. 'My youngest is a year old. Since he started walking, every time I feed the dog he comes running and tries to eat the dog's food. I keep him away when I can, but if I turn my back he's right back in the dog's food bowl. He really likes Iams,' she finished helplessly.

'At least it's not a cheap brand,' the other woman said, shrugging. 'My kids eat dirt. Count your blessings.'

Laughing, Andie continued to the counter with her loaded tray of dirty plates and cutlery. The television mounted on the wall was muted, but as she passed by one of the truckers seated at the long counter said, 'Hey, turn up the TV. That's a weather bulletin.'

Shifting the weight of the heavy tray to her hip, Andie picked up the remote and hit the volume button. Immediately the voice of one of the local meteorologists filled the room, and the din of conversation died down as everyone turned to look at the screen.

'–Weather Service has issued a tornado watch until nine p.m. for the following counties in east Kansas. This watch does include the Kansas City area. The dynamics of this storm have been impressive–'

She took the tray on to the pass-through where the waitresses left the dirty dishes to be collected by the kitchen staff. She hadn't dealt with any tornado watches when she'd been living in New York, but now that she was back in the Midwest the whole drill had quickly become as familiar as if she'd never left. Spring was welcome, with its longer days and warm relief from the bitter cold and blowing snow, but spring weather was volatile: warm one day, cold the next, with warring air masses chasing each other back and forth. Just last week they'd had another three inches of snow. Now the weather was warm and humid, and giant thunderheads were building high into the sky.

Keeping an eye on the weather was second nature to everyone in the Midwest and the South. 'Tornado watch until nine tonight,' she sang out to the kitchen crew.

'Lord,' another of the waitresses, Denise, said

as she wiped her hands before reaching into her pocket for her cell phone. 'Joshua was going to spend the night with one of his buddies. I'd better make sure he lets the cats in the house before he leaves.'

'The cats will be fine,' Andie said absently. 'Just tell him to make sure he turns off the stove.'

'Stove? Joshua doesn't cook– Oh!' Her eyes went round as she realized Andie had kind of drifted off mentally, which they'd learned was a signal. Cassie had shot off her mouth, telling some of her trucker pals about Andie's near-death experience, and some of those pals had asked the other waitresses about it, and even though some of them had considered her slightly psychic before, now they were *really* paying attention to what she said.

Furiously Denise punched the buttons on her cell phone. 'Voice mail!' she muttered with annoyed frustration. Instead of leaving a voice message, she texted her son; teenagers found it almost impossible to resist reading a text message, whereas they could ignore voice mail with ease.

Her phone rang within two minutes. 'No, I don't have a spy camera set up at home,' she said after listening to an outraged teenager squawking so loud Andie could hear the tone of it from ten feet away. 'But it's a good idea, thank you for giving it to me. Now go home immediately and make sure the stove is off, do you hear me? Immediately! Joshua, if you say one more word, you'll not only go home, you'll stay at home. Is that understood? You may say "yes."'

With an air of satisfaction, Denise disconnected the call and winked at Andie. 'Thanks. Now he thinks I either have spy cameras all over the place, or I'm psychic. Either way, he'll think twice before he does something he shouldn't be doing.'

'Glad to be of service.'

With a little start of inner surprise, Andie realized that she felt good. She liked being able to help people even in small ways, though preventing a kitchen fire that could have burned down Denise's house probably didn't qualify as 'small,' certainly not to Denise. She liked working and paying her bills. Physically, she felt damn good, not just for someone who had been impaled and died, but better than she'd felt in years. She was active, she had plenty to eat, she slept well. If she could see her way clear to using that two million dollars for her own benefit, well, life would be better, but her conscience wouldn't let her do it.

Whoever said money corrupted had had it the wrong way around. Money was okay; money was good. Having it was way better than not having it. The corruption came from the person, not the money itself. She would love to use at least part of the two million to buy herself a nice house and a new car, but every time she had herself halfway talked into doing it some bitchy little inner voice would say 'Nope, can't do it.'

But the money was sitting in her bank account, tempting her every day and she knew she had to get rid of it before a weak moment caught her when the bitchy little inner voice was on a coffee break or something. She just wished that this one time, doing what she wanted to do and what was right had both happened to be the same thing.

Ah well. She still had her jewelry, and she hadn't stolen it, so selling it and using that money shouldn't be any problem. The amount wouldn't be anywhere close to two million, but she'd still have a nest egg – unless the inner voice told her to repay what she'd used of the two million, in which case she was shit out of luck. Doing right definitely wasn't easy.

A thunderstorm rolled overhead about five p.m; that was usually a busy time at the truck stop, with people getting off work, but the heavy sheets of rain kept people in their cars, inching along the interstates and surface streets. Stopping might have been the better option, but no one wanted to get out and get soaked. Even the big rigs kept rolling past. The customers who were already in the truck stop stayed put, lingering over a last cup of coffee or deciding to have a slice of pie after all, but overall both the kitchen staff and waitresses had time to catch their collective breaths.

Business remained slow. Storm after storm marched across the city, and though they dodged the bullet regarding tornadoes, the thunderstorms were magnificent. Huge sheets of lightning flashed overhead, and straight-line winds blew trash like missiles across the parking lot. Andie had always kind of liked thunderstorms, so when she could she'd go to the windows and watch.

Around dark the storms eased and the rain lessened, and business picked up a little. Mother Nature wasn't finished with the fireworks, though; the last line of storms marched through, providing a little more drama even though this one wasn't nearly as intense as the earlier storms had been. One particularly brilliant and long-lasting flash of lightning lit the sky and automatically Andie looked out the windows.

If the man had been walking toward the restaurant, she wouldn't have paid any attention to him. But he wasn't walking; he was just standing there as motionless as a rock, while the lightning flashed around him. She couldn't make out any of his features, he was wearing a long rain slicker and was nothing but a dark shape, but the bottom dropped out of her stomach and her breath caught, and she *knew*. She had this reaction to one man, and one man only.

She forced herself to turn away from the window as if she hadn't seen anything out of the ordinary. She wanted to run screaming, but letting herself panic was the last thing she needed to do; look what had happened before.

The way he was just standing there, staring inside, reminded her of how Cassie had described the man she'd seen last month. Had he been watching her even then? How long had he known where she was? At least a month, she was certain. So what was he waiting on? Why hadn't he made his move?

She couldn't begin to understand what he was doing. Maybe he was toying with her, like a cat with a mouse. Maybe he was playing some kind of game, waiting to see how long it took her to spot him. If she ran, it would trigger his pounce.

When the next bolt of lightning flashed she couldn't stop herself from whirling to look out the window, but the dark figure was gone. No one stood outside watching her through the rain, almost daring lightning to strike him. She would almost have thought she was seeing things – almost, if not for the fact that Cassie had seen him, and if not for the way her nerves were twitching and her stomach flip-flopping.

She made herself finish her shift. She made herself take orders, refill cups and glasses, clean away the debris. While she did, she thought about what his appearance meant, and she faced some facts she'd been avoiding for the past eight months.

When her shift ended, she sought out Glenn, who worked longer hours than any of them. Good short-order cooks were hard to come by and Glenn didn't want to hire someone who was just adequate; he did too much business for that. If he couldn't find two other cooks who met his exacting standards, then he worked doubles, without complaining.

'I need to talk to you,' she said as she pulled off her apron and tossed it in the laundry basket. 'In private, if you can spare a minute.'

'Do I look like I can spare a minute?' he groused, his beefy face shiny with sweat. He cast an expert eye over the two order slips hanging from clothespins on a line in from of him. 'These two won't take but a minute, so cool your jets until then. Go wait in my office.'

She went into his office and sank down on one of the straight-backed chairs, sighing with relief as she got her weight off her feet. She stretched out her legs and bent her feet back toward her as far as they would go, feeling the pull in her

Achilles tendons as they loosened. Then she rotated her ankles, and next her shoulders and neck. God she was tired; tired of running, tired of looking over her shoulder, and there was only one way she'd ever be truly free.

Glenn came hustling into his office and closed the door. 'Okay, what's up?'

'I saw a man out in the parking lot tonight,' she said, jumping right into the middle of the subject. 'He's been stalking me for almost a year, and now he's found me again. I have to leave.'

Glenn's face went dark red. 'Point him out to me, and I'll make damn sure he never bothers you again,' he growled.

'You can't protect me from him,' she said gently. 'I don't think even around-the-clock guards could stop him. The only thing I can do is stay one step ahead of him.'

'Have you been to the police?'

'Glenn, you know restraining orders aren't worth the paper they're written on,' she chided. 'If he's caught violating it, then it's a felony misdemeanor or something like that, I don't know the right term, but a restraining order never stopped anyone from doing something he really wants to do.'

He chewed on the reality of what she'd just said, scowling as he finally admitted she was right. 'Damn, I hate to lose you. You've turned into a good waitress. Provided some entertainment around here, too. Got any idea where you're going?'

Andie took a minute to get past the idea that she'd been providing entertainment, though she

270

supposed he might have found a certain amusement in her threat to skewer some guy's balls on a fork. 'No, I'll drive until I find somewhere that feels safe. I'll shake him for a while, but he knows how to find people.' She knew exactly where she was going, but it was better that Glenn stay in the dark.

He heaved himself out of his chair and went to the electronic safe behind his desk. Keeping his bulk between her and the readout he punched in the numbers; there was a whirring sound, then a click as the lock opened. 'Here's what I owe you,' he said, counting out some cash from the day's take. 'Drive carefully, and Godspeed.' He flushed again, then leaned forward and gave her a quick peck on the cheek. 'You're a good woman, Andie. If you ever see your way clear to come back, there's a job waiting for you.'

Andie smiled and impulsively gave him a quick, affectionate hug, then blinked back tears. 'I'll remember that. You take care, too.' She stopped suddenly, her gaze losing focus as she stared at him and through him. 'You need to change your routine,' she blurted. 'Stop taking the cash by the night deposit on your way home.'

'Well, damn it, when else am I supposed to take it?' he asked irritably. 'The bank's right on the way home and it isn't as if I have a lot of time—'

'Make time. And use a different branch for the next week or so.'

His mouth opened, then he pressed his lips together in a grim line. 'Are you having one of them visions?' he asked suspiciously.

'I don't have visions,' she denied, her tone as

irritated as his. 'It's common sense. You've been taking a chance going to the night deposit at the same branch every night, and you know it. Make better decisions, and you won't get shot.'

She'd actually had the thought that he'd get knocked on the head and have a concussion, but getting shot sounded a lot more dramatic and serious, so maybe he'd listen to her. He still looked obdurate, so she muttered, 'Go ahead and be bullheaded then,' and left his office before she started crying. She was really fond of the stubborn jackass, and she hated the idea of anything happening to him, but at the end of the day the decision was his, not hers.

She had enough big-time decisions to handle on her own she thought as she trudged out to her Explorer. The other second-shift waitresses were leaving at the same time, so she wasn't alone and she supposed that was as safe as she was going to be. She didn't see him, but then she hadn't expected to. He was gone. Just as she felt his presence, she also felt his absence. He didn't know she'd seen him, and the cat had gone off to take a nap somewhere, confident the mouse would stay in its hole.

She felt oddly ... calm, now that her decision was made. The first thing she would do was take care of dispersing that two million dollars, because if she got killed before she did anything then the money would just sit there, not doing anyone any good. St. Jude's could always use the bucks, and she would be helping sick kids. There. Decision made. It was so easy she wondered why she'd wrestled with the problem for so long.

Her second decision was that she would never be free as long as Rafael was alive. He would keep the assassin hunting her, and in the meantime he himself would keep on bringing drugs into the country, ruining lives, killing people, while he raked in the dough. She couldn't let him continue.

She'd been a coward when she lived with him, making sure she never looked deep enough to find any hard evidence that could be used against him, deliberately ignoring the opportunities she'd had to discover more about what he was doing. She hadn't wanted to know, and as a result she had no knowledge she could take to the FBI that might result in his arrest. Rafael had the money to fight the legal system, anyway; even if he was arraigned, he could keep the case dragging on in court for a long time.

But she knew him, knew the brutality he hid under his three-thousand-dollar suits and designer haircut. She knew his ego, and the rules of the world he lived in. If he actually saw her, if he knew she was alive and right under his nose, it would drive him nuts. He might lose all sense of caution, because his machismo couldn't tolerate letting her go. He'd stop at nothing to kill her.

The FBI might be able to keep her safe. She hoped so, but with a sense of fatalism she accepted that they might not. One way or another, though, she had to do what she could to stop Rafael, to break up his business. *This*, then, was the cost of her new life – and the price might well be her life.

25

At first he thought she hadn't seen him. Rather, he knew she'd seen him, but he thought she hadn't recognized him. He'd gone to his car immediately, swearing at himself for being so damned stupid as to stand outside knowing a lightning flash could expose him at any minute. He'd felt compelled to watch her, though, and in the end the temptation had been too strong; she'd been laughing, and he'd realized how much he wanted to hear her melodious laugh again. So he'd stood there for a minute, and the next thing he knew a sheet of lightning lit up the night and she turned to look out the window.

The parking lot was lit, but the rain had seemed to absorb a lot of the light and he'd parked in a deep well of shadows between two rigs, in the area normally used only by the truckers. He could still see in the windows, though; that and the area of shadow were why he'd chosen that spot. He lowered a couple of windows just enough to let in some fresh air and keep the windshield from fogging, then sat in the dark and watched, waiting to see if she ran, but she had gone back to work and for a little while he'd let himself think she hadn't recognized him. Then his instinct kicked in; did he want to take that chance? The answer was a definite no.

He hadn't wanted her to ever know he was watching her, watching over her. She was terrified of him, with good reason. The one thing he didn't want to do was frighten her again, or cause her more pain. Now he thought he probably didn't have a choice. He had to see her, let her know she had nothing to fear from him, before she ran again.

She couldn't get away from him, unless she jettisoned the phone and the SUV at the same time and he wasn't able to pick up her trail, which was unlikely. But she'd wear herself out running, and she wouldn't let herself settle anywhere. Drea was a woman who needed to settle; she needed a home, and friends, a life where she felt safe and normal. He didn't want her to live in fear; he didn't want her thinking she had to run for her life.

What would she do, when she left work? Would she immediately rabbit, or would she continue to act as if she hadn't seen him, hoping to fake him into relaxing his guard. The second choice would take iron nerves, but she'd panicked before, and had the accident. He couldn't let himself forget, ever, how sharp she was. She'd learn from her mistake, and she wouldn't do the same thing twice.

He bet she'd go home. She'd probably sacrifice the Explorer, leaving it sitting in the driveway while she packed a few clothes and walked away in the wee hours of the morning. She would keep a supply of cash handy, just in case she had to leave everything on short notice, because she planned ahead.

He checked the time. It would be a couple of

hours yet before her shift ended, and he didn't want to leave the rental car parked on her street for that length of time, or this early in the night. People were still up, still watching television. Lights would begin winking out as soon as the ten o'clock news went off, because these people, by and large, weren't part of the Leno and Letterman crowd. That was when he would move in. For now, he was in a good spot to watch and wait. If patience was a virtue, then he had at least one to his name.

At ten-thirty, he chose a moment when she had her back turned before starting the car and pulling out of his shadowed parking space. When he got to her house, he parked down the street and walked back. The rain had slackened to a drizzle which allowed him to wear the concealing slicker but meant he had to be careful about dripping water anywhere she might see it.

She normally used the front door; she left the porch light on there, and she was protected from the weather. The kitchen stoop was uncovered, a bare and exposed two steps of crumbling concrete. The steps were already wet, so dripping on them wouldn't matter. A storm door protected the inner wooden door from the elements, and it was locked. He had it open in five seconds. The inner door had a simple doorknob lock, the kind that wouldn't keep out a ten-year-old, and opening it didn't take as long as opening the storm door. He let himself in, removed his wet slicker and put it in the tiny laundry area just off the kitchen, then he mopped up the water he'd tracked in.

The little duplex didn't afford many places

where he could conceal himself. He didn't want her to see him when she first let herself in the door or she would bolt off the porch and run. He wanted her inside, the doors locked, which would slow her down and give him time to grab her, talk to her.

Logistically, the duplex apartment was a nightmare. The front door opened straight into the small living room, where what furniture she had was shoved against a wall because floor space was so limited. The single lamp she left burning was enough to light the entire room. Next was a tiny hallway, if it could be called that; it was just long enough to accommodate a closet on the inside wall, and he suspected the space had once belonged to the living room but some remodeling had been done when the house was turned into a duplex. There were no doors closing off the hallway; it flowed into the eat-in kitchen, where space was even more cramped because some of its area had been taken for the laundry. Next was the bedroom and bathroom, both of which were barely adequate for squeezing in the necessities.

He wanted to be between her and any door before she saw him. He also had to be close enough to get his hand over her mouth before she screamed the house down and the neighbors called the cops.

She would be terrified, at least at first; he hated that, but he couldn't help it. She had to listen to him.

The best place to position himself was in the kitchen, against the wall. She would walk right past him, but there was no door to get behind, no china cabinet. In his favor was the fact that she didn't normally turn on a light in the kitchen; she went into the bedroom and turned on the light there, then backtracked to turn off the lamp in the living room. If she followed her routine, he would wait until she was almost to the bedroom, so he could get between her and the kitchen door.

There were a lot of things that could go wrong. If she was spooked, she might turn on the light in the kitchen. He had to be on his toes, ready to react to whatever she did. She would fight. No matter what, Drea was a survivor. She didn't give up. She'd fight until she couldn't fight anymore. He'd have to control her, without hurting her, until she either reached that point or he could get her to listen to him. He'd never held back in his life; the very concept was alien to him. If he fought, he fought to win. But with Drea, he wouldn't be throwing any punches. She, however, wouldn't be suffering under the same restriction, so he was prepared to absorb some damage before he got her under control. Part of him hated that she'd be so frightened but beneath that was something he had to acknowledge: anticipation.

He'd have left her alone forever if life had shaken out that way. But it hadn't, and finally – *finally* ... he'd be touching her again, holding her close, even if only for a brief moment. He closed his eyes against the piercing heat of memory; of feeling her soft inner muscles clenching around him when she came. For four hours she'd been his, her slender arms locked around his neck, her legs around his hips.

Just for a little while, he'd be able to touch her again. He had no delusions about what would happen after he calmed her down and set her straight about any harm she thought he meant to do to her. Whether or not they ever had any more contact would be entirely up to her – and he knew how that would go.

He checked his watch. He had another twenty minutes, maybe half an hour. If he wanted to know for certain where she was, he could get his laptop from the car and track the locators he'd planted in her phone and vehicle, but he'd bother with that only if she didn't show up on time.

He settled in a kitchen chair to wait.

Andie drove past her house twice before she pulled into the driveway. She hadn't seen anything out of the ordinary, but then she didn't know what he was driving, so she had no way of spotting his car. The cars parked along the side of the street were all dark and silent and, as far as she could tell, empty.

She was taking a chance going into the house. She knew that. He could have followed her home at any time during the past month, assuming that when Cassie had seen him was when he'd first found her. For all she knew, he could have found her months ago. But she had to retrieve her jewelry and small store of cash, because that was what she'd have to live on. She'd have to buy another fake ID, she realized with a sinking heart, and that cost a big chunk of change.

Nothing moved in the dark, silent neighborhood; no dogs barked, warning of a stranger slipping quietly down the street. She could drive away, she thought, or she could go inside. She needed to go inside. He was either there, or he wasn't. He was either behind that big oak at the edge of the yard, or he wasn't.

Mustering her courage, she took a deep breath, grabbed her bag, and got out of the Explorer. Normally she locked the vehicle, but this time she didn't in case she had to run for it and every second counted. The yellow porch light, instead of comforting her, made her feel exposed as she fumbled with the door key, finally managing to get the lock open.

The shabby little living room looked normal. The apartment was as quiet as usual. She stood listening for a moment, but didn't hear any telltale scraping or breathing. Not that she would, she realized. He was too good for that. Her heart was pounding so hard she wasn't certain she'd have been able to hear anything over the thunder of her blood, anyway. Her chest felt tight, as if she needed to gasp for air. Just thinking about him did that to her, every time. He didn't even have to be there to scare her half to death.

The jewelry was in a bag in her dresser drawer. She'd just go into the bedroom, grab the jewelry and throw some clothes in her suitcase, and leave. She'd be out of there in two minutes, tops, and every second she stood there was a second she might not be able to afford. She took another deep breath and strode quickly toward her bedroom.

A hard hand clamped over her mouth while an arm passed around her waist and jerked her back against a body so hard the impact actually hurt her. She hadn't heard a whisper of sound, felt a rush of air, literally nothing to warn her. He was just suddenly *there*, behind her, and the blood rushed from her head as he whispered, 'Drea.'

26

Thick gray fog clouded her mind, pushing out all rational thought. She reacted like a wild animal, hurling herself backward with all her strength, trying to knock him off balance, dislodge the hand that was over her mouth so she could scream, *anything* to escape. Sobbing wildly, she arched and kicked, clawed, slung her elbows, jerked her head back trying to catch him on the mouth or jaw, none of her efforts coordinated or planned; every move was made by sheer instinct, a rabbit trying to escape the jaws of the wolf. She could hear him saying something, but nothing after that first utterance of her name made any sense at all, or was even recognizable as words.

The darkness was overwhelming, both in the kitchen and in her mind. She knew she'd left the lamp on in the living room but no light seemed to penetrate this far; her terror blinded her to everything except the need to fight, to get away. Somehow, somehow, her desperation lending her strength, she managed to tear herself partly from his grasp. She was off balance, disoriented; when all of her weight abruptly shifted to one side she couldn't get her feet under her and she fell, somehow getting tangled in one of the kitchen chairs before crashing to the floor. The chair overturned and went sliding; she rolled, trying to scramble to her feet, trying to scream, but she didn't have enough air in her constricted lungs, and all she could do was make a small bleating noise.

He was on her like a panther, his weight bearing down on her, flattening her to the floor again. Once more his hand clamped over her mouth. She jerked her head, trying to open her mouth and bite him, anything to get free of his iron grip. At the first scrape of her teeth he tightened his fingers on her jaw, applying pressure to a sensitive point that made pain explode through her head.

Even though the pain was almost paralyzing she tried to fight. When she tried to punch him in the head he shifted so his elbows pressed down on her arms, pinning them down. Desperately she wiggled, trying to pull her legs up between them so she could use the power of her thigh muscles to shove him up and away. With a quick swivel of his hips he wedged one of his knees between hers and shoved it to the side; another swivel and he had both legs between hers, shifting his weight from first one side to the other as he slid his knees upward, lifting and spreading her legs until her thighs were helplessly draped across his while his heavy torso held her down.

Horrified, she realized he was aroused; his erection, trapped by his pants, rode painfully against her pubic bone. He shifted, just a little, easing himself downward so he was no longer hurting her there, but she preferred the pain to the feel of that thick bulge riding her as if he were trying to enter her through the fabric of her pants. Dear God, was he going to rape her, too?

She couldn't bear it, couldn't bear that *he*

should hurt her that way. Of all the men she'd ever met, only he had actually touched *her*, had moved so effortlessly past all her protective barriers that he'd broken a heart she would have sworn was untouchable. He'd taught her differently, taught her the hard way that she wasn't as impervious as she'd deluded herself into thinking. Knowing he'd been hired to kill her was tough enough, so tough she had broken down to the point that she lost control, but somehow rape was worse, showing not just a lack of feeling but a total sense of contempt. She would rather he kill her outright.

Her futile struggling slowly diminished, and her useless attempts to scream turned into choked sobs. Tears leaked from the corners of her eyes, ran down her temples into her hair. She couldn't bear to look at him, couldn't bear to see his face even if drenching tears had allowed it, so she squeezed her eyes as tightly shut as she could.

And, in that first moment of stillness, heard the deep murmur of his voice. 'I won't hurt you,' he said, his lips moving against her ear. 'Drea, be still. I won't hurt you. I'll never hurt you.'

At first the words were as incomprehensible as they had been originally, and even when she finally understood the words she couldn't grasp their meaning. He wouldn't hurt her? Did that mean he was going to painlessly kill her? That she wouldn't suffer?

Big of him.

Anger, life-saving anger, surged through the pain and terror and she somehow lunged one more time, wrenching her head to the side and sinking her teeth into any part of him she could reach, which happened to be the side of his forearm, just past his thick wrist. The hot, metallic taste of blood exploded in her mouth, as if she'd bitten into a penny. He said 'Fuck!' in a strained tone, forcing the word between his clenched teeth, and with his other hand he applied pressure to those points in her jaw again. Despite herself her jaw loosened, and he pulled his arm from between her teeth.

'Do me a favor,' he muttered. 'If you feel you just have to hurt me somehow, punch me in the eye instead of biting me. At least then I won't need a tetanus shot.'

Her eyes popped open and she glared at him in outrage. He glared back at her from a distance of about ten inches, just far enough that she couldn't head butt him, at least not with her limited range of motion. Despite her earlier impression of utter darkness, the kitchen wasn't completely dark; the light from the living room made a dim, mellow swath across the linoleum floor, let her see the strong shadowed planes of his face and the glitter of his darkly brilliant eyes.

Silence stretched between them, taut and heated. After a moment he drew a slow, controlled breath and let it out the same way. 'Can you listen to me now?' he finally asked. 'Or do I have to tie you down and gag you?'

Surprise sparked through her, and she stared at him in confusion. If he was going to kill her, he could just do it, he didn't have to tie her down and gag her. He'd won; she was at his mercy – if he had any, that is.

Could he have meant ... had he possibly meant that he wasn't going to kill her, period?

He hadn't had to jump her, she realized. He could have shot her at any time, if killing her had been his purpose. She had operated for so long under the assumption that he intended to do exactly that, that she felt as if the ground had evaporated beneath her. If what she'd thought was reality wasn't real at all, then what the hell was?

If his hand hadn't been over her mouth, her jaw would have fallen open. Slowly, carefully, her movements hampered by his grip, she first nodded her head, once, up and down, then just as slowly shook it.

Taking the movements exactly for what they were, her answers to his questions, in order, he said, 'Then pay attention. I'm not going to hurt you *in any way.* Is that clear? Do you understand?'

She nodded again, the motion just as restricted as it had been the first time. He hadn't relaxed his grip one iota.

'All right. I'm going to let you up now. Do you need help?'

She shook her head, though she honestly didn't know. Slowly he released her, massaging the pressure points in her jaws as he did so, easing her through what could have been a spike of agony. He rolled lithely to a crouching motion and slid an arm behind her shoulders, lifting her to a sitting position.

Completely stunned, Andie sat silently on the floor. After supporting her for a moment he asked, 'All right?' When she nodded, he stood in that graceful, controlled way of his and went to the sink, turning on the water and holding his arm under the flow. 'Turn on the light,' he said, not looking at her.

Still in shocked silence, she scrambled up and went to the doorway, where she flipped the wall switch. After the relative darkness, the sudden flood of light was so bright she stood blinking, trying to take in the unbelievable fact that the man who had so terrified her for months was standing calmly at her kitchen sink, soaping the blood from his arm and hand.

Hesitantly she approached, stopping several feet away because she couldn't quite bring herself to get within reaching distance. She stared at the wound on his arm, the dark, purpling edges where her teeth had punctured his skin. Her head swam and she reached out, gripping the edge of the counter for support. She had done that, she who had never before been violent in any way.

She began trembling as the adrenaline that had flooded her body began to dissipate. The shaking started at her ankles and climbed to her knees, then rapidly filled her so that even her internal organs felt as if they were quaking and shivering. Her teeth clattered like marbles bouncing down a brick path. He continued running water over his arm, not looking at her even though he had to hear the rapid clicking of her teeth. Icy with reaction, she hugged herself and clenched her jaw in an effort to still the motion and quiet the noise. 'Do-do you really need a tetanus shot?' she finally asked, her voice small. Of all the asinine things she could have said, why she picked that one was beyond her understanding.

'No,' he said briefly. 'My vaccinations are up to date.'

She stared at him, going under for the third time in the sea of confusion. He couldn't mean childhood vaccinations, like for measles and chicken pox, and the only other kind of vaccinations that came to mind were like rabies shots for animals. Nothing was making sense; either she was in shock, or she was in an alternate universe. The alternate universe had her vote, because it was impossible that he was standing there in her kitchen. The edges of reality blurred when he was anywhere around; his presence was so intense that he seemed to draw all of her attention the way a magnet drew steel shavings, leaving everything else faded and out of focus.

'V-vaccinations?' She sounded like a stammering idiot, but she was still shivering, and it was all she could do to control her chattering teeth.

'For going out of the country.'

She felt like an idiot, because of course she knew that he did a lot of his 'work' outside the country, and smart people going into third-world countries made certain they had all the appropriate vaccinations. Then she felt like an idiot all over again, for focusing on mundane stuff like whether or not his shots were up to date, but the shift in her reality was so abrupt and so drastic that she couldn't absorb it all at once, and she felt capable only of taking in the small stuff.

Her gaze drifted over him, outlining his height, the broad set of his muscled shoulders. The short sleeves of his dark green polo shirt revealed the corded strength of his arms, but she didn't have to see his muscles to know how strong he was. He was a neat, well-dressed man, his shirttail tucked in, a thin black belt buckled around his trim waist. His black pants had a sharp crease in them, and his black soft-soled shoes were clean, despite the fact that earlier he'd been standing in the rain. Almost hungrily she stared at his thick dark hair, still cut short, and the darkening of beard stubble on his jaw; she drank in the details of his appearance, and this freshening of her memories was both painful and a relief.

She knew the scent of his skin, as if she smelled it every day, as if she woke up to see his dark head on the pillow beside her. She knew the timbre of his voice, low and ever-so-faintly raspy. She knew his taste, how he kissed, the softness of his lips, the shape and length and thickness of his penis. She knew he still scared her more than anyone she'd ever met – but she didn't know his name, he didn't want her to know even that much about him, and she was damned if she'd ask again even though the pain of not knowing almost choked her. That was where at least half of her fear came from, not just because he was cold and lethal but because somehow, for some insane reason, he could break her heart and she'd always sensed that.

She had to ask. Even knowing she was setting herself up for more pain, she had to try one more time, and if he wouldn't tell her anything this time then she'd know that she had to stop this stupid yearning after the impossible. She might not be able to stop the feelings but she could stop the hopeful expectations that led her to stare at him like a teenager staring at a rock star

'I don't know who you are,' she whispered, the sound thready and broken.

He glanced briefly at her, then tore a paper towel from the roll beside the sink and began drying his arm and hands. 'Simon Goodnight.'

She was so startled that she said, 'That's not your name!' and almost laughed, then she almost cried, because at least he'd said *something*. She swiped at her eyes, wiping away the tear that trickled down.

He shrugged. 'It is for now, just the way you're Andie Pearson, for now.'

'Andie is my real name. Well, Andrea is. I was always called Andie, when I was a kid.'

'Simon's my real name,' he replied, blotting the blood that welled in the puncture wounds.

Which meant the Goodnight wasn't, and she was glad, because that was a helluva name to carry around. Why had he chosen it? Out of some sly sense of humor, or because it was so unlike him that it was, in a way, another layer of camouflage? She almost laughed again. Forget about Smith and Jones; they were Butts and Goodnight, and if that didn't sound like a vaudeville team she didn't know what did.

Then she stared at the blood on the paper towel, and the urge to laugh immediately shriveled to dust. 'You need stitches. I'll take you to the ER.'

'I can do it myself, when I leave here,' he said in dismissal.

'Sure, why not do a Rambo?' she snapped, turning to the battered refrigerator and jerking open the freezer door. Taking out a pack of frozen peas, she tossed it to him. He'd turned to watch her, probably to make sure she didn't do any-thing other than what he was willing to allow, so he wasn't surprised by the toss and easily fielded the peas. 'Then put that on the punctures so the edges won't swell, or you won't be able to show how tough you are.'

He looked amused, not because he actually smiled, but just for a second the corners of his eyes creased a little. 'Not that tough; I use an analgesic spray to deaden the area first.'

Meaning he'd sutured himself before. Before she could quite get her head around that, he tilted his head toward the table.

'Sit down. We need to talk.'

Automatically she started to take the nearest chair but he took her arm with his left hand, picked up the overturned chair with his right, and positioned it on the far side of the table, closest to the wall, before urging her into it and taking the other chair himself. That placed him between her and the door, a habit that might have been in-grained but a move that was definitely deliberate. If she'd had any intention of running she'd have been pissed, or upset but she was neither because short of the house catching on fire she didn't think she could summon the energy to run.

Twisting around, he leaned back in the chair just enough to grab the dish towel she had hanging on one of the cabinet pulls. Wrapping the pack of frozen peas in it, he put the makeshift cold pack on the table and rested his arm across it. 'Did you quit your job?' he asked.

'Yes,' she said, because there was no reason not to tell him. She was both alarmed and angry that he was so damned hyperintuitive, figuring out what moves she would make before she made them. This wasn't a game of checkers laid out on a board with a limited number of pieces and a limited number of spaces. She could have done anything. She could have gone straight to the airport, or just started driving, and not come back here at all. But of all the things she could have done, somehow he'd known exactly what she would do, and he'd been here waiting for her.

'Maybe you can get it back.' He flicked his glance at her, a quick touch of the dark opal gaze that in an instant cataloged everything about her. 'You don't have to run. Salinas thinks you're dead.'

Andie hugged herself again, covering her elbows with her hands and trying to retain what warmth she could. She was still icy cold, though at least her teeth had stopped chattering. 'Then why did you hunt me down? Why have you been watching me?'

'I didn't have to hunt you,' he replied coolly. 'I've always known where you were.'

'Always?' she echoed. 'But how?'

'I followed you when you were released from the hospital.'

He'd been there? All that time, he'd been there? She blinked at him, the light from the overhead fixture suddenly too bright and revealing, and made her own intuitive leap. 'You're the one who paid my hospital bill!' she charged, her tone as hostile as if she were accusing him of cutting in line at the local Wal-Mart at Christmastime.

He gave a little flip of his hand, dismissing the

charge as unimportant.

'Why?' she demanded. 'I could have paid it. You know I have the money.'

'I didn't want his money paying for your care.' For all the expression or emphasis he put in the words he might have been ordering a hamburger, but that dark gaze was on her again and she felt the burning intensity of it. She couldn't tell what he was thinking, she knew only that suddenly she felt like squirming in her seat and a slow roll of heat began dispelling the chill that shook her.

'But ... why? He hired you to kill me. If it hadn't been for the wreck, you would have— I know you would have, and you know it, too!' Her voice rose on the last few words and she broke off anything else she might have said, resisting the urge to yell at him.

'Maybe. I don't know.' His mouth set in a grim line. 'I could say I never took the job, and officially I wouldn't be lying, but I can't say for sure what would have happened if you hadn't had the wreck. As much as I'd like to think I wouldn't have done it, I have to say I don't know for certain.'

'Why didn't you take the job?' She knew she was pushing, but she didn't care. She was angry at him for a bunch of reasons, not the least of which was that he seemed so cool and in control when she was a mess of raw nerve endings, and she felt as if at any time she might break and run screaming down the street. 'I was nothing to you. I'm still nothing to you.'

He simply watched her, his expression as unreadable as always, which made her even angrier. 'How much did he offer you? Wasn't it enough?

293

Was that the problem?'

'Two million,' he said calmly. 'The money wasn't the issue.'

Two million! She felt the air wheeze out of her lungs. Rafael had offered the same amount she'd stolen, and he had to know he wouldn't be able to get the money back because of the tangle of banking and tax laws and regulations, bringing his total liability to four million. She stared at the man sitting across from her and wondered how he could have *not* immediately accepted the job.

'Exactly what *was* the issue, then?' she demanded.

He stood, sighing as he pushed his chair back. Planting one hand on the table and sliding the other under her hair to cradle the back of her head, he bent and covered her mouth with his. Her mind went blank and she froze, still hugging her own arms, her head tilted back by his grip on her hair and her mouth taken, opened, and molded by the pressure of his. His tongue probed, and numbly she accepted it, welcomed it with hesitant touches of her own tongue.

He released her and sat back down. Unmoving, Andie stared fixedly at the table. In the silence she could hear the clock ticking, hear the hum of the refrigerator, the muted crash as the automatic ice maker dumped fresh cubes into the ice bin. It was ironic, but she, who had seldom been at a loss as to how to handle a man or what to say to turn any situation to her advantage, was at a total loss. She had no idea what to say, and she doubted this man had ever been handled in his entire life. She sat in helpless silence and refused to look at him.

'I guess you were wrong about the "nothing" part,' he said, his tone suddenly grim.

27

Once she would have been ecstatic at that grudging admission of some sort of feelings for her, but all she could think was, *Why now?* Why had he shown up now, when she finally had her decisions made and her goals set. Neither the decisions nor the goals in any way included having a man in her life, especially this man, and in fact she didn't know if anything like that was being offered. He had simply made a statement, in more ways than one. There was no place in his life for a woman, at least not on a permanent basis, and if she ever did find a time and space for a relationship again, if she lived through what she'd decided to do, she wouldn't settle for anything less than permanency.

She'd gone without a man for months now, and she liked the solitude, the sense of self she was gradually regaining. She wasn't anyone's girlfriend, or arm candy, or companion; she belonged only to herself. The time when she would have unhesitatingly gone with Simon – she had to get used to that name – was past. Between them now was death and reawakening, and the knowledge that while she was still the same basic person she had been before, her outlook had changed. The happiness and security she wanted was within herself, not something he or anyone else could give her.

Suddenly she realized that he'd been there when she died, the knowledge jolting her into abruptly snapping her head up to stare at him. She remembered seeing him, his normally impassive expression for once unguarded, and stark with ... what? Something she couldn't grasp. He'd said something, but the memory of what he'd said was lost in the much larger memory of that pure, white light, and wasn't important anyway. What was important was that he knew what had happened to her. He knew she'd died. He'd taken her things and left her there – so why had he come back? After what he'd seen, why would he have even *considered* the possibility that she might have survived?

'I died,' she said flatly.

His eyebrows lifted just a little, as if he were mildly surprised by the sudden change of subject. 'I know.'

'Then what made you check on me? Most dead people get buried, and that's that. You should never have known I'm still alive.'

'I had my reasons.'

Reasons he wasn't going to tell her, that was clear enough. Agitated, she pushed both hands into her hair, scooping it back from her face and tugging, as if the pressure on her scalp would pull her thoughts into order. The slight narrowing of his eyes told her he wanted her to drop the subject, just let it go, but she couldn't.

'You knew I was dead. No mistake. You don't make mistakes like that. So aren't you even a little bit curious about how I'm sitting here right now? I know I'm a *lot* curious about why *you're*

297

here, if it isn't to kill me, because I'm not buying that I was suddenly important to you. Once was enough, remember?'

'I don't do relationships,' he replied, his tone completely unruffled. 'In that context, once was enough. That doesn't mean I wasn't attracted. I stayed hard for four hours, remember?'

Oh, yes, she remembered, every detail and every sensation, so intense and detailed that it was like being back in the moment. She felt her face getting warm. 'That was just sex. It has nothing to do with what I'm talking about.'

'Usually not,' he agreed, giving her another of those little almost-smiles that, on anyone else, would have been a full-out laugh.

Her face got even hotter. Exasperated because she was trying to find out something and he was distracting her with sex, she slapped her hand down on the table, the sound like a small shot. 'Stay on subject. *Why did you look for me again?* What tipped you off?'

'I did an Internet check of the newspapers to see if you'd been identified. Instead, I found out you'd survived.'

'What difference did it make, whether I'd been identified or not?'

'It was for my own curiosity.'

That was definitely an unrewarding answer, if she'd been expecting anything heartwarming. She should always, always remember that he didn't operate on the same level as most other humans. 'But you didn't tell Rafael.'

'Why would I? You survived, and he was permanently in the dark, so I left it that way.'

'Why did you bother tracking me? You paid the hospital bill, that was more than enough for you to do. Why not go your merry way after that and let me get on with my life?' She shot the question at him, determined to get an answer if she had to stake it out of him, though she bet that would be something to see if she attempted it.

'I did an occasional check to make sure you were all right. If you hadn't seen me tonight, I wouldn't be sitting here now, but you did and I had to let you know that you don't have any reason to run.'

'What difference did it make to you whether or not I'm all right? I'm well, I have – had –a job, I have money. You could have checked once, and let it go.' *She* should let it go, instead of gnawing at the subject, but she couldn't. On the surface his answers were satisfactory, but she had an uneasy feeling there was more behind what he'd been doing. He wasn't just anyone; he was a man who answered only to himself, who lived outside the law and wasn't subject to the usual human emotions. Maybe the reason he'd kept a check on her was for the exact reason he'd said, but maybe there was another reason, one she should fear.

He didn't answer immediately; instead he watched her with unnerving silence, his gaze hooded. Then he caught her gaze with his and she almost jumped, so unnerved was she by the intensity in his eyes. 'I watched you die,' he said softly. 'There was nothing I could do to save you, no way I could help. You were so far gone I couldn't even tell you I was sorry, that I hadn't meant for any of that to happen. But I saw your face, saw your expression when you looked past me and saw ... something else, something that had to be the most beautiful thing you'd ever seen. You whispered "angel," then you died.'

'I remember your face,' she murmured. 'And the light behind you.'

'I sat with you for a while. I touched your cheek. You had no pulse, no breath, and your skin was already going cold. I called 911, and I waited until I could hear the sirens before I left. We aren't talking about a few minutes, Drea–'

'Andie,' she murmured. 'I'm not her anymore.'

'You'd been gone for at least half an hour, and you weren't submerged in an icy lake to slow all your systems and funnel oxygen to your brain. There was no way the medics could have revived you, and in fact they didn't. You started breathing on your own, *almost a fucking hour after you died*,' he said grimly. 'You don't have any brain damage. *Any*. Not even minimal. So now I have to believe in miracles, because you're a living, breathing, walking, talking miracle, and that means there's something else out there after all of this, isn't there?'

A luminous smile spread across her face. 'Yes,' she said simply.

'Then get used to it, sweetheart, because the miracle has a permanent bodyguard.'

She continued to sit at the kitchen table after he'd left. They had talked some more, and when he thought he had completely convinced her that she had nothing to fear from him ever again, he'd left. She had actually reached that conclusion

300

way before he had, but he was naturally wary and untrusting.

So many different thoughts were roiling through her brain that she could barely sort them. Her very first thought was one of pure relief: Rafael thought she was dead. She didn't have to worry about him at all, ever again. He hadn't sent Simon after her; he wasn't still trying to have her killed. She was free.

Free! For the first time in her adult life, maybe in her entire life, she was truly free. She had thought she was free when she left Rafael, but now she knew the difference. Being free was about more than just eating what you wanted, or not having to play dumb anymore.

She was free to be happy.

She didn't think she'd ever been happy, not even as a child. Certainly she'd never been care-free. As a child she had enough food in her stomach and clothes to keep her warm, usually, but she had always climbed out of the school bus and reluctantly trudged up the driveway to wherever her family was currently living, because she never knew what awaited her there. Were her parents quarreling, too drunk to care if their kids heard them call each other whore and bastard? Would supper be anything more than what she could scrounge for herself? Would her dad lurch into her on his way to the bathroom and shove her down for being in his way?

And later, she'd had other worries. Would her mom's boyfriend of the moment try to shove his hand between her legs when her mom's back was turned? She'd tried, just once, telling her mother about it, only to be told that she was just like her fucking father and to stop lying. After that, she'd become an expert at avoiding her own home whenever any of the boyfriends were there, and to climb out her bedroom window in a flash if any of them showed up after she was already home. By the time she was twelve she was a master at evasion, at hiding, at getting away.

She'd gotten away, all right, but she'd never been free – until now.

The future stretched before her, not a future without worry or troubles, but a future undogged by Rafael and the fear that he'd found her. At first all she could focus on was the sense of freedom, the bone-deep relief that she wouldn't have to spend the rest of her life looking over her shoulder or offering herself up as bait to set a trap for Rafael.

By the time she showered and dragged her weary body to bed it was after three, but she couldn't shut her mind off and go to sleep. Too much had happened in such a short length of time; she'd gone from the sheer terror and exhaustion of her struggle with Simon to bewilderment to lust to relief to joy bouncing from point to point without enough time at any one reaction to even begin to absorb what each one meant to her life from now on.

She lay awake in the darkness, staring at the ceiling and reviewing everything that had happened from the time Simon first grabbed her. Other than her relief at being free of Rafael, Simon was uppermost on her mind.

He put her in a quandary, representing the

most potent temptation that she could face. She would never be indifferent to him. If he crooked his finger at her and said 'Come with me,' she had no confidence that she wouldn't do exactly that – somehow she'd have to find the strength to resist him. He was a paid killer; hooking up with him wouldn't, by any definition, be keeping to the straight and narrow. The hooking up wasn't the problem, though she couldn't even *think* of sex now with anything other than caution, because she'd screwed up so bad in that department before. He was the problem. Who and what he was, everything about him, was the problem.

She had the sudden thought that she should turn him over to the cops, and dread immediately knotted her stomach. She didn't know if she could do that to him, even though it was the right thing to do. Then she realized that, not only did she not know any of the specifics and therefore couldn't tell the cops anything that would be of use, what little she did know had taken place outside the country. She didn't even know what country or countries he'd been in, though she supposed the authorities could find out just by looking at his passport, assuming he didn't have more than one passport, which she was fairly certain he did. After all, he made a living slipping undetected in and out of countries.

He'd bulletproofed himself, she realized, at least as far as law enforcement in this country went. He was safe from arrest because there was no known crime that could be laid at his feet. Even if she could provide specifics, the cops would likely find no evidence that he'd been out of the country at that particular time.

Turning him in would accomplish exactly nothing. Tears of relief stung her eyes when she realized that. She didn't want to turn him in; she didn't want him to spend the rest of his life in prison. Maybe she should, but she wasn't a saint, and she'd have to be to so totally ignore her own heart.

Further muddying the waters for her was the fact that, although murder was supposed to be the ultimate no-no, altogether he seemed like a far more decent human being than any of the scum her mother had dated. On the scale of badness, which weighed the heaviest, murder or abuse?

The law said murder. But, damn it, there were some people who didn't deserve to live, and it stood to reason that if a drug lord hired Simon to kill someone, that someone was likely a rival drug lord. How could that be a bad thing? Anything that depleted their numbers had to be good for humanity. Was it bad because Simon made the kills for money rather than out of any notion of bettering the world by lowering its scum-to-human ratio? Motivation couldn't be everything, because there were a lot of people who, with the best of intentions, did a world of harm.

This wasn't something she was going to figure out in an hour, and she was too tired to keep worrying at the details. The good news was that she didn't have to do anything right now. She didn't have to decide anything about Simon, and she didn't have to do anything about Rafael. She was free to–

Her thoughts hit a dead stop. *Rafael.*

So, just because *she* was safe, it was okay to let him continue as always, importing the drugs that wrecked people's lives, the drugs that addicted and killed, and getting monstrously rich in the process? Just because she was safe, she had no obligation to do what she could to put an end to Rafael's operation?

No. The answer in her gut was immediate and emphatic. She had more of an obligation than anyone else on earth, because she had lived off that money, benefited from it, and because she was in the unique position of not only knowing Rafael as well as she did, but she was the one person on earth whose presence would goad him into doing something stupid, something that could give the cops a solid charge to hang on him.

She had to do it. No matter what the risk, this was something she had to do.

Her thoughts circled back around to Simon. He now felt obligated to protect her, which could play hell with any plans she made to poke a figurative stick in Rafael's eye. She didn't want Simon involved in this; it was her debt, her obligation. How he would see the situation, however, was something else entirely.

Would he try to stop her? Beyond a doubt. Even worse, she suspected that he usually succeeded at whatever he set his mind to. She didn't have to stretch her imagination at all to see him holding her captive somewhere, or whisking her out of the country so she couldn't get to Rafael.

Same old song, different verse: she had to get away from him.

Reassured that she wouldn't run, he'd relax his

guard, she thought. Maybe not right away; he was wily and suspicious, and he might watch her from a distance for the next couple of days. So she'd hang around, make a few preparations, lull his suspicions until he felt safe in leaving. She had no way of knowing exactly when that would be, but he was human; he might be tougher and smarter than most, but he was still human, and he still had to eat and sleep and pee just like everyone else. He had to occasionally let his guard down. With luck, even if he was still hanging around, she could be on a plane and gone long before he realized she wasn't there.

He'd be able to track her; so far, he'd seen through every move she made, every step she'd taken to change her appearance and identity. She had no hopes that he'd suddenly turn stupid and she'd suddenly turn into a talented escape artist, but all she needed was a couple of days head start, maybe not even that long, and she would be in New York.

She would contact the FBI. Rafael had to be under almost constant surveillance, and surely the feds were frustrated by their ability to put together a solid case against him. Surely the agent in charge would jump at the opportunity to use her in some way.

Once she was in the FBI's hands, she would be beyond Simon's reach.

28

When he got to his hotel room, Simon booted up his laptop and checked her location, just to be certain he'd convinced her she was safe and she wasn't already on the road running for what she thought was her life. Good – both the Explorer and her cell phone were where they were supposed to be, and stationary, so the odds were she was in bed. He set the program to send a message to his cell phone if the locators began moving, just in case she tried to pull a fast one.

He'd like to be there with her, but when he kissed her he'd felt a reserve on her part that said she wasn't going down that road with him again, at least not yet. He didn't like waiting, but he would – for a while, anyway. He'd raised patience to an art, honing it into a form of weapon as he outwaited both man and nature in the hunt for each target, but now that the veil of secrecy between him and Andie was down, his instincts told him to move fast and hard. She had gotten by in life by making herself pleasing to men, by submerging her own needs, her likes and dislikes, and mirroring back only what the man wanted to see. She needed time, yes, but she also needed to be wanted for herself. She needed to be courted, pursued, the tables turned; she needed a man to curry *her* favor.

Patience was just another form of persistence.

Maybe that meant he was a bastard for not getting out of her life and leaving her alone, after all he'd done and all the pain he'd caused her. So what? He'd rather be a bastard and have her, than be a gentleman and let her get away.

If she hadn't responded to him at all he'd have dealt with the loss and left her alone, but she'd been all but squirming in her chair, and he knew enough about women to know she'd been re-membering how it had been between them. He knew enough about her, gleaned from the afternoon they'd spent together, to know how she looked when she was turned on. She wanted to be indifferent, but she wasn't, any more than he was indifferent to her. He'd wanted to be; he'd wanted to forget her as soon as he walked away from her. For the first time in his life, that hadn't happened. He dealt in reality, not in roses and wishes, and what was between them was real – unexplored, undeveloped, but real.

Reassured that she was staying put, at least for the time being, he got out his first-aid kit and carefully disinfected the bite wounds in his arm, then sprayed the area to numb it. The analgesic was only topical, but it took enough of the edge off the pain that putting in the stitches didn't bother him. He'd had splinters that hurt worse. After he dabbed an antibiotic on top of the stitches, he slapped a couple of adhesive bandages over them, then carefully repacked the small kit, taking note of which supplies needed to be replenished. The first-aid kit went everywhere with him, and had possibly saved his life a couple of times. In the tropics, an open wound, no matter how minor, could fast become life-threatening.

Then, yawning, he popped a couple of ibuprofen before stripping off his clothes. Turning out the light, he sprawled across the bed. His phone would signal the arrival of a message, and wake him, if she decided to make a run for it, but he was fairly certain she wasn't going anywhere tonight. If she had anything in mind, she'd probably try to fake him off by staying put for a few days. She was sneaky, but he was sneakier. He went to sleep knowing that, for now, things were under control.

Andie slept late – big surprise there – and finally stumbled to the kitchen for coffee at half past eleven. She had a headache, maybe from the adrenaline crash, or maybe she just needed a dose of caffeine. She was usually out of bed around eight, giving her time to do her chores or errands before going to work, so she was about three hours past the time she usually had her first cup of coffee.

She took two aspirin, then took her coffee into the living room. Turning on the secondhand television she'd bought, she curled up in the corner of the sofa, at the moment not wanting to do anything more than sip her coffee and wait for the aspirin to start working on her headache. She watched a little of the noon news, enough to learn that more thunderstorms were expected that afternoon, then, despite the coffee, she nodded off again.

Two sharp raps on her front door woke her. Maybe it was the neighbors, she thought sourly, belatedly concerned enough by all the banging around last night to find out if she was all right. She could certainly hear them thumping around, so she knew they should have at least heard when she knocked the chair over. But had anyone checked to see if a burglar had broken in, or anything? If she'd heard the same noises from their side, she'd have at least beat on the wall and yelled to ask if everything was all right.

She paused before unlocking the door, raising a slat of the blinds and looking out. She found herself staring straight at Simon, because he stood square in front of the door. Her breath wooshed out of her lungs at the impact of his physical presence, sort of like looking out and finding a large wolf standing there. His gaze met hers through the glass, and he lifted his brows as if to say, *Well?*

Dismayed, she let the slat drop and stood there for a minute, trying to decide whether or not to open the door. She'd hoped he had already left town. What was he hanging around for? What else was there to say?

'You might as well open the door,' he said through the wood. 'I'm not leaving.'

'So what else is new?' she grumbled, turning the lock and pulling the door open. He came in, a smile ghosting around his mouth. 'What?' she demanded, pushing her sleep-mussed hair out of her face. She hadn't even dragged a brush through it yet, and she didn't care.

'I came to see if you wanted to go out for lunch. I guess not,' he said with a faint undertone of amusement.

Andie yawned and turned back to the sofa, pulling her legs up and tucking her bare feet under the cushions. She was still wearing her pajama bottoms and T-shirt, so, no, she wasn't going out, for lunch or anything else. 'I guess not,' she echoed, frowning at him. 'I haven't had breakfast yet. Thank you for asking. What do you want?'

He did a one-shoulder shrug. 'To take you to lunch. Nothing more.'

Like she believed that for a single minute. 'Yeah, right. You probably don't breathe without an ulterior motive.'

'Staying alive is all.' He lifted his head, sniffing the air. 'Is the coffee fresh?'

'Fairly.' She checked the time. She'd napped longer than she'd thought. 'It's about an hour old, so it should still be good.' She could use more coffee herself, so she got up and went into the kitchen, taking her cup with her. 'How do you take yours?' she called as she opened the cabinet door and reached for another cup, raising her voice so he could hear her in the living room.

'Black,' he said right behind her, and she jumped, almost dropping the cup. He reached out to catch it, his hand closing around hers to steady her grip. Immediately, she pulled out of his grasp and lifted the coffeepot from the warmer, filling both their cups.

'Make some noise when you walk,' she finally said flatly.

'I could whistle.'

'Whatever. Just don't sneak up on me.' She was more unnerved than she wanted him to see, because the moment had reminded her vividly of when he came up behind her on the penthouse balcony and had sex with her right there, not even turning her around to kiss her. At the time, he couldn't have made it plainer that she was nothing but a piece of ass to him, yet she'd let herself be seduced by sheer pleasure, and over the course of the afternoon built it up in her mind until she thought he would actually take her with him. She still felt scalded by the humiliation of his rejection.

She set down the cup and took a slow, steadying breath. 'I think you should leave,' she said baldly. 'I need you to leave.'

'Because I kissed you last night?' His gaze was shrewd as he studied her.

'Because you are who you are and I am who I am. I know what I was before, but since the wreck I've been alone–' Hell, he knew that; he'd been keeping tabs on her all this time. 'And I think being alone is what's best for me. I don't make good decisions when it comes to men. Sad, but true.'

'I'm not asking you to make any decision. You have to eat, don't you? Let's go to lunch. Or breakfast. We can always go to a pancake restaurant.' His tone was mild and undemanding, and if she hadn't been on her guard she might have been lulled into a false sense of safety. How dangerous could a pancake restaurant be? The problem was, there was no such thing as being safe with this man, at least not from him, and the reason for that lay as much within herself as it did with him.

She shook her head. 'I don't want to go

312

anywhere with you.'

'If you do, I'll answer any question you ask.'

She froze, furious with herself because the offer was too tempting to resist, and he knew it. Intellectually she knew she should stay far, far away from him, but let him dangle the opportunity to find out anything she wanted about him and she was all over it like a hawk on a bunny rabbit. He watched her with amusement glittering in his eyes and quirking the corners of his mouth, and he was so damned attractive like that, his guard down and his normally blank expression banished, that she actually quivered from the strength of his pull. Still, she tried to hold the line. 'I don't want to know anything about you.'

'Sure you do, like how I got the tattoo on my ass.'

'You don't have a tattoo on your ass!' she snapped, glaring at him. She'd seen his ass, and as fine as it was she hadn't been struck blind; she'd have noticed a tattoo.

He began unbuckling his belt.

'Don't do that!' she said, alarmed. 'You don't have to–'

His lean fingers grasped the tab of his zipper, pulled it down.

Andie lost the thread of what she was saying.

He turned around, hooked his thumbs in the waistband of his jeans, and worked them down. His shirttail drooped over the round, muscled curves; he reached behind himself to pull up his shirt and there it was, high on the right cheek, some sort of abstract design that looked like a weird, curly maze. Her fingers twitched from a

313

sudden, intense need to reach out and touch him, not because of the tattoo but because she wanted to feel the shape and coolness of his ass under her hands again.

She clenched her hands into fists and tried to sound unperturbed. 'Strange design. What does it mean?'

He pulled up his pants and tucked his shirttail inside, turning back to face her as he zipped and buckled, his gaze amused. 'I'll tell you over food.'

'Damn it,' she snarled, whirling on her heel, and she went to the bedroom to get ready.

She was out in ten minutes, having done nothing more than brush her teeth and hair and exchange her pajamas for jeans and a pullover shirt with only one button left open at her throat because she didn't do low-cut anything now, the scar on her chest a constant reminder that things were different. She didn't bother with even minimum makeup, because she wasn't trying to impress him or anyone else. Shoving her feet into a pair of flip-flops, she looked down at her unpainted toenails and gave a little snort. Her appearance was the polar opposite from the way she'd looked when Rafael gave her to him, but if he didn't like it, then he could kiss her ass and leave.

He smiled when he saw her; actually honest-to-God smiled. 'You're so damn pretty,' he said.

The compliment was so unexpected, so at odds with what she'd just been thinking, that she skidded to a stop, her mouth falling open in shock. 'I, uh, thank you. But … *are you blind?*'

'No, I'm not,' he answered as seriously as if the

question hadn't been rhetorical. He reached out and touched her hair. 'I kind of miss the curls, but I like the color. You're not as flashy now, not as brittle. That's good. Your mouth still ... never mind.'

'Never mind, what?' He was playing her like a hooked fish. She knew it, but that didn't make any difference. What about her mouth? She shouldn't ask because the answer had to be sexual and she didn't want to go there, but ... *what about her mouth?*

'I'll tell you over food,' he said.

It wasn't until they were sitting in a booth in one of the area IHOPs, menus in hand and coffee steaming in front of them, that she realized he'd said he would answer any question, but not that he'd answer honestly. Annoyed with herself for not thinking of that catch earlier, she slapped the menu down on the table and gave him a frustrated glare. 'Answering any question is one thing, but will you tell the truth?'

'Of course,' he said easily, so easily that she knew she'd been had.

'You're lying.'

He put his own menu down. 'Andie, think about it. What do I have to hide from you? Or you from me?'

'How would I know? If I knew everything about you, then I wouldn't need to ask any questions, now would I?'

'Good point.'

He smiled at her. She wished he would stop doing that. When he smiled, she forgot he was a hired killer, forgot that ice water ran in his veins, and that by walking away from her he'd hurt her more than any man ever did. But thinking about him walking away also made her think about the tattoo on his ass, and how she could possibly have missed it.

'So, what does the design of your tattoo mean?'

'I don't know. It's a temporary kid's tattoo. I put it on this morning.'

She was in the middle of taking a sip of coffee and she choked, clapping her hand over her mouth and nose and trying not to spray coffee all over the table. As soon as she managed to swallow, she began laughing at how adroitly he'd baited her into doing what he wanted. 'That's cheating, and I fell for it. I *knew* you didn't have a tattoo.'

The waitress sailed up, pad and pen ready. 'You guys decide what you want?'

Andie ordered scrambled eggs, bacon, and toast, and Simon went for the same thing except with added hash browns. As soon as they were alone again, she set her cup down so she wouldn't embarrass herself by snorting coffee if he had any other surprises tucked up his sleeve, or in his pants.

There were a lot of questions she wanted to ask him, but some she didn't dare because she wasn't certain she wanted to hear the answers. Now that she thought about it, being given the power to ask any question she wanted, and get an answer, was a bit daunting. It would be daunting with anyone, but with this man she felt as if she were poking a tiger with a stick, which, even with the tiger's permission, could be a dangerous activity.

316

She started with the easy stuff, for her own sake. 'How old are you?'

His brows lifted a little in surprise at her choice of question.

'Thirty-five.'

'Your birthday?'

'November first.'

She fell silent. She wanted to know his real last name, but maybe that was something she was better off leaving alone. His secrets were darker than hers, the boundaries that defined him more violent and starkly drawn.

'That's it?' he asked, when no further questions came at him. 'You wanted to know how old I am and when I was born?'

'No, that isn't all. This is harder than I expected.'

'Do you want to know how old I was the first time I killed someone?'

'No.' She hastily looked around to see if anyone had overheard him, but his voice was too low to carry and no one was giving them horrified looks.

'Seventeen,' he continued relentlessly. 'I discovered I have a natural talent for wet work. I gave it up last year, though, after sitting in a hospital chapel and crying because I had just stood outside your hospital room and listened to you talking to your nurse, and I knew you were not only alive but somehow whole. I haven't taken a job since.'

29

Damn him, damn him, damn him.

Andie cursed him for the next two days, not only because she didn't see him at all even though somehow she knew he was still there, keeping watch, but because, sitting in that booth at the IHOP and listening to him expose his soul, she'd fallen in love with him. Of all the ill-advised things she'd done in her life, falling in love with a hit man, even a retired one, had to top the scale. If she had ever needed verification that she should stay far, far away from any romantic relationship because she was incapable of making a good decision when it came to picking out a man, there it was, proof positive.

She hadn't cried, though she'd wanted to. He'd made his heartbreaking confession so calmly, in such a matter-of-fact tone, that he'd enabled her to keep her composure, and after a while she'd been able to ask more questions, such as where he was from (he was born on an army base in Germany) and if he had any family (he was an only child, and both his parents were dead). Even if he'd had any close family, she thought, he would still have chosen to be alone. She'd sailed alone herself, so she knew what it was to confide in no one, to trust no one. She still didn't trust, at least not very much. She had made no close friends since settling here in KC., which was really pitiful, but on this level she completely understood him.

He was atypical in a lot of ways. He didn't care for professional sports of any kind, which also made sense; team sports wouldn't appeal to a loner. He didn't have a favorite color and he didn't like pie. Maybe he saw preferences as weaknesses that could be used against him and he'd deliberately disassociated himself from many of the likes and dislikes that people used to define themselves and their boundaries; maybe he had always had that distance between himself and everyone else.

Yet he had reached out to her, more than once. On the afternoon they'd shared, he'd seen how frightened she was, and he'd reassured her with tenderness, seduced her with pleasure. He'd *made love* to her; though at the time neither of them had seen it that way. When she'd had the accident, he had stayed with her as she died, watched over her until someone else could come.

She never dreamed about the accident, seldom visited her vague memories of dying. First came that incredible light, somehow both pure and vivid, and then she'd been in that wonderful place. Her recall of both was detailed down to scents and textures, but what came between those two happenings was sketchy and out of focus. Maybe it was because she was sitting across from him, staring at his face and making memories, that abruptly she saw the scene as clearly as if it were taking place in front of her eyes. In her mind she heard him whisper '*God sweetheart,*' and saw him touch her hair. She watched him wait with her. Looking directly at her own body was nearly impossible, as if there were some sort of shield around her, but she could see him oh so clearly. She could see the anguish he struggled to control, the pain he could barely acknowledge.

Like a bolt once more going through her chest, she knew why he'd looked up the newspaper accounts of her accident. He had wanted to find out where she was buried, so he could put flowers on her grave.

'Andie.' He reached across the table and caught her hand, cradling it in his rough palm. 'Where are you?'

Inside she was shattered, but she had pulled herself back to the present, away from memories she didn't want to have, but bringing with her another piece of understanding of the man sitting across from her, the man who was trying to be less remote, who was willingly exposing himself by answering any question she asked.

She couldn't bring herself to ask any other questions, and in silence they finished what remained of their meal. He watched her, his expression once again still and blank, though she couldn't say he'd been wildly expressive before. He'd let himself show a little amusement, and occasionally his gaze would settle on her mouth and pure heat would burn in his eyes, but other than that nothing of what he was thinking or feeling had come through.

He'd taken her home, and gone up on the porch with her, but stood at a slight distance that somehow told her he didn't intend to come in even if she invited him, instead he walked to the other side of the duplex, rapped sharply on the front door. What was he doing? Her brows knit in puzzlement as she watched him. Fifteen seconds later, he knocked again. No one came to the door.

'What are you doing?'

'Making sure no one's home. The car's gone, but one of them could be at home.' With that sentence he confirmed to her that he'd watched the house enough to know a couple lived in the other side of the duplex, but not enough to know that both of them worked second shift, like her, and were usually gone by one o'clock.

'Why? What does it matter?'

'People are nosy. They listen when they shouldn't.'

'So?'

'So this isn't any of their business.'

Curious, completely in the dark, she watched as he pulled out his wallet and extracted a card. 'In case you have trouble accessing the money,' he said, extending the card to her.

It was her old driver's license.

She stared at the license, at the picture on it, and her fingers trembled as she reached out to take it. She had thought Drea was gone, dead even if she wasn't buried, but there she was again: the mass of long blond curls, full makeup job, slightly vacant expression. She wasn't that person now. Most people would have to examine the photo very carefully to find the resemblance between Drea's face and her own.

'I'm giving the money to St. Jude's,' she said

numbly. 'I have a bank account here. I was going to do an electronic transfer to this account, then go to the bank and get a cashier's check made out to St. Jude's. The IP number would be different on the transfer, but I have the password and...' Her voice trailed off. She was chattering, not paying attention to what she was saying. He'd know about IP numbers and electronic transfers though he probably did his banking offshore. She probably wouldn't have any trouble making the transfer, though she'd thought about calling Mrs. Pearson beforehand and alerting her. By returning her old driver's license to her, though, Simon had guaranteed she wouldn't have any trouble doing whatever she wanted with the money even if Mrs. Pearson no longer worked at the bank.

'Thank you,' she whispered, clutching the license even though she never wanted to see that photograph again. 'Why did you keep it?'

He didn't answer the question, because evidently her carte blanche in that area had ended when they left the restaurant. Instead he said, 'I have a plane to catch,' and left her there on the porch. She watched him drive away, then went inside and sat down on the couch, thinking about the last two hours.

He had a plane to catch, her ass. She didn't believe him for a minute.

She hadn't seen him since, but she had learned that that didn't mean anything. He was there, somewhere, still keeping check. He didn't trust her not to run, even though he'd gone out of his way to reassure her she had nothing to fear.

On that score, at least, Andie did believe him.

She was safe. She was free to live her life in the open, free to stop looking over her shoulder, free to do whatever she wanted even though she would be smart to avoid New York City until Rafael was either dead or in jail. The odds of seeing any one particular person in a city that size had to be tiny, but screwier things had happened; she was living proof of that.

Evidently she wasn't smart, because going back to New York was exactly what she intended to do. First, though, she had to slip away from her self-appointed bodyguard.

The one thing she could do that would most reassure him she was staying put would be to go back to Glenn's and ask for her job back, which she was certain Glenn would be glad to give her. Unfortunately, that was the one thing she couldn't do, because she had every intention of leaving within the next few days and she didn't want to mislead Glenn that way.

Instead she concentrated on taking care of business. She did call Mrs. Pearson, who expressed heartfelt relief. She'd been worried when no action had been taken on the account since she'd last seen Andie, and her e-mails had gone unanswered; she was afraid something had happened. Something *had* happened, but Andie didn't go into it. Instead she reassured Mrs. Pearson that everything was fine. They chatted for a while, and at one point Andie thought Mrs. Pearson had mentioned that she had a grand-daughter who would be born in a few months. When she said, 'Congratulations on that grand-daughter,' though, Mrs. Pearson gasped.

'How did you know there's a baby on the way?'

'You told me,' said Andie, a little uncertainly. 'Didn't you?'

'No, I haven't mentioned it. We won't find out if it's a boy or girl until next month.'

'Oh. I would have sworn–' She broke off, and hastily covered her slip, because the explanation wasn't something she wanted to go into. 'No, I remember now who mentioned having a granddaughter. I'm sorry, I'm a little scatterbrained this morning. I must need more coffee.'

After she got off the phone she made the electronic transfer, then periodically checked her account until the transaction showed up. Once the certified check was on its way, by FedEx, to the children's hospital, she felt as if an immense weight had been lifted from her shoulders. That money had been a pain in the ass from the moment she took it, which she supposed was only fitting.

Mingled with relief, though, was a sense of regret. Too bad she couldn't have kept it, because a part of her really would have liked being rich, even with stolen money – *dirty* stolen money. Maybe she'd get extra points for getting rid of it, because that so went against the grain. Being virtuous was as big a pain in the ass as having the money had been.

But the money was gone now, taken care of, and she could move onto the next item on her list. She didn't have a lot of cash, and she needed some, so it was time to use the jewelry Rafael had given her.

She got the phone book and started looking for

a diamond broker. She could hock the jewelry but she would realize only a fraction of its worth, and the pawn shop would make a killing because she wasn't interested in redeeming any of the pieces. She had to sell the jewelry; and she didn't want to take the time to auction it off on eBay.

She'd settled on a course of action and she felt driven to complete it, to get to New York and set the plan into motion. It was time.

A week later, with money in her bank account – though not as much money as she'd hoped – and a newly issued bank credit card, she booked a flight to New York for the following day and set about putting the duplex in order, in case she never made it back.

She cleaned out the refrigerator, getting rid of all the perishable food in the house. If she didn't come back, she didn't want the landlord, in a month or so, opening the door to the overpowering stench of rotted food. She swept and mopped and neatened, and tried not to cry. The shabby secondhand furniture she'd bought to furnish the duplex wasn't much to look at, and she didn't own the place anyway, but the duplex was still her first real home. It was *hers;* she'd picked out everything in it, from the cheap cookware to the chenille bedspread. She'd bought the lamp in the living room at a yard sale, for five bucks, and the soft throw draped across the arm of the couch for a dollar at yet another yard sale. The scent of the air freshener was the scent *she* preferred, the soap was the soap *she* liked.

She packed all her clothes. She didn't have much; every stitch she owned fit into two suitcases, and that included what makeup she'd bought, which wasn't much. She had delighted in not wearing much makeup, in not having to care if anyone saw her less than perfectly dolled up and tricked out. The last remnants of permed curl had long since grown out of her hair, which she had let remain dark. She didn't want to be blond again; Drea was blond; Andie had no-nonsense brown hair.

When the apartment was clean and her suit-cases packed, she had two more errands to run. The first was to a large mall, where a wig shop was located. She would have to be Drea again, to get Rafael's attention, but she wanted to be able to whip off a wig and quickly become someone he might walk past without recognizing.

There weren't any wigs in the shop that matched the way she'd worn her hair then. She chose one that was close enough: a little longer, a little straighter, and the shade was more platinum than golden, but it would do.

Her final errand was more subterfuge, but of a different kind. Just in case Simon was still watching her, she went to the grocery store where she usually shopped, and stocked up on some nonperishable stuff. Buying food would reassure him that she intended to stay where she was. Also, if she actually got to return to the duplex, having food there would be a good thing.

The next morning, she drove to the airport, parked the Explorer in the long-term parking lot, and began her return to New York. Her seat, booked at the last minute as it had been, was a middle seat in the very last row. She sat crammed between a largish gentleman and his equally largish wife, who had evidently chosen their seats hoping no one would get the seat between them and they'd be able to spread out more comfortably. They were out of luck, and so was she.

After spending a little over three hours waiting for a connecting flight, it was mid-afternoon by the time she finally landed at La Guardia. She collected her luggage, rolled the cases out to the ground transportation area, and stood at the curb waiting for the hotel shuttle to arrive. The spring day was cold, about fifty degrees, and with the breeze the windchill was probably forty-five.

When the shuttle arrived, four more people got on it with her, but none of them seemed to be traveling together, so they all rode in silence toward the skyscrapers of Manhattan.

She loved the city, Andie thought as she watched the skyline getting closer. She loved the people and the busy pace, the sights and sounds and smells. Kansas City wasn't a small town, by any means, but it wasn't anywhere near the scale of New York. Maybe, if things worked out, she could move back here.

Or maybe not. She wouldn't be able to get a high-paying job, and Manhattan was expensive. The money she had from the sale of the jewelry wouldn't last long here. She had to be practical, because she had no particular skills or job training, and wanting more than what she could provide for herself was what had led her to men like Rafael in the first place. From now on, she would content herself with what *she* could afford.

She checked into the Holiday Inn, and when

she was in her small, rather dingy room she hauled out the gargantuan phone book and began looking for a number. 'United States Government,' she murmured, then found the group of listings and began running her finger down the column. When she got to the number she wanted, she kept her finger on it while, with her other hand, she turned on her cell phone and waited for it to find service. When it did, she punched in the number.

There she was. He'd found her. She'd finally turned on her cell phone.

Simon's fingers flew over the keyboard of his laptop, typing in commands. He had relocated to San Francisco, and remained there longer than he'd ever been in any one place. Now that he wasn't active in the business anymore, he had no need to keep moving around. He hadn't exactly put down roots, but he'd modified his habits somewhat.

He had left Kansas City when he'd told Andie he was leaving. He didn't want to crowd her; he'd given her a lot to think about, and she had some adjustments to make. He had kept track of her and been reassured when her movements seemed to be mostly routine, though it bothered him that she hadn't gone back to Glenn's. The fact that she hadn't put him on alert, and he'd kept an unusually close watch on her movements.

His cell phone had buzzed before dawn, though he wasn't immediately alarmed. Kansas City was in a different time zone, so it was well after dawn there. But he got up and tracked the Explorer, and when its movement stopped at the airport he'd broken out in a cold sweat. She was getting on a damn plane, and he was a thousand miles away, unable to do a fucking thing about it.

He hadn't hacked into any system in months, hadn't needed to. He didn't know which airline she'd used, which hampered him, but he began systematically searching them all, just in case she either hadn't taken her cell phone with her or didn't bother turning it on until she needed to use it.

When the locator in the phone was powered up, he immediately typed in the commands that would tell him exactly where she was, and when the map popped up on the screen he felt icy sweat pop out on his skin.

She was in New York.

30

The next morning, Andie worked her way through all the barricades and security checks at Federal Plaza. She was given a visitor's ID and an escort, shown where to wait, and eventually she went into a small office. Special Agent Rick Cotton got to his feet when she entered, shaking the hand she held out. He had a nice firm handshake, not too tight and not wimpy, but at first glance she didn't see what was so special about him.

He was middle-aged and graying, though still trim, and he had a calm, mild expression. The impression she got from the way others acted around him was that he was liked, but there was no sizzle of electricity that said he was a mover and shaker. She knew sizzle, because she'd been in very close contact with it one summer afternoon last year. The force of Simon's personality dominated any room he was in, while Rick Cotton would barely be noticed.

'Please have a seat, Ms. Pearson,' Agent Cotton said, indicating a battered-looking straight-backed chair. 'I believe your message said you have some information about someone named Rafael Salinas?'

If those cards got any closer to his chest, Andie thought, he wouldn't be able to see them himself. He wanted her to show her hand first, which was fine with her.

'My name isn't Pearson,' Andie said. 'It's Andrea Butts. I used to go by the name Drea Rousseau, and I lived with Rafael Salinas for two years.'

She saw the shock in his face before he could school his expression. He blinked, staring at her. 'I had long, blond, curly hair then,' she added helpfully.

He said, 'Just a moment,' and picked up his phone and dialed an extension. He said, 'Drea Rousseau is sitting in my office,' and replaced the handset.

He sat silently, and so did she. She honestly had no idea if she would be of any use to the FBI, or they to her, but they were the logical place to start. Offering herself as bait would work only if someone was watching the trap, otherwise the bait was just a meal. She might not be able to do anything about Rafael; if she couldn't, then at least she had tried.

A sandy-haired man opened the door and came in. 'Ms. Rousseau,' he said, 'I'm Special Agent Brian Hulsey; I'm in charge of the Salinas investigation now. Would you step into my office, please?'

Andie paused, her head cocked a little to the side as she studied him. He hadn't knocked before entering Agent Cotton's office, and she had caught the slight emphasis he'd placed on the word 'now,' which had been completely unnecessary unless he was making a point to the agent who had been in charge of the investigation before. Office politics, she guessed, with ego and a power display thrown in. Agent Cotton, on the other hand, looked mild and unperturbed. No ego here, and he wasn't interested in power.

'No,' she said, drawing the word out a little as she reached a decision. 'I'll talk with Special Agent Cotton.'

Special Agent Hulsey said, 'You misunderstand. Agent Cotton is no longer in charge of–'

'I didn't misunderstand anything,' she replied, her tone going cool. 'English is my first language, so I know a lot of the words.' English was also her only language, but he didn't need to know that.

His face turned red. 'I apologize. I didn't intend to imply–'

'That I'm stupid? That's okay. A lot of men make that mistake.' She smiled at him, a sweet smile that, if he'd been paying close attention, would have made his blood curdle. 'Rafael Salinas was one of them.'

'I assure you, Ms. Rousseau–'

'Butts,' she said, putting hard edges on all the consonants. 'My real name is Andrea Butts. I thought you knew that.'

'Of course I–'

She hadn't let him complete a single sentence after he'd introduced himself when he came in, so she saw no reason to start now. 'Special Agent Cotton,' she said firmly, 'or no one. Your choice.'

There it was, dumped in his lap. He either delegated his role in the investigation to Special Agent Cotton, or he would be the one responsible for losing the contact that could possibly bring down Rafael Salinas once and for all. He would see the first choice as an almost intolerable affront to his authority – he was the type – but the second choice could be a career-killer.

'I'll get it cleared with the assistant director,' he muttered resentfully, walking out of the office and leaving the door open.

Andie got up and closed the door with a firm thud.

'I didn't like him,' she confided as she resumed her seat.

Special Agent Cotton allowed himself a little smile, but all he said was, 'He's a good agent.'

'I assumed so, or he wouldn't be stationed in New York, but I can also assume the same thing about you.' Agents vied to be posted in the larger cities, with D.C. and New York at the top of the heap, where the action was and where everything was high visibility.

'I work with some very sharp people. It's easy to look good when all the people around you are on their toes.'

What Andie got from that was that he was willing to spread the credit around, while Hulsey wasn't. She was satisfied with her decision in sticking with Special Agent Cotton.

'If you don't mind, I'd like to call in an agent who worked with me when I was assigned to the Salinas case,' he said, lifting the phone again. 'His name is Xavier Jackson, and he's a genius at what he does. It was his bad luck to be partnered with me, but we still talk sometimes even though we aren't on that case now.'

She gathered they'd been reassigned because they hadn't produced any results, though she'd bet the farm that Hulsey hadn't done any better than they had. No wonder Hulsey had been adamant that she talk with him rather than

Cotton; she would have been a big feather in his cap, and maybe just what he needed for the case to reach the tipping point and actually produce some prosecutable evidence against Rafael.

She and Cotton chatted casually while waiting for Genius Jackson. Some fifteen minutes later there was a polite rap on the door; and a wait until Cotton raised his voice and said, 'Come in.'

Xavier Jackson was young, maybe her age, and lean and dark and handsome, his features faintly exotic, his skin olive-tinted. He was a more dapper dresser than most of the FBI employees she'd seen in the building; though he wore the de rigueur sober suit and white dress shirt, his tie was a deep, rich red with a tiny design that, when she looked closer, turned out to be highly stylized horses in an even deeper red. Instead of the flat rectangular fold of white handkerchief, his breast pocket sported a few subtle peaks in the same rich red. Altogether he was subtly more flashy, his movements faster, his accent was as undefinable as that of a television news anchor. The expression in his eyes was decidedly sharklike, but unlike Hulsey, his attitude toward Agent Cotton was that of respect.

Neither of them was going to die anytime soon. She got that, plucked the sudden conviction out of the air as if it were a ripe apple dangling in front of her, but saw no need to tell them. Jackson thought he was bulletproof, and Cotton was looking forward to retirement and having more time to spend with his wife, doing things he enjoyed. No death worries darkened their minds, so she didn't introduce the subject.

Jackson gave her an incredulous look. 'Are you really Drea Rousseau?'

She laughed, and he immediately said, 'Oh, yeah, I recognize that laugh.' Curiosity burned in his eyes. 'I thought you might be dead. You just disappeared.'

'On purpose,' she assured him. 'Running for my life.'

'Salinas wants you dead?'

'He did. After I left town, though, I was in a car accident and the news release mistakenly said I'd died in the accident, which was actually a lifesaver because Rafael called off his hounds.' There had been only one hound, and he'd been the one to report to Rafael that she was dead, which was true, but her glib skirting of the truth was much more believable than what had actually happened.

'So he thinks you're dead,' said Cotton. 'You're safe. Why come back to the city, back to his territory?'

'Because if I know anything about him that would help you build a case against him, help put him in prison, then it would be wrong for me to play it safe while he goes on bringing drugs into the country every week. Rafael's smart,' she said. 'You might never be able to get enough evidence against him, unless you somehow catch a break. I might be that break. I don't know that I am, but I'm willing to give it a shot.'

'Do you know who his accountant is? The real one, not the one who does the books for the public stuff?'

She shook her head, knowing the accountant, and his, or her, location, would have been the

335

linchpin to Rafael's entire operation. 'I never heard a name mentioned. He was careless about a few things – like his bank password – but not about that. I don't think any of his men know, either. They talked in front of me, but they never mentioned anything about books, or an accountant.'

'Did he ever disappear, and not take any of his men with him?' That was Jackson chiming in.

'Not that I know of, though he could have left with his usual guard and ditched them somewhere afterward. But like I said, I never heard them talking about anything like that. Rafael's paranoid about going out by himself. He thinks the streets are knee-deep in rivals waiting to knock him off. He wants to be surrounded by other bodies, at all times.'

They both peppered her with questions, about any detail they could think of. They talked for hours, with Andie pitching in any detail she could think of but she began to despair because nothing seemed to be enough to hang on him. She'd been afraid of that, afraid she might have to resort to more desperate measures.

'There's one option I have to mention,' she finally said, when even the two agents seemed discouraged because their golden opportunity to nail Salinas was turning out to be a dud. 'It isn't a federal charge, but the idea is to get Rafael out of business and off the streets, right? If he sees me, he'll go nuts. I'm supposed to be dead. When I left, I ... took something that was very important to him.' Yeah, she could honestly say that two million dollars was important to him, but equally important to someone like Rafael was the affront she had landed to his ego. Come to that, his ego might be *more* important. He'd convinced himself that he loved her, and she'd thrown that love in his face. 'If he can, he'll kill me where I stand. So how can we use that against him?'

'It won't work,' Jackson said softly, after Drea Rousseau left – a vastly changed Drea, but it was definitely her. 'Even if we could use a civilian as bait, which the AD would never allow anyway, an attempted murder charge doesn't carry a severe-enough sentence to keep him off the streets for much more than a year or so – and that's if he even did any jail time.'

'I know,' said Cotton. His voice was tired. 'I know. We still can't nail the bastard, even with her help. And God forbid if we set her up as bait and he actually did shoot her down in the street. I couldn't forgive myself if that happened.'

Andie stopped at a diner for lunch, so dis-couraged she could barely swallow the soup she ordered. She had been so certain she could come back to New York and, in short order, somehow have Rafael either in federal custody or dead. She had honestly been thinking 'dead,' as if there would be some big dramatic shoot-out, which would certainly juice up a slow news day; and Rafael would be killed. Looked at logically, now that she was here, she couldn't say how she had arrived at that scenario. This wasn't like the sud-den impressions she had concerning other people; she'd never had one relating to herself.

337

Her plan, if it could be called a plan, had been big in scope but very sketchy on details. Now that she was here, she felt pretty foolish. She hadn't thought anything out, which was so unlike her she could only shake her head. She wasn't brave, she wasn't intrepid, she wasn't any kind of heroine, but she had conceived of this grand scheme without having any way of carrying it out. What the hell was wrong with her?

Unless she really was meant to die here – unless her death would be the avenue by which Rafael was finally put away for good.

Blindly she stared out the window at the street, with its endless stream of pedestrians. She wasn't afraid of death, but she was afraid of not being good enough to go back to the place where Alban was. She had tried hard to become a more worth-while human being, to work for what she had in life, to stop using her looks and sex to get what she wanted, but only eight months had passed. Eight months, stacked against fifteen years, was bound to be on the light end of the scale. If she died now, had she gotten enough attagirl points to make a difference?

Maybe her death, a final death, was the true test. A greater love hath no man, and all that. If it came down to it and her death was what it took to bring Rafael down, then she would do it. Somehow she'd get the courage to do it.

But oh, she didn't want to leave Simon. Despite their history, what was between them felt new and tremulous, barely explored. And despite *his* history, despite telling herself that he was the bad choice to end all bad choices, she wanted to place

338

her hands along his beard-roughened jaw, look into the dark opal colors of his eyes, and watch tenderness bloom where before there had been only emptiness.

She wanted the time to get to know him, really know him. She wanted more than the superficial knowledge he'd given her during their question-and-answer session at the IHOP. She wanted to tell him silly jokes and make him laugh, she wanted to share meals with him, she wanted to be with him as he changed from a man who sutured his own wounds to someone who could let others help him.

He was so alone. If she died, what would happen to him? Would he stay on the path he'd chosen, or would he return to his old ways? She didn't believe she was so unique that he could never find anyone else he could love, but the question was: Would he? Would he try? Or would he wall himself off even more solidly than he had been before? She knew the answer to that, because she had seen how completely he shut down all the overtures she'd made during their afternoon together, refusing even to tell her his name. He hadn't wanted her to kiss him, either; she remembered how he'd frozen, at first, as if about to push her away. But he hadn't; something in him had craved being held, being kissed, and when he had started kissing her in return she had felt as if she'd never before been kissed so deeply, so hungrily.

If she hadn't seen him at the truck stop, if he hadn't gone to her place to reassure her, if he hadn't kissed her, she would have always thought of him with the pain and regret she hadn't been able to shake, but she wouldn't *long* for him. Thoughts of him wouldn't make her regret doing what she knew she should do.

After finishing her soup, she left the diner and took a bus across town to the Holiday Inn where she was staying. The route went fairly close; she had to walk only a couple of short blocks. She got into the squeaky elevator alone, and rode up to her floor. A housekeeping cart was parked at the end of the hallway, and from the open door she could hear the drone of a vacuum cleaner.

Inserting her key card, she opened the door and froze, holding it open.

'Don't scream.' Simon loomed in front of her, his expression enigmatic.

She swallowed the sound just in time as he pulled her against him and closed the door, putting the chain in place and then turning the deadbolt. 'What are you doing here?' he growled in a very annoyed tone.

'This is my room. I was about to ask you the same question,' Andie said, gulping, dropping her purse on the floor and throwing her arms around his neck. Tears stung her eyes and she almost burst out crying, but she blinked them back. If she hadn't been thinking about him just then, thinking how much she wanted to see him, she could have restrained herself, but the relief at hearing his voice and feeling the muscled hardness of his body against her was too intense, her longing too close to the surface. She might die soon, and she wanted to have him again before she did. Going upon tiptoe, she pressed her mouth to his, moaning a little at his taste and the well-remembered softness of his lips.

He had hesitated before when she kissed him, but he didn't hesitate this time. His arms tightened around her and he swung her around, half-carrying her and half-pushing her past the bathroom and into the main part of the room—

—where the bed was.

He broke the kiss long enough to lean down and catch the bedspread, whipping it completely off the bed and to the floor, then he took her down across the bed with him.

His kisses held the same heat, the same hunger, that she remembered. He covered her with his heavy weight, pressing her into the mattress, and Andie coiled her legs around him, sliding her thighs up his hips to cradle him between them. Slowly he began rocking his erection against her even as he levered his torso up enough that he could begin taking her coat off. 'You'd better be sure about this,' he murmured, his gaze meeting hers. 'There's no going back.'

The intensity in his narrowed eyes shook her, burned her. She framed his face with her hands, just as she had imagined doing, and took the leap. 'I love you, Simon.' She wanted to say it at least once, in case she didn't have another chance to tell him. She wanted him to know that he was loved, that he was cherished, that he wasn't alone.

He faltered then, his arms abruptly wobbling and refusing to support his weight. He sank down on her, breathing hard, his forehead pressed to hers. 'You don't have to say that,' he muttered, something in his tone so humble it broke her heart.

'It's true. When you wouldn't take me with you, I fell apart. I cried for hours.' She stroked his hair, her hands tender. 'I could barely think, I hurt so much, and I had to convince Rafael I was upset because I'd realized he didn't love me, and that you'd said I was too much trouble and didn't touch me at all.'

His head jerked up a little and he stared at her, nose to nose. 'You mean he bought it?' he asked incredulously.

'Of course. I have a talent for lying,' she said, her mouth twitching a little with amusement.

'Damn. I knew you were good, but that's world-class.'

'Thank you.' She laughed, raising her head for a quick taste of those soft lips again. She felt them curve in a smile, and her heart squeezed.

Gently he nipped her chin, stroked his hand down to grip her thigh and pull it higher. 'Let's get out of some clothes. I really, really need to fuck you for a while.'

'How long is a while?' She began unbuttoning her blouse, but abandoned the effort to work at his buttons, because she'd much rather feel his skin than her own. 'Want to go for a personal best?'

'You mean more than four hours?' He shook his head, smiling. 'I can't. Not this time. Let's shoot for twenty minutes.'

'Slacker. I know you can do better than that.' She didn't need twenty minutes, she thought, her hips lifting and rubbing against him, seeking the hard ridge of his erection. Five minutes would do it. All her internal muscles clenched as she suddenly remembered how it felt when he entered her, pushing deep. His penis was thick enough to make her feel stretched, even then; how would it feel now, when she had been celibate for months? It was as if her sex drive had dried up, because she hadn't even thought about sex since the accident – until he showed up in her kitchen, and she realized it hadn't dried up, it had just been dormant because she was preoccupied with other things.

She got his shirt unbuttoned and pulled it free of his pants. The broad span of his chest, the light sprinkling of hair, enticed her and she spread her hands over it so that the hair tickled her palms and her fingers found the small flat coins of his nipples, centered with tiny nubs that hardened as she stroked them. His cheekbones darkened with color as he braced himself over her, letting her play.

Enough of that. She really, really liked his chest, but what she wanted most was in his pants. Abandoning his nipples, she went for his belt buckle, all but ripping it open. 'Watch out for the zipper–' he managed, then rescued his erection from her dangerous eagerness to set it free. She was suddenly frenzied, batting at his hands in an effort to get to him.

'Move,' she muttered. 'Let me have it.'

'Slow down. You can have it– Shit. Wait a minute.'

'No. Hurry.'

'Get your clothes off, too.'

He rolled to the side and impatiently she

surged to her knees, tugging and tearing at her clothes and tossing them aside. As soon as she had her jeans and underwear off she tossed them aside and straddled him, concentrating on something that was far more rewarding.

'I love you, Simon,' she said as she grasped his penis and guided it between her legs. She used his name deliberately, reinforcing that she loved *him,* the man, not just the sex. White-hot anticipation tightened her stomach muscles. She sank down, just enough for the swollen head to push against her opening. The heavy pressure burned as her flesh gave, opened, molded around him. It hurt, but she didn't care. She pushed some more, hungry for more, then tantalized herself by lifting slightly.

A growl rumbled in his throat and he grasped her hips, pulling her downward with a quick jerk that pushed him all the way inside her. His head arched back, his eyes closing as he savored that moment of penetration, then he relaxed his grip and his body and a beautiful smile curved his mouth as he said, 'There. Go for it, sweetheart. It's all yours.'

31

'Why did you come here?' he asked.

'How did you find me?' she countered.

They were lying naked amid the tangle of sheets and pillows, drowsy and relaxed and finally able to concentrate on something other than getting as close as possible to each other. He was still holding her close against his side, her head cradled on his shoulder as if he couldn't yet bear not to touch her.

They were both new to this, to the sense of utter joy in someone else. Andie couldn't stop touching him either, astonished at how fast things had changed between them, that she was now free to touch him and kiss him, bury her face against his neck and inhale the wonderful heat and scent of his skin. She kept having little episodes of unreality: she was actually here with *him?* Her body had joyously accepted his presence, but her mind hadn't quite caught up yet to this sudden change. The man she had gone in terror of for so many months was now her lover. Not just her lover, but her love. However ill-advised it was, she loved him. They didn't have the comfort of having known each other for years, dating, learning all the details and quirks of personality and tastes. Instead, every time they'd met, the contact had been intense and fraught with emotions neither one of them had any experience in handling. She was as much a novice as he in this business of loving, so all of this was difficult to take in.

To begin with, she felt giddy. Drunk. Drunk on him, on sex, on relief and joy and pain all rolled together. When he touched her, she felt cherished – she, Andie Butts/Drea Rousseau – who had never been cherished before in her life, who had never been loved, never been valued. The full realization that he valued her, that he was concerned with her pleasure, her comfort, her wellbeing, was almost more than she could take in.

Just as disconcerting was the depth and strength with which she cherished him. She would do anything to protect him, to care for him and smooth life's bumps out of his path. If she felt this way about him, she could only imagine how this emotion would feel turned around toward her, in a man whose middle name was 'intense' and whose every instinct was that of a predator. How would he react if he knew she intended to put her life in danger. Not very well, she was afraid. No man would, not even an average Joe, and he wasn't average by any measure she could imagine.

She would have to tell him why she was here. She wouldn't deceive him. This new, wonderful thing between them deserved better than that, but not right now. For right now, if he thought the time had come for questions and answers, then she wanted her own questions answered first, to prevent him from distracting her after he got *his* answers.

She tilted her head back on his shoulder, looking up at his face as she sifted through the possibilities. 'Even if you have a tracer on my

Explorer, that would track me only as far as the airport parking lot,' she said, thinking aloud. 'You wouldn't know what airline I used or what flight I took to where. I suppose if you're a good enough hacker–'

'I am,' he interjected, without any hint of ego or bragging, simply stating a fact.

'You could eventually find out, but that would take time unless, by sheer luck, you found me in the first couple of databases you hacked. But then, after you found I'd come to New York, you'd have to find out where I'm staying. Considering how many hotels and motels are in this area, and that you have no idea what name I'd use to check in, there is literally no way, using a computer, that you could find me so fast.'

He didn't say anything, his expression one of interest as he watched her think through the situation.

'You have a tracer on me,' she said. 'It's the only explanation. Not on the Explorer, but on me.'

'I have one on the Explorer, too,' he admitted without shame.

'So where is it?'

'Think logically.' His mouth curved in amusement. 'You'll come up with the answer.'

'It would have to be on something I keep with me. My purse, but women change purses all the time. Something in my purse. Oh, hell – my cell phone.'

'GPS technology is a great thing. I can locate you within a certain number of yards, and with my computer can even get the address where you are. For instance, why were you at the FBI building?'

'Talking to the FBI. Duh.' She accompanied the 'duh' with an eye-roll, just to tease him. She suspected he'd never been teased much in his life, and he needed some playfulness. 'How did you get a tracer on my cell phone? When did you get your hands on it?'

'Months ago. I went into your apartment early one morning, when you were sleeping.'

He'd been in her apartment, in her *bedroom* – because she'd kept her purse close at hand, just in case – and she'd never known it. If an untimely lightning flash hadn't revealed him standing in the parking lot at the truck stop, she never would have known he'd been watching over her like a guardian angel, keeping his distance but always making certain she was safe. But thank God for that lightning flash; because of it, he was here now, his arms around her.

'You didn't have to come to New York to talk to the FBI,' he pointed out. 'There's a field office in Kansas City.'

'But none of the agents there have been keeping surveillance on Rafael,' she said. 'I had to come here.'

'The FBI has phones.'

'Simon, I had to come *here.*'

'Your being here is dangerous,' he said, ignoring her tone of voice, which invited him to drop the subject. He turned on his side facing her, so their bodies were pressed full against each other. 'Even with your hair different, even though you aren't staying in Salinas's part of town, you shouldn't be here. There are thousands of people on the street who are involved, one way or an-

348

other, in his business. A good many of them knew you by sight. The FBI watches them; they watch the FBI. Salinas could already have word that a woman who looks a lot like you has been meeting with the feds.'

She actually hadn't considered that any of the people on the street could be photographing anyone and everyone who entered the federal building, though she should have. Certainly foreign interests involved in espionage and intelligence would he interested. Rafael – yes, she could see him going to that extent, too. He hadn't gotten where he was in the drug trade by overlooking the obvious. Trust was nonexistent, even in his own organization.

He cupped her chin in his hand, tilted her face up so he could read every nuance of her expression. 'For the third time, why are you here?' His hand lingered, smoothed a strand of her hair behind her ear.

'You know why.' She sighed and turned her cheek against his palm. 'Whatever I can do to help them get him, I'll do. I spent the morning talking to two agents, going over every detail I can remember.'

'Why is getting Salinas, in particular, so important? A lot of people deal drugs. They're scum, he's scum. He's worse than some, but I've met others who make him look like a choir boy.'

That was a scary concept. Andie shuddered a little. 'He's the one I know stuff about. I don't know those others. And I profited from the drugs by living with him. I have to make up for that, try to make things right.' She wouldn't tell him yet that she'd offered to act as bait in any trap the FBI could set up. Agents Cotton and Jackson hadn't been enthusiastic about the idea, for various reasons, and if the idea ever came to fruition there was no point in getting Simon riled up for nothing. She had the sneaking suspicion that riling Simon could be a dangerous thing to do – not to her, but she didn't want him wiping out the entire building at Federal Plaza.

But if – big *if* – Cotton and Jackson came up with a plan, she'd have to tell him. Trust came hard to her; and even harder to Simon. She wouldn't abuse something so precious and new.

Today, though, there was nothing to tell him. For the rest of the day, and the night, she had nothing more important to do than simply be with him. They might not have much time together, so she wanted to make the most of it.

Andie went from being miserably unhappy to almost glowing with joy at Simon's presence. They napped, made love again; by then the afternoon had worn away to evening and she was hungry. After showering – together – in the unremarkable and slightly stained tub, they walked down the street to an Italian restaurant.

Simon didn't have a bag with him, so he put on the clothes he'd worn there. Andie hadn't unpacked, on the premise that her suitcases were cleaner than the dresser drawers, so she flipped open the unzipped top of a suitcase to rummage for clean underwear. The wig box caught her eye and she hurriedly tossed a shirt over it. Thank goodness she hadn't taken the wig out to brush it, and a wig box was fairly small and–

'What's that?' Simon asked in an expressionless voice, gently appearing at her shoulder. He reached into the suitcase and with one finger lifted the shirt that covered the wig box.

'It's a shirt,' Andie said, though she knew damn well that wasn't what he was asking.

He didn't reply. Instead he took the box from the suitcase and opened it, pulling out the wig and shaking it so the long blond strands fell free. He held it up, the synthetic curls wrapping around his forearm.

'It isn't exactly the right color, but it's close,' he said, still in that remote, deliberately flat tone as he turned the wig back and forth, studying it. 'And it isn't as curly.' He dropped it back into the suitcase and turned his narrowed gaze on her. There was only one reason for her to have a long, blond, curly wig, and they both knew it. 'I'll be fucked and damned if I'll let you play bait for any stupid-ass trap the feds have dreamed up.'

Andie squared her shoulders. She believed she was doing the right thing, so she had to stand by her decision. 'The feds haven't dreamed up anything. I suggested the idea – which they didn't go for.' She didn't tell him it wasn't any of his business what she did, because it was, the same way he had become her business. She had given him that right when she told him she loved him.

'Damn good thing. I haven't killed anyone in law enforcement yet, but that would be a good place to start.'

If most people said something like that, it would be safe to assume they were exaggerating and blowing off steam. Not so with Simon. He stated facts, and he backed up his statements. Andie reached out and caught his hand; he let her, but he didn't return the pressure.

She cupped his hand in both of hers and cradled it to her chest, just over the scar that ran from beneath her collarbone all the way to the end of her rib cage. An hour ago he had kissed that scar with the tenderness of a mother kissing a newborn, and she knew they had both been thinking about what had happened to her, and the walking miracle she was now. 'I have to pay for this,' she said softly. 'It came with a price, and part of that price is doing what I can, anything I can, to stop Rafael. I can't walk away and do nothing just because I've fallen in love with you and would like nothing more than to spend the rest of my life sailing the ocean with you, or whatever the hell it is you do. I have to pay this debt. I have to earn this second chance.'

'Earn it some other way. Work in a soup kitchen. Give all the money to charity–'

'I've already done that,' she said. 'Before I came here.'

'Taking care of loose ends, in case you don't survive?'

Sarcasm lent a knife-edge to the words, but she said, 'Yes,' and saw him flinch. The reaction was gone so fast it might have been an illusion, but she knew better and her heart ached for him.

'I don't want to do anything that will take me away from you. I have another appointment with the agents tomorrow, and I promise – I *promise* – that if there's any other way at all, I won't en-

352

danger myself.'

'That isn't good enough. I don't want you anywhere near him regardless of whether or not he ever spends so much as an hour in jail, or if he dies rich and happy at the age of ninety. I've already watched you die once. I can't do it again, Andie. I won't.'

He pulled his hand from hers, turned, and walked to the window, though the view was of nothing more interesting than a narrow alley and the back of another building. Silently she finished getting dressed. There was nothing she could say to reassure him unless she lied, and it was ironic that she, a world-class liar, couldn't bring herself to betray his trust. She had promised as much as she could; beyond that, she could only hope for the best.

They walked to the restaurant, where they ate in silence. It wasn't a sullen silence, or a resentful one, but more as if they had both said all there was to say and anything else would be beating a dead horse. At the same time, she didn't feel like making small talk and he wasn't a small talk kind of guy; neither did she want to make plans for their future when they might not have one, which pretty much left her without anything to say.

But he held her hand as they walked back to the Holiday Inn, and after getting mostly undressed they sat on the bed, propped against the stacked pillows, and watched television. She went to sleep in the middle of a show, her head resting on his stomach.

The next morning, she called Agent Cotton and requested that they meet somewhere other than the federal building. Simon's warning about people watching the FBI building to see who entered made Andie uneasy, the way it made her uneasy when she was shopping and noticed one of the floor security personnel watching her. *She* knew she wasn't doing anything wrong, but she still didn't like being watched; it set off some sort of primitive alarm.

What bothered her more was the possibility that Rafael had a paid informant working there, and he already had word that a woman claiming to be his ex-mistress was talking to the agents. That would give him time to think and plan, and take away the shock value of seeing her again. If she had to sacrifice herself, damn it, she didn't want it to be for nothing.

'How about Madison Square Park?' Cotton suggested. 'I'll be in the area, so that'll be a nice place to talk. I'll be waiting at Conkling's statue at one o'clock.'

Simon left around ten, merely saying that he was going to get his suitcase and he'd be back. She didn't know where he had to go, but she waited until a little after noon before leaving, and he still hadn't returned. She wrote a note and left it on the desk. He didn't have a key card, but that hadn't stopped him the day before, so she wasn't worried about returning to find him standing in the hall waiting for her.

The day was warmer than the day before, with the wind sending fat white clouds scudding across the sky, but she was glad to have her coat. She stuffed her hands in her pockets and settled into the brisk walk of the city dweller, arriving at the park a little ahead of time. She went to the southeast corner, where the Conkling statue was. She didn't think Senator Conkling had done anything more remarkable than freezing to death in the 1888 blizzard, but evidently that was enough to warrant a statue.

Both Agent Cotton and Agent Jackson were waiting for her, their overcoats buttoned against the wind. 'I hope you like coffee,' said Cotton, extending a takeout cup to her. 'I brought cream and sugar, too, if you need it.'

'Black is fine, thanks.' The warm cup felt good in her chilled hands; she took a tentative sip, not wanting to burn her mouth with too hot coffee.

'Let's sit down over here,' said Cotton, indicating a bench nearby They walked over and she sat between the two men, both hoping and dreading that they had come up with some viable plan.

'Have you thought of anything else to tell us?' he asked, his gaze constantly cataloging their surroundings. Cops, even federal ones, always had restless eyes.

'No, but I wanted to talk to you about the plan I suggested–'

'Don't bother,' said a quiet voice behind them. 'It's a non-starter.'

Both of the FBI agents visibly started, whirling out of their seats to confront what could, for all they knew, be an attack. Andie had recognized his voice as soon as he spoke, and surged to her feet, too. She hadn't been expecting him; making himself so visible to two FBI agents, letting them get a good look at his face, wasn't a good idea.

He stood just behind the bench, his hands in

the pockets of a black cashmere overcoat, his eyes hidden by very dark sunglasses. She had no idea how he had gotten so close without either of the agents noticing him; he hadn't been in sight when they sat down, and they had been there, she figured, less than thirty seconds, so that meant he'd been moving fast.

After a short, startled silence, Cotton sighed and removed his own sunglasses. 'I'm Special Agent Rick Cotton,' he said, introducing himself and flipping out his ID. 'This is Special Agent Xavier Jackson.'

'I know your names.' He didn't tell them his, not even an alias. Nor did he take his hands out of his pockets. Cotton made a brief movement as though to offer a handshake, but evidently saw that the polite gesture wasn't going to happen and aborted the motion.

'I'm not at liberty to discuss Ms. Pearson's business with—'

'It's okay. He knows all about it,' Andie said. She didn't introduce him. If he'd wanted the agents to know his name, or any name at all, he'd have introduced himself. She wanted to heave a huge, frustrated sigh. If he had just told her he was coming to the meeting and given her a name beforehand, this situation could have been handled much more smoothly.

Agent Cotton wasn't pleased with Simon's presence. He said to her, 'This isn't a good time. I'll be in touch with you about your plan. I think something can be worked out.' He nodded at Simon, then he and Agent Jackson strode briskly toward the street.

Astonished, because she hadn't thought they would think there was any viability to a plan that could involve getting her shot, Andie bowed her head and stared at her feet as she fought the sting of tears. She couldn't look at Simon, couldn't face that impassive expression.

'Let's go,' he said, taking her hand and linking their arms. He was silent during the walk back to the Holiday Inn, though they had plenty of opportunity to talk. He'd stated his position, and he didn't see the need to keep restating it.

She still felt compelled to offer what comfort she could. 'It'll be all right,' she finally ventured, to be met by a wall of silence.

32

Jackson was silent as he and Cotton walked down the street toward their car. He was patient, waiting until they had closed the car doors behind them and buckled their seat belts before he asked, 'What was that about?' He couldn't think of any reason why Cotton would deliberately mislead Drea Rousseau – he had a hard time thinking of her as 'Andie' anything – about the feasibility of any plan involving using her as bait. If Salinas were in hiding and they were trying to draw him out, maybe, but that wasn't the case. Physically, they could put their hands on him at any time. Their problem was getting evidence against him that would stick, and short of filming him killing her, there was simply no way to use her. The Bureau wasn't going to set her up as a sacrificial lamb, so the whole idea was a nonstarter.

Cotton studied the street, the people around them, before asking mildly, 'You didn't recognize him?'

'Recognize him? Should I have?'

'He's the man on the balcony.'

Jackson stared at Cotton, astonished. 'The man on the balcony,' as they called him, had been a source of frustrated conjecture for months. He had simply vanished, and they'd never discovered how. Jackson sat back in the seat and looked straight ahead as he mentally compared the man in his memory to the one he had just seen standing in the park. 'I'll be damned. Good eye, Cotton.' He drummed his fingers on his leg. 'She's probably been with him all this time.'

He hoped she had been, anyway. He'd never admit it to anyone, but he had a kind of soft spot for her. When she'd been with Salinas, he'd pitied her, because she'd been like this pretty, useless doll that Salinas dragged out whenever he wanted to play with her, but otherwise had no interest in her. Whoever the balcony guy was, though, she loved him. Jackson was a hard-core realist, but being a realist meant he recognized what was right in front of him. When the guy had appeared right behind them, as silently as a damn ghost, both he and Cotton had damn near had coronaries, but when she'd turned around her face had taken on a luminous expression – exasperated, but luminous, as if the sun had just come out in her world. She might be a tad pissed off at the sun, but she was glad to see it all the same.

She was different, and it wasn't just the shorter, darker, straighter hair. It wasn't that she no longer dressed to show. In a way she was more eye-catching now than she had been before, but not because of the flash. There was something in her expression, a serenity, that hadn't been there before. Sometimes her attention seemed riveted to something in the distance; once he'd turned around to check if someone was behind him, but there was nothing, and when he turned back she had refocused on him. That was another thing:

when she looked at a person, she really *looked*, deeply and thoroughly. With that stare turned on him, he'd had to fight the compulsion to look down and check his zipper, to see if that was making her study him so intently.

Reading the guy wasn't as easy as reading her. Hell, his expression hadn't so much as flickered, and the damn sunglasses hadn't helped. He'd been as blank as a store-window mannequin. But Jackson had looked back and seen the guy take her hand and link their arms, and something in the way he'd touched her told Jackson that the feeling between them was mutual.

Jackson was glad, for her sake. From the conversation she'd had with Salinas on the balcony that day they knew that he'd given her services to the guy as if she were just a whore to him. They knew she'd been extremely upset. Then, the next day, she was gone. They knew she hadn't packed her clothes and moved out, because they kept track of everyone who entered and exited the apartment building. The last time they'd seen her, she had gotten into a car with one of Salinas's thugs, and when he came back she wasn't with him.

When she'd disappeared, there had been a lot of upheaval in Salinas's routine, and Jackson had wondered then if she'd been killed and her body disposed of, for reasons they could only guess at. Thinking of those days immediately following her disappearance, he suddenly made another connection. 'Hey! Remember that meeting Salinas had in Central Park? We couldn't get a shot of the other guy's face. Remember? I think that was him, then, too – the man on the balcony.'

Cotton considered the possibility, dredging his memory for the few details they had of the man Salinas had met, and he gave a single, considering nod. 'I think you're right.'

What that meeting could have been about was anyone's guess. Remembering the chain of events, though, Jackson thought Drea had walked out on Salinas and gone to the other man, and Salinas hadn't had any idea where she was. Maybe he'd arranged the meeting to ask, or even to hire the other man to find her. The Bureau had no idea who the man was, or what he did, so the possibilities were endless.

He couldn't resist a challenge, never had been able to. His agile mind began running through all those possibilities and scenarios, testing time against the few facts available, discarding some, expanding others, entertaining himself so thoroughly that it wasn't until later that he realized Cotton hadn't answered his question.

Simon felt the chill of his old friend Death creeping over him. He wasn't a man who agonized over his choices; he identified them, analyzed them, and then made the best one and moved on. This choice, however, left the tang of bitterness in his mouth. It wasn't that he regretted it, because he didn't, couldn't. But he didn't like it at all, didn't like being forced into it, even though he'd have made the same choice without outside intervention. He would protect Andie, period. That was his bedrock.

He took her back to the Holiday Inn and

escorted her to her room; he had to see for himself that she was safely there and that no one had broken in. Then he framed her face with his hands and kissed her, long and slow, letting the taste of her and the feel of her soothe him.

'I have things to do,' he said when he finally lifted his mouth. He wanted to take her straight to bed and lose himself in the hot clasp of her body, but he was nothing if not disciplined. 'Don't wait up for me. I don't know how long I'll be.'

Her blue eyes darkened with concern as she stared at him. 'Don't go,' she said suddenly, even though she had no idea what he'd be doing. He'd noticed that her instincts, always sharp, had gone beyond sharpness into another realm, as if she knew things that she couldn't possibly know. Was she even aware of how much time they spent staring into each other's eyes, until he sometimes felt their separate identities blur? He didn't think so. In most ways she was still very much of this world – a little crabby, a little impatient, a lot sexy – but every now and then she went away, not inside her head but somewhere out in the ether, and when she came back she always looked a little more radiant.

However it had come about, she read him better than anyone ever had, as if she had an inside track to his head.

'I'll be back as soon as I can,' he said, kissing her again. 'Wait for me. Don't let those FBI assholes talk you into anything before I get back. Promise me.'

Her brows snapped together and she opened her mouth to blast him for demanding a promise from her when he wouldn't honor her request. He laid a finger across her mouth, his eyes crinkling at the corners in amusement. 'I know,' he said. 'Promise me anyway.'

She narrowed her eyes at him, then turned to look at the clock. 'Give me a definite time. I'm not buying that "I have things to do, I don't know how long I'll be" crap. Two hours? Five?'

'Twenty-four,' he said.

'Twenty four!'

'It's a definite time limit. Now promise.' Twenty-four hours wasn't a stretch, either; he'd need every one of them. 'This is important to me. I need to know you're safe.' That got to her, because she loved him. She *loved* him. The unreality of it shook him, yet the rightness of it went straight to his core.

Because she loved him, she grudgingly said, 'All right, I promise,' even though she didn't like it one little bit. He kissed her again and left, standing out in the hall until he heard her chain the door and turn the deadlock. By the time he got to the elevator, he'd already placed the most crucial call of all.

'This is Simon,' he said when Scottie answered the phone. 'I need a favor, probably the last one ever.'

'Whatever you need,' said Scottie promptly, because it was due only to Simon that his daughter was alive. 'And it's your call whether or not it's the last one. I'm always here, for whatever you need.'

He explained what he needed. Scottie thought a minute, then said, 'You got it.'

That taken care of, he began analyzing the

situation more minutely. The two things you needed in order to kill someone were a weapon and the opportunity. All the other details fell into one of those two main categories. Getting a weapon was no problem; getting an untraceable weapon, and a good one, was easy if he had enough time, but time was the one commodity he didn't have. Normally he would spend days working out the details, the logistics. This had to be done fast, then he would grab Andie and get out of the country while he could.

That pissed him off, too. He didn't like being forced to leave his country, and he knew going into this that he might never be able to return. If he worked everything just right, maybe. Only time would tell.

If he'd maintained his apartment in the same building as Salinas, he wouldn't have any problem, but he'd let it go months ago and relocated to San Francisco. Likewise he didn't have time to establish Salinas's routine, so he'd have to initiate the meeting. Drawing him out wouldn't be a problem, because Salinas had already been trying to contact him about another hit. Now he'd never know what big scheme Salinas had going on, he thought, then gave a mental shrug because it didn't matter. Salinas wouldn't live to see it through. Somewhere in the world, someone would live another day.

He'd have to do a street hit, which greatly increased the risks. On the plus side was the weather, which was still cool enough that coats were needed. On the minus side was that he'd not only have to carry his weapon, but adding a sound suppressor to it greatly increased the weapon's visibility by doubling the length.

Having to suppress the sound added all sorts of complications to his plans. To begin with, using a pistol meant he had to be close, and Salinas was always surrounded by his men. Because of how their mechanisms worked, a suppressor could turn a semiautomatic pistol into a single-shot weapon by preventing the slide from unlocking, but because a pistol meant close work, he had to have more than one shot available to him, in case one or more of Salinas's men were trained well enough to function through the surprise and initial confusion. He'd need an advanced suppressor that overcame that problem, or he'd have to use a different type of weapon.

The more the sound was suppressed, the harder it would be for them to pinpoint the location of the shooter. He'd go with a smaller caliber weapon, he thought, a blowback design with a fixed barrel; they were more effectively suppressed. He'd never yet seen a real weapon that could be suppressed to Hollywood standards, but with all the street noise added in, the resultant sound wouldn't immediately be recognized as gunfire. Most bystanders would have no idea they'd heard a shot, at least at first, because it was neither the soft spit of what they'd heard in movies, or the sharp crack of unsuppressed gunfire. When Salinas fell and his men grabbed for him, the bystanders would be confused, and they'd either mill around watching or they'd rubberneck but keep walking. Salinas's men would pay more attention to the walkers, figuring the shooter would be among them, trying to slip away. Instead he would be right there in the middle of them, under their noses.

Between now and then, however, he had a gargantuan number of tasks to accomplish.

A little after noon, Rafael Salinas emerged from his apartment building, surrounded by his usual coterie of seven. His driver was parked at the curb, motor running. One guy, his long hair tied back with a thin strip of leather, came out first, his head swiveling in all directions. He surveyed the street and the pedestrian traffic, though most of his attention was reserved for cars. Seeing nothing suspicious, without turning around he gave a brief nod of his head, and seven more men exited the building: Rafael Salinas walking in the middle of six men who used their bodies to block sidewalk traffic so Salinas could go in a direct path from the door of the building to the open door of his car. People stalled, tried to side-step, growled 'Get out of the way!' or worse, all of which was ignored. One bent old guy with a cane lurched a little off-balance.

A bus rumbled by and there was a barely audible *pop* over the roar of the diesel engine. Rafael Salinas stumbled, his hand going out as if to catch himself. A second *pop*, right on the heels of the first, made several people look curiously around, wondering what that noise was. Salinas went down, a red spray arcing from his throat.

The first man out of the building realized something was wrong and wheeled in a half-circle, his hand already emerging from his jacket, clutching a semiautomatic.

Pop.

The first man, a red blossom growing on his chest, reeled back into the driver. The weapon fell from his suddenly limp hand and went spinning across the sidewalk. People realized something was wrong and a few random screams pierced the air, followed by a flurry of pedestrians suddenly running or diving to the sidewalk. The old guy with the cane was pushed down and he landed behind the back bumper of Salinas's car, half on the sidewalk and half in the street, his cane several feet from his outstretched hand. His lined face wore a startled expression as he tried to crawl for his cane, only to sprawl on the ground when his strength gave out.

'There! Go!' One of the remaining men pointed down the street, where a young guy was flying through the crowd, trying to get as far away as possible. Two of Salinas's men took off in pursuit. All of them had weapons drawn by now, pointing them at first one person and then another in a serious lack of muzzle discipline. They circled around Rafael Salinas as if they could protect him now, despite the evidence of their eyes. The red spray from Salinas's throat had stopped; his heart had beat only a few more times after the first bullet ripped into him. The second shot, thrown off by Salinas's sudden lurch forward, had caught him in the throat.

The old guy tried once more to get his feet under him. 'My cane,' he kept bleating. 'My cane.'

'Here's your fucking cane,' one of the goons said, kicking it toward him. 'Get outta here, gramps.'

367

The old guy picked up the cane, his gloved hands trembling, and with difficulty levered himself to his feet. He hobbled behind the next parked car and stood there staring around as if he didn't understand what was going on. 'What happened?' he asked several times. 'What happened?'

No one paid any attention to him. Sirens began blasting as New York's Finest tried to bull their way through traffic. The old guy worked his way through the crowd and continued on down the street – back in the direction he'd come from. Fifteen minutes later, a uniformed cop found the murder weapon, a pistol with a sound suppressor threaded onto the barrel, lying on the pavement under Rafael Salinas's car.

Simon called Andie's cell phone. 'Get packed,' he said quietly. 'We're leaving.'

'Leaving? But–'

'Salinas is dead. You don't have any reason to stay. Now get packed, because we have to move fast.'

Numbly she closed the phone. Rafael was dead.

She wasn't stupid; she didn't need things spelled out for her. Horrified, she realized exactly what Simon had done. In a daze she gathered her toiletries and dumped them in a suitcase; as she hadn't unpacked, getting ready to go took only minutes.

Simon appeared at her door within half an hour. The closed, set expression on his face kept her from asking questions. He took the suitcases and she followed him in silence, her eyes as bleak as his.

Two hours later, they took off from a small private airfield in New Jersey, with Simon in the pilot's seat. Andie had never been in a small plane before, and she didn't like it. She sat frozen, her hands gripping the edge of the seat as if she could keep the plane up by keeping a tight hold on it. The late afternoon sun was at about two o'clock in her window, telling her they were heading southwest.

As time wore on and they didn't crash, she lost the sharp edge of terror that had paralyzed her. She managed to say, 'Where are we going?'

'Mexico. As fast as possible.'

She absorbed that, looking at his stony profile. He wasn't angry with her, but he had shut himself off, and she felt helpless to reach him. 'I don't have a passport,' she finally said.

'Yes, you do,' he replied. 'It's in my bag.'

Silence fell once more, a silence she couldn't seem to overcome even when he had to land to take on more fuel. Life as she had known it was over, and she thought there probably wouldn't ever be any going back. Simon would be wanted for murder, and she wouldn't let him take his chances in a courtroom. He had done that for her; she wouldn't let him sacrifice anything more, not one minute of freedom, no matter what.

No matter what.

'You ain't gonna believe this,' the tech said, swiveling around in his chair. 'That camera's out.'

'What?' Jackson turned on him in disbelief. He could almost feel his hair lift as anger surged through him. 'Are you telling me the one feed we need the most, out of all the cameras in the city, is *out* and no one fucking *noticed?* How can you people not notice a fucking *blank screen?*'

'Because the fucking screen isn't blank,' the tech shot back at him, his tone hot with annoyance. 'Don't get in my shit, buddy.' He swiveled back to his keyboard and began furiously typing commands. 'Here, come here and see for yourself. Look.' He pointed at the screen, at the silent black-and-white images marching with unknown purpose.

Jackson forced himself to rein in his impatience. Getting this guy's back up wouldn't accomplish anything, and the hell of it was, he thought whoever had killed Salinas deserved a parade. He wouldn't turn this into a personal crusade, but he had to do the investigation. 'Is that the camera?'

'That's it.'

'Looks to me like it's working,' Jackson said, but he dialed back the sarcasm until it was barely noticeable.

'That's because you aren't paying attention, *Special Agent.*' The tech was as good at sarcasm as Jackson was. 'Okay, there. See that guy drop his briefcase?' He stopped the action, backed up, played it again. Jackson watched a portly businessman trying to balance a drink, eat a hot dog, and carry his briefcase without breaking his stride. When everything began slipping, he held on to the drink and hot dog, and let the briefcase drop to his feet and go skidding across the sidewalk.

'I see him. What about it?'

'Keep watching. I'll speed it up for you.'

370

The tech tapped a key, and the people onscreen began scurrying around like ants. About ten seconds later he tapped another key and they slowed down to normal speed. A few seconds more, and Jackson watched the portly business-man sacrifice his briefcase again.

'Shit!' he said. 'Shit! It's a damn loop!'

'That's right, it's a damn loop. Somebody got into the system and got the feed, looped it, fed it back to us. Whoever it was is damn good, is all I can say.'

'Thank you for your help,' Cotton said quietly, giving Jackson an inscrutable look. 'Mister–?'

'Jensen. Scott Jensen.'

'Mr. Jensen. We'll get back to you if any other questions come up, but I imagine you have your own housekeeping to do for the time being.'

Scottie Jensen said, 'You got it,' in a grim tone, and turned back to his keyboard.

Jackson looked startled at Cotton's lack of pursuit down an avenue that should definitely have been investigated, but he quickly masked his reaction. As they silently returned to their car, a more thoughtful look replaced his agitation.

What he was thinking was out there – way out there. The Rick Cotton he knew was a by-the-book guy, as straight-up as anyone he'd ever met. He didn't have any evidence, and if he voiced his suspicions to anyone he'd be laughed out of the Bureau. All he had was his instinct, and it was shouting at him.

He didn't say anything, not then. He kept silent after they returned to Federal Plaza, went through all the expected motions. Details turned

371

over and over in his head, nuances of expressions that he'd caught, the timeline involved. Everything fit. Nothing was provable – hell, he didn't know that he *wanted* anything to be provable, or that he'd act even if there was – but he knew what had happened, knew it down in his bones.

And so did Cotton.

He waited until the day was finished. Cotton headed home to his wife, and Jackson ate dinner in the city, then walked some, absorbing the lights and constant movement around him. There was always something new around the corner, wasn't there – with people as well as with things. More so with people, come to think of it.

Reaching a decision, he fished his cell phone from his pocket and punched in a number. When he heard Cotton answer, Jackson said, 'He did it, didn't he? You knew he would.'

Cotton was silent a moment, then very calmly asked, 'What are you talking about?'

Jackson disconnected the call, not wanting to say anything more. He walked some more, his hands in his pockets. The night air was getting colder by the minute, but he needed to walk a while longer.

First and foremost was the decision he had to make. Would he say anything? The immediate answer that resounded in his head was a firm 'Hell, no.' There wasn't a damn thing he could prove, even if he'd been so inclined, and he wasn't.

The guy who'd killed Salinas deserved a parade, not an investigation. He'd done it to protect the woman he loved, and, hell, there was something noble in that, wasn't there? Cotton had sensed something right away, when their meeting with Drea had been interrupted, and going on pure instinct had set the wheels in motion by intimating that the FBI might want to use her as bait. That had been pure bullshit; Jackson knew damn good and well that had never been an option. The only way they could ever have built any case, using her, was if Salinas went bat-shit crazy and killed her – and the guy from the balcony knew that. He loved her, and he wouldn't risk her, so he'd taken matters into his own hands.

How had Cotton known the guy was capable of doing something like that? The plan had been slick, but the execution of it had required not just a big set of balls but some titanium ones. They didn't even know the guy's name, or anything about him. They didn't have a fingerprint to run, or a facial analysis to try to pin him to any of the locations where shit had gone down. But Cotton had summed him up in one brief, very brief, meeting, and within seconds had a human weapon aimed directly at Rafael Salinas.

In that one moment, Rick Cotton had performed above his own capability, and all Jackson could do was mentally salute. 'Way to go,' he murmured to the night.

Rick Cotton slept well that night. Soon he'd be retiring from a long and undistinguished career, but this one time he'd gone beyond his own limits and he felt good about it. He would go even further, doing what he could to stonewall any investigation. Those two deserved their chance at happiness, and he'd try his best to

373

make certain they got it.

Sometimes there was a difference between the law and justice, and sometimes justice had to step outside the law. The proof of that, he thought just before he fell asleep, was that he didn't work for the Department of Law; he worked for the Department of Justice ... and Justice had been served.

The last few days had been strained, as if they didn't know how to act with each other, which Andie supposed they didn't. On one level their intimacy went deep; their acquaintance had been marked by drama and passion, and deep pain. On a more mundane level, there was a lot they still didn't know about each other, and only time would remedy that. For now, they walked cautiously around what felt, to her, like a huge elephant in the middle of the room, not speaking of it or acknowledging it was there even though they both went out of their way to avoid it.

She didn't know what he was thinking, what he was feeling. He was self-contained anyway – that was the understatement of the year – and since they'd left New York he'd walled himself off, emotionally. It hurt her to be around him and not be able to touch him, but *not* being with him would hurt even more. Oh, she could touch him physically, but the mental barrier he kept between them reminded her of the afternoon in the penthouse, when she had tried desperately to reach him and he'd turned away.

She knew him better now, knew she had nothing to fear from him – the opposite, in fact.

No matter what, this man would place himself between her and danger without a second's hesitation.

Watching him one afternoon, watching him prop his shoulder against the door frame and stand motionless for long minutes at a time, staring out at the sea, her heart squeezed with pain for him. He was so alone, so willing to take all the risks himself in order to protect her, yet once he'd taken those risks he had distanced himself from her. Did he blame her, for forcing him to kill again after he'd sworn he wouldn't?

She knew how she would feel if someone forced her to do something that would keep her from returning to that perfect place of joy and seeing her son again. She would feel bitter, and alone, and as if there was no longer any point in trying. Was that what Simon was dealing with now?

She stared at his back, trying to read his mood, get some impression of him, but he was as closed to her as she was to herself. He was too close, she supposed; she couldn't get any insights into his future any more than she could her own.

Backlit like he was, she couldn't make out his features, but he was surrounded by a nimbus of light that turned his thin white shirt translucent, letting her clearly see the lean, muscled shape of his body. She stared at him, feeling the blood drain from her head until she swayed on her feet and the world around her slowly faded away until there was nothing but him and the light.

He had stood between her and death one other time, his pain and love shielding her, sending a signal, perhaps, that had weighted events in her favor. She had loved, and she had been loved. Her love for her child had been the biggest factor in the decision to let her have another chance, but Simon's love for her had also been felt.

They were linked; what she did affected him, and what he did affected her. If anyone had asked her if she'd fallen in love with him that afternoon they were together for the first time, she'd have said an emphatic no, but the truth was she had felt their link even before then and that was why she'd been so terrified of him. She had recognized him, somehow, on some molecular level that defied logic, and known that he would force her to once again take the chance of loving. But if he hadn't, would she be here now? Or would there have not been enough love to balance the emotional wasteland she'd become?

Conversely, by loving him, was she also shielding him as he'd shielded her? He loved, and he was loved. How much difference would that make in his life? Already, she would say, the difference was huge, but love was like an aggressive ground cover, spreading and taking up more and more space, choking out weeds. Because of love, he'd stopped hiring out his services as a hit man. Because of love, he was trying – and she sensed what a gargantuan effort it was for him – to open himself up to her, to let her inside the iron shields that separated him from the rest of the world. He was more comfortable alone, but for her he was willing to step outside that zone in a big way, to live the rest of his life exposed and vulnerable.

For her, he was willing to kill again, and count the cost well worth it, so long as he was the one who paid and she didn't have to.

She didn't think she made any sound, no gasp or sob. He'd known she was in the room behind him, of course, because she hadn't been trying to sneak, and the house was small anyway, so small he probably knew where she was every minute. But he was so attuned to her that abruptly he turned, every muscle alert, ready to go into action once he identified the source of whatever had upset her. He saw her swaying there, her face paper white, and reached her in a few quick strides to wrap those strong, supporting arms around her.

'What's wrong? Are you sick?' Even as he spoke he was lifting her off her feet, cradling her to his chest. There was no distance between them now, no reserve in those dark eyes that could look so icy.

'No, I'm fine,' she said, winding her arms around his neck and holding him close, holding herself close to him, two actions that might look like one but were very different in intent. 'I love you, Simon Goodnight. Simon Smith. Simon Jones. Simon Brown, Simon Johnson, whatever your name is, no matter what, I love you.'

His arms tightened around her and she saw something ease inside him, some burden get a little lighter. 'No matter what? Even if my real name was Clarence or Homer or Percy?'

'Well, then I might have to rethink this,' she said promptly just to tease him, and was rewarded by one of his little smiles.

'Cross,' he said, so easily that for a split second she missed the significance of what he was saying.

'Cross? That's it for real? Truly?'

'Truly.'

She rubbed her cheek against his shoulder. 'Thank you,' she said, because the trust represented in that simple action, telling her his name, was enormous. 'You can let me down. I'm all right.'

'You looked as if you were about to pass out.'

'No. You know how it hits you sometimes, how much you love a person, and it's almost too much for you to hold in? Like that.' She pressed her lips to the underside of his jaw, loving the smell of him, the feel of his skin cool under her lips but with his vital warmth just below the surface.

He released his hold on her legs, letting her slide down to a standing position, but he simply rearranged his grasp on her and pulled her fully against him as he bent his head to kiss her. She went on tiptoe to meet him halfway, her hands clasping around his neck, stroking beneath his collar. His erection pushed against her and a heated mixture of excitement and anticipation began stirring deep in her belly. Though they had slept together since arriving here, he hadn't made love to her, and she hadn't felt able to bridge the distance between them to reach him.

She felt able to now, though. He was right there, in her arms. Sliding her hands from his neck, down his chest and belly, she unfastened his jeans, slid his zipper down, and discovered he was commando. Humming a little with delight, she wrapped both hands around his length, wringing a guttural sound from him that made her shiver.

Moving swiftly, once again he hoisted her in his arms, breaking her grip on his penis. 'Bed or couch?' he asked.

'Bed.' Oh, the bed. She needed room to do to him everything she wanted to do.

He carried her into the small, sunlit bedroom and dumped her on the large bed that took up most of the space in the room. She laughed, trying to shuck off her own jeans while she was still bouncing. He stripped off his shirt and stepped out of his jeans and that was it for him, so he turned his attention to helping her with the rest of her clothes.

She wasn't wearing a lot, herself; the heat was too intense for layers and layers of clothes. Jeans, underwear, and a loose tank top was all she could tolerate. He pulled the top off over her head, then immediately palmed both her breasts. 'These are so pretty,' he murmured, brushing his thumbs over her nipples and making them flush with color as they firmed beneath his touch.

He made her feel pretty all over, the way he looked at her as if he could lick her from head to foot. She had never *felt* pretty, even though the mirror told her differently. Sometimes she had looked like a million bucks, but inside she'd felt worthless. But when Simon touched her, when she felt the tenderness with which he handled her, as if she were something precious beyond reason, then – *then* – she felt pretty.

He spread her legs and moved over her, settling his heavy weight into the vee of her thighs. She sighed in contentment. She could have done with some foreplay, but she also enjoyed his urgency, and the sense of pressure, of being stretched, as he slowly pushed into her mostly unprepared body. Her legs quivered around him, then tightened as her body lifted to his and she took him deeper.

Magic. Making love with him had been like magic, right from the start. Her body soared in response, in delight, in sheer, bone-melting pleasure, because that was the difference – not having sex, not fucking, but making love, so caught up in being with him that her protective mechanisms had shut down and she had just let go.

She did so now, flying from unprepared to orgasm so fast she felt she would have spun apart if he hadn't been holding her locked tightly to him. When her brain cleared and her body relaxed in utter contentment she returned the favor, holding him steady with arms and legs as he stiffened and shuddered and lost himself in pleasure.

They dozed, and when Andie woke it was to the uncomfortable reminder that they weren't using condoms. Most men would simply be happy they weren't having to suit up, but Simon wasn't most men, and she wondered if he was hoping they might have children. Her heart constricted, because some pains never lessened, never went away.

'I can't have children,' she said into the silence, and put her arm over her face so she wouldn't have to see his if disappointment shadowed it.

'Neither can I,' he replied calmly.

Stunned, she lay frozen for a few seconds, wondering if she'd heard him correctly. When she could move, she peeked out from under her arm to find him lying there watching her with something like relief in his eyes. 'What?'

'I had a vasectomy years ago. I didn't think my genes were something that needed to be passed along.'

He was probably right, she thought, and burst into tears. Damn the man, he could make her cry when nothing else in the world could. But wasn't that something he'd do, calmly analyze the situation and then take steps to protect the world from his progeny, which might carry the peculiar combination that made him so lethal, but without his coolness of thought, his restraint?

'I–I had to have a hysterectomy when I was fifteen,' she said, hiccuping and crying and talking all at once. She got up and went into the bathroom, got a tissue to blow her nose. While she was there, she took care of another area that needed attention, then wet another washcloth and took it to him.

'My own genes aren't anything to brag about,' she said, still sniffling a little. 'It took a miracle to get my attention, and you can't count on miracles all that often.'

'One to a lifetime, probably.' He gave her a wry, crooked smile. 'And I've already had mine ... with you.'

She lay down beside him again, cradling her head on his shoulder and placing her hand on his chest. Feeling the strong, steady beat of his heart made her feel better, more secure. She would always feel better when he was near, their bond making her stronger; she hoped she had even half that effect on him, because it wouldn't be fair if she got all the benefits and he gave and gave with nothing coming back to him.

'I don't expect much,' he murmured, staring at the ceiling while he stroked her hair 'At the end. If remorse is a requirement for redemption, then I'm not there. I don't imagine I ever will be. All I can offer is ... revenge, maybe, and retribution. I can offer restraint – unless you're threatened, and then all bets are off. But I don't feel remorse. Some people need killing, and I did the job. So ... this life with you is probably all I'll have, but it's enough, sweetheart. It's enough.'

The damn tears started again, and Andie smiled at him through the blur as she leaned forward to kiss him. His heart beat strongly beneath her fingers and she flattened her palm over that vital, rhythmic surge. 'Don't count yourself out,' she advised. 'I have inside information, and in the end, I think, you'll be fine.'

It would be a long road for both of them, she thought, suddenly seeing a span of years stretching out in front of them. She got only a sense of time passing, no specific incidents, but years and years and years. They had time, and they had each other.

The publishers hope that this book has given you enjoyable reading. Large Print Books are especially designed to be as easy to see and hold as possible. If you wish a complete list of our books please ask at your local library or write directly to:

Magna Large Print Books
Magna House, Long Preston,
Skipton, North Yorkshire.
BD23 4ND

This Large Print Book for the partially sighted, who cannot read normal print, is published under the auspices of

THE ULVERSCROFT FOUNDATION

THE ULVERSCROFT FOUNDATION

... we hope that you have enjoyed this Large Print Book. Please think for a moment about those people who have worse eyesight problems than you ... and are unable to even read or enjoy Large Print, without great difficulty.

You can help them by sending a donation, large or small to:

**The Ulverscroft Foundation,
1, The Green, Bradgate Road,
Anstey, Leicestershire, LE7 7FU,
England.**
or request a copy of our brochure for more details.

The Foundation will use all your help to assist those people who are handicapped by various sight problems and need special attention.

Thank you very much for your help.